I Can't Let Go

The Brothers of Chi Town, Book 1

CHERYL BARTON

Published by: Cheryl Barton Publishing, LLC

For permission requests, write to the publisher, addressed to: "Attention: Permissions Coordinator," at the address below.

Cheryl Barton Publishing, LLC
P.O. Box 962
Reisterstown, Maryland 21136
www.crbarton.com

Ordering Information:
Quantity sales.
Special discounts are available on quantity purchases by corporations, associations, and others. For details, contact the publisher at the address above.

Orders by U.S. trade bookstores and wholesalers.
Please contact prez@crbarton.com

ISBN: 1948950065
ISBN-13: 978-1948950060

OTHER ROMANCE NOVELS BY CHERYL BARTON

Bachelor Series

Bachelor Not for Sale
A Designed Affair
A Perfect Combination
Love at Last
Twelve Bachelors for Sale – Coming 2019

Amorous Occupations Series

The Artist
The Bookkeeper
The Chef
The Dancer
The Electrician

A Lovers' Heart Series

Heartthrob
Heartbeat
Heartbreaker – Coming 2019

Stand Alone Romance Novels

Holly for Christmas
Snowbound
Cupid's Arrow
One Wish
His Halloween Promise
Home for Thanksgiving
Holly for Christmas
A Better Man
Bossy
Un-Break My Heart
Love on Top
Take a Knee
Love at First Sight
My First Love
Black Love

Dear Reader,

Thank you for sticking it out with me and following my journey to helping couples find the love they were always meant to have. In this first installment of a new series, *"The Brothers of Chi Town"*, you get to meet Carter Garrison, a gorgeous, wealth hunk who loved and lost the perfect woman because of his lack of judgment in realizing he didn't need to have his cake while eating it, too. He had all of the best in Sienna until she ended their marriage without looking back.

I love Carter's character because he really did mess up as a lot of people in relationships do, but the difference was, he was immediately remorseful and he didn't have to admit his wrongdoing, but he did. The struggle to get back the life he'd lost was real and after the time he suffered being away from Sienna, all he needed was one opportunity to prove to her that he had learned his lesson and wanted a chance at loving her again, the way he should have the first time around.

Can we really get over an indiscretion of the worse kind, looking beyond it and into what real love is about? Can and should forgiveness be given?

A lot of people struggle with this. I wanted to write this story because there are stories we come across in the media where celebrities didn't give up on cheating spouses, but stuck around and saved their marriage. In *"I Can't Let Go"*, here is my take on discovering the meaning of real, true love, fighting for it and never letting go!

Happy Reading!

Cheryl

Prologue

Carter Garrison felt as if he were in the fight for everything in life that gave him purpose. In a way, he was. Life as he knew it was coming apart at the seams and usually, he was quick on his feet to resolve any kind of situation, but today, he had no control and for the first time in his life, he felt lost. The outer Carter was speaking softly, trying to pull the intensity of the situation back to a place where he and his wife could talk and the inner Carter was screaming at himself for being a screw-up. He hoped the outer Carter would help their level heads take control. So far, he'd had no luck, but he was still trying. He found himself apologizing profusely to Sienna Garrison, his wife and the love of his life. He was begging and pleading, yet nothing worked to bring about a better resolution than what he was being confronted with. Yeah, he was a screw-up, a stupid fool and his chickens had come home to roost.

As he sat on the side of the bed in the large master suite of their bedroom that he had been sharing with Sienna for the past four years, he watched her go through her dressers and angrily walk in and out of the large walk-in closet, snatching and packing up as many of her belongings as she could get her hands on. To his anguish, she was preparing to finally leave him. Carter wasn't ready, and if he had more time, he might be able to convince her to give their marriage another try. Her anger was fierce and he wasn't winning. His eyes trailed over her every move as she hurriedly and haphazardly tossed clothes on the bed that she planned to take with her when she walked out on their marriage. Each item she added pricked his heart a little bit more as the pain of what was to come sank in slowly.

He was losing her and nothing he said or did was working to change that.

For half of their marriage, they'd shared their lives together in their three thousand square foot, French country style home, which boasted four bedrooms and four and a half baths that he'd had built for her as a second wedding anniversary gift. He couldn't imagine being in the house without her, but from the look of things, he was about to find out.

He knew he'd messed up, but he never thought she'd leave him. He wanted to work their problems out, though he knew she wasn't the problem – it was *all* him and his lack of respect for her, something he never would have equated to him when it came to Sienna. He did the unforgiveable, the unjustifiable, and he was paying the price knowing if he didn't convince her to stay, he would never get her back again.

Carter never doubted that he was meant to be with Sienna and even though he screwed up, in his heart, he was still meant to be with her and no one else. Nothing was supposed to break their love, but in his ignorance, he'd found that thing that had shattered their perfect love. He had done the one big thing that Sienna was finding unforgivable. He needed to fight for the love he knew was still there, though it was clouded over by his indiscretion.

Looking at Sienna from across the bedroom, he saw anger that was evident even to a man in outer space looking down from high above the Earth. After the way he'd betrayed her, she had every right to be furious with him, but that didn't mean he wasn't going to use this one last chance to keep his marriage together. He was undoubtedly a fool, but he was a fool who was deeply in love with his wife despite the mistake he'd made. He was fighting for his marriage.

"Sienna, baby, I'm sorry. Please listen to me," Carter proclaimed from deep in his heart. He didn't speak loud or defensively, but in a voice that was calm and soothing. He didn't want to upset her more, though he wasn't even sure that was possible. He couldn't remember a time since they'd met that he'd *ever* seen her this angry before. He was determined to apologize as many times as needed to keep her from leaving him. He'd been saying it over and over again and yet, here they were with her finally deciding she couldn't stay any longer and her only option was to leave him and their life. She was walking away.

"You cheated on me!" Sienna turned and screamed at him. When she looked his way, he saw tears streaming down her face, running through and staining her cheeks as they ran down her face through the light make-up she often wore. He wanted to get up and embrace her to make the tears go away, but touching her was not an option. She hadn't allowed that for some time and he respected that. Not holding and making love to her has been brutal. He gave her the time and space from him that she needed and so far, she had at least stayed in their house. She needed time to cool off, yet it never happened. There was no doubt that she wasn't going to accept an offer of support and affection so he fought the desire to reach for her. It was bad enough that he was in the same room with her and not letting her pack in peace the way she thought she would be able to.

He contemplated apologizing once again, but instead, took a moment to consider what he could say next and contemplated over the words he would use to not continue to fuel the fire that brimmed. He was in a life or death situation and whatever he said could make Sienna stick with her decision to leave him for good or perhaps forgive him and try to continue working through his grave error in judgement. The fact that he stopped before the act was finished didn't mean much because he never should have begun. He never should have been in a hotel room with a woman that wasn't his wife. He never should have touched or let another woman touch him in an intimate way. He thought telling Sienna and coming clean was a good idea, but what he didn't expect was her level of rage over the incident. He may be thirty-one years old, but he scolded himself for not doing the mature thing when he was faced with a decision to either stay faithful to his wife or take advantage of what had been placed before him pretty much on a silver platter – woman willing to do anything for him despite the fact that he had a wife at home.

Though warranted, he was still surprised that after a month and a half, she was as angry as she had been the day he'd returned from the basketball All-Star weekend with a somber story about what he'd done and how sorry he was.

He'd never seen Sienna angry before, not at him or anyone else. They'd had their disagreements over the years but never any real fights. This was a real fight and he was glad that there were no boxing gloves around because she would have knocked him out and he would have accepted every single punch. He had done the one thing he knew would tear them apart, and he knew it. In one night that he truly regretted, he ruined everything he and Sienna had built in their four years of marriage and ten years as a couple after meeting during undergraduate school at the University of Illinois at Chicago. Ten years together and he couldn't imagine his life without her, yet he was faced with that very thing.

"I know baby and I'm sorry. I've been saying I'm sorry for over a month and I still mean it. I'm so sorry for what I did. Please, don't do this. Don't leave like this," Carter pleaded.

When Sienna whipped her head toward him, temporarily stopping the act of packing more clothes, Carter raised his hands in surrender to let her know he understood her anger and that she had every right to every ounce of it aimed in his direction.

"Do not say you're sorry for sleeping with another woman while you're married to me," she spoke harshly. "Four years we've been married and ten years together, and you decide that now is a good time to have sex with someone else!" Sienna yelled loudly.

Carter tried to stay calm, hoping it would diffuse her anger, but it wasn't working. He may be cool and collected, but she was enraged.

"I stopped it. I told you I stopped it," he implored.

"You stopped it, but not before you joined your body with hers. Just because you didn't complete the act doesn't mean you didn't *cheat*. The moment you put your penis in another woman, this marriage was over. I gave it all I could, but I can't continue walking around here like the images of you with another woman are going to go away."

"I'm not saying I wasn't wrong. I stopped when I..."

Carter didn't finish his thought as Sienna slammed the suitcases shut and turned back around to him.

"You stopped when? When you thought about me? I know, you've told me that a hundred times, but you know what you should have done? You should have thought about me and stopped before you even got to that point. You had no business in a room with a woman engaging in anything. The moment you walked into that hotel room and women were present and none of them were me, you should have left. You should have been home with your wife! What was it about our sex life that wasn't working for you? Did I not satisfy you? Was I not enough for you? Was cheating so easy and convenient that you simply decided to say what the hell, why not?" Sienna queried with a brutal tone.

Sienna had to stop herself from grinding her teeth together. She couldn't help clinching them as she spoke, making sure all of her anger poured out in every word. Here was the man she loved more than anything in the world and all she could see were images of him on top of another woman, loving her the way he... She couldn't think about it anymore and shook it off as fast as she could. She'd made love with her husband a countless number of times, and all she could see when she thought about it was the image of another woman on the receiving end of the kind of love he gave her that often brought tears to her eyes the feelings were so profound and powerful. How dare he even think of giving any part of himself to another woman?

"It was a lack in judgement that I'm sorry for. It just happened. It wasn't planned, and I stopped it," he said again.

Sienna picked up the suitcases and sat them on the floor to extend the handles in order to roll them out. She had already loaded a few other bags into her car before Carter arrived home and found her packing up her things to leave. She was hoping to not have this conversation, thinking he would be at the car dealership he owned until later that evening. Maybe this was what he needed in order to know what he was losing. He'd thrown away what they had for some nameless woman!

"You did it!" she shouted. "Stopped or not, you did it and trust me, at whatever stage you were before you stopped it, it still happened and I can't do this anymore. The counseling only made me angrier, and I can't be here with you any longer!" she shouted. Sienna knew her words spat out like daggers to his heart and that was exactly what she wanted. He needed to not only hear but *feel* her pain.

"You haven't given counseling an honest try. Our marriage deserves more of a chance than the few sessions we've already had. I know we can get beyond this," Carter pleaded.

The minute the words left his mouth, Carter knew he was fighting a losing battle and encouraged her rage even more.

"You didn't think our marriage deserved more when you slept with another woman did you? Before you answer, let me answer for you---*no!*"

Sienna turned toward the bedroom door. Carter started to jump up, but with his six-foot five height over her five-foot eight frame, he didn't want to seem intimidating. He needed to let her control the talk, but he wanted her to calm down enough to actually have a real conversation.

"Please don't leave like this. I will apologize forever, just don't leave me, Sienna. I can't live without you. Don't leave me," Carter said softly hoping to change her mind.

Without looking back, Sienna kept her eyes on the opened bedroom door and spoke softly.

"You left me the moment you made love to another woman. My dad and uncle will be by tomorrow to get the rest of my things. Unless you want to have to deal with them and I'm sure you don't, I suggest you make it a late day at the dealership," she said.

No more words were needed. Sienna left the bedroom and headed for the steps to take her through the kitchen and out through the garage. There was no need to leave out of the front of the house and risk giving her neighbors a show even though there was quite a bit of property separating them from the next home.

Carter sat with his hands in his head knowing this was the end of his marriage. His world was crashing around him and there was nothing he could do about it. He had to let her go because he could say everything he thought she would need to hear, and it wouldn't be enough. With the cat out of the bag, his mistake would always be between them and because of that, he knew Sienna would never be able to forgive him.

He could hear the click-click of her heels as she crossed the hardwood floors of the entryway as she made her way to the kitchen. He wasn't ready for this day and prayed it would never come.

For the past month and a half, they slept in two separate bedrooms in their home as they tried to deal with what he had done. So far, he had pled and pled his case for love and until today, he thought he was making progress toward them getting past his imprudence, but today, she told him she needed space and couldn't get it with them living in the same house. He hadn't expected to come home to find her packing when he decided to make it an early day of work. If he hadn't shown up when he did, he would have come home to her never coming back again.

Hearing her heels now clicking across the Century Mosaic Italian Marble Bianco kitchen flooring, he jumped up hoping to make one last pitch for his marriage before she got in her car and sped away.

Taking the steps two at a time, he rushed down and then through the house to the kitchen. When he opened the door between the kitchen and the garage, his heart dropped as he watched Sienna drive way with the bright red lights of her Mercedes being the last sign of her. Hurrying to the end of the driveway, he hoped she would turn and he could capture her eyes and plead with his own for her to not leave. When she turned the corner without looking at him, he knew it was over. His marriage had officially ended and the fault was all his because he'd hurt the one woman he should have loved and never stepped out on. He hurt the one woman he should have always protected, especially from any harm he could bring to her. The harm he ended up inflicting was to her heart and he would never forgive himself. He knew Sienna would never forgive him either. All hope left with her and was driving away. Where he stood now, feeling alone and angry at himself, he knew it was a place he deserved.

1

Eighteen Months Later

It was unseasonably warm for October in Chicago at eighty degrees, but Carter knew that it still wasn't the time to remove his brown bomber leather jacket and start behaving like many other people around him dressed as if it were a hot summer day. As he drove through the busy Chicago streets in his black Mercedes AMG-S65 with old-gold and black leather seats, the colors of his fraternity, on his way to the high-end Garrison Motors Mercedes Benz car dealership he owned, Carter shook his head at those he saw strolling along in shorts and tank tops. He knew that in a few days when the temperature dropped to a normal twenty-degree day, there would be a lot of visits to emergency rooms of those suffering from the flu. When he was a kid back in high school, he would have behaved the same way, but as a responsible adult, he knew better. The flu and even pneumonia were real and the out-of-the-ordinary weather wasn't to be trusted.

Cruising along, he was thankful for the reprieve from the usual Chicago freeze because the warm weather aided in increased sales at the dealership. He'd even recently hired a few new salesmen to help with all of the interest his business had been getting after friends of his who were professional ball players as well as the number one rap artist in the country had bragged on social media about his dealership and its famous customizations.

Along with the dealership, he also owned a car customization business, *Chi Brothers Customization*, with two locations because of how in demand its services were. Adding to his lucrative dealership and customization business, he also still owned the two auto body shops he and one of his best friends, Dexter, had opened up a year after they graduated from college. Between the dealership and the customization business's two locations, he'd made a nice life for himself, so much so that he was working on a new dealership location to expand his offering of high-end vehicles to the most elite around the world.

Earlier in the year, he was able to provide a fleet of Mercedes to a sheik from Morocco who needed ten Mercedes-Benz S-Class Pullman stretched limousines and thanks to a baller who was married to the sheik's daughter, the dignitary was referred to him. At one million dollars per car, plus the cost of the requested customizations, he was a very wealthy businessman. He smiled at the things people wanted added to already expensive cars, but he obliged and his bank account thanked them. He still couldn't believe the sheik had requested actual fish tanks be added to the cars. Thankfully, he knew the right people and got it done. Friends who bought from him and referred him were why he was working on opening his new location within the next six months. He'd come a long way from a country boy born and raised in Meridian, Mississippi, until his parents moved to Chicago while he was in high school.

After graduating college and completing his Master's

degree in business, he used the money loaned to him by one of his best friends who played professional football, to open his two auto repair shops. He and Dexter made lots of money throughout their college years repairing cars on the side around campus and knew they'd make a money-spinning business venture if they had the funds to do so. They repaid that loan back with interest in no time at all.

The current year for him on the business front was his most successful so far. Six years in the automobile industry and spending the last five as an owner, he was ending the year on a high note. He felt good about the prospect of opening the new dealership months earlier than originally planned.

Pulling onto the lot of the dealership, he sat back and watched the hustle of his salesmen who were working hard with the crowd that showed up early to get deals on his end of the year sales event. He already knew sales for the year would be double the sales from the previous year. For that, his staff would think he was king when he issued end of year bonuses just before the holiday season. He was glad to be the kind of owner people enjoyed working for and when he was successful in business, they were successful as well, which was how it should be.

Just before getting out of his car, Carter spotted a couple who looked at each other lovingly as they made the decision to buy their first high-end luxury car. He remembered them from the day before and knew that they wanted to go home to discuss the cost. The husband wanted to get the car for his wife, but she pushed back on the cost knowing that her husband also needed a car and the expensive Mercedes should be put off for a while. The husband spoke of how much he loved her and would do anything for her, including getting her the car that she'd dreamed about and he decided now was the time. Because of the way he spoke about his wife, Carter respected the man and potential client. He, too, remembered loving a woman so much that he would do anything for her. Too bad, he'd gotten so caught up in being a big shot a few years back, that he ruined the trust of the only woman he'd loved.

Walking into the dealership, he greeted those he came across as he made a beeline for his office. In just an instant, seeing a loving couple had him thinking of a love he had to let go of.

Sienna Garrison, now, most likely back to Sienna Richards, had been that woman and every single day since he had lost his mind and done the unthinkable, he'd thought about her and how much he still loved her. He wished he could go back in time and not screw up his life and marriage. After all, he knew she probably called him all kinds of names every day in her mind and definitely out loud to close friends and family. He'd been a fool, and he deserved the ache that settled in his heart and wouldn't leave.

Closing his office door and taking the seat behind his desk, Carter had planned to catch up on work, but found himself not able to focus. Sienna was in the forefront of his mind, and even if he could shake it, he didn't want to. Eighteen months after the separation, which included months after the divorce and not one word from or sighting of her. He felt like a drug addict going through withdrawal. He missed her as much now as he did the moment she left him, but it seemed like Sienna never looked back.

"Call on line three, Carter."

Hearing his name called by his assistant, he picked up, needing the distraction from once again feeling sorry for himself.

"Dexter, what's up brother?" he said, already knowing who would be on the other end.

Carter had been expecting this call from his best friend who was more like a brother than just a friend. He already knew how the conversation was going to play out since Dexter had a habit of calling to grill him after he missed another evening of hanging with the fellas. He had expected Dexter to be at the dealership for an early morning meeting with their team, but remembered he was doing a site visit at the location for the newest dealership, their first partnership together on such a venture. Currently, they were partners only on the customization business and the auto body shops. When Carter blew them off the night before, he had basically expected this early morning call and prepared to take it.

"Not much. I'll be heading your way in a few. I had an early morning meeting at the auto body shop and it ran over. You already know why I'm calling though, so try not to act absent-minded," Dexter said.

"I know, I was expecting this grilling. I want to talk to you about the fleet for the new dealership and the possibility of expanding the customization business by opening a branch in Los Angeles and one in Miami. We're already scheduling clients months out because of all the business and we're expanding quicker than we can deal with, but that's going to change. Let's have a sit-down on top of the other meeting that's already scheduled today."

Carter liked that he could focus on the dealerships while Dexter focused on the customization and auto body shops.

"Yeah, we could have celebrated your success if you ever stop coming up with excuses every time the guys and I hang out. You need to stop ignoring your friends. You're divorced from Sienna, not from your boys," he said.

Carter felt the sting of the statement. It didn't matter how many times someone brought up the fact that he was divorced from the love of his life, the pain was always the same.

"Man, you know how busy I've been with business. I can't continue to expand if I'm not focused on what needs to be done on my end," he proclaimed.

"I know and I hear you. The guys keep asking me what's going on with you. You can't possibly still be mourning the end of your marriage to Sienna. Or is work really keeping you that busy? It's been a few months since the fellas and I have seen you out socially. Sienna didn't get everybody in the divorce. A few of us are still in your court!" Dexter jibed.

Carter shook his head and smile. Only Dexter could find humor that would make him smile when it came to his divorce.

"Don't hate on a brother out here trying to make moves. You know how I do and, besides, the other location is ahead of schedule. I've been crazy busy getting as much done before bad weather hits this region and all construction comes to a halt. How did the site look when you checked it out?" he asked.

"Looks great. You're right that the construction is ahead of schedule. An early summer opening should work out," Dexter said.

"I'm counting on that," Carter replied.

"Good, now off of business and back to the personal.

What's really going on with you? We're getting a pickup game of basketball together at the gym this weekend. You own the dealership, and I know you can get away whenever you want to. Those minions can run things while you get a day off."

"I'll see what I can do. I could use a game to remind you fools who's boss on the court," Carter joked.

"Man, you can't remind us of anything. You have a lot of explaining to do. You and Sienna divorced and all of a sudden, you divorce everybody associated with the life you had with her. I was around before you even heard of a Sienna. In fact, I was with you that day on campus when you met her and said the next minute that you were in love. You can't divorce me. Did you get my message about the wedding? On second thought, I'm not going to ask you did you get my message. I know you got it and you ignored it like all of my other messages."

Carter remembered the message and his reaction to hearing that Sienna was going to be there and she was bringing a date. He knew Dexter was warning him before he heard it from someone else or decided to show up and see it for himself.

"Yeah, I got it and I got the wedding invitation from Keith and Kim. Responding slipped my mind. I'm not sure I can make it. I told you how busy things are for me right now," Carter explained and hoped the lie would suffice.

Knowing Dexter, it wouldn't.

"Bruh, you lying to your best friend? I know you better than that. This is all about Sienna being there with someone. She left you over a year ago, and the divorce has been final what? Six months now? You should expect she would move on. I'm not throwing salt on your wound, but Sienna is a stunningly beautiful woman. She wasn't going to be on the singles market for long. It's time for you to get over her and move on. Get back out into the dating world and you won't feel the sting every time you think of her being back out there and possibly with another guy. It's going to happen and I don't want to see you walking around like a zombie forever."

The last thing Carter wanted to do was discuss Sienna and her dating situation. He didn't want to know about it or hear about it. She may have left him and then divorced him, but he still loved her as much as he had when they were married.

"I'm serious, Dex, my Saturday's are crazy and you know that's a big day for any car dealership. If I hang out with the guys this Saturday, I can't be out of the dealership two Saturdays in a row."

"Man, Keith is going to disown you if you don't show up, so you may as well go ahead, bite that bullet and let him know you're coming. It'll be good to be in the place with all the fellas together again. There's been a lot going on since your disappearing act. I know he wanted you to be in the wedding, but he wanted to give you some space after the divorce. The entire chapter of the frat will be there and you can't be the missing link," Dexter said.

"I had some things to sort you, you know that. I'm good though, and he and I did talk about that. He mentioned being in the wedding, and I declined, but you're right, I can't not go. I told him I would be there."

"Alright. Lance's band is playing a gig tonight. He would appreciate the support if you have an hour or two to spare."

Lance was another one of their fraternity brothers who was all about his music. It had been a long time since he'd gone out and supported his brother's efforts. Carter needed to get back in the fold and stop avoiding everyone. He didn't have any blood brothers, but his friends and fraternity brothers were as close to brothers as he could get. He knew he was wrong for avoiding them and he needed to shake it off.

"Cool. I can do that. I have a crazy day, but I can definitely come out and support. Text me the time and address, and I'll drop by."

"Good. I'm sitting in on the drums, so tonight is going to be extra live. This is a good opportunity to check out that new supper club downtown. I'll text you as soon as we hang up. I'll let you go so you can sell every car in your showroom and on the lot and I'll swing by later," Dexter laughed.

"Yeah, whatever. Later."

Carter hung up and knew the rest of his day was shot. Until Dexter mentioned it, he hadn't thought a lot about the fact that Sienna was dating someone and would be bringing him to Keith and Kim's wedding.

They had all been friends since college, but after the divorce, he had distanced himself from everything and everyone involved in their old crowd. If he and Sienna weren't a couple, he didn't want her to be the one who didn't inherit the friends, so he backed off. If she was bringing someone, it must be serious and that wasn't sitting well with him. His mind went back and forth with whether to go or not to go. He wanted to see Sienna, but he wasn't sure he could handle seeing her with another man.

Carter fumed when he imagined some other man touching and kissing Sienna. His blood was boiling at the thought and he already wanted to hurt the guy. He had a real reason for not going to the wedding. Seeing Sienna dancing in someone else's arms or seeing her laugh and smile at something he may say to her could cause him to latch out, not at Sienna, but at the man who dared put his hands on Sienna in any way. Carter knew he was a lost cause. He needed to stay as far away from that wedding as he could in order to keep himself out of jail.

Shaking it off, he had work to do and making his rounds around the showroom was first on his agenda. He had plenty of time later to continue to feel sorry for himself.

2

Sienna looked over the file in the box on the door outside of the room where her next patient was waiting. Being a dentist had been a dream of hers since she was a little girl and tried to extract teeth from all of her dolls. Opening her own dental practice was one of many highlights in her career.

The morning had been a busy one and after taking a week of vacation away from the office, she was happy to be back, and the heavy schedule of patients coming in meant that many had waited until her return before scheduling an appointment instead of seeing one of the other dentists on the team, including her partner in the practice, Constance. Sienna didn't like being away from the office, but there were days when she felt she couldn't breathe and knew she needed some time off.

Divorce wasn't easy and taking a vacation didn't make it any easier. She wanted to focus on moving forward and being happy, but found herself focused on her doomed marriage and not really enjoying herself as much as she could have. She needed a little time away to deal with the personal turmoil she'd suffered with the divorce from the man she thought she'd be married to for the rest of her life. Though the divorce was six months ago after a year of being separated, the weight of it all felt fresh and she figured some time to get herself together was needed.

In her time off, she didn't go away as much as she relaxed at home and thought through how to get her life back on track as a single woman again. What actually happened was she spent a week sulking, crying, and wondering how things could have gone so wrong. A year and a half later, she was still hurting, not just over her ex-husband's indiscretion, but also over the emptiness she felt daily. Carter had hurt her deeply and the lasting impact of her disintegrated marriage was a hard pill to swallow. When after a week, she hadn't done anything but lounged from one room of her house to the other, she was happy to be back to work and on a regular routine.

Knocking and then opening the door, she smiled when she saw that her first patient was one of her favorites.

"Ms. Olsen, it's good to see you," Sienna said happily.

"Dr. G, well, it's about time you were back. I called to make an appointment for last week, and I was told I could either see one of the other dentists or wait for you to return from vacation. I've never known you to take a vacation before."

Sienna smiled. She missed the banter with Ms. Olsen.

"Nonsense. I've taken vacation before. You haven't noticed because you weren't scheduled for an appointment when I would be out. How are you and I see you're finally getting that annoying tooth pulled?" she asked, opening the folder and taking a quick look at the write-up one of the office assistants had prepared for her.

"Yes, the pain is getting bad and no need to say I told you so. Did you have fun on your vacation?"

"I did. It was relaxing," Sienna lied knowing she did nothing but sulk.

"Did you go away with that sexy husband of yours? You know, even at my age and all of the years I've been around, I have never seen a man more handsome than your husband."

Sienna was used to Ms. Olsen having selective memory, and now that she was in her late eighties, she often forgot things more frequently.

"Ms. Olsen, we're divorced six months now and have been apart for a year and a half. I've told you that a few times already."

"Divorced?"

Sienna stepped back when Ms. Olsen shot straight up in her chair.

"Yes, we're divorced."

"Now, that's nonsense. You were only married a few years and who divorces a man like your husband?"

"Handsome or not, we're divorced. He is good looking, but he's not the only good-looking man around."

"Honey, stop it. You adore that man. Something really bad must have happened."

Sienna didn't want to get into her personal business with a client, so she quickly changed the subject.

"Tell me, are there any other problems I need to know about? I have you for one extraction today. I'm going to have my assistant take one more x-ray of your mouth so that I can get some films, and then we'll get you numbed up and ready to get that tooth out. Are you sure you're not ready for me to pull the last few remaining teeth and give you a full plate? I know you like the idea of having a few of your own original teeth, but your mouth would feel much better with them all out."

"I'm going to get another tooth added to my plate, right? I can't walk around with that tooth missing in the front of my mouth. I might have the rest pulled in a few months, but not right now. I like being able to brag to the others at the nursing home that I still have some of my own teeth. None of them can say that," she laughed.

Sienna smiled at her to reassure her.

"Yes. We'll get that taken care of. You'll be as good as new with a one-hundred-watt smile."

"I hope so. I may find myself a sexy husband like you did. I'm still sexy even in my eighties!" Ms. Olsen declared.

"Yes, you are and I told you he's not my husband anymore."

"I can't believe you divorced him. I would never have divorced a good-looking man like that. You must be seeing someone new or something, huh?"

"No, not at all."

"Then you're still in love with your husband."

Sienna didn't want to continue the conversation about her private life.

"I'm going to have someone come in and get the films done and then I'll be back in to take the tooth out."

Before her client could start in again on her private life, Sienna opened the door and stepped out into the hallway. After giving her assistant some instructions, she rushed to her office and closed the door behind her. She was hoping to get through a day without thinking about Carter. Six months ago, she thought the divorce would help her finally move on, but that didn't happen. Instead, she started hanging out more with her friends, some that she and Carter had together as a couple. There were times it helped her get over the loneliness she was going through missing being married. Each time she went out, she secretly hoped she would run into Carter, but he never showed up to any of their group outings. That shocked her. She wondered what he was doing instead of hanging out with their friends. Life had changed for them both and though she wasn't dating, she'd been going out more than usual and had drawn the interest of some men. As hard as she tried to be interested in trying her hand at another relationship, her nerves wouldn't let her take that next step into her new reality of being a single woman again. She still had a lot to learn.

She had been married to Carter for four years before they split and before him, there had been no other. They met during her freshman year in college and had hit it off instantly and were inseparable from that point on. Their perfect life had come crashing down one evening when he revealed he'd done something. Although he knew she would never forgive him, according to him, he told her because he didn't want to keep something he'd done a secret from her. That equated to a lie in his book and that wasn't him, which made it hard for her to understand how he could have done something that would hurt her to her core.

Though she had not seen him in months, she wondered if he were seeing anyone. She had no right to ask or even know about Carter's private life. She shouldn't be concerned since she was the one who initiated the separation and the divorce. She wouldn't have to think about what Carter was doing now if she'd fought harder to deal with the problems instead of opting to leave him all together.

While she was on her week away from the office, she came to the realization that she'd made a mistake divorcing Carter. Yes, he had hurt her, even devastated her, but was it really worth ending her marriage? She had begun to doubt herself and even started longing again for what they'd had. Then she thought about what caused all the turmoil and she moved between being okay with her decision and regret. She couldn't figure out which side of the fence she wanted to be on. Perhaps it was due to how much she missed Carter, who had not only been her husband, but her best friend. Being in love for years was hard to let go of, but she had to try and figure it out. She could no longer live in the past. There was so much happiness in their past and still one fleeting moment ruined it all. How could Carter risk losing all that they had built together? It wasn't about the material things or the wealth, but, for her, it was about the love. In the blink of an eye, he made a choice that opened a seam in the heart of their love.

She couldn't seem to really get over the hurt and as usual, here she was again debating about her decision to end things and whether she'd made the right decision. She had to stop letting what happened control her every waking moment. She had a job to do. She had no doubt in the quiet of the night when she was alone and wondering what Carter was doing now that they were apart, she would have plenty of time for her continued pity party. For now, her focus had to be on work.

Standing up and straightening her clothes, she grabbed the file for her next patient and went to work. Before diving in, she inhaled deeply, let it out, plastered a fake smile on her face, and forced thoughts of Carter to the back of her mind.

**

Carter walked into the crowded supper club, one of the hottest new spots in Chicago. Thankful that Dexter had left his name at the door, he was able to get ahead of the long line of people waiting to get in when a spot opened up.

Walking past the bar and through the tables that surrounded the dance floor in front of where the band was playing, he found the reserved table that Dexter had set aside and was surprised to find himself at a table with two beautiful women. It was, no doubt, something Dexter cooked up.

"Good evening," he said sitting down in one of the two empty chairs and looking up at Dexter as he played the drums behind Lance and the rest of the band members. He saw a distinctive grin on Dexter's face that needed no words. Without telling him so, Dexter had provided a female friend for him, and Carter wasn't happy about it. Turning his attention away from Dexter and back to the women so that he didn't appear rude, he faked a smile at them, not because he was purposely trying to be discourteous, but because he was upset that Dexter hadn't warned him ahead of time.

"Well, hello. You must be Carter. I'm Amy and this is Deanna. We're friends of Dexter."

Carter knew immediately which woman had been invited out for the evening for him. As Amy talked, she reached across the table and laid one of her hands with its long, manicured nails painted in hot pink on top of his and left it there.

"It's nice to meet you both and yes, I'm Carter," he replied.

He watched as Amy slowly let her eyes caress every inch of

him before she leaned closer, not allowing the other woman to hear her.

"You're more handsome than Dexter said. In fact, you are the sexiest man I've ever met. I can't believe you're single," she said.

Carter wasn't interested even though he could admit that Amy was beautiful. To him, there was nothing more beautiful than an African-American woman, but he hoped she didn't come out with a false impression of him being interested in anything other than supporting his friend's band.

"Thank you for the compliment. I think you're beautiful, too. How long has the band been playing? I'm hoping I didn't miss too much," he said trying to change the subject.

"They should be close to taking a break," Amy replied.

"Can I get either of you ladies a drink?" he asked signaling for the waiter.

"I'll take a white wine," Amy said.

"I'll have the same," Deanna replied.

When the waiter arrived, Carter took that time to remove his hand from under Amy's as he used it to reach for his wallet to pull out his credit card. After ordering the drinks for the women and none for himself, he was told all drinks for his table were already covered. Putting his wallet back, he leaned back in his chair and focused on the band. His thoughts couldn't linger past the fact that during the previous few months, all of his friends had tried hooking him up with one woman or another. Though there was nothing wrong with any of them, nor were they a turn-off for him, he had a problem seeing beyond his lingering love for Sienna. He had let her go by signing the divorce papers, but in his heart, she still thrived in living color. He didn't know how long it took most people to get over their ex-spouses after a divorce, but for him, he couldn't imagine there being another woman for him.

"I hope we can talk when the band takes a break. The music is pretty loud and I'd like to know all about you," Amy said, leaning over.

Trying to focus on the band, he smiled at Amy and turned his attention back to the stage. Out of the side of his eye, he could see Amy was no longer focused on the band, but her focus was squarely on him. He was all for women being as aggressive as they needed or wanted to be, going for what they wanted. In any other situation, he may have been interested.

Carter had tried dating a few times after the divorce from Sienna, but nothing led to anything other than a few nice dates. When the opportunity for intimacy came up, he used that as a time to walk away. He didn't want to lead any woman on while his heart still belonged to an ex-wife who wanted nothing to do with him.

The band finally wrapped up and he watched as Lance took to the microphone to tell everyone that the group was taking a thirty-minute break and would be back soon. A few minutes later, Dexter joined them at the table.

"I assume you met these two beautiful ladies. Lance will be over in a bit. He had some business to discuss with the owner," Dexter said.

"We were trying to get acquainted, but this band was playing so good and loud that it was impossible," Amy chimed in, and they all laughed.

"Funny, Amy," Dexter said.

"What? I'm just saying, you told me you had a friend you

wanted me to meet and that's exactly what I'm hoping to do," she said.

Carter said nothing, but looked over at Dexter knowing the look on his face needed no words.

"We're going to the restroom," Amy said standing and signaling for Deanna to join her.

When they were out of ear range, Carter turned to Dexter, removing the pleasant smile he'd had courtesy of the women at the table.

"Are you out of your mind? Tell me you were drunk out of your mind when you came up with this brilliant plan to set me up with Amy. You know I'm not interested and now that I'm about to get up and go home, you'll have to explain to her that I didn't leave because of her, but I left because I don't appreciate being set up. I don't have a problem meeting woman."

Carter tried to reign in his anger with Dexter knowing he meant well, but still, he knew better than to try and get his mind off of Sienna by introducing another woman. He didn't want another woman. He was a long way from being ready.

"I know you don't. Out of our entire group, you're always the one the women have their eye on, but you've been down in the dumps lately and I thought a nice night out with some beautiful women would be what you need to finally get over Sienna. You have to admit it's been a long time, and you're still depressed about your divorce. It's time for you to snap out of it and get back out there," Dexter said.

Same old story, Carter thought. All of his friends thought the answer to his woes was to casually hook up with women. That's what got him in trouble in the first place, listening to friends. He was beginning to lose patience with anyone who thought there was another woman out here for him other than Sienna.

"I'm not down in the dumps and I'm not trying to get over Sienna. You know how I feel about her and another woman won't change that," he explained.

"What? Do you have some major plan of getting her back? You told me you haven't seen or talked to her since the divorce. She's bringing a plus one to the wedding and since Reese is coming with her own plus one, it's not her and they are best friends. When are you going to let this go? I'm just saying, you're messing up the bro code. You're not supposed to let a woman get the best of you, especially one that left you. If she hasn't forgiven you by now, I don't think she will. You're free and single, but you're living like a monk. I'm only trying to help my brother out. I need the old Carter back, not this shell of Carter that I keep getting. Get it together and get back on the horse, literally."

Carter laughed when he saw Dexter smirk.

"I know you don't mean any harm, but you're going to have to fix this with this woman. I caught some of the show and you guys were great. I came out to support you. If I wanted a quick hookup, I don't need any of you to do that for me. Don't think because I'm going through something that I've lost my mojo. I need it to work on Sienna, not some other woman. I know I'm a glutton for punishment but let me be that guy. No one-night stands or hookups," he said.

"You're not looking for a hook-up, right? Is that it? Amy is more than that. I've been kicking it with Deanna for a few months now and I've gotten to know Amy. She owns two hair salons and is looking to expand, so she's got great business acumen. She's not wild and crazy, plus she has got it going on. I *know* you see how fine she is. Are you *blind*? She and Deanna practically live in the gym and it's not even all about that for you, I get that. You're not superficial. I'm only explaining to you that I thought the two of you would really hit it off."

"I hear you, Dex, and I appreciate the fact that you're looking out for me, but I'm serious when I say that I'm not interested, and it has nothing to do with who Amy is or is not. I'm sure she's a nice woman and she is definitely fine. There are beautiful women everywhere, but when I see my life with a woman in it, I see Sienna. Until I no longer see that, I can't get hooked up with any other woman. It wouldn't be fair to Amy or any hypothetical new woman, for that matter, that I'm still carrying a torch for my ex-wife."

Carter leaned back in his chair and brushed his hand across his chin. He couldn't figure out why Dexter wouldn't let him handle his life his way. He got that he and the rest of their friends were concerned about him, but setting him up with one woman after another wasn't the answer.

"I got it. You love Sienna, and you're not ready to move on yet. You know I don't mean any harm by caring about you as your best friend. I wish I could help fix this for you. I know how you feel about Sienna, and even if it doesn't seem like it, I respect your love for her. I'm just trying to help my brother out so that he can move on with his life beyond a woman who has made it crystal clear that she's through with him," Dexter explained.

Carter leaned forward, closer to Dexter so that he was clear in his intent and there would no longer be a need for anyone to try and hook him up in the future.

"I'm never going to be able to move on. I love that woman

with everything in me. As much as I would like to say that loving Sienna was no longer a factor and that I'm ready for another woman, the truth is, that would be a lie. I know she left me. I know she divorced me. I know it's over as far as she's concerned. I have yet to deal with that reality in my heart. Everything that has happened so far is on paper. Man, I'm still madly in love with her and I need you and everyone else to stop trying to rush my heart to forget about her as if another woman would do that. Right now, that's not a factor. I can't say what will be the case months or years down the road, but today, let it go. I made a mistake not just that night in that hotel, but also the day I agreed to let her divorce me. I gave in too easily and I never should have. I should have stayed and fought because Sienna is worth it. She always has been. I've been thinking about her lately, especially knowing I'll see her at the wedding next weekend. I thought about it all day today and yeah, I decided to go to the wedding. I need to see her, even if it's on the arm of another man. I need so see Sienna. I want my wife back. I know I messed up, but I'm hoping she can forgive me. If I need to grovel, I will do whatever it takes. My life is shot to hell without her and it's taken almost two years for me to really feel what it's like to not have her in my life and I can't stand it. It's driving me crazy. It's not just want; it's a *need*. I'm not whole without her."

Dexter leaned back in his chair and from the look on his face, Carter knew he finally understood.

"Wow. I not only hear you, but I felt those words. All this time, I've been thinking that the answer to your woes is to help you move on and find a woman to soothe your hurt, when all along, the only answer to your happiness is still

Sienna. I always respected the love you and Sienna had for each other. If that connection was as deep as I thought it was, if what you want is Sienna back and on some level she's able to forgive you, I say go for it and you'll never have to worry about me hooking you up ever again. It's all love brother. I still remember when you met her and we shared that dorm suite back in college. I never knew any other guy who met a woman and after four years of college, pledging, parties, playing sports and having every temptation thrown at you, you *still* had eyes only for Sienna. Again, I respect that more than you know," Dexter said.

That's all Carter needed to hear. He knew over the past few months, he started sounding like a broken record when he would confess his undying love for Sienna, but he didn't care. Until he had her back, his life was no longer complete. He needed her back.

"I appreciate that. I'm going to head out."

"Man, at least sit through the next set. You were only here for what one or two songs? I promise to fix this with Amy, but don't leave yet. Plus, I know Lance will want to see you."

"I can see Amy has ideas of her own and I don't want the night to be awkward."

"Don't worry about it. Stay, have a few beers, chat with the ladies and before they get back to the table, I'll take of this."

Carter didn't want to ruin anyone else's night. There was no reason he couldn't hang around for a bit and enjoy the company. He didn't want to hurt Amy's feelings, but he wasn't interested. If Dexter could smooth things over, he was good.

"I'll hang for a bit, but you talk to Amy. I'm cool with sitting here and having a good time, but she needs to know you were preemptive in telling her you were setting her up with me."

"I got you covered."

"Cool. I may not stay until the end of the next set, but I'll be here for a few more songs. If I don't catch you by the end of the night, I'll see you at the pickup game this Saturday," Carter said.

"Cool. You'll miss Lance."

"I'll give him a ring. If I'm gone when you're finished, tell him I had to leave. The band sounds great. It's good to see you sitting in like you did back in college."

"Yeah, it feels good to be up there. I had to remind myself that I'm not just about cars. The love of playing the drums still lives in me. I'm going to say hello to a few other people and catch Amy and Deanna real quick. Thanks for coming out to support," Dexter said standing.

Carter sat for a while and when Amy and Deanna returned, he stood and smiled at them.

"Ladies," he said and sat.

"No hard feelings," Amy said leaning over to him. "Dexter thought we could have some fun, but there are times when things aren't meant to be. We're good," she said and smiled.

"I'm sorry. I don't mean to make things awkward."

"Not awkward at all. If nothing else, we can all listen to some good music, eat some good food and enjoy the evening," Amy said and then turned to Deanna.

When he saw the waiter, Carter ordered a beer and waited for the band to start up again. Without even focusing on her too much, Sienna came to his mind. When they were married, they often enjoyed places like this supper club. They would dance until the owner would practically put them out.

They would leave, go home, making love all night. He knew he could find satisfaction in the arms and the body of another woman, but that's not what he wanted.

Thirty minutes later, after the band played several more songs, Carter excused himself, telling the women he'd had a great time hanging with them and that he was calling it a night. Standing, he headed toward the front door, saluting Dexter and Lance as he left. His heart wasn't into the evening. Every song played reminded him of Sienna. She might think the worst of him right now, but Carter believed he was redeemable. He had to be and he had to hold on to the idea that somewhere in her heart, a little love for him still lived. A little is all he would need.

Carter felt lonely as he made his way back to his car. This isn't where he wanted his life to be. Every day, he relived the moment when he'd made the worse decision of his life. He thought about Dexter's comment about him moving on, but until he had a chance to have an encounter with Sienna to know that she hasn't thought about him all this time, he still held onto the hope that he was right to not let go of the love he knew was meant for him.

He wasn't letting go just yet.

3

Rising from the bed after a restless night, Carter swung his legs over the side, but didn't attempt to stand. He'd spent much of his night thinking about the mistakes he'd made with Sienna starting with his decision to go away for the NBA All-Star weekend. Having nothing but time now to think about that weekend and that night, he couldn't blame anyone but himself. No one forced him to stay in that bedroom with that woman knowing why she was there. He went along with it for what? To prove something to his friends? The only person he ever needed to prove anything to was Sienna and there was no longer a need to do that; she was gone.

After leaving a club a few weeks ago after hearing his friends' band playing, he had been unable to get his mind off of Sienna and found himself driving around Chicago just passing the time before heading home for the night to his place where loneliness lived. No one would think that him being successful and knowing women who would love nothing more than to be asked out by him or even invited back to his place for a night of sex, he was actually lonely. It was a self-imposed loneliness, a state that he currently deserved. What brother in his right mind would screw up as bad as he did? He knew he wasn't the first one, nor would he be the last.

Before finally turning his car around and heading home, he made a detour, far out of his way and took the drive out to the home he had shared with Sienna where she still lived. When he approached the house, he could see that she had the curtains in the living room wide open, something he told her to never do. Though the community was an exclusive one with lots of security and he knew the house had a state-of-the-art system, he still worried about her. He drove slowly around the bend and moved at a snail's pace when he finally got close enough to actually see the numbers on the front of the house above the front door. Looking again at the window, he leaned up just in time to catch a glimpse of Sienna as she walked by the window. He didn't want to be seen, so he continued on, but smiled knowing he had finally gotten a look at her, even if it was only brief. His heart leaped with love the moment she came into view. He looked back at the house and saw that she was closing the curtains.

As he drove away, Carter felt more determined than ever to earn his way back into Sienna's life. He'd been able to get his mind right and back on business until last night when he realized the next morning, he would have to face Sienna again, at Keith and Kim's wedding. He'd sent his reply that he would be attending and he wouldn't back down. He'd worked late at the dealership and he got home, he walked relentlessly around his house, barely thinking. He was nervous and wondered if Sienna would even say anything to him. He'd spent his evening trying to play out the next day and how, no matter what he saw, he would remain calm and not ruin the wedding with his jealousy.

When he finally arrived at home, he did everything to take his mind off of the current state of his existence. He tried looking over work; that didn't work. He attempted to play a few video games and couldn't find one that held his interest; that didn't work. He thought about calling to check on his parents, but realized the time was close to midnight; that wouldn't work. In the end, he took a shower, grabbed a beer and watched television until he could barely keep his eyes open. Now, in the light of day, his mind was back on Sienna and what he'd done to ruin his own marriage.

He was friends with some of the top athletes in the professional basketball league and he let his status with them go to his head when he tried to fit in. Was he trying to fit in because he'd never really had the kind of fun that weekend availed to him? Getting involved with Sienna in college and focusing on no one but her, did he really feel he was missing out on something by falling in love and marrying young? He knew that wasn't the case at all. He was attempting to show off and be one of the boys, but it came back to bite him viciously. That may have been the ballplayer's way of doing things, but that wasn't him. He loved Sienna, and even though he would have been able to take that incident to the grave one day by keeping silent in theory, in reality, he couldn't live that kind of lie.

Since the divorce, he had not seen or talked to Sienna and his life was empty. He never thought he would feel this way after losing her and the impact of her absence showed him what a fool he was.

Getting up after trying for hours to get some sleep, he walked into the bathroom to get a shower before heading to

Keith's afternoon wedding. If what he heard was true about Sienna, she would be at the wedding, and he would see for himself that she had really moved on. He didn't want to know or hear anything about her having a boyfriend or any semblance of a man in her life. Whoever he was didn't matter because it was never supposed to be anyone but him. If he hadn't screwed up so badly, he would be escorting the most beautiful woman in the world to the wedding. They were supposed to be living a life of bliss as many of their friends were now doing, but he threw it all away. He didn't lose Sienna simply because he told her about that night; he lost her because of what he did that night and he would never forgive himself for what that betrayal did to her. He never wanted to see her that hurt ever again.

Walking across the gray tiles of the bathroom floor, he flung open the door of the fully glass-encased shower and turned the water on hot. He didn't have pajama bottoms or a top to remove because even though he slept alone every single night, he still slept in the nude. He missed how Sienna loved doing that, too. He loved being able to pull her close to him during the night and feeling the warmth of her bare, shapely flesh against his.

Walking to the vanity, he wiped the essence that formed on the mirror from the steam and looked at himself. He had become a shell of the blissfully happy man he had been until the day Sienna had left him. He could have had plenty of women to choose from to build a new life with or to warm his bed at night, but that's not what he wanted. He'd been thinking about Sienna more than usual because he knew it didn't matter how long they were apart, how much time had passed, he loved her and would never love another woman.

Seeing his reflection, he was sick of himself for how he'd wrecked their life together, and now, he was dealing with the consequences.

Turning around and walking into the shower, he shut the door behind him and instead of making haste with the shower to not be late for the wedding, he leaned forward, placing the palms of his hands on the gray and white tiled wall allowing the hot water to cascade down his back. He thought back to that night in a hotel room almost two years ago, a place he should not have been in, and punished himself for his actions again. He still remembered every single word of the conversation that nigh and the visual played like a 3-D movie in his head.

'Carter, she won't know. I'm telling you, get yours tonight and then forget it ever happened.'

He listened to the words come out of the mouth of the one hundred and twenty-million-dollar ballplayer and rather than argue, he started thinking about the possibilities of the scene before him. Was it the alcohol or something else that had him thinking about the proposal? Carter knew he'd only had one beer which wouldn't cloud his judgement. He didn't want to be the prude in a group of professional athletes who he'd come to consider as close to him as brothers. The number one draft pick of the season was standing in front of him, flanked by not one, but two incredibly beautiful women, obviously medically enhanced with body parts that peered at him through fabric that barely covered them. What he saw was more like scraps of clothing than actual outfits.

What they came for was evident in the way they were looking at him. Everything in him said he should turn around, leave the hotel, hop on the first plane and get back to his wife.

'Theon, seriously, I can't man. Sienna would kill me if she ever found out and that is the least of what she'd do,' he decreed. He tried to defend against making the wrong move.

'What are you worried about? Her leaving you? Dude, she'll never find out and trust me, she would never leave you. You are a very rich man with all these connections I'm going to hook you up with. This is one of the biggest weekends in basketball, and you're going to meet guys who have nothing but money to throw away on expensive cars and upgrades. You, my brother, are about to be one of the luckiest brothers here and this is one of the perks,' Theon said pointing at the two women he had his arms around.

'Theon, you know I can't, brother.'

'Nonsense. Now, stop second guessing yourself and have some fun. I'm married too, and you don't hear me worrying about my wife. Wives know what goes on and as long as we're taking care of home, they look the other way. If your wife somehow finds out, buy her something nice, big, and expensive so then you'll be fine. Don't throw away the chance to have the ride of your life,' Theon sneered. 'When I say the ride of your life---Candy here is a full-time gym instructor with energy you won't believe. A few rounds with her and you won't even remember your own name. Have at it and you can thank me later.'

Theon pushed the woman at him and without any gesture from him, she plastered her body up against his and whispered into his ear about all of the nasty, kinky things she wanted to do to him. Before he knew what was *happening, he looked up and Theon and the other woman were gone and he was left in the bedroom suite with Candy. No one else was around. No one would know what went down in the room besides the two of them. Maybe Theon was right. He could indulge in a little fun.*

With the bedroom door closed, he found himself still standing with Candy rubbing up against him, using her hands to get familiar with his body. When she stepped back a few inches, his eyes followed her as she reached up and untied the string around her neck that held her tight red dress in place. His eyes widened the moment the dress fell to the floor revealing she had nothing on underneath. He watched her withdraw a condom from her little gold bag before tossing it to the floor.

'Ready for the ride of your life?' she asked.

Before he could even second guess himself again, he remembered Theon saying his friends were paid for their silence and no one would ever know. He allowed Candy to push him down on the bed and watched her sink to the floor in front of him. That was the moment he should have gotten up and left, but he didn't. Theon's words played over and over in his head that no one would know, so he made the wrong decision and figured, when in Rome...

Haphazardly breaking out of his self-induced, loneliness-imposed, individualized crater of his very own pity party that had him feeling down on himself, Carter then added a little more heat to the water, and, for the first time in a long time, he was taking back the life he wanted. He was done being the guy who cheated on his wife and now found that he couldn't stop thinking about her or wanting her. He wanted her back. He didn't have a plan, but one would come to him. That night with that woman could have been worse, he could have gone all the way. There had to be a way that Sienna could see his good qualities outweighed what happened that night. At least, that was his hope.

Grabbing the shower gel, he poured it over himself and used his hands to work the gel into a lather. He'd had enough of dealing with repercussions he didn't have to. If in fact there was no hope with Sienna, he wasn't going to buy into it. He wouldn't become some obsessed stalker, but he knew he'd made a mistake not fighting for the love of his life. He'd let her go too easy without doing everything he could to prove to her that, yes, he had messed up and he wasn't going to deny that, but Carter had failed to prove that he was also madly in love with her and there was no other woman in the world for him. He wasn't ready to let go of her for good. He hoped that time really did heal old wounds, as an old saying went, because if there was any chance that he could get his love back, he was going to do it and if it required begging on his knees, he would spend every dime he had on knee pads. He only hoped he wasn't too late. Now rushing, he finished his shower so that he could get to the wedding. For the first time in months, he was going to see Sienna again face-to-face and he needed to be ready, mind, body and spirit.

**

"Hey Sienna! I'm glad you made it."

Sienna put on a bogus smile for a woman she didn't care too much for. Bridgette was a gossip and meddler who enjoyed stirring up drama.

"Thank you, Bridgette, and it's good to see you again," she lied through her plastered-on smile.

"Did you hear that Carter finally responded that he was

coming to the wedding today?" Bridgette asked.

Sienna exhaled and kept her phony smile in place. This had to be a record for Bridgette when it came to stirring up mess.

"That's nice. Listen, I'm going to go inside the church and grab a seat on the aisle so that I can get some good pictures of Kim when she comes down the aisle. I'm sure we'll get to chat more at the reception," she said and tried to walk away, but didn't get far.

"Oh, sure, no problem. I was going to do the same thing. Who's the handsome guy with you?" Bridgette said louder drawing attention to them. Leave it to Bridgette to make a scene so that everyone would look at her. She tried to walk away as if she didn't hear her, but to her dismay, Bridgette followed her up the steps to the church.

Exhaling, Sienna started to turn and respond when Brien answered for himself.

"I'm Brien, a friend of Sienna's. Go ahead and get us seats," he said to Sienna, giving her a way out.

Sienna exhaled, happy to be away from Bridgette or anyone else who wanted to inform her of Carter's presence at the wedding. She expected it, but hoped it would happen after the wedding. She hadn't even made it in the church yet. She was thankful for a friend like Brien who intervened, most likely sensing the uncomfortable tension in her. She looked back just as Brien turned to Bridgette.

"Bridgette, right?" he said stalling until Sienna was out of the line of sight.

"Yes. It's nice to meet you, Brien."

"Yes, it is. Enjoy the wedding," he said and walked the rest of the way into the church. He could see from the surprised look on Bridgette's face that she was expecting more of a conversation, but he didn't give her one. He simply wanted to give Sienna the time to get far away from Bridgette's meddling.

Going into the sanctuary, he looked around until he saw Sienna waving to him from one of the pews.

"Thank you for saving me," she said moving over to give him room to sit down.

"I could sense your lack of patience and disinterest in having a conversation with her. It took her two seconds to mention your ex-husband. I take it she's not a friend?" he asked.

"She's far from it. I'm nice to her because we have friends in common, but we're not friends. Thanks for coming to the wedding with me."

Brien smiled and patted her hand.

"That's what friends are for. You sure you're okay running into Carter today? You haven't told me much about your divorce, but I assume it wasn't a good end to your marriage."

"I wouldn't categorize it that way. What broke us up was pretty intense, but going through the divorce wasn't like some *Lifetime* movie. It was amicable and though I wasn't asking for anything because my dental practice is very profitable, he gave me the house we lived in and paid it off so that I wouldn't have payments. He also paid off my car and gave me a really good financial settlement," she explained.

"Wow! Really? I think I like this Carter guy."

Sienna laughed when she saw the smirk on Brien's face showing he was trying to make her laugh.

"He's a good guy."

"Yet, you're divorced." Brien surmised.

"He messed up, and I couldn't forgive him at that time."

"Oh, I see. Have you forgiven him since then?" he asked.

"Yes."

Sienna surprised herself with how quickly she'd said that. She really had forgiven him and had a lot of time to think about what happened and knew they had a history together that outweighed what he'd done, but she had never admitted it to anyone and still wasn't ready to do so. Saying yes was all she was willing to share about it.

"That's good. People are human and they make mistakes. We shouldn't expect perfection from imperfect people. You have to know what you can live with, get over and move on from. Life is short, honey!" Brian exclaimed.

Just as she was about to respond, music started which signaled the ceremony was about to begin.

As she turned to look up the aisle to see who would be coming down first, her eyes looked across the room into the pew on the other side and her gaze landed on Carter. For a few seconds, she forgot how to breathe. She hadn't seen him in months and with a quick look, all the love she'd had for him and missed having with him surfaced as she locked eyes with him.

Everyone was still sitting and she had a clear view of him and his handsome face. She noticed he'd finally let his goatee grow in and it was perfectly trimmed. Even from where she sat across the hall, his light brown eyes pulled her in. His hair was still cut close like she loved and there was a time when she would spend hours caressing it. Shining brightly was the diamond stud in his ear that she'd given him for their first wedding anniversary. She had one to match and even though she knew it was there, she reached up to her own ear and quickly touched the matching stud in the third hole. Knowing he could see her, she speedily put her hand back in her lap. When his lips curved into a grin and she caught a look at his pearly white teeth, her heart felt like it was about to leap out of her chest.

Still the most handsome man she'd ever seen, Carter looked like a snack for every hour of the day. Seeing him stirred up feelings she had tried to forget about in the six months since they signed the final divorce papers. The one thing no one could ever take away from him was how good he looked, only enhanced when he wore a designer suit as he was doing today.

When she tried to look away, she couldn't. It was as if his eyes were a snake charmer and she was the snake mesmerized by his aura. Carter Garrison was the epitome of an African American Greek god.

"Who is that?" she heard a woman a row behind her say. Sienna looked over at Brien who had also heard the comment. Sienna smiled when Brien turned and looked at her before looking to where her gaze landed.

"That's Carter Garrison. He's one of Keith's friends. I've been trying to get that brother to notice me for months, but every time the guys get together to go out, Carter is never there, which makes for a wasted trip for me."

"How do you know him?" the first woman asked.

"My sister is dating a guy who works at Carter's dealership and the bride, Kim, and my sister are good friends. I know that's a lot, but the bottom line is, he's single and gorgeous –-a tall delicious glass of perfectly aged wine. Wait until you see the stance on this guy with those sexy ass bowlegs. I mean, you will never see a sexier man. I bet he's god when he's naked," she added.

"Girl, you need to set your sights a little lower. That man isn't going to be interested in you. I bet he has women for every day of the week. What happened to the guy you were dating?"

Sienna cringed because even though the women were trying to whisper, she could hear every word.

"Oh, we're still dating, but Carter is a man a woman has for life, not just dating like I'm doing."

"Girl, stop it and be quiet. The wedding is about to start. You can ogle him at the reception."

"Please, bump that! I'm trying to climb that tall tree to plant a sign," she laughed and then quieted.

Sienna smiled when Brien took her hand and gave it a light squeeze. Hearing women talk about Carter like that wasn't new to her. Since the day they met back in college, women had always fawned over him, something that had never bothered her because she felt secure that he loved her and only her. The fact that he cheated on her dispelled the notion that he only had eyes for her. Despite that, she was thinking about him as a familiar tingle surged through her body the moment that she saw his handsome face and sexy grin. They were all Carter. What she couldn't see, but used her memory to reprise was how sexy he looked when he walked, exuding more potent sexuality than any one man should ever possess. He still had it and though she's never told anyone, she still wanted him. Her body was on fire, a sign that reminded her how long it had been since any man had touched her.

Sienna exhaled and shew her lustful thoughts away. She was in a church and needed to re-focus, at least for the moment.

As the bridal party began walking down the aisle, Sienna turned and fixated on that and not on how good Carter looked. The sight of him took her back to her own wedding day when he stood at the front of the church waiting for her to join him as they prepared to make a commitment to each other, something he didn't live up to.

"Are you okay?" Brien leaned over and asked her.

"Yes."

Sienna couldn't think of more to say because just as she was about to stand, she looked up and over at Carter again and once again, locked eyes with him. She stood just as he stood, yet the trance wasn't broken. She couldn't move as the intense connection between them obliterated everyone else in the room. His stare was hot, piercing, and penetrating as if he were looking at her soul. She remembered that was all he needed to do to capture her attention. His eyes were magnetic. When he gave a slight wave to her accompanied with another smile, she grinned back and gave a quick wave. She then broke the trance and looked up the aisle where Kim was being escorted down the aisle by her father.

Sienna could feel her heart beating rapidly, almost out of control in her chest, as she shuffled uncomfortably from one foot to the other. She had to be appearing as if she was rocking. She tried to focus on Kim since it was her day, but her eyes drifted between Kim coming down the aisle and Carter standing on the other side of the room, his eyes locking on hers.

He looked good, really good. She huffed, unable to control herself.

Trying not to seem too obvious that she was checking him

out, she took in the charcoal gray suit and purple shirt he wore. She remembered how good he looked in a suit, especially one as fashionably chic as what he had on ––– knowing he pretty much looked hot in anything he wore. He had always been her own personal walking fashion show. Images of him at times when she would watch him dress had her body unnecessarily heating up. The coldness of the day outside and the fact that the church was cool led to no reason for the sudden warmth. The only explanation she had was her reaction to seeing Carter again.

Shaking off her trip down memory lane, she turned her attention to Kim as she passed by her row. Seeing her in her beautiful gown and veil, Sienna's mind was transported again back to the day when she and Carter had married and how happy that day had been. With Kim and her father a row ahead of where Sienna sat, she had no reason for letting her eyes linger back to Carter when everyone else had now turned to face the front of the church. She turned her body slightly, but for the life of her, she could not make her head turn forward. Carter was still looking at her as if he were trying to mentally send her a message. She was vividly remembering their wedding day and not just that. Seeing him looking sexy across the room, she also remembered their wedding night and how meticulously he had removed her wedding dress from her body, making sure he touched and kissed every part of her.

Shaking off the visual and again, scolding herself for not remembering where she was, she turned fully around to face the front of the church. Now wasn't the time to swoon over her ex-husband.

"You're sweating," Brien whispered in her ear. "Are you

alright?"

Sienna cleared her throat while hoping it would also clear her head, enabling her to focus.

"Yes. Carter's looking at me. I can't say anything because I'm looking at him, too."

"Ah, hence the sweat. I've finally seen your ex-husband and from what I see, I'm sure he's making more than just you sweat. Are you sure you're okay?" he inquired again.

"I am. I wasn't expecting to have this kind of a reaction to seeing him after all this time. He looks amazing, and he knows my look. He knows what I'm thinking and it's all about him," she whispered.

Brien turned and looked directly at her this time.

"From the sweat to the look on your face, I'd say you're still in love."

Sienna started to claim denial, but changed her mind. The moment she saw Carter, she already knew Brien's comment was true. She'd never stopped loving him, despite the fact that she'd divorced him. For months, she'd avoided any contact with Carter, allowing herself to grieve the end of her marriage in peace. They had officially been apart for almost two years and seeing Carter today, she now knew that it had been too long. It was easy when she didn't see or talk to him, but today she couldn't escape to her private cocoon where only memories lived. Carter as here and she was still in love.

4

The wedding reception was in full swing as Carter made his way through the throngs of people on the dance floor. After dining on a meal of roasted salmon stuffed with Maryland crab cakes, green bean amandine, and basil and parmesan encrusted potatoes, he'd gotten up to hit the dance floor.

After seeing Sienna at the wedding and now at the reception, he was feeling rejuvenated. He'd seen her looking at him the same way he'd been looking at her and there was something in her eyes that he recognized as want; as desire. She may have been sitting with another man, but there was no mistaking that there was something still left unfinished between them. He did wonder who the guy was she was with. Was he a friend or a lover? He didn't know and the last thing he wanted to do was come in between her and a new love, but if that wasn't the case and he had a chance, he needed to know. The thought of the guy being a lover had him feeling sick. No man – *no man* other than him was to ever touch Sienna in that way. Now he knew how she felt at the idea of another woman touching him.

Carter hadn't spoken to Sienna in a long time and though

the divorce was amicable and not nasty and dirty, he wasn't foolish enough to think that he was one of her favorite people. He'd hurt her deeply and there were some hurts you never get over. He was hoping the hurt he caused her wasn't one of those and that somewhere in her heart, there lived at least a little bit of forgiveness. All he needed was a little room left for him; just a little.

Carter was filled with a small amount of hope when he smiled and waved at her during the wedding and to his amazement, he saw a genuine smile on her face as she waved back. That was something he wasn't sure would happen and hope was also what he needed. When it came to having Sienna in his life again, even as a friend, he lived off of hope.

Leaving the dance floor, he spotted Sienna through the crowd and headed in her direction. He didn't see her date with her and hoped that approaching her at the reception with a lot of people around wasn't a mistake. He had once been married to her and surely, they could be in each other's presence and have a conversation even if it was for her to tell him to stay away from her or to even suggest that he take a quick hike to hell. He had to find out if anger still thrived in her. He wouldn't know if he never tried to say anything. They had been married and there was no need to act like strangers, especially since they each knew the other was there.

"Hello, Sienna," Carter said softly the moment he was close enough for her to hear him over the loud music coming from the band. He didn't know if she was going to speak back or even acknowledge him. He would give her a few minutes and if he got nothing, he would walk away. A non-response would mean she wasn't ready yet and he was prepared to respect that. Waving across a room to him was one thing, but talking to him in person was another. With her back to him, he couldn't read her face to know how receptive she was to his presence. When she didn't turn around, he figured she didn't want to hear anything from him or even see him. After waiting a few seconds longer and seeing her not making an attempt to turn around, he turned to go back the way he'd come.

"Hi, Carter."

He stopped and turned back slowly, hearing her voice. She had also turned around to face him, yet her eyes weren't directly on him. She was looking beyond him, kind of shy like, but he was fine with that. She at least said his name. His heart practically leaped out of his chest, unprepared for the wallop of a punch to his gut he felt seeing her beauty up close after so long. He wanted to smile to let her know how happy he was to see her, but he played it cool to not push her away. If nothing else, he wanted to be sensitive to how she felt seeing him again.

"Hi, Sienna. How are you?" he said walking a little closer to her. The interaction seemed to be comfortable for her. He moved even closer.

"I'm doing fine. I was surprised to see you at the wedding and here at the reception. It's been a long time since we've been in the same place knowing we have a lot of the same friends. You haven't been around," she said.

Carter smiled when she finally looked him square in the eye and to his delight, she wasn't scowling at him in that unforgiving way she had throughout the divorce proceedings. He wanted to reach out to her and pull her into his arms, longing to hold her and to touch her again, but he didn't.

Instead, he placed his hands in the pockets of his pants to avoid making a fool of himself if he would reach for her and she would step away.

"Yeah, I've been pretty busy with work and haven't had a lot of time for socializing. You're looking as beautiful as ever. How's the dental practice coming along?" he asked, curious and a bit intrigued. He knew how hard she worked to open up her own dental office and was happy to have been by her side to help with whatever he needed to see her dream come to fruition.

"It's going really well. Constance and I now have a total of twelve full-time dentists and a lot of additional staff now and my calendar has stayed full with patients, sometimes more than I can handle."

Happy for her, Carter smiled brightly.

"I'm glad to hear that and hap for you. You've worked really hard to make it a success," he said.

"I can see from your pearly whites that you've found a really good dentist, and I'm glad," Sienna said.

Carter wanted to say he hated having to find someone else and only wanted her. He restrained himself knowing they would both think over why he had to switch dentists and so far, they were being cordial. He wanted to keep it that way.

"Well, none will ever be as good as you, but he's a good second runner up," Carter joked.

For a few seconds, their eyes locked and then they both looked away as if they were struggling with what to say next. Carter was just happy they were saying anything to each other.

"How are your parents?" Sienna asked.

"They're doing great. Of course, my mom has asked about

you. She's wondered if we ever see each other. I can finally tell her that I've seen you and you're happy. How are your parents?" he asked.

"They're great as well."

"Keith and Kim really did it big with the wedding. I'm glad they finally took the leap," he said.

"I know. I thought those two would never get married. She looked absolutely gorgeous," Sienna said.

When Sienna beamed, Carter's heart swelled even more. There was no doubt she still held his in the palm of her hands.

"She did, but she didn't compare to how beautiful you were on your day," he said.

Too late, he thought to himself. He'd said it before thinking about making a reference to their wedding day. Carter knew now wasn't the time to bring that up, but he wanted her to know that he wasn't shying away from the fact that she was still the most beautiful woman in a wedding gown he'd ever seen. He wished he could go back and never make that huge error in judgement because they would still be living as husband and wife and probably either already pregnant or talking about getting pregnant.

Before they were married, they had a plan in place to focus on their careers and get them really jumping so that when they decided to have children, she would be able to stay at home for as long as she wanted to in order to bond with and raise their children without putting them in daycare. That was important to both of them. He ruined all of the hopes and dreams they had for their love.

"Thank you. I was thinking about that day when I was at the church," Sienna.

Carter saw her blushing and figured she was probably not only thinking about that day, but that night and how they had barely gotten any sleep before the sun had come up.

"That day was perfect and you were perfect in it. When I saw you as Kim was coming down the aisle, I couldn't focus on her; I was too busy remembering how incredibly beautiful you were that day and still are," Carter said.

Sienna looked up at him.

"I guess that wasn't enough?" she asked.

Sienna surprised herself and didn't know where that question came from. Though she meant to say it as a statement, it came out as a question. She didn't move when Carter came closer and leaned down close to her ear.

"You were and always were enough. I messed up, but that had nothing to do with who or what you are. I hope what I did never has you questioning that. No man, not even me, should ever make you feel like there is something wrong with you. I'm the one who screwed up and messed up our lives. You are and will always be enough for any man, including me," he clarified.

Carter leaned back up when she smiled. Though he'd hurt her more than anyone ever has, he wanted her to know how genuine his words were.

"Thank you for saying that."

Carter had been smiling until he looked over her shoulder.

"I think your date's looking for you. I see him looking around and I don't blame him. I wouldn't let a gorgeous woman like you out of my sight either. I was a fool once for not appreciating you enough. I hope he knows how lucky he is. Are you happy?" he asked, capturing her gaze.

Carter needed to hear the words and also see if in her

eyes. He longed to hear her say that being around him again and having him this close was messing with her head. He wanted to imagine her stomach doing flip-flops as she struggled with no being able to deny that she still held some love for him. He wanted to hear her say that their time apart since the separation and divorce left her with a lot of time to think and seeing him now and hearing how sorrowful he still is, would have her questioning if she had tried hard enough to save their love. The love they had ran deep and with the connection they were currently experiencing, to him it still did. There was something in the way she was breathing and looking at him that told him there was more behind her eyes, but she wasn't ready to share it with him. He knew her look. He'd known it since college. She was struggling, but the time wasn't now.

"I am as happy as I could be right now. I'm at a place of peace, if that makes sense," Sienna finally said.

Carter didn't know whether to be happy or sad knowing she was so content without him, but if she was happy, then that was all that mattered to him. Knowing that they could be in the same space and there not be tension was enough for him for now. He'd stayed away to give her space. Now he knew that the air between them wasn't cloudy.

"Sienna, I wish you every bit of happiness that you deserve and I hope we can stop avoiding each other as if we weren't married before. Seeing you happy means the world to me," he said. "I'll let you go. It was great seeing and talking to you again." For one last time, Carter leaned close to her ear again. "Please don't stop talking to me and smiling and waving at me. I've been miserable without you, but that makes it a little better to bear with what I've done to us," he added.

Sienna turned to wave at Brien to let him know she was finishing up.

"You want me to be happy and I want the same for you. I thought I would be able to not care if you were happy or not, but I do care. I want you to be happy, too. I hope you're trying and have forgiven yourself," Sienna said.

"Seeing and talking to you just made my day and my start to happiness."

"It was good seeing you, Carter."

"Likewise," he said just before she turned and walked away.

Carter stood in place until she turned one last time and waved at him before she disappeared into the crowd of people on the dance floor. He then turned and went back to his table feeling good that he made the right choice in approaching Sienna. He didn't want anything to be awkward between them. Just as he was about to sit down, he looked across the table at Dexter who was grinning from ear to ear. By the time he actually sat, Dexter had already moved over to the chair next to him. He prepared himself for the onslaught of questions Dexter was about to throw at him.

"I saw you talking to Sienna. How did it go?" Dexter inquired.

"It went fine. We talked about general stuff, nothing too deep. I asked her if she was happy."

When he didn't say anymore, Dexter nudged him.

"And? What did she say?"

"Bro, what is your problem? You look like you're excitedly waiting on the punchline. She said she was at a place of peace. Her boyfriend started looking around for her and then our conversation was pretty much over."

"Yeah, I see them dancing on the dance floor. You missed that when you walked this way."

Carter turned his head so fast in the direction he remembered she went in that he felt a quick pain in his neck. He let his eyes follow the direction of where Dexter was looking and saw her. At that exact moment, the fast tempo song changed to a romantic slow one and where he hoped he wouldn't have to witness Sienna in another man's arms during a slow song, he was now in the midst of such a moment. His heart crashed and burned in his chest. His entire body stiffened at the sight of them. He had no right to be upset, but it pained him to see her go so easily into someone else's arms and from her bright smile, she was loving it and so was her date. He on the other hand, wasn't.

"You cool?" Dexter asked.

"No comment," Carter said through clinched teeth. He was trying his best to not let his reaction show. If he knew his friends as well as he thought he did, they also saw Sienna with another man and were wondering and watching for his reaction. He wouldn't give any of them the satisfaction.

"Okay, as long as you're cool. I'm checking to make sure you don't make a move to hurt that guy. I can see how you're looking at him and can only imagine what's going on in your head."

"Naw, I'm cool," Carter lied. "Nothing violent is flowing through my veins. That guy has every right to have Sienna in his arms right now, just like any guy would have. She's single and downright gorgeous and tonight, that guy is the luckiest guy in this room. That even includes Keith, who just got married. Sienna's date is still the luckiest because in his arms, he holds the most precious woman any man could ever encounter. Because of me, he gets to hold her like that and this is my punishment for being the biggest jackass that ever lived," Carter groaned, painfully aware of how his heart ached.

The pain he was going through increased when he thought he could see a glow in Sienna's eyes as she and her date talked and danced.

"Don't be too hard on yourself. You made a mistake and because of the incredible person Sienna is, she isn't making you pay for it by throwing it in your face when she sees you."

"No, I paid for it when she divorced me. She would never continue to focus on that. She's not that kind of woman. She is the kind of woman a man treats better than I did. I really screwed that up. I mean, I really, really screwed that up, and for the past six months, I've thought about nothing else or no one else but her. I want my wife back," Carter admitted. It was ironic that the moment he uttered the words, his eyes locked with Sienna's again as they had in the church and when they were talking and if there was a way to mentally send her what he was thinking, he was trying his hardest to do so. He sorrowfully accepted the vision in front of him with her and another guy. Still, he wasn't ready to give up; guy or no guy.

Watching her in the arms of another man pretty much ate him alive and he deserved the hurt and the pain his heart was going through. This feeling was his penance for what he'd done to her, the one woman he should have loved with every fiber of his being, which meant never betraying her.

"Are you ever going to tell me what happened All-Star weekend? I mean, I know what you did, but how did you get to that? What made you actually do it?" Dexter asked curiously.

Carter had never told anyone other than his father and Sienna about what he'd done that day. Most people had an idea, but as far as the exact details, he'd only spoken that to two people. Dexter was his closest friend and until now, he wasn't ready to trust even him with the details. It had been almost two years ago.

"You already know I cheated, but it wasn't an all the way kind of cheating, if that makes sense," Carter said.

That was the best Carter could do and when he saw the perplexed look on Dexter's face, he knew he was being mysterious about what cheating really was. Were there levels to cheating or was any amount of cheating just cheating?

"It doesn't, so explain," Dexter retorted quickly.

"Ok. You know Theon and a bunch of his teammates had a huge after party where there was drinking and half-naked women. I had never partied with a crowd like that, full of professional ballplayers and it was definitely wild. I didn't realize these guys have all kinds of hookups all the time when they're away and that weekend was no exception. He showed up to my room with two women and one he'd snagged for me. I knew I shouldn't have, but I got caught up in the atmosphere and the moment and I let my body control my mind. I knew it was wrong and even more so when I let her slip a condom on me. It was pretty much over before it really got started. Things progressed really fast and she got right down to business. She started pleasuring me with her hands and the next moment, she was on my lap on the bed. The moment I joined my body with hers, I came to my senses and knew I shouldn't be there and not with any woman other than my wife. I moved her off, zipped my pants up grabbed my overnight bag, which I had never unpacked and got out of there. I headed straight for the airport and caught an early flight and went home. Guilt ate at me even over the few seconds I penetrated her, since I knew it was wrong. Even though I didn't go beyond a few seconds or anywhere near completion---*if you catch my drift*---the fact that I did it at all was enough to ruin my marriage to the most incredible woman, ever."

Carter exhaled his frustration with himself once again. Each time he thought about that night, he hated himself a little more because of it.

"I know this is a crazy question, but with the little that did happen and it seems like you stopped it right away, why did you tell Sienna? Why not just let it go and keep your happy marriage?" Dexter asked.

Carter turned completely around and faced Dexter, taking his eyes off of Sienna. Being a sucker for punishment, he kept looking at her and her date and fumed more and more each time he saw them.

"Because that's not who I am. I owed Sienna the truth. I had never lied or hidden anything from her before and I knew the risk of telling her. I honestly thought we would be able to work through it, but that didn't happen. She couldn't stop picturing me, even for a few seconds, inside of another woman. I have no excuse for what I did, but I damn sure do miss her. I miss Sienna every single day. She was it for me and there's been no one since."

"What?" Dexter stated louder than he'd planned. He knew Carter wasn't interested in being hooked up by any of his friends, but he didn't know that meant that he hadn't been seeing anyone at all.

"You heard me," Carter said turning his attention back to Sienna. He couldn't seem to take his eyes off of her. It didn't help that she looked amazing in a purple dress with bling accents that fit her curves, accentuating just how gorgeous she was.

"Are you saying you haven't been with anyone this entire time? No woman at all?" Dexter said.

Carter saw the disbelief on Dexter's face, but held his stance. He wasn't ashamed to say he wasn't as much of a player as Dexter was. Knowing what he lost, he didn't want anyone other than his wife, even if she no longer wanted him.

"Correct. None, and I'm not interested in any other than the one I'm looking at right now. I've gone out on dates, but nothing intimate. I can't stop thinking about Sienna and she is who I want in my life and in my bed."

Carter was annoyed as Dexter poked him in the arm. He was already looking at him, so the extra gesture wasn't necessary, but it was pure Dexter. He had to make a big show of everything.

"You do know you're divorced right? I mean, is there something about the fact that it's over that you don't quite get? She left you and divorced you. I think your chance of getting back in her good graces is slim to none. The reason she divorced you is still there and that won't change. Don't think I'm not supportive of you because you know I'm always in your corner, but I'm concerned that you're not getting it."

Carter gave Dexter an impatient look and then turned back to Sienna.

"I hear you and usually I would see the glass as half empty

as you are seeing it, but I don't," Carter said.

"Bruh, have you seen how happy she is with this guy? Look at them? I think she's moved on," Dexter said.

"I see it and I see them and what I see is a man with his arms around my wife and I don't like it. Sienna has always been the only woman for me and she always will be. I'm a clown and a fool for messing up the way that I did. I don't regret telling her because that was the right thing to do. I do regret ever going to All-Star weekend with Theon and his teammates. I don't care how rich they've made me over the years with the number of cars they've bought and had customized, nothing was worth losing the love of my life. I intend to get her back and I don't care how much begging, pleading and making promises that I'll have to keep forever if I have to; I want my wife back. I don't know how or when yet, but it started tonight when I spoke to her. She wasn't disgusted by me, nor did she act as if she couldn't stand to be in my presence. We were cordial and if there is any way that I can get her to forgive me enough to try at anything again, especially friendship, then I'm here for it all. I'm here for every bit of having Sienna in my arms like that again."

Carter was feeling pumped. He had no real reason to be, considering he was the one in the chair and Sienna was dancing with a man. The fact that they could again be affable was a good start. He didn't care what any naysayers had to say, he was a determined man.

"I hear you and I am behind you one hundred percent. You're right that you and Sienna were meant to be together, and I'm sorry about what happened to your marriage. One thing I can say is that the love is still there. We've been sitting here watching them dance like two stalkers and I've noticed that every single time she's looked this way, she focused her attention on you. I think you're not the only one still feeling the tug. All I'm going to say is that this time when you marry Sienna, I'd like to be the best man again. I've been there from the beginning. I'm always going to be in the wings for you both," Dexter said.

Carter smiled and nodded when Dexter gave him a hard pat on the back.

"You caught that in her gaze, did you?" he asked.

"I did and if I wasn't a believer all this time, I am now. She sure is beautiful."

"Yes, she is and always has been. Everything about her is perfection."

"Best man, Carter. That's all I'm saying."

"It's already in my plan," Carter said and for the first time in a long time, he felt optimistic.

When his eyes once again connected with Sienna's he was sending her love, even if she didn't know it. He was sending her his determination that there may have been a divorce, but he wasn't letting go just yet. He was in this thing called love to win it again and only with her.

5

"Mom? Are you here?" Sienna yelled the moment she walked into her parents' house. No matter how busy her days were, she always made time to drop in on them to check in.

"Yes, I'm in the kitchen," her mother hollered back.

Walking into the kitchen, Sienna sat in the high brown leather chair at the beige and brown marble island as her mother cut the stem off of the flowers that she had laid out in front of her. Her mother loved having fresh flowers on tables throughout the house and with the look of the cloth covered island, it seemed she was replacing all of the flowers today.

"Hey daughter of mine. Is there a reason I haven't seen you in almost two weeks? The last time I saw you was the night before Kim and Keith's wedding."

"I know and I'm sorry. I've been busy with the practice and trying to find a new building for the office park and community center. The last deal fell through," she said full of disappointment.

Her mother stopped moving and looked over at her.

"Fell through? I thought it was going well and your father said the location was perfect for what you needed. What happened?"

Sienna loved knowing that if no one else had her back, Lars and Connie Richards did. Her father and mother were the best.

"The guy who owns it is being a prick. He keeps raising the price knowing how badly we want that spot and what it would mean for all of our plans. Rather than keep playing these games with him, Constance and I have been looking for another location."

"Will the two of you still be the only partners or are you looking for others? Whatever you get is going to be a large spot and you'll need a lot of help. You're tripling the size of your staff, right?"

"True. We're taking on more staff, but no other partners, at least not any time soon. I'm trying to not let this business with the building stress me out. Our business plan is great and our offer was even better. Where's dad?" she asked looking around as if her father would appear out of nowhere because she asked for him.

"He went to the store to pick up a few things for me. Did you need him for something? He should be back within the hour."

"Nothing pressing. I wanted to see you both. I have some time."

"Good. Tell me about the wedding? Was it nice? I know Kim was stunning!"

"It was great and Kim looked beautiful. Anyone could see her happiness from the moon. I took a lot of pictures on my phone. I left it in my car, but I'll get it before I leave so that you can see how gorgeous she looked."

"No one will ever be more beautiful than you were on your

day. That's still the second most momentous moment of my life, the first being the day you were born. I was as happy as you were on that day."

When her mother's hands stopped moving as she held the scissors mid-cut, Sienna knew she was thinking of a way to take her words back, but there was no need. Sienna's wedding day was what dreams are made of and she would never discount that because of divorce.

"I see that look on your face and it's okay. I'm not squeamish at the thought of my wedding. Really, it's okay. Besides, Carter said the same thing to me at Kim's wedding," she said, matter-of-factly. Saying Carter's name flowed from her mouth as if it was the most natural thing. She saw the surprised look on her face knowing he had not been a topic of discussion between them for a long time.

Not only did her mother stop cutting the flowers, she sat the scissors down and turned her full attention to the conversation. Sienna knew she'd get that reaction and figured it would be best to get his name out in the open and get it over with. There was no way she'd have a conversation about the wedding and reception and not bring up the fact that Carter was there and since seeing him, she hadn't been able to stop thinking about him.

"Carter? You saw Carter at the wedding?"

Sienna shook her head and reached for the jar of cookies her mother always had on the counter. She needed a distraction, something to do with her hands. She was nervous and a bit uncomfortable talking more in-depth about Carter. Most of the conversations she had shared with her mother about him since they separation were not good ones, but now, she didn't have horrible things to say about him. She could say his name and not be angry.

"I did and we actually talked; it was friendly."

"Really? I'm surprised. Every time I've asked you since the divorce if you've seen him, you like to change the subject. You easily say his name now. Does that mean you're moving beyond the anger?"

"Mom, I moved beyond that anger a long time ago. I don't hate Carter, and I'm not angry at him. After all of this time and having months and months to think about it, I can't walk around angry forever. I would live in misery if I carried that burden around day after day. It was what it was. I won't lie and say even after all this time, it doesn't still hurt, but the sting isn't as painful," she acknowledged.

"I wish you hadn't acted so quickly back then with the separation and divorce. The way he loved you...I know he was sorry and he made and error in judgement, but it's something we've all done."

Sienna stopped eating the cookie she'd pulled out and looked up at her mother quizzically.

"Are you saying me filing for divorce wasn't warranted?" she asked quickly and defensively.

"I'm not saying that at all. You made the decision you felt you needed to make for your own happiness and I respect that. I would never, ever question or cause you to doubt that. You know what was best for you and if it was to divorce Carter, then so be it. I will always support whatever you do in life," Connie said.

"What would you have done if daddy had done that to you? I know you mom, and you would have done exactly what I did. You don't tolerate a man taking you for granted, let alone cheating on you. It's about self-respect," she said.

Sienna thought her mother would have responded right away, sharing her convictions, but she didn't. Instead, she removed her gloves and reached around to take off the apron she had around her hips and came around to the side of the counter where she sat. She didn't know what was going on, but her mother still hadn't said anything in response to the question she asked. She'd been doubting herself a long time and even had doubts the morning she signed the final divorce papers. She wanted to change her mind, but she'd gone so far by then, she didn't see any room for going back. She never told anyone she was no longer angry over what happened and saw that even Carter wasn't perfect, but she wanted him to be. That was then.

"Come with me. Let's sit at the kitchen table and talk for a minute," Connie said.

Sienna followed her by stepping down from the stool and joining her at the table.

"Are you alright, mom? You look puzzled. Did I say something wrong?" Sienna asked concerned.

They were having a good conversation and now Sienna was worried. Her mother looked stressed about something.

"I'm going to share something with you and I need you to promise you won't be judgmental and that you will never share that I told you this. I made a promise to someone that I would never tell you this so that you wouldn't change how you see your father."

Sienna looked at her questionably. This had to do with her father?

"Daddy? What about him?" she said shuffling in her seat. She waited through the seconds of quiet while her mother gathered her thoughts.

"Years ago, your father had an affair."

"What!" Sienna shouted and leaned back so far in her chair that it almost toppled over.

"Sienna, remember what I said. No judgment and he's your father. Just like Carter, he's not perfect, and we shouldn't expect perfection. I'm not making any excuses for him here, just an observation."

"I love daddy and nothing would ever change that."

"That's good because he loves you more than anything in this world. He would hate for you to look at him differently and I don't expect you to."

Sienna tried to calm her rushing heart. Her father had an affair. She was shocked.

"I won't. When did this happen?" she asked.

"A long, long time ago. You were about five years old. It was with a woman he worked with. It wasn't an almost incident like what happened with Carter. This was an all-out affair that lasted about four months before I found out about it. I thought my world was coming completely apart and, in that instance, he didn't tell me like Carter confessed to you. This woman came to my house and told me because she wanted him to leave us and go with her. *Permanently.* When your father found out she had come here, he was furious and more apologetic than I've ever seen him. For six months, he didn't live with us, but you didn't know it. He had moved into an apartment and would get up every morning and come here so that he would be here with you in the morning and he would come by after work and stay until you were in bed before leaving to go home to his place. We didn't want you to know anything about our struggles. My first reaction was to divorce him, but we talked about the problems we were having and decided to try counseling like you and Carter did. We did that for another six months and eventually found our way back to the love we knew was always there. His slip-up was much more severe than what Carter did and I loved him. I only knew love with your father."

Sienna was stunned. She couldn't believe they kept this secret from her for years.

"I had no idea anything had ever happened," she said.

"We wanted it that way. He was my everything. He was wrong, oh he was dead wrong, and it took me a long time to forgive him. Besides that, he'd slipped up with some crazy chick. Thankfully, she moved on and out of state after he let her know he wasn't leaving his wife and child for her. I also encouraged him to apologize to her because he'd led her on for his own selfish reasons. He was doing what he saw other executives doing and he got carried away. He never did it again because he realized how close he'd come to losing you and me. I'm telling you this because I want you to know that things are forgivable, even that. Your father's affair lasted months, and eventually, I forgave him completely and we got our marriage back on track. We had problems and we talked them out so that we could work through them and remember the love. Counseling and hard work at our marriage helped a great deal. I'm sorry it didn't work out that well for you and Carter. I really thought it would, but it didn't. You know I love him."

Sienna didn't know what to say. Her father had an affair that lasted months and hadn't confessed until he was found out. Counseling and hard work had worked for them. Hearing how they made it through was giving her confirmation that she didn't try hard enough with her marriage to Carter.

"I can't believe Daddy did that to you. I'm sorry you had to go through that," she said comforting her mother.

"Baby, believe me, that has been water under the bridge for a lot of years and I never thought for one second that your father didn't love me. He got caught up and I have to tell you, I've had men approach me before and I can see how easily anyone can be tempted."

"You were tempted?" Sienna asked.

"I'm human, dear, your dad is human and so are you and Carter. I'm not condoning or dismissing what he did, but I will admit I prayed that you would find your way back to each other before the divorce happened. I'm sorry you had to go through that. You know how furious I was at him for what he did, but I stood on the outside of your marriage. Only you could decide what would make you happy."

"Wow. I had no idea you went through that. Just, wow," Sienna exclaimed.

She exhaled loudly and leaned back in her chair, exhausted just listening to her mother's story.

"I survived and stayed in love with your father."

"I'm shocked that you did. I never would have thought you would have."

"No judging," her mother said.

Sienna lifted her hands in surrender. The last thing she would ever do is judge her parents for deciding to make love their priority.

"None, mom. I would never do that because that was you and daddy's situation and had nothing to do with me. You both have loved me unconditionally and because of you, I have been able to live, love and thrive. Why didn't you tell me this when I told you what Carter did and how I was planning to divorce him?" she probed.

"Would my telling you then have changed your mind?"

Sienna paused. Since her father wasn't home and her mother was sharing from the depths of her soul, she wanted to do the same thing. She looked down at the floor and then back up at her mother.

"I think I messed up terribly, mom. I had changed my mind before the divorce, but pride wouldn't let me stop myself. I had gone that far and was feeling good about having all the power. I felt like people who knew what happened could look at me and see how strong I was and that I wasn't fazed. I thought more about others seeing me than I thought about how I saw myself. I knew my filing for divorce would hurt Carter and at the time, I needed him to hurt. Then I realized, he wasn't the only one hurting."

"Are you saying you didn't do all you could have done to save your marriage? Is that what you wanted?"

Sienna hunched her shoulders, still unsure of herself.

"We tried counseling and there were times that I didn't want to hear what was being revealed, mainly because it made me take a hard look at myself and I didn't like what I was finding out about me. After the divorce, I was sad and empty beyond anything I thought I could survive. I was the one who gave up on counseling and I was the one who stopped talking. Carter tried and he said and did so many things to let me know how sorry he was for what he did and how he would never, ever do anything like that again. I also realize now that we were young and even though that's no excuse, it was a hurdle. We had never had any real problems other than small squabbles, but nothing big like that. I didn't know what to do. I should have remembered my vow of for better or worse and I didn't. I was hurting and I wanted him to hurt. The only way I knew to do that was to divorce him because I knew he didn't want that."

Sienna could feel the tears welling up in her eyes as she thought about how much Carter begged and pleaded with her and his words fell on deaf ears because she was filled with vengeance. She looked up when her mother reached out and took her hands in hers and held on tight.

"You told me he didn't actually go all the way, if you know what I mean, with that woman and the moment he got back home, he told you what happened. You said he didn't even stay the rest of the weekend, but caught a flight back home to you. Do you remember the day you came home and told your father and I about this guy you met one day walking across campus? We didn't want you focused on a man but on your studies. You weren't hearing any of that. All you wanted was that guy; all you wanted was Carter Garrison. From that day until that weekend when he messed up, you knew nothing but love for him. It hurt me to know what happened, but even more to know that something like that caused your divorce when I remembered what I had been through," Connie explained.

"Was it easy to forgive daddy for what he did to you?" Sienna asked.

"It took a lot of forgiving your father knowing that all those late nights and trips away he was with another woman and it wasn't just once. It was over and over. It took a long time, but yes, I forgave him because our love was deeper than our faults, especially his. Your father is an incredible man just as Carter has always been, and for me, that was worth fighting for. Back then, I told my sister and two of my friends and all of them had something to say with the bottom line being I should divorce him and take all the money. They were vicious with their comments. These are women I thought I could confide in and it wasn't that I wanted them to say what I wanted to hear, but all they heard was affair. They began planning a funeral for my marriage. There were a few things I learned from that---one was, at that time, all of them were single, so they had no idea what being in a marriage was like and what it meant to take vows seriously; even when something happens and those vows are broken. Second, I realized that it's easy to speak of walking away when you're not in that situation. I had to make the decision based on your father and me. What I can say is that it was a major lesson learned for both of us and our marriage was stronger and happier than it had been. We chose to fight and we fought hard and, in the end, love won. I can't imagine my life without him and I chose to forgive and keep love and I didn't care what anyone thought. No one could live my life other than me. I can say, I never knew total happiness until your father and I went through that bad patch in our marriage."

Sienna sniffled and tried to hold back her emotions.

"I should have fought, Mommy. I should have fought harder. I should have listened. I should have *tried!* Carter tried to fight for us and I mean he tried hard, but I was so angry, I couldn't see past the fury. The image of him and another woman was hard to bear. I couldn't eat, I couldn't sleep, I couldn't do anything, but focus on that every time I saw him. What I couldn't see was how truly sorry he was. I forgot that he wasn't perfect. He had been so perfect for so long. He was the perfect guy, the perfect boyfriend and the perfect husband until that moment and I forgot about all of the good times. That one moment ruled my life and my decision," she said, sadly.

"Baby, it's easy to say that right now, but back then, you didn't see life that way."

Sienna shook her head up and down, knowing how right her mother was, but still, she was without Carter because she didn't fight; she didn't love the moment they finally had bad times.

"I saw Carter at the wedding and so many memories of how good our marriage was came flooding back in. Like you and daddy, our love was deep and the best there was. He slipped up and fell outside of that perfect circle I put him in and I couldn't come back from what he did."

Before she could stop them, tears streamed down her face as her mother reached up to clear them away.

"I don't like to see you this unhappy and unforgiving of yourself. I know it was a hard time for you and your emotions were all over the place. You still love Carter, don't you?"

Sienna nodded, trying to keep herself from openly crying. No one had asked her that before and hearing the question, there was no need to doubt what was in her heart.

"Yes, I do. I've known it for a long time, but not seeing or talking to him made it easier to deal with. The moment I saw him, the love came flooding back like someone had turned on a faucet to my heart. I haven't been able to stop thinking about him since the night of Kim's wedding."

Her mother rubbed the back of Sienna's hands in an effort to soothe her.

"There are some choices we make that we aren't happy about, but we're forced to live with because that's the path we choose. I'm sorry you're going through this. It sounds like you had a chance to talk to him. Is he doing well? I know your father has seen him a few times and they've talked and been cordial. I can also tell your dad misses Carter. He misses having that son. I hope one day you'll be able to heal and perhaps get married again. I still want grandchildren," her mother said, causing them both to laugh, lightening the mood of their depressing conversation.

Sienna wiped the remaining tears from her eyes.

"I definitely see grandchildren in your future," she said.

"Good. Now, let's get some ice cream from the freezer and pig out while we wait for your father to get back."

"I'm glad you and Dad worked things out. I can't imagine not having the life and love I had growing up."

"Not to slight you in any way, but when I said my vows, I meant every single word. My marriage to your father was meant to be forever, good or bad."

"I wish I had realized that before it was too late for me with Carter."

"Is it?" Connie asked quickly.

Sienna looked at her questionably.

"Is what?" she asked.

"Is it too late for you and Carter?"

Another question no one has ever asked her and she never thought about it. She saw divorce as final and therefore, anything else never came to mind.

"I'm sure he's moved on to someone else by now. A man that good looking and successful has no problem finding a woman who will appreciate him."

"You appreciated Carter, so don't say that. He hurt you and you lashed out the only way you felt would ease your pain. Now you're dealing with another kind of pain – the pain of wanting him after he hurt you."

"Ugh. What is wrong with me? How can I still love him?"

"Because like the love your father and I have, your love with Carter was meant to last forever, through the good, the bad and the ugly. That was an ugly time. It was hard."

"It was hard and I shouldn't want him and he shouldn't want me," Sienna said.

"That's not what I asked you."

Sienna locked eyes with her mother, the one woman she could be vulnerable with.

"Yeah, mom. I think it's too late, but I will forever love him. At least now, we've broken the ice of talking since the divorce and I no longer have to avoid seeing or being around him. Unlike you and dad, I divorced him, you stayed and worked your way through it. You did it together. I immediately separated myself from Carter and I let my hurt keep me from seeing that we may have been able to work things out. I think it's too late," she said somberly.

"Keep your head up. Perhaps, daughter of mine, it's not too late."

"I treated him horribly."

"Yes, you did."

Sienna thought her mother would have had more to say, but she didn't. She watched her smile and then get up and went to the refrigerator. There was a strange look on her mother's face that she couldn't read. Something told her that her mother would one day ask her that question again.

Maybe she would have a different answer; maybe.

Putting it to the side, she got up and went in search of two spoons. Ever since she was a little girl, her mother used ice cream to heal all wounds. This was definitely an ice cream kind of moment.

6

Almost two months after seeing Sienna at the wedding, Carter was still going to bed at night and waking up in the morning with her on his mind. He hadn't seen or talked to her since then, but he knew that she'd visited his parents a few times. After Kim and Keith's wedding, his mother told him that Sienna had reached out to her to have lunch, missing them as much as they missed her, even though Sienna was no longer married to him.

Sienna was the only daughter they had since he was their only child. He was happy to see that she and his parents could still have a great relationship.

A few times, he'd come across Sienna's father and they were able to have good, quick chats. He didn't think her father had ever mentioned to her that he was still in contact, but he didn't want to forget how good her parents had always been to him, even after he hurt their only child. Those few brief chats had her father talking glowingly of Sienna, a sure sign that at least those family bonds were still strong. Her father had been extremely upset with him early on, but he believed Lars could see how sorry he was and, in some way, he felt like Lars understood. It was a vibe he got, but he didn't dwell on it.

On a typical Thursday, he would spend the day at the dealership or go to check out how the new building for the new dealership was coming along, but today, he was meeting with Dexter to talk about a larger location for one of the repair shops. His mind may be distracted, but he still had business to take care of.

He walked into the main repair area of *Chi Brothers Customizations*, the auto customization business they owned together. He preferred letting Dexter run the shop while he focused his attention on the dealership. He sent many referrals to Dexter, but opted to remain more of a silent partner than one who was hands-on. They had good managers running the repair shops and both of them checked on those locations often. He looked around for Dexter and as he walked toward his office, he turned when he heard Keith's voice. He spun around and walked in the direction of his voice near one of the car bays. When he got there, he saw Keith talking to one of the guys who worked for him and in the middle of the floor was Keith's pride and joy, a new Navigator truck that had been recently purchased right before the wedding.

"Back from the honeymoon I see," he said greeting Keith.

"Hey, what's up Carter. I wasn't expecting to see you here. I figured you didn't come around here too often. You might get dirty or something. This isn't like that pristine clean Mercedes showroom floor."

"You got jokes," Carter said, greeting him with the greeting one frat brother always gave another on sight. Though they had been friends for a lot of years, even before college, they grew closer when they pledged the same fraternity at different colleges. "What are you doing here?" Carter added.

"A wedding gift from my beautiful new wife was upgrades to my truck. Malcolm here is taking real good care of me. I was dropping it off and was going to hang with Dexter until Kim picked me up. She went to check on her boutique."

Carter knew about Kim's boutique. He'd bought a lot of things for Sienna from there. Kim owned one of the hottest clothing boutiques in downtown Chicago.

"Oh, she hooked you up huh? Which package are you getting?" Carter asked.

"The platinum of course, which is everything from new rims to seats with iPads in the back of them. Let's just say I'm getting the works. How's everything going?"

"Great. I'm busier than ever, but I'm maintaining as much normalcy as I possibly can," Carter relayed.

"Now that we're back, we're hoping to hang out with the gang this weekend. Christmas is next week, and everyone goes their separate ways. I was going to have Kim stop by the dealership when I left here because I assumed you'd be there instead. I know you've divorced the whole group when you and Sienna parted, but if you decide you want to give us all a second chance to have you in our presence again, we'd like to see you at the gathering," Keith said.

"Man, not you too. I've been getting that from everyone. What did you all do? Get together and decide to all jump on me at once? I got it; I hear you."

"Nothing has been the same with you missing, though I was happy to see you at the wedding. What happened? Did you and Sienna agree in the divorce that she got all the friends? She may not come to everything, but at least we see her. Unless it's on the basketball court where it's just the guys, you're ghost. What's up with that? Still avoiding Sienna?" Keith asked.

Carter wasn't avoiding her as much as he was allowing her room to heal without seeing him everywhere she went. He hadn't seen or talked to her since the wedding reception, but she'd been on his mind daily. One of the problems with the divorce was that they had a lot of friends in common and though their divorce wasn't a bitter one in the end, he backed off so that she could feel comfortable around the friends they once shared. He would rather be the person on the outside and not her. He did miss hanging with the group.

"I'm not avoiding Sienna. I actually had a chance to talk with her at your wedding reception and it wasn't awkward. You know she got my mother in the divorce," he joked.

"So, they're still tight, huh?"

"I think even tighter. It was a little touchy at first, but for the past few weeks, they've been handing pretty tough. I stopped by the house the other day and my Pops said they had gone out for manicures, pedicures, shopping and lunch. They used to do that a lot when we were married. My mother gave me the third degree for what I did to ruin my marriage and, of course, as she should have, she took Sienna's side and I got why. Just last night, I was going to stop by and when I turned down their street, I saw Sienna's Mercedes parked in front of the house. I kept going and went home."

"Oh, so you're avoiding everybody? Now, I don't feel so bad about being treated like the crazy uncle who lives in the basement," Keith ribbed.

"I'm just trying to make things more comfortable for

Sienna. In time, things will get back to normal," he said.

"Is that how you really feel? You working towards getting back to normal? Are you dating yet? Papers were signed, what, six months ago and you're not back out there yet."

"That's because I love my wife," Carter admitted out loud.

"What? You do realize she's not your wife, right?"

"That doesn't mean I don't love her anymore. She divorced me and I gave in because I wanted her to be happy and being with me after what I did, I knew she'd never be happy with me again."

"You know, I never thought it would be you. I hope I'm not going too far left and all in your business, but there are guys in our group who I could point a finger at and say if he hasn't cheated, he will soon enough. But never you," Keith shared.

"I know and I still can't give anyone a valid reason why I did it. I had sex with another woman, no matter how brief the encounter was, and I hurt my wife, the one woman I vowed I would never, ever hurt. I feel like she's finally getting over it and getting her life back and I want to be sure I'm staying as far away to give her room to breathe."

"Kim told me you were still in love with Sienna. When we were on our honeymoon, she told me she saw you at the reception and she knew immediately that you were still in love. The two of you had what we all thought was the perfect marriage - the perfect love."

The perfect love is exactly how he would categorize what he had with Sienna and what he was planning to have again, if possible. Avoidance was not the answer.

"We did. Life is what it is and I'm no longer walking around avoiding running into her. I'm free this weekend, so you'll see me. I'm going to go check in with Dexter. I'll see you Saturday," Carter said.

"It'll be good to have the whole gang together again."

Carter was thinking the same thing and he was going to get the chance to see Sienna again. That alone added more pep to each step he took across the concrete floor. He had no doubt she would be there.

**

Sienna raced down the steps to the front door where Reese was leaning on her doorbell. She loved her best friend, but the fact that she could never show up without ringing the bell like a mad-woman was driving her mad.

"Girl, stop ringing my bell like that!" Sienna yelled after opening the door and moving so that Reese could glide in as she always did as if she owned the place.

"Well, if you gave me a key like a true best friend would, I wouldn't need to ring the bell at all. I know some friends who accommodate their best friends that way and no one is a better best friend than I am to you," Reese said, joking.

"Except for me as your best friend. I'm number one in that column and if I gave you a key, I'm afraid I'd wake up and you'd be in my kitchen cooking and eating at all times of the night. You know you have no boundaries," Sienna laughed.

"Boundaries are for chumps. The good part of me always being around outweighs the bad of me cooking up all of your food. Besides, you're in this big ass house and it takes you forever to come to the door to let me in. I hope a psycho in a mask like the guy on those Halloween movies isn't chasing me in your house one day. I'd be dead before you open the door!" Reese yelled.

"Girl, you would be dead anyway. If I see someone chasing

you with a mask like in those movies, all bets are off. It's every woman for herself. I'm running through this big house and finding a hiding place!" Sienna boasted as they both laughed uncontrollably.

"Whatever, chick. I can't believe you decided to stay in this house and not sell it so that you could downsize. You live here all alone and that doesn't bother you? It would eat me alive to roam around this mansion alone night after night."

Sienna followed behind Reese's steps as she went to her favorite room, the entertainment room off the kitchen. She stood in the doorway and watched Reese work to get comfortable as if she were at home. First, she took off her shoes before grabbing the remote and turning on the gigantic wall-sized television. Adding in the surround sound, the sound vibrated off of the walls. She was done for when Reese opened the top to the leather ottoman, pulled out a blanket and covered herself as she relaxed back with her feet crossed at the ankles on the ottoman.

"Comfy?" Sienna asked.

"I would be if you brought me something to eat. I'm starving. I know you cooked something because you knew I was coming over. What are we having?" Reese asked.

Sienna shook her head and smiled.

"I made lasagna. Would you like some?" she asked as she turned toward the kitchen.

"You know better than to even ask. I not only want some, but I want to take some home to have for tomorrow. You know I hate to cook," she laughed.

"Yeah, I know and I was prepared for that. There is a complete pan just for you to take home."

Going into the kitchen, Sienna uncovered the lasagna and

grabbed plates to heat them each a plate. Grabbing the bowls of salad that she'd already made, she took them into the room and sat them in front of Reese.

"Those look good," Reese said.

"By all means, don't get up to help," Sienna joked, adding a smile to show humor and not seriousness.

"Do you really want my help? I can barely boil eggs without them exploding. Okay, that's a lie. I cook like a chef, but that's when I'm home. I come here to be waited on. You know you do not want me in your kitchen. You won't have any food left. I will, however, get up to wash my hands and get ready for this delicious food," Reese said getting up and walking into the kitchen. "Are you going to Kim and Keith's house this weekend? She told me she was calling you today."

"She called and I told her I would think about it. I have a lot of work to do on the office park. You know that deal fell through and Constance and I have to find new locations to check out."

Sienna smirked at Reese's sad face.

"I was hoping that would work out for you. I know how badly you wanted that location. That guy is making me want to throw bricks through his car windows!"

Sienna laughed.

"Don't even think about it. I know you're the friend that I could count on to help me hide the body, but no violence! Something else will come through."

Sienna was a little down after finding out that the real estate developer she was hoping would sell her and her partner in her dental practice a building and land they could use to expand their practice. She and Constance both wanted to add a medical center to the existing practice for the South side of Chicago community as well as a community center where the kids could find safety in learning during after school programs. They could also provide a place for exercise through the many athletic programs she was also hoping to start.

"I know and I don't want to talk about business tonight. You came over for girl talk and we never include business in that," Sienna said.

Reese walked close and leaned back against the counter.

"Okay, then let's talk Carter Garrison. I know you saw and talked to him at the reception weeks ago and we have yet to talk about it. You've been so busy you've been ignoring your best friend. What's up with that?" she laughed.

"I said I was sorry about that, but you know how things have been with trying to expand. I have big dreams and this guy is shattering them time after time."

"Nope, no business, remember?" Reese said.

After Sienna placed their food on plates, Reese grabbed them and walked back to chill in front of the television where they could really talk.

She waited to eat until Sienna sat with her.

"Okay, you asked me about Carter. Yes, we talked at the reception."

"Was it tense? Did you want to scratch his eyes out? I know you hadn't seen him in a while."

"It was nothing like that. It was nice and polite."

"What did you talk about?" Reese asked.

Sienna was glad she was prepared to be grilled tonight. Plus, talking about Carter was getting easier and easier.

"Just general stuff about how we were doing and about business and how we're both doing really well on that front."

"Nothing personal?" Reese asked in between spoons full of lasagna.

"He mentioned how much he missed me and wished me well. I wished him well, too. We also talked about how we didn't have to avoid each other and I know that we don't."

"Well, he sure did look good," Reese said and whistled.

Sienna looked at Reese sideways and continued.

"He did, didn't he? He's always been gorgeous and that day was no exception. Goodness how memories of being with him played with my mind that night."

"I also noticed that bling on his wrist. I've seen others like that and I do believe it was a Rolex GMT Master and it was all platinum. That man sure can walk around looking like a runway model. He's still sporting that diamond in his ear, too, just like you wear yours. Coincidence? I think not!" Reese shouted.

"It's not a coincidence. The set has special value to us and I always wear mine. As far as I know, he has always worn his. You know that. Have you ever seen him without it?"

"Right, but it's a keepsake from your wedding anniversary, something you no longer have. I thought one of you would stop wearing it, though I'm glad you haven't. You may never admit it, but a piece of you still longs for Carter. I know how much you loved him and even though I also know how much he hurt you, that love between the two of you was deeper than any love I've ever been able to experience that up close and personal between two people. You know how my mother spent years man-hopping. I know what happened to ruin things, but what about now? What about after separating and divorcing and now almost two years later? How do you feel now? Do you still hate him?" Reese asked.

"I could never hate Carter and I never will. Despite what happened, he was the love of my life and that will never go away until someone else takes his place in my heart," Sienna explained.

"That'll never happen as long as you hide yourself away and stay removed from dating anyone."

"Just because I don't go out on a date almost every night of the week like you...well, it doesn't mean that I don't date," Sienna explained.

"Really? When was the last date you went on and don't say Brien because he doesn't count?"

Sienna took a few moments to think about it and suddenly realized how long it had been, but at least she did go on one.

"There was Dennis."

Reese sucked her teeth.

"He doesn't count. He was crazy and quite stalker-*ish*. What did you do to that man on one date that made him fall in love with you?"

Sienna laughed and almost choked on her food.

"Stop it," she laughed.

"I'll get us a bottle of wine, but keep talking," Reese said getting up.

"I didn't do anything. It was a nice date, but I didn't feel the vibe that he felt. Before the end of the date, he told me he felt like I was the one. That creeped me out."

"Why? People fall in love at first sight. Why couldn't he?" Reese hollered from the kitchen.

"I'm not saying he couldn't have, but I wasn't ready for all that. I was fresh out of my marriage and I wasn't ready for anything more than getting back into dating. He was going all serious on the first date. It was too much."

"Okay, who else?" Reese said coming back in with two glasses and a bottle of white wine, pouring them each a glass full.

"I went out with that guy from my gym," Sienna said.

"Please. You went to the movies and you barely got the chance to talk other than in the car. You never called him back. Listen, I'm not saying you will never find anyone else, but you still miss Carter. You still love Carter even if you won't say so out loud to me. I know you miss him and it has to be awkward being in this big ol' house without him. Your life was here with him which is why I don't understand you not moving from here, especially after he paid it off so that if you wanted to move, you could sell the house and make a big profit on it. Instead, you stayed. I know I can't get you to tell me that you still love him and it's okay. I know it matters to you what people think, but I'm your best friend. I won't think of you as weak or a doormat if you still love and want your ex-husband back. Bottom line is, Carter is a good guy who made a mistake that he's paying for every day that you're apart. The way he was looking at you at the wedding and reception was proof positive that he's been empty without you. I see it in you, too."

Sienna stopped eating and sat her plate on the ottoman.

"Okay, I do miss Carter. I miss him every day. You want me to tell you I'm miserable without him? Because it's true and I am. It's not that no one else is interested in me because that's not the case. I know he messed up, but I'm wondering if divorce was too extreme for what he actually had done. It's like giving a man a life sentence for robbing a store when he didn't do something as extreme as killing a man. I've thought about it and I've struggled with it. I don't know how to get beyond questioning what I did because I was fiercely angry and I knew I could hurt him and have him in pain like I was. Then, over time, that pain went away. The anger went away. The justification for going straight to divorce seemed out of place. I ended my marriage and like Brien said, Carter isn't perfect. We all have imperfections. The thing that I didn't think about was whether or not I was willing to take the good with the bad and work on what we had that was so good. Now, it's too late, and yes, I miss him. I miss him every day, even more after I saw him at the wedding. Seeing him made it real again," Sienna explained.

Reese sat her plate down and took Sienna by the hands. They were the best of friends and if Sienna needed honesty from her best friend the time was now.

"Listen to me. You did what you felt you needed to do at that time in order for you to feel better. Almost two years ago, it was the best thing for you. Almost two years later, you have had time to think about everything that happened and you realize there was more to your marriage than that one indiscretion. See, whether divorce was extreme or not, it happened, but that doesn't mean it has to be the end. Hear me when I say, that man still loves you and I can see it in your eyes and hear it in your voice that there is still love for him in you. The question is, what can you do about it if you could? Are you willing to take a leap and find out if your happiness still lies in your love for Carter?"

Sienna didn't want to admit that she'd been thinking that very same thing, yet still didn't have an answer.

"Do I need to answer right now?" she asked. She was tired of the conversation and wanted a relaxing evening.

"Nope, because I don't want my lasagna to get cold and

I'm starving. You know I only get to eat when I come over here. You still make the best Italian food."

Reese picked up her plate and began eating again.

"I miss him, Reese."

"I know. You couldn't know because you avoided the man for like a year. I know you live out here with the rich folks and he lives in the heart of downtown Chicago in that nice bachelor pad. You're at least still in the same city and eventually your paths were going to cross again. It's going to keep happening. Are you always going to act like you are done with him or are you thinking of at a minimum, learning how to exist in Chicago together and do it with ease?"

Sienna didn't answer as Reese turned the volume up on the television, giving her time to let their conversation sink in. Grabbing her glass of wine, as she no longer had an appetite, Sienna sipped and focused on the television while the silence of their conversation hovered and thoughts of Carter controlled her mind.

7

Sienna ordered a glass of white wine, her favorite, and joined in the fun and laughter at the table as everyone gathered in the dining room of Kim and Keith's holiday decorated home. After her girl chat night with Reese, she was ready to insert herself back into the collective with her friends and hoped that Carter would find his place among them, too. Reese had her thinking about a lot of things and though she ended their marriage, there was no reason they couldn't co-exist and do so happily. She needed the night out and was happy that her friends hounded her until she agreed to come out for the night as long as someone gave her a ride. A light snow was beginning to fall and it looked like they were going to have a white Christmas in a few days. She'd had a long day at work and wasn't in the mood for driving to their house, which was almost an hour from where she lived. Luckily, Reese agreed to pick her up and drop her back off at home at the end of the night.

Seeing how beautifully Kim and Keith's house was decorated had her longing for the days when she and Carter went all out decking out their home which included a large, live tree with decorations from top to bottom and also in every room. Now, with the size of the house and living in it alone, she didn't feel the need to have that many decorations, but she did get a tree, albeit an artificial one and some modest decorations.

The mood at the party was lively and festive and everyone was having a good time, including her as she made her way from room to room conversing with friends she hadn't seen in a while. She gave them all the same excuse that she'd been overwhelmed with business, which was the truth.

Fun for her had been almost non-existent over the past two years. Her life was finally getting back to normal or as normal as it could be now that she was a single woman again. Never in her wildest dreams did she think she would ever find herself in this position after marrying the love of her life.

Seeing Carter at the wedding was a shock and she was even more surprised at how comfortable she was talking to him. Throughout the divorce, they had been civil to each other though when they originally split up, she couldn't stand the sight of him. That changed over time and throughout the divorce proceedings, he didn't make any demands and offered her things she wasn't planning on taking. Deep down, she knew that was the kind of man he was, but her anger blocked her from seeing the good in him. Even now, she couldn't keep her eyes off of the front door every time the bell rang. She'd heard Carter was coming and her stomach had been in knots all evening as she waited for his arrival. His showing up didn't exactly mean he would focus on her all night, but she longed to see him again anyway.

She knew she looked strange to everyone every time

someone new walked in the door. She no longer felt sorry for herself for her role in the end of her marriage. He may have briefly cheated, but she was the one who filed for divorce ending any chance at reconciliation they could have had. At least now, they could be around each other in the face of their friends.

She was about to take another sip of her wine when she glanced up and right in front of her stood Carter, looking like the perfect gift under any woman's Christmas tree. She'd been so busy thinking about him that she hadn't seen him come in.

"Carter's in the house!" she heard Keith shout and the room cheered. She tried looking away but couldn't. When their eyes met, she got that tingling feeling all over that she always got when he was around and looking at her with those light brown eyes.

Tonight, in place of the gray suit from the wedding, he wore all black and exuded a level of sexiness reserved only for him. When he removed the black leather jacket, she saw that he wore a shirt with the top few buttons opened, allowing her to glimpse the beginnings of that hairy chest she loved laying on top of. She used to love how it felt when they made love and the hair on his chest would caress her already sensitive skin. She inwardly shivered at the thought.

"Hey, Sienna! Let's dance," Dexter said as he stood to pull her up with him.

"Sure," she said and caught a quick glance at Carter who feigned not looking at her.

Taking the seat Sienna left vacant, Carter found himself sitting next to Reese. He watched as Sienna and Dexter did the latest dance moves. Watching her smile and laugh made him feel good, though he wasn't pleased knowing that she was this happy without him. He knew it was selfish, but he hoped she was struggling as much with being away from him as he was with being away from her.

"You're staring, Carter," Reese leaned over and said.

"She really is happier without me, isn't she?" he asked, not able to take his eyes off of how she laughed and danced around. If anyone knew Sienna well, it was her.

"No," she said without missing a beat.

Carter whipped his head.

"What?" he asked.

"No," she said again while not looking his way.

"Are you answering me or is your attention someplace else?" he asked.

Reese turned and looked at him directly.

"You asked me a question and I answered you," she said.

"Right, but did you hear what I asked or did you just automatically have that response prepared?" he asked, hopeful.

Reese poked him in the arm.

"Carter! You are not this dense, my brother. Really, stop it. Let me see if I can break this down so that you can understand. Now, pay attention," she said. "You asked me if Sienna was happier without you and my response without having to think about it is *no*. Got it?" she asked and then turned her attention back to everyone dancing.

"She's not happy? What's wrong? Did someone hurt her? Who do I need to kill?" Carter boasted, genuinely concerned, while also adding in a bit of humor.

"What's wrong is she's not with you and I'm not sure I can ever forgive you like she did, considering your actions. You ruined the only perfect image I had of a married couple by thinking with the wrong head," she said. "Sienna isn't happy. She's not moving on and she's still in love with you, but you didn't hear that from me. She misses you even after all that's happened."

"What do you mean she hasn't moved on? I thought she was dating someone? That guy she brought to the wedding? That's over already?" he asked.

Carter's pulse quickened. Was it possible he wasn't the only one of the two of them who was miserable with them apart?

"Brien? Oh, he's some pharmaceutical guy or something, just someone she knows. They're good friends, but not dating. She says she's not ready to date or get seriously involved with anyone. She still loves you, Carter, and with as crazy as I think that is, you were the best thing that ever happened to her. I personally don't think she's giving herself a chance to move on, at least not yet. Eventually she will, but not at the moment. So, again, in answer to your question, no, she's not happier without you---not yet she's not."

Carter didn't say anything else as he watched Sienna dance with Dexter and saw her having a good time. It was good to see her laugh and smile again. He had missed seeing her face.

"She looks happy," he said, low, not really to Reese but more to himself.

"Just as you've avoided seeing her for months and don't try to deny it, she's been doing the same thing wondering if she would run into you with some woman. I noticed you came alone to the wedding. Does that mean you're not seeing anyone?" Reese asked.

"I'm not seeing anyone because I still love her. There isn't another woman in this world I want, but her. You're her best friend. Would you tell me if there was a way for me to ask her out where she would say yes and not slap me in the face for even asking?"

This time he watched as Reese turned her head quickly as he had done and saw when she massaged where she probably suffered a quick pain in her neck as he had. He smiled knowing he'd caught her off guard.

"You're serious?" she asked.

"I'm more serious than I've ever been. Look at that beautiful woman out there. I need and want her in my life. If there's any chance with her, I'm taking it. I have no problem starting over again. If she tells me no, I'll live with that, but I need her to tell me there's no hope at all. Can you help me out? I know I'm asking a lot considering what happened, but she is still my everything even if she doesn't know it."

"Brother, I'm in your corner. You and Sienna together is how it was always supposed to be."

"What do I do?" he asked.

"You know, she's been thinking about getting a newer Mercedes, but hasn't because out of some misplaced loyalty to you, she didn't want to go to a rival dealership. On the other hand, she didn't feel comfortable going to your dealership. So, her answer is to either keep the car or get something other than a Mercedes, which is ludicrous because we all know how much she loves that brand. The two of you are going to have to figure out how to function in each other's company without awkwardness."

"I can help her get a new Mercedes, or if she wants, she can go to a rival dealership and that would be fine."

"Yeah, I know that and you know that, but someone needs to tell her that. Are you going to tell me how much you're still in love with her? I assume that's going to come up."

"Reese, you know I will never stop loving Sienna. She was it for me, and yes, I know I didn't prove that by cheating on her, but it's true."

"Can I ask you something very personal?" Reese said turning again to face him.

"Anything," Carter said and prepared himself for whatever she asked.

"Was it only that one time? Have you ever cheated on Sienna any other time?"

"That was the one and only time. I didn't plan it, set out to do it or thought about ever doing it again. I messed up really bad. I can't take it back and I can't make her forget about it. I'm just thankful that she forgave me."

"She had to do that or she would never move on, even though she's not there yet."

"I love her so much," he admitted.

"I know you do and you want her back, don't you? Not just to take out or to date, but you want her back as your wife, right?" Reese asked.

Carter didn't answer that question right away. He'd been thinking it, but hearing someone else say it then made it all real.

"Yes, I do."

"I'm in your corner with that. My girl has been miserable without you and it's all about the heart. Her heart still belongs to you. You better make this right. I could say that I think you have a chance, but only Sienna can tell you that. Just be you, and I think you're in there. I'm in your corner," she said. "I see somebody giving me a special eye. I'm going to go see if he's as good up close as he is sending me signals from a distance," Reese excused herself and stood.

Carter shook his head. Reese, the player, was still in effect. Just as she walked away, Sienna and Dexter returned. He moved over one seat to give Sienna her chair back. He smiled when Dexter made himself disappear.

"Hello beautiful," he said leaning closer to her. He smiled when she turned her head around to face him and was grinning as brightly as he was.

"Hello, yourself. We have to stop meeting like this. We go months without seeing each other and now twice in the past few months. I guess I should get used to seeing you. I'm sure everyone is happy to see you back around," she said.

"I hope that's a good thing."

"It is. It's good to see you. Did you see where Reese went to? I swear she is a master at disappearing. She must have met some guy and is probably in a corner someplace getting his life story," Sienna said.

"You know your friend well. Some guy looked at her and she went to check him out," he said.

"Typical Reese," Sienna said, joking.

"Are you having a good time out with everyone tonight?" he asked.

"I am. I hate to think that you haven't been out with the gang because of me. They're as much your friends as they are mine and no one took sides, at least not openly."

"I'm sure everyone took your side as they should, but you're right that no one has openly. We have great friends," Carter said.

"Yes, we do and right now, I wish my best friend would

come on because it's getting late and I have to get up early tomorrow."

Carter looked around.

"I think I see her over at that corner table talking to that guy she was eyeing."

"I guess I'll get comfortable for a little while longer. She looks engrossed in their conversation."

"I was about to take off myself and if you don't think it's out of sorts, I can give you a ride home. It's just an offer and it is late."

Carter didn't feel bad about his small fib. He had just arrived, so he wasn't already planning to leave, but he would if it mean he had some time alone in his car with Sienna. Even if they didn't talk, being in her presence was enough.

"I could call an Uber. I can't ask you to do that. I'm sure you have some place to go or something else to do besides ferrying me around," Sienna said.

"An Uber? Alone? That's not a good idea. Besides, you didn't ask; I offered. I don't have anything else to do. Plus, I think I'm a little more trustworthy than an Uber driver, but it's up to you. I've had enough for the night after a long day at the dealership and I need to get home to get up early for a meeting in the morning before the store opens. Reese mentioned you were looking for a new car. You know we may be divorced, but I still have the best supply of Mercedes in the area. If you want to look at the current stock, you can come by the dealership and I'll make sure you get exactly what you're looking for. If you would feel more comfortable, I'd understand if you went to a different dealer. We have to figure out how to live normal lives since you left me."

Sienna looked over at Carter and noticed a smile he was

trying to hide from her.

"I see you got jokes," she said.

"I'm just saying that we don't have to act like we don't know each other. If you want a new Mercedes and we both know I own a Mercedes Benz dealership, then why wouldn't you check out the inventory? It would be a win-win."

"Really? How is that?"

"Well, you get the car you want and I'll get the chance to see your beautiful face again. When is a good time for you?" he asked.

"Are you serious?" she asked.

"You tell me when and I'll make myself available to help you out. The new models have finally arrived. You'll get a first look at the models for the new year."

"A new car in the new year would be nice."

"Well, let's plan for you to stop by sometime. Are you still off on Sundays?" he asked. It was the one day he knew she loved to sleep in after a full week of patients, especially Saturday which was her busiest day. Parents were off work and kids were out of school making it an easy time for appointments.

"Yes."

"Great. It's a date. Well, not actually a date. You know what I mean," Carter said stumbling over his words.

"I appreciate it," she said.

"Now, about that ride home? The offer still stands."

Sienna smiled. She was ready to leave.

"Sure. Let me say my goodbyes and I'll let Reese know she can go straight home. I'm hoping she'll do that before the snow really picks up."

"I don't know. I see her with her eyes on the prize. She's

got a laser focus on some guy and I have a feeling she's here for the duration."

"She can do that, but I want to be home before the weather gets too bad. Give me a few minutes to grab my coat, and I'll meet you at the door?" Sienna asked and pointed towards it.

"Yes, you will. I'll be the one standing at the door looking anxious."

When Carter smiled, her world lit up. Yeah, she missed him and hoped the car ride wasn't a quick one.

8

Coffee was a must and Sienna went in search of her favorite latte, immediately turning on her coffee maker as soon as she walked into the kitchen. She was up earlier than she'd planned and she knew why---she was anxious about going to Carter's dealership.

Three weeks after the new year and she had reached out to him to see if she could schedule a day to come in and check out the cars. The morning she'd called the dealership, she paced around her kitchen until the receptionist finally got him on the phone. She had picked up the phone to dial and hung up several times before finally letting the call go through. They had gone from not seeing or speaking to each other for months to her meeting him to talk about her purchase of a new car. She was surprised to hear that Reese had mentioned her desire for a new car to him. She should have known when she saw them talking while she was on the dance floor that they were talking about her.

One day while working out together, she mentioned to Reese that she was thinking about replacing her current silver two-door Mercedes with a larger version. She had always loved the brand but felt strange going to Carter's dealership to get a new one and then there was the idea of taking her business to a rival dealership knowing, eventually, Carter would probably find out and then assume she'd done it out of spite.

After giving her a lift home from the party before the Christmas holiday, she walked into her house, exhausted from the festivities, but too wired up to fall asleep. She was comfortable being at the party and interacting with Carter, but then they were in the close environment of his car and she didn't know what to make of how easily they conversed. That was the closest they had been in a long time.

A light snow had fallen outside and the temperature had turned colder in the few hours she was at the party. Carter didn't rush to get her home, but drove as they easily talked and laughed about a comedian on the satellite channel in his car. They talked about the latest Marvel Comics movie because that was one topic they had in common since the day they'd met.

As she walked across her college campus one day, Carter approached her and introduced himself. He explained he didn't mean to interrupt her, but he wanted her to know that she was beautiful and he'd like to take her out on a date. Back then, Carter had the eyes of every woman on campus, and she was ecstatic to know that he was interested in her. Once she agreed to go out with him, she couldn't believe her luck when he chose an *Iron Man* movie, knowing that she was a big sci-fi fan and loved those type of movies. Over the years of them dating and after they got married, they were always at the theater on the first day any sci-fi movie was released, especially when the Marvel Comic movies started rolling out.

In the car, there was no way to share everything that they'd missed out on in each other's lives and the fact that they each wanted to share blew her away. They were like two best friends who hadn't talked in two years, and in the time it took to take her home, they tried to talk faster than usual. There was no tension over their breakup and divorce and no mentioning of what happened in the past. Instead, they focused on a stress-free, tension-free car ride and for that she was thankful. They could have easily fallen into a trap devolving into an argument, but they knew the past was the past and should stay there.

They talked about their parents and how well they were doing. When she asked about his parents' upcoming anniversary, she was surprised to hear that he hadn't begun planning anything. He wasn't known to be the kind of person to plan lavish parties, but his parents were celebrating forty years of marriage in two months and she knew how much he loved and adored them. When he told her he was going to send them on the trip of their dreams and take them out for a nice dinner, she didn't press the issue. If they had still been married, she would have taken over planning a large party. Forty years was a major milestone.

Still, she let the subject go since it was no longer her concern.

Arriving at her house, the same house they once lived in together, other than getting out to open her car door, Carter didn't stick around. He watched her go inside and she looked out of the window as he drove off. The moment between them in the car wasn't awkward and it felt really good being able to talk to him so openly again. That was something she missed.

Now, she was up early and nervously watching the clock. She still had a few hours before she would head out to the dealership, but in the meantime, she couldn't stop going back over everything that had happened between them from the day he came home from and the All-Star game to the moment she'd seen him at the wedding. As she did, old feelings flooded through her.

The day when she'd finally realized she couldn't stay in the house with Carter any longer, she'd been at work, a place where she'd begun spending a countless number of extra hours in order to avoid more confrontations with Carter. That day had been a few months after the incident and they had been sleeping in separate rooms in the house they shared together.

She had originally agreed to counseling after many days and nights of them fighting, her crying, and him apologizing copiously. Nothing seemed to work and, in the end, counseling didn't either. She had refused to allow Carter to give her all of the explicit details of what happened. She would only let him tell her that it *had* happened. The counselor, on the other hand, felt that she needed to hear him explain everything and get it out in a controlled environment, but what little she heard only angered her more. Sienna didn't understand how he could ruin what they had for some clandestine rendezvous with a woman he didn't know, spurred on something said by a ballplayer who was well-known in the media for having women on the side and who had a wife who didn't care as long as he kept her in glitz and glamour. Sienna wasn't that kind of wife and she expected more from her husband.

That final day, she'd gotten up and left the house earlier than usual, avoiding running into Carter, who like her, had begun spending an increasing number of hours at work, staying away from their volatile home life. She'd gotten halfway through her day and thought it crazy that they were living separate lives under the same roof. Worse, at times when they did talk, she couldn't help going off on him like a lunatic, which was completely out of character for her. She tried talking to her mother, but didn't get much input. Her mother, though supportive of whatever she decided to do, didn't tell her what to do and that had been what Sienna thought she needed at the time. It was selfish of her, but she wanted someone to tell her it was okay to leave and file for divorce. That way, if later on, like say now, she had begun second-guessing the divorce decision, she would have someone else to blame other than herself. She needed that in order to take the pressure off. Now, she found herself not only lonely, but specifically lonely for Carter. There was no one else to blame.

Seeing him and talking to him took her back to the days when their marriage was in a good place. They had the best of times taking vacations whenever they wanted because they ran their own businesses. They would engage in sexy encounters wherever and whenever the mood struck them, including times she'd gotten in the car for a road trip with no panties on and the things she did as he drove almost caused a crash a time or two. On another road trip, they were actually parked outside of their hotel and the amorous feeling overcame them so strongly that they'd made love in the back seat when their room was only a walk inside and up the elevator. No room or surface was ever off limits in their house and she laughed at times when she had to remember to grab cleaner and wipe down surfaces where the night before their lovemaking had gotten out of hand. Those times when that happened, Carter moved from one surface to another, pleasuring her to the point that she didn't care where they were as long as he didn't stop.

She laughed to herself as she remembered the night of one of Reese's birthday parties, since she threw one for herself every year, where she and Carter had disappeared into what turned out to be a linen closet and once they exited, Reese scolded them for how disheveled their clothes were, including Carter's zipper which was still down with the edge of his shirt poking through. After her admonishment, Reese told them she couldn't wait to find a man who was ready all the time and was up to rendezvous like them.

There were times when Carter would show up with flowers and a gift, just because. He would unexpectedly come to her office and bring lunch knowing that she often skipped lunch due to her heavy schedule of clients.

She loved cooking for him, and some days when she thought he would be working later than usual, she would rush home to cook one of his favorite meals only to find him standing in their kitchen in nothing but an apron, already cooking dinner for the evening. She would go in search of another apron while running to their bedroom to grab a quick shower and quickly strip. They loved cooking in the nude as long as there was no hot grease involved.

That would have been tricky.

Their connections and happy times were deeper than the passion too. For example, they had a mutual love for their parents that was unlike the relationship she saw a lot of their friends having. Some people saw their parents and spent time with them when it was convenient, but she and Carter made sure their parents were an intricate part of their lives, stopping at their houses throughout the week just to sit with them and catch up. They had the worst schedules sometimes, but family was everything to them. They couldn't wait to start their own family and before the incident, they had begun talking about her going off of birth control so that they could start trying for children. She was hoping to have years at home with their children, raising them herself and thinking about her dental practice later down the road. She would keep her partnership status, but hire more staff to accommodate her absence. Constance understood and agreed that family was more important than anything. That never happened because life had opened up under their feet and swallowed their love, tossing what was left of them back and forth until she couldn't face coming home to him and going through the routine they had fallen into.

Leaving the office early the day she left him, Sienna had called her mother to see about staying with them while she figured out what her next move would be. Her mother didn't say much other than to tell her that she could always come home if that was what she wanted.

She went home and began packing her bags. She was able to get three suitcases full of items packed and placed in the car. By the time Carter came home unexpectedly, she was working on two more. He tried to talk to her, but she wasn't listening. She left that day and filed separation papers within a few days. A week later, she received a note from Carter's lawyer that he was moving out of the house so she didn't have to move out permanently if she were uncomfortable with that option. Carter's kind gesture caught her off-guard and the reaction was two-fold. Either he was being his usual giving self and letting her live in the house while everything was sorted out *or* he was showing her that since she walked out on him, he was all for moving on and putting their life behind him by getting his own place. She agreed to move back into the house and found out that Carter had first moved into a suite at the Four Seasons Hotel and then, a few weeks later, he purchased a large, luxury condo. The day that he officially changed his address on paper, Sienna realized how permanent her decision to leave him was. He had officially moved on, not by renting a place, but by purchasing one. She knew how expensive it was to rent and knew that Carter was frugal with how he spent his money and would never waste it on renting a place to live for long.

She still remembered the day she picked up a copy of *Essence* magazine and right on the front was Carter Garrison, who they toted as man of the year, not just because of his striking good looks, but because of his business practices and how he'd turned his businesses into huge money-makers. He was saluted for his desire to hire men who had been incarcerated and were finding it hard to find a job. He paid for them to take trades to work on cars and all of the men were doing great. He was also celebrated for mentoring men on the power of never giving up.

He'd done several lectures around Chicago at high schools that had low graduation rates and it was later discovered that he was starting a foundation to award college scholarships to Chicago high school students who showed promise and determination but who were lacking when it came to funds. She always knew Carter was a great man and had a heart for the people just as she did. That compassion drew them together.

He slipped up and tore their lives apart and now she didn't get to live out her fantasy marriage with the man of her dreams.

Though the process of the separation and divorce took eighteen months, that time seemed to fly by and one day she looked up and the judge was granting her wish to go back to her maiden name and all was final. Even though she asked to go back to her maiden name, she still had not changed any of her important documents to reflect that. Something deep inside of her wasn't ready for that last and final step. Was she trying to tell herself something? She didn't know, but what she did know was that she needed to get ready for her meeting with Carter about her new car. It didn't matter what the past held, whether good or bad times, she looked forward to seeing him again.

**

Carter knew the minute Sienna had walked through the doors of the dealership. All of a sudden, where there had been chatter out on the main floor, he noticed complete silence. Most of the staff had been working for him back when he and Sienna were married, so they remembered who she was and probably wondered what she was doing at the dealership knowing they were now divorced.

Cutting through the thickness of the silence, he entered the main showroom floor and walked right up to her.

"Hey there," he said and held back the urge to hug her. As usual, her beauty stunned him and today, she wore a navy wrap dress that accentuated her luscious figure. He couldn't help but admire the hour-glass figure she had always been able to maintain. She was shapely in all the places a man loved, and no one loved to dress up as much as Sienna did. Today was no exception.

"Hi," she replied and smiled.

Carter's heart skipped a beat the moment she smiled up at him. He took in his fill of her. Her hair was swept up into a loose ponytail with tendrils streaked in her usual chestnut blonde, a color that went well with her dark brown, natural shoulder length hair. Sienna could definitely be the next top runway model. On her feet, were her staple high-heels and this time, they were a sexy pair of gray and navy boots. Her long, gray leather coat topped of her look. He would never tire of looking at her beauty.

"I'm glad you made it," he said, stopping his slow perusal of her looks to remember to engage her in a conversation before his stare turned creepy.

"I'm sorry I'm a little late. I hope you didn't think I'd changed my mind," Sienna said.

Carter tried not to let his face show that he was worried exactly about that. He had been expecting a call from her saying she couldn't do it. When she walked in the door, it was like Christmas morning and finding his favorite toy under the tree.

"Not at all and you're not late. Come into my office and let's talk about what you're looking for. I didn't know how much time you had today, so I pulled some photos of a few I thought you'd like, but if you have time to look at more, I have as much time as you need."

Carter stopped short of saying he hoped she would take all day. He'd love nothing more than to be able to spend more time with her.

"I have more time than I originally thought. Constance and I were supposed to look at this new property today, but someone else made an offer that was accepted, which is why I'm dressed up instead of in my usual sweat suit and tennis shoes. You know my usual relaxing day attire."

Carter sat down behind his desk as Sienna sat across from him where he'd laid out several photos of new models of cars he thought she'd love.

"Property? You're moving your practice?" he asked.

"We're looking to expand. We've already added to the staff, but we've been talking about doing more for the community by moving the practice to an office park and also opening up a community center to offer either free or discounted dental and medical services. We want to have after school programs for neighborhood children on the southside that include sports camps, computer labs, reading rooms, before and after school meals and so much more. We have been able to get several doctors on board who are interested in opening up offices at the office park and also offering free and discounted services that state services don't cover. You know I've always been about helping the less fortunate," she said.

Carter was impressed with the idea and one thing he'd always known and loved about Sienna was her heart for helping people. Since she was a dentist, he knew she already provided discounted and free services because of who she was. For the clients who couldn't always afford to pay, they were often so grateful for Sienna's services that they made donations to help cover the cost of her free services when they could. She also had a knack for getting those who were more fortunate to donate larger sums of money to cover expenses for those who didn't have much. Sienna was a force and he was proud of her.

"You've always been about helping others. Do you have any other locations in mind other than that one?" he asked.

"We had one, but that guy has turned out to be a pain. He owns a building and surrounding land that would be perfect for our needs. We've been in negotiations with him for a few months and he is now playing hardball by raising the price of the building when he found out our plans for it and the interest other companies have for being a part of it. I don't know how he got information on our plans, but from the change in his response to us, I have a feeling he knows everything and is trying to get a lot more money out of the deal," she explained.

Carter didn't like what he was hearing. There was a guy trying to take advantage of Sienna and her business partner.

"Tell me about this guy," he said. If he could figure out a way to help her, he would.

"His name is Oscar Jankowsky. He owns a lot of prime real estate in Chicago. In the beginning, he was welcoming and willing to negotiate and then one day, he stopped talking to us directly and sent a representative to handle everything. As of right now, we've backed out. The bank doesn't even think the property is worth what he's asking for it and they won't finance it. I wouldn't want them to at that price when I know he was willing to offer it at a lower price weeks ago. Through the grapevine, I've heard that a few others are making bids for that property and he purposely priced it out of range. It's frustrating because the property is absolutely perfect for what we need. We can't pay more for it because we'd need the additional cash flow to pay for the remodeling of the space to add on a basketball court, swimming pool, the computer labs, library books and quiet rooms, not to mention all of the space that needs to be converted to medical space."

"Sounds like that would have been a perfect location on the southside."

"Yes, and in the heart of a community that could use some revitalization. The plan, once we secured a spot, was to reach out to local and national companies for sponsorship to help defray some of the costs. We have to get through the first phase first which is securing a location. There are a few more we are looking into, but that one was prime. I'm sorry that we won't be able to bring those services to the community. You know it's been a dream of mine to do more for those we serve."

"I know. Before you leave, give me the information on this property and this Jankowsky guy. Let me see what I can find out. What you're trying to do would greatly benefit that community and anyone who loves Chicago should want to be a part of helping with a project like yours."

When Sienna smiled at him, Carter's world seemed perfect. That's a look he had been missing out on every single day.

"You would do that? Look into this?" she asked, surprised. He was already helping her with her car and now this.

"Divorced or not, I would never sit back and allow anyone to take advantage of you or what you're trying to do. I have a guy who I work with when it comes to scouting out land for new business opportunities and he found me the best location for the new dealership. I'll see what he knows about this guy and see if there's a way to get to him."

"New dealership?" she asked.

"Right, you wouldn't know. I'm opening up another dealership soon and also thinking of expanding the customization business into other states to help handle the extra business we're getting since the endorsements from celebrities. We have cars scheduled months out."

"I heard about that job you did for that other sheik after he referred you from the one a few years back. He not only purchased a fleet of limos from you but also had them customized too, right? That's major. I'm happy for your success."

"Thank you. I'll always be happy for yours and if I can help with this in any way, trust me, it will get done. I'll call Bobby today and have him put out some feelers. If the spot you really wanted isn't available, he may be able to help your realtor find something just as nice."

Sienna didn't know what to say. She was speechless that after all they'd been through, Carter was still helping her out in any way he could. She knew who he was didn't have anything to do with what he'd done. He was still one of the greatest guys she'd ever met, one with a heart of gold. He always wanted to be a part of the betterment of people, especially African-American young men.

"Thank you."

Sienna wanted to say more, but words were caught in her throat. She was shocked that after the way she didn't give them a chance, he was still adamant about her having an opportunity to achieve success by any means possible. That was what she loved most about him and compassion for his mistake is what she had been missing when she left. She had a right to be angry, but what happened to forgiveness? What happened to being hurt, being angry, being livid, but also putting in real effort to decide if what they had that was good was better than walking away? She didn't do that and being with Carter now and remembering all the good, she'd failed herself. More than that, she'd failed him.

Worst of all, she'd failed their love.

"Now, let's get to this car," Carter said, jarring her back to their conversation.

"Okay."

"Take a look at what I have in front of you and if you want to see more, we can do that, too. I'm all yours today," he said and waited for Sienna's reaction.

"All day?" she asked. Sienna pulse quickened after seeing his big, bright beautiful smile. She wasn't the only one excited about their time together, even if the reason for the closeness was only car shopping.

Carter leaned forward to be sure she knew he was serious.

"All day today and the next if we need it," he said, he said, lowering his voice. He didn't know where the need to sound sexy came from, but fixating his gaze on her, he saw a beautiful reason to do it. There was no way Sienna could know how much this exact moment meant to him. He'd gone so long with no contact with her and he wasn't taking her presence at his dealership for granted.

9

Carter sat in his office, pondering what his next move would be. His mind was focused on this guy who was trying to take advantage of Sienna with a business deal. He contemplated how to insert himself without totally taking control. The only person who could help him was his own realtor. He picked up the phone and dialed him.

"Bobby!"

"What's going on Carter? I know you're not looking for another property already? You're making me a very rich man!" Bobby jested.

Carter laughed. His realtor was the greatest and had found and secured his last two properties and he had no doubt if anyone knew who Oscar Jankowsky was, he would.

"No, not at all. I have enough to handle right now. I'm calling to see if you can get me some information on a guy name Oscar Jankowsky. Do you know him?" he asked.

After helping Sienna get her new Mercedes, one she found on his lot and drove home with that day smiling like she'd just won the lottery, he thought through his anger over how that Jankowsky guy was strong arming her. He wasn't having that and after taking a drive and looking at the property himself, he agreed it was a perfect location and had everything she would need as far as space to do what she wanted.

"Yeah, he owns a lot of properties. You haven't heard of him because the commercial properties you're always looking at for expansion are much larger than what he owns. He owns a lot of buildings, but not a lot of open space like for car lots. I hear he's a tough negotiator. He has something you're looking at?" Bobby asked.

"No, Sienna is."

"Sienna? As in your ex-wife Sienna?" Bobby asked.

"Yeah. She found a property that would be great for a new office park, community and medical center. She had her eyes on a building and surrounding land and after knowing how much she wanted it, he raised the price above the amount her bank would finance. In other words, this guy is playing hardball."

"And I know that's pissing you off. You may be divorced, but I know how you feel about her. You're not going to let anyone take advantage of her."

"Damn right I'm not. He picked the wrong one to try and swindle. She and her business partner are trying to do something big for the community---especially the kids---and that site would be perfect. I drove by there earlier today on my way into the office and she's right; it's perfect."

"What are you going to do, strong arm him into lowering the price? You know the fellas and I can go rough him up like they did back in the day in Chicago," Bobby laughed.

Carter laughed off the insinuation, but he knew if he called on his boys, they would have his back.

"Not this time, but I will keep that idea close to the vest just in case one day I need it. No, what I want to do is find out why he would try and turn what could have been a good sale into a dirty deed; a way for him to make a bigger profit. She told me things were going well with negotiations until he raised the price to a ridiculous amount claiming he was getting offers higher than hers. She was able to find out he was lying and then just out of spite, he rose the price even higher. By then, she figured he didn't even want her to have it anymore."

"Well, you know he's friends with the owner of the Chicago pro basketball team. I've seen pictures of them together at a few games. You're tight with a lot of the players especially the star of the team. Maybe you can talk to him and see if he can make some waves and sway that deal in Sienna's favor. If you're trying to get back into her good graces, then that's a way in," Bobby suggested.

"Man, I would like nothing more than to have her back in my arms, but I don't want her out of any obligation to me because I helped her out. I want her there because she wants to be and her heart leads her back to me."

Carter had been feeling more optimistic lately than he had in a long time, but Sienna wanting him had to be about love and nothing else.

"You know I've got my fingers crossed for the two of you because even though you slipped up, something we all have done, it could have been a lot worse. I think she overreacted but that's your love and I won't judge."

"Man, she had every right to be as pissed as she was because I was dead wrong and nothing was worth losing my woman. Not even for the few minutes I'd lost all of my common sense."

"I know how remorseful you've been and one day it'll all work out. In the meantime, check your connections. I think this Jankowsky guy even sold Jermony his mansion."

That had Carter thinking. He and the number one player on the team, the highest paid basketball player in the country, may be his way in to helping Sienna out.

He and Jermony had become good friends after a referral on some cars. Friends like Jermony were why his businesses were thriving, not just from his own purchases, but from the weekly visits and calls he received from celebrities around the world who were referred by Jermony. Carter would start with a call to him.

"You could be right. I'm going to give him a call. I know he's in town this week. I have a meeting with my new mentees and interns. I'll check with you later. Thanks for the information. It gives me a place to start," he said.

"Glad I could help and if it helps at all, good luck with Sienna. You two were always meant to be together. That kind of love can survive anything."

"From your lips to God's ears."

Carter hung up and immediately dialed Jermony. He had a few minutes before his meeting. He was bringing in a new group of high school graduates to shadow him and a few other professionals he was able to line up around Chicago. Before each young man went off to college next fall, they would spend the summer as paid interns learning what it meant to work hard and have a plan for success. He was excited to meet the new group and get them ready for the summer ahead with a few months to work it out.

He dialed Jermony who answered quicker than he

thought he would.

"Carter, what's up, bro?"

"Not much is shakin'. I wasn't expecting you to answer that fast. How's the family?"

"Pregnant again," Jermony said and laughed out loud.

"Seriously? What's that number four?"

"Yeah, number four in six years. We've been busy. You need to come by for a pickup game while I'm in town. Besides, I want to talk to you about a customized Navigator truck. I need it completely overhauled with more amenities than any truck should have, but you know me; only the best."

"I can do that. You know I got you. Listen I need a favor," Carter said.

"Anything, what's up?" Jermony asked.

"Oscar Jankowsky. I hear you might know him?"

"Yeah, I do. I not only bought two of my houses from him, but he owns the construction company that did the complete overhaul on the properties. You looking for a new house?"

"No, he's been giving Sienna a hard time about a purchase price on a property he owns that she's been trying to secure for a new office park and community center to benefit the community where her dental practice is. They need to expand and a property he owns would be perfect. He raised the asking price several times, putting it out of range. I was told you knew him and I was hoping you could get him to drop the price back to the original amount."

"Wait, dude is trying to rip off that sweet, sexy ex-wife of yours? We can't have that. Consider it done. I'll give him a call and hit you back when I hear from him. I don't see it as a problem. I've sent a lot of business his way. That fool has gotten stupid rich off of a lot of players and you know we always overspend, so he should be able to accommodate my request. Text me the information on the property and I'll hit you up in a few days. That good?" Jermony asked.

Carter had no doubt he'd be able to count on him.

"You know it and I appreciate it. I may not be married to Sienna anymore, but the last thing I'll ever allow is anyone to take advantage of her desire to do good work."

"We're boys. You're a better brother to me than my own two brothers. Don't forget the pickup game of basketball and besides, your godsons will forget who you are if you don't get by here to see them."

"How long are you in town?" Carter asked. He was going to carve out some time for them.

"About two weeks and then I'm back on the road. I'll be back when Kris has the baby, too. Coach is allowing me a few days to be here for that since she's having a c-section and we know the date. I'll hit you up when I'm back and we can get a few beers or something at that time too," he said.

"That's a plan and I'll do a drive by before the week is out. Tell Kris I said hey and kiss little Krissy for me. She's only one and you're already working on another."

"One day when you start having kids of your own, you'll understand. My kids are my world and as long as Kris wants to keep having them, I'm going to keep doing my part," he laughed.

"I hear you. Thanks again for helping with this Jankowsky matter. If this works out, Sienna will be happy and I'll be happy because she'll be happy."

"Are you seeing anyone yet?" Jermony asked. "I know you're still hooked on Sienna, but she did divorce you. Kris has a friend who would be perfect."

"No, I'm not, but I'm good. I've done some dating, but I don't want to put any woman in a position to get hurt when my heart still belongs to Sienna."

"I understand. Got those knee pads ready for the day when you'll need them? I see some begging and pleading in your near future!"

"I'm already on it and if I need more, I have enough football playing friends who can loan me some. Whatever it takes, she's worth it. Lately, we've talked more than we talked the last few months we lived together but separate in the house. I'm keeping hope alive."

"You're Carter Garrison. You can woo a woman from miles away, so I'm sure Sienna is in for the wooing of her *life*. Do it, bro. You deserve that love back and besides, I'm ready to see you sprout some little Carters and Siennas. I can't have all the kids!"

Carter chuckled.

"If I had done things right, I'd probably be a father already, but that's water under the bridge. I can't go back, but if I can go forward and make things right, you'll be one of the first to know."

"Bet. Holla!" Jermony yelled and hung up.

Carter leaned back in his chair and was about to head out to his meeting when his phone signaled a new text message. Scrolling through to the app, he saw a message from Sienna which caused his heart to beat faster. Even though he had a new cell number, he always kept the last number he had for her in his phone just in case she kept her same one and some day he got up the nerve to use it. They had been communicating about her car by her calling him at the office even though he had given her his new cell phone number. He assumed she would never use it.

Clicking on the message he smiled at a picture of her standing next to her new dark blue, brand new E-300. He was looking forward to sending her car to be customized. He knew that he would do anything for her and the way she was smiling at him in the picture, he just fell in love with her even more, if that were possible. Seeing the wording of the text under the picture, he read it out loud.

"This is because of you and I'm grateful. Sienna."

He paused.

"Anything for you, baby. Anything," he said out loud to himself.

Carter felt like a lovesick puppy and he didn't care who else saw it. This was Sienna and though he felt like he was starting from scratch with her, he didn't care. He would do it again and again if it meant she was back in his life.

10

"You did what?" Reese screamed into the phone.

Sienna expected Reese to get all crazy, but even she topped her usual over the top response.

"I sent Carter a text with a picture of me standing next to my new car," she admitted nervously.

"You sent him a text?" Reese asked louder than usual.

Sienna pulled the phone away from here ear, looked at it as if she were looking directly at Reese impatiently and then put it back close to her ear.

"Reese, pay attention, please. I know that's hard for you sometimes but try. I said that and you're repeating me."

Sienna shook her head and could picture Reese up and running in place with excitement. That was the kind of friendship they had.

"I know, but I'm making sure I know what I'm hearing. You sent Carter a picture, which means you used the cell phone number he gave you. You told me he'd given you the card that night after the party when he drove you home. You said you stared at the card for hours, but you still only contacted him at work. You wanted to keep working with him on a professional level. You know this means you've gone from professional to personal, right?" Reese insinuated.

Sienna paced back and forth across her bedroom floor, probably wearing a hole in the rich burgundy colored carpet. It was after midnight and she should have been asleep, but instead she was wide awake.

"You are so dramatic, Reese!"

"Tell me everything and don't leave anything out. For starters when did you send it and before you answer that, tell me how it all started. Wait, let me grab a glass of wine and get comfortable first," Reese said on the other end of the phone.

Sienna waited until Reese let her know that she was ready. She could hear her moving about through the phone.

"Okay, I'm ready."

"Wine in hand?" Sienna joked.

"Yes, and my ear is plastered to this phone. I don't even have my speaker phone on because I don't want to miss anything, so spill it all. I need the juice, the tea, coffee, all of it. Give it up!" Reese declared.

"So, dramatic," Sienna sighed as if she was already exhausted.

"Girl, don't act like you met me yesterday. I've been about the dramatic all my life. Now, *stop* stalling and tell me."

"Okay. On my way to work yesterday---a few days after I got the car---I was rushing to work since I was running late. I pulled the car out of the garage and was heading down the driveway when I stopped. I was thinking about Carter, which I do every time I get in the car."

"Chick, please. You think about that hunk of a man when

you're not in that car. Don't try and play me like that. Now, back to the story."

"Whatever! Anyway, I saw my neighbor's son walking by heading to the bus stop where a bus picks him up for school and I asked him to take my picture. He happily obliged and I got out, took off my coat because you know I had on a sexy dress."

"See, you were already thinking in terms of sexy when you decided to take off that coat and show all that lusciousness to Carter. You want that man, don't you? Mmm, hmm."

Sienna laughed, but didn't admit to anything.

"As I was saying before you rudely interrupted me. I took off my coat and posed next to the car and smiled with the brightest smile I could muster up at eight in the morning. When I saw the picture, I was excited, yet hesitant to send it to him. I told myself I wanted him to see how beautiful the car was."

Reese exhaled loudly on the other end.

"If that were true, then you didn't need to have someone take the picture and you didn't need to be in the picture. You wanted Carter to not only see the car, but to see you too. Now, who is being dramatic!" Reese exclaimed.

"Whatever," Sienna sighed.

"I want you to stop living in that dream world you're living in and step into reality girl. You wanted that man to see you. Who gives a crap about a car? There's a million of them on the street every day. He looks at Mercedes Benz cars all day long."

"Can I finish my story before I hang up on you?" Sienna reprimanded with humor.

"Yes, please. I'll try and be quiet this time, though I'm not making any promises. You know how I do."

Reese made some sound with her mouth that caused Sienna to pull her phone away from her ear again and look at it.

"What in the world was that sound?" she asked.

"Oh, I was trying to make that sound that Cardi B. makes when she's being extra sexy. You know I admire her straight in your face, no chaser attitude. She's the hottest thing around right now. Don't tell me you haven't heard her make this sound where she rolls her tongue?" Reese asked.

Sienna laughed.

"Oh, I've heard it, but the sound you made was nothing like that. Practice, girl, so that you're representing her well" she quipped.

"Whatever! Story please?" Reese inquired.

"Right. Maybe I wanted him to see me and the car together and I wanted him to know how much I appreciated the deal I know he would never give to another living soul. I didn't know how much he would read into the photo, but I went with it anyway. After getting back in my car and closing the garage door, I sat for a few minutes and thought of the perfect text. I crafted ten drafts before finally settling on something that showed how much I appreciated him."

"Yeah, yeah, you said that and I still don't believe it, but I'm your friend, so I'm listening."

"Really, Reese? Are you listening? Seriously, when did talking start sounding like listening?" she joked. With Reese, there was never a dull moment, even at midnight.

"Girl, finish this story. I feel my uterus aging waiting on these details."

"Oh, the images you plant in my head. I wish you

wouldn't," she joked.

"*Sienna!*" Reese hollered.

"Alright, already. I stared at the picture and text message and held my finger over the send button before actually hitting it once I exhaled the breath I'd been holding. I threw the phone in my bag, afraid to read anything he would send back. I was nervous like some high school girl. I got about halfway down the block and stopped. My legs were shaking and I started to sweat and the car was still cold. I had to take a moment to calm my racing heart. I was about to pull off when my phone pinged. I had a text message and I already knew it was him. No one texts me that early in the morning besides you, and I know you had a hot date the night before and you probably weren't up yet."

"Don't hate because you're in a dry spell. That Carter got something, something for that, though. I'm just saying."

"Ugh, you work a nerve, girl."

"Yeah, so what did his message say?"

"It said, he was happy I loved the car and he was happy to help. I smiled, but was a little disappointed that was all he said."

"Well, all you said was something about the car. You don't get what you don't put in."

"Don't start quoting passages you read on the internet like you're Buddha or somebody. I was about to put it back in my bag when it pinged again. His second message said that though the car was beautiful, the sexiest and most gorgeous part about the picture was me. I was on a roll by then. I replied thank you and added a smiley face. He replied back with one word."

There was a pause and Sienna knew she was driving Reese

crazy.

"I hate you. You know this silence is *killing* a sista!" Reese screamed and huffed loudly.

"I know. You know I had to get you back for all of your drama tonight. In response, he typed the word, *anytime*, and I walked through my entire day on a cloud."

"I bet you did. Whew, that was better than the best love story I could have ever read. You're growing up my young Padawan," Reese joked.

"Ugh, you and *Star Wars*. So, what do you think? Too much?"

"Nope. Just enough. It's okay to have Carter in your life. Others may have something to say about it, but who the hell cares what someone else thinks. This is your life and if you want to be friends with your ex-husband, do it. I'm all for that. Whew, that drained me and I'm up early in the morning for a flight. I'll be back in a few days and I'll check on you then. Whatever you decided to do, I don't want you to second guess yourself. This is your life, honey, and whatever you want, you get it and don't let anything get in the way. Remember, one life to live, so make the best of it and *get yours*!" Reese screamed.

"Love you, my sista!" Sienna said. "Thank you for being my voice of reason and the best friend any girl could ever have."

"Love you back, now get some sleep, so that you can dream about that man. You know you want to!"

Sienna hung up and laughed as she headed to grab a late-night shower. She turned the water on and was about to get in as steam filled the room when she heard her cell phone ping again. She had no doubt it was Reese with something she forgot to tell her. Grabbing it, she was surprised to see the text was from Carter. She clicked on it and read it.

'I know it's late, but I'm just getting in from work and I wanted to tell you that I have been looking at the picture you sent me since the moment you sent it. Thank you for texting me. I know I'm reading more into this than I should, but it means a lot to me that you used my cell phone number. It meant everything. Have a good night and I hope to hear from you again soon, even if it's another picture of the car. Just make sure you're standing in it, too.'

Reese smiled as her heart warmed. She started typing a message back, but instead, took a leap that she knew only someone like Reese would take. She hit the dial button and bit her nail nervously waiting for him to answer. He picked right up.

"Hello," Carter said.

The deep, luxurious sound of his voice was melodious and she tingled from head to toe. He still had that impact on her. There were times, like now, when his voice vibrated through her as if the sound was making love to her. *So enticing*, she thought.

"Hi. I hope I'm not calling too late. I was going to text you back, but since it appeared we were both awake, I figured I'd call. Is that okay?" she asked.

"You can call me anytime you want, day or night. I will always pick up. How are you?" he asked.

"I'm fine. I was up talking to Reese and you know how that can be."

"Drama central?" Carter asked.

"You got it. I love her like a real sister though. Even though she has a sister, Nicky, she still treats me like I'm number one."

"She's a good friend to you and I remember her sister. She has a brother too, right?" he asked.

"She does. He lives in New York, but they're still really close. How are you?" she asked.

Still naked after undressing for her shower, Sienna sat on the leather seat at the foot of her bed and smiled. She was talking to Carter.

"I'm good and right now, good has gone up to great because you called me. It's wonderful to hear your voice. I hope my text didn't disturb your evening. I know it's late, too, but I was thinking about you and wanted to send the text before I went to bed."

"It was nice to receive and I'm glad you liked the picture. The car is amazing. I loved my old car, but having this one is on another level when it comes to luxury."

"I'm glad you like it. I told Malcolm to expect a call from you when you want the windows tinted and anything else you want done. He's got you covered. Dex will get him right on it."

"I appreciate that. How is everything coming on the new location?" she asked.

"That's going great. I'll be over there most of the day tomorrow checking out the work. This will be an even bigger location and I'm excited about that."

"More Mercedes?"

"No. I'm moving into Bentleys, Jaguars, Ferraris, Rolls Royce's and much more. I'm really high end and that's based on the demand. I'm getting a lot of requests and though I've always been able to find what people need through other dealers, I want to get them what they need directly from me."

"Wow, you have really expanded your brand."

"More and more every day."

"I'm happy for you. I really am happy to see that you're doing big things and that you're content."

"I am doing big things and it's rewarding, but it doesn't make me happy."

"No?"

Sienna knew the feeling. As much as she loved her work, something was missing from her life and it was keeping her from being her happiest.

"No, but I won't bore you with that. Where I am right now, I'm at peace, like you, but I could be happier and one day, I will be. Until then, I'm enjoying life."

Sienna wondered if that meant a woman. She wouldn't ask, though she was dying to know if he'd found anyone even on a casual level. Reese would pry, but that was a part of herself that didn't exist. She would let it go and not get into his personal life. She was afraid of what the answer would be.

"I can understand that. Well, I don't want to keep you. I know it's late and we both have work in the morning. Maybe we'll talk again soon?" she asked.

"If you're okay with that, you can count on it. Have a good night, beautiful," Carter said.

"You, too," Sienna replied and hung up. Forgetting she was naked, she stood and danced around her room before walking into her bathroom. She couldn't remember a time when she'd felt this good. There must be something in the air, she thought, stepping into the steamy shower.

11

Days later and Carter was still happily distracted with thoughts of Sienna. Alone in his office, he pulled out his cell phone and looked at the picture she'd sent him. He marveled at her beauty and wondered how much of an idiot did a guy have to be to lose someone as beautiful, intelligent, kind, sweet and as remarkable as Sienna. He was a special kind of idiot because he did.

Hearing a noise at his office door, he looked up as Jermony cleared his throat. The country's number one basketball star was standing in his office.

"Hey, Jer, what are you doing here?" Carter asked.

"I came by to see how the dealership was coming along, and I see you are doing things big. When does the second location open?" Jermony asked.

"Early summer."

"All high end?"

"Nothing but the best," Carter said.

"Good because my lady wants a new Bentley and you know how she loves everything personalized. I asked her what she wanted as a push gift for the new baby and that's what she wants. Let me know when you have time to talk about what she prefers in color, style, interior."

"Of course. Because of you and all of those ballplayers you send my way all the time, I'm the number one dealership, not just in Chicago but in Illinois. The cars go out of the lot quicker than I can get them in which is why I need the second and possibly, eventually, a third location. So, what's up?"

Carter relaxed as Jermony took a seat and stretched out his long legs.

"Two things. I want to talk about my truck, which I'm going to leave at your shop when I fly back for my game. I'll let you know what I want done with it before I get back on the road. The second thing is to let you know Oscar Jankowsky has backed off on being a jackass. He not only dropped the price of that property back down to where it was originally, but I also talked him into doing me a solid by donating the time and materials for any upgrades Sienna wants done to the office park. Tell her to go all out with her needs and it's covered. Trust me when I say that you won't have any problems out of him again in case you see another property you want. He was happy when I dropped by his office yesterday and then his smile turned to a frown when I told him I wasn't happy with him. He begged me to let him fix whatever was wrong. When I say he's made millions off of me and my referrals, that's not a joke. I told him what you told me about the deal with Sienna's practice and before I could finish the story, he asked me what he could do to fix things. I told him I had a number I wanted him to sell it for and that it would be great if he could donate the upgrades in the name of supporting the community. He was more than willing to help. It's done."

Carter couldn't believe what he was hearing.

"Are you serious? I know part of the reason she needed to keep the cost down was because of the cost of renovating the property and adding outdoor and indoor basketball and tennis courts. The dealership is going to donate all of the computers for the new computer lab, something I haven't told her yet, but I know it's needed. She'll be happy to hear that she can now make the deal thanks to you."

"You mean, thanks to you, the man who loves her more than anything. When are you going to get your wife back? Kris and I were talking about the two of you this morning. I know you slipped up, but life is too short to walk away from real love like the two of you had. We can't wait to hang out with the two of you again."

"Let me ask you something," Carter said. He hoped he wouldn't be prying.

"Sure, anything."

Jermony leaned forward in his seat.

"Have you ever been where I've been? You know what I'm asking, right?"

Carter didn't want to say the words. He was tired of doing so, but he knew Jermony would catch on.

"Yeah. You're asking have I ever stepped out on Kris. Too many times to count and when she found out, it was after my first season, after our first kid but before the rest. When I say she was angry, man, I've never seen her like that. My second season was about to kick off when she found out through the media. There were pictures and I mean there were pictures of me in the act, man, and it wasn't just with one woman.

There were a lot of them and a few times, more than one woman at a time. It was brutal," Jermony explained.

"But you're still together," Carter exclaimed.

"We are, but it wasn't easy. She left me and there wasn't a thing I could do about it because the season was starting and I was in training and then on the road. When I could get a short break, I would fly to North Carolina where her parents lived. When she left me, she went back home and I was devastated. I had purchased her a house there, but she didn't even want to stay in that. I had a good season, but it could have been better if I didn't have to work on my marriage at the same time. We were young and I was stupid thinking I was a big shot on and off the court. She was gone for the whole season. I wanted her back and was willing to do anything. I made sure I barely talked to any women for any reason, not even reporters. I would call her every night and when I had more than two days off, I was in the air to wherever she was. She wouldn't let me stay with her, so I stayed in that big house by myself, alone and lonely for my family. Those were some hard months. Over time, we worked it out and I never strayed again. She and I have been together since junior high school. She was with me when I had nothing and living in a rat-infested apartment with my mother and brothers. I couldn't lose a woman who never wanted anything more from me than love and honesty. I'm thankful I got another chance to prove I could be trustworthy. I know you're struggling with losing Sienna, and she's already divorced you. Still that was only a piece of paper. True love finds a way."

Carter had been hoping upon hope that those words were true.

"I appreciate you telling me that and I'm hoping that's true. I can tell she forgave you. You certainly don't let Kris breathe!" he joked about her being pregnant all the time.

"Man, she knows how much I wanted kids. Other than you and Dex, I didn't have any friends growing up and all I wanted was to have a brood of my own."

"What about your brothers?"

"Yeah, I love them, especially when their hands aren't open for me to drop bills in them. We're brothers, but I've always been closer to you and Dex."

"What about your sister? Have you found anything out about her yet?"

Carter remembered having a conversation a few years back about Jermony being told his father had another child, a daughter who would be a few years younger than him.

"No, and we're keeping that on the down low because everyone will claim to be her if word got out that I have a long-lost baby sister that I never knew about until a few years ago. I want to find her and the private eye I hired is all over it. For now, Kris is happy being pregnant and popping out babies, and, trust me, I'm just as happy as she is."

"I know you are. You've always wanted kids and lots of them."

"So have you. I'm still expecting to get that call one day telling me I'm going to be a godfather, so get Sienna back and stop playing around!"

Carter laughed.

"I hear you and trust me, if it's possible, I'm all over that. I can't wait to tell her about the property. She was going to start looking at others, but I know that this one was her first choice and to hear the renovations are going to be donated, she'll be over the moon."

"I'm glad I could help. Let's talk about this truck so that you can call and celebrate with Sienna."

Carter felt like he was sitting on top of the world. He knew how much that real estate deal meant to Sienna and he was happy he could help turn things around for her. Seeing her happy and having her dreams come true was still important to him.

"Let me hear what you want in this truck and I'll get someone on it right away."

**

Seconds after Jermony left, Carter pulled out his phone and called Sienna. It was early in the day and he assumed she would be at work and he would leave her a message on her phone. Instead, she picked up on the second ring.

"Hi, Carter," he heard her say and hearing her voice gave him the chills. The woman did that for him and he loved it.

"Hi, Sienna. Did I catch you at a bad time?" he asked.

"Not at all. I'm actually off today. I'm hanging out with my mom today doing some shopping. My dad's brother had an accident and he flew to Seattle to check on him."

"Which brother?" he asked.

"Uncle Charlie."

"Is he alright?"

"He's fine. Something about a squirrel carrying a nut or something and I think the squirrel won," she joked.

"That's hilarious. How's your mom?" he asked.

"She's good. Lonely with my dad gone, so I'm keeping her busy today."

"I won't hold you. I'm calling to let you know that you should be hearing from Oscar Jankowsky in the coming days.

He has an offer you won't be able to refuse, nor would you want to. He's dropped the price for the property just at and maybe a little below the first offer you made and he's agreed to donate all of the upgrades to the building that you'll need. I want you to go all out and think of everything you want that office park to be. He's donating all of the materials and the team to completely overhaul whatever you want. He wants to do his part to support the Chicago community knowing what you're doing will help a lot of people. I guess he's now cool like that!" Carter joked.

"He's cool like that, he's cool like that, he's cool like that, he's *cool!*" Sienna sang the lyrics to one of their favorite songs by an old school group called *Digable Planets*. She laughed loud when Carter joined her in singing it. The song took her back to their days together. For years, even after the group was pretty much never heard from again, he played that song in the car, around their house and pretty much everywhere they went. It was still one of her all-time favorite groups.

"You remembered, huh?" he asked.

"Yes. You played that song so much that I would wake up singing it."

"It's a great song."

"I can't believe you got him to change his mind."

"I didn't do it. I reached out to Jermony and he did it. He sent a lot of money Jankowsky's way and he owed him."

"That's amazing. Constance is going to be ecstatic, just like I am."

"I'm happy I could make you smile."

"You seem to keep doing that. I can't remember a time where I've been this happy. Thank you so much. I know you didn't have to do that for me, but you did."

"I'm glad I could help."

"Can I at least buy you dinner or lunch or something? I want to be able to say thank you. You seem to be saving me a lot lately," Sienna offered.

"You're well worth the save and lunch or dinner would be fine, but only if you allow me to pay. You know how I am. I can't let you buy me dinner. Are you free tonight? I know you're hanging with your mom, but anytime works for me," he said.

Sienna thought about it and though she was hanging with her mother all day, she would be free later in the evening.

"I'm free after seven or so. My mom likes to be back home to watch Steve Harvey's game show and I know she would never miss that."

"That sounds good. I went to this new supper club downtown a few weeks back. They have live bands every night, and the food is really good. Would you like to meet there?" he asked.

"That sounds good. Want to meet around eight to be sure I can get back home to change? I'm wearing a sweat suit and that is not supper club dinner attire."

"Eight is great. I'll text you the address. I'm looking forward to seeing you."

"So am I. See you tonight."

After hanging up, Carter felt like he was strong enough to climb the highest mountain in the world. He had to pinch himself to make sure he wasn't dreaming the fact that he just scored a date with Sienna. Well, he saw it as a date, but he didn't care what it really was. He was going to be out with Sienna tonight and if he thought he was going to get any work done now, that idea was gone. He was so excited that he couldn't stand to be closed in by his desk chair. He needed to get up and walk it out. He felt like he was gliding on a rainbow of excitement. Date or no date, in ten hours, he would be having dinner with the most beautiful woman in the world. Tonight, he was going to be the luckiest guy in the world.

Carter moved around his office as if he was about to skip around because that's how excited he was. To really be silly, he broke out in the Carlton Banks dance from the television show, *The Fresh Prince of Belair*. He was for once, dancing as if no one was watching. Little did he know that someone was.

"What in the world is going on in here?"

Carter stopped moving and turned to see Dexter entering his office. He tried to be more subdued, but inside, he was screaming and jumping for joy.

"What?" he feigned.

"Don't try it. You were here dancing, but not really dancing. What in the *'brother can dance but wasn't really trying to dance'* kind of mood are you in?" Dexter joked.

Straightening his suit jacket, Carter turned and faced Dexter square on, sitting on the edge of his desk to try and contain his excitement.

"I'm having dinner with Sienna tonight," he gloated and tried to pat himself on the back, but didn't quite reach it.

To say that Dexter was as shocked as he was would be an understatement. They stared at each other as if the words he spoke were still floating in the air between them.

"What? You're doing what, now?" Dexter asked for clarity.

"You heard me right. I'm having dinner with Sienna

tonight. We're meeting at that supper club in the city. I don't know who out here in the divine world is looking out for a brother, but whoever it is, kudos to them," he said and pumped his fist in the air.

"You're serious. How did that happen?"

Carter ran everything down to him about the building and how Jermony came through for him.

"She actually offered to take me to lunch or dinner as a thank you for helping her get the building and surrounding land. This guy is even throwing in all of the repairs and upgrades for free. Jermony worked his magic as the big money man and Jankowsky caved in immediately. All I know is, I'm having dinner with her tonight and nothing, I mean nothing will keep me from it. I hope you didn't show up for an extended chat today because today is not your lucky day. I'm getting out of here early so that I am there when she pulls up."

"Fool, it's still morning, but I understand your excitement. I'm happy for you. I don't know where it will lead, but I'm happy for you. Look at you? I haven't seen you smile like this or been this excited in years. This is the Carter I was hoping you'd get back to. I knew only Sienna would be able to get you there."

"You're right about that. She is everything. She's still my world even if she doesn't know it. I'm not going to push her into anything or get all in my feelings. I'm going to enjoy her company and let things go in whatever direction they'll go in. She called me the other night and we talked like we did when we were back in college, getting to know each other."

"You and Sienna may need to get to know each other again. I hope you're patient enough for that."

Carter waved him off. He was nothing if he wasn't patient when it came to Sienna.

"Bruh, I'm as patient as I have ever been. It's been too long since I've seen her in an arena like dinner and music, let alone sit across the table from her and what I won't do is waste any of my time trying to rush her. I'll go at a snail's pace if I have to. Right now, I'm happy about dinner and I won't look beyond that."

"You know I'm pulling for you. Listen, I came by because I was in the neighborhood and to let you know I have the information on the possibility of some great out of state locations for the new customization shops we were talking about. You up for checking out what I found?" he said displaying the folder he'd walked in with under his arm.

"Really? Yes, I'm here for that. That's great news. I want to get that moving as soon as possible. I want to get Bobby in on this and he can help us get more information on the out-of-state locations. Today, is a good day," Carter said standing and walking around to his chair, still with an extra pep in his step.

"Man, anything could happen and you would still be having a good day. You are consumed with love for Sienna, and that's a good thing. Let's look over everything and get you out of here for your date which is hours away," Dexter said.

Carter shooed at him, knowing that he didn't care what time of day it was and how far away the date was, his day was full of Sienna and no one could take that kind of happiness away from him.

"Bet!" Carter said and grinned with a smile he knew would be permanently plastered on his face for the remainder of the day.

12

Sienna wished she had nerves of steel so that nothing made her nervous or uncomfortable. She could use that right now as she drove through the streets of Chicago to meet Carter for dinner. She still didn't know where the words came from when she asked Carter out to lunch or dinner. She'd been excited after hearing she and Constance would be able to move ahead with their plans.

After her call with Carter, she had been looking forward to getting a call from Oscar Jankowsky sometime later in the week, but to her amazement, her realtor called while she was out with her mother and gave her the good news. She was over the moon with excitement.

Thinking about being out with Carter, she was surprised at how brazen she was taking the step to ask him out. She wasn't sure if he considered this a date and she refuses to define it. She really did want to thank him for all that he had been doing to help her first with the car and then with the property. As the day went on, she didn't regret doing so because she actually looked forward to seeing him and thanking him in person.

Not only was she getting the building, but she didn't have to figure out how they would pay for the upgrades. Getting together with Constance and her realtor later in the week was going to be the second highlight of her week. The first was going to be the moment she sat down across from Carter and enjoyed a relaxing evening out. The good thing about her thoughts about him was that there was no pressure for anything. It was as if they were friends and not seeing each other as potential mates. They had gone down that road and it had ended badly, though amicably. There was no reason they hadn't talked since the divorce other than she wanted to hurt him. She was well beyond that and now they were learning to exist in a world where they didn't have to cross to the other side of the street when they saw each other.

Turning the last corner, she saw the sign for the restaurant and smiled when she saw Carter standing at the valet stand waving to her. As she pulled up, he came around to help her out while signaling for the valet to get in and park her car.

They rushed to get inside of the restaurant because of the cold. Once inside, he helped her out of her coat.

"Are you trying to kill me?" he leaned over and whispered in Sienna's ear causing her to blush. Even with the chestnut brown coloring of her skin, he could see that she was flushed. His eyes trailed her body from head to toe and he wanted to pant openly. "You are stunning in this red dress," he added.

Sienna smiled, happy that after going through over a dozen different dresses for the evening, she settled on the red because it was bright, friendly and accentuated everything from her model-like physique to the way the red dress matched to her long reddish-brown hair flowing around her shoulders. While out with her mother, she'd taken a little extra time to get her hair done and to get a fresh, new color. Most days she wore her hair up in a loose bun, but tonight, she was feeling extra sexy and wanted her attire to match her mood. Seeing the look on Carter's face let her know that she'd chosen a winner.

"I'm glad you like it. I bought it over the Christmas holiday along with a few others and I had yet to have an occasion to wear it," she explained.

"I'm glad you chose tonight. Next time warn a brother so that I can prepare my heart. I love the new hair color," he added and did a fake move of grabbing his chest like he was really having a heart attack from her beauty.

"You noticed?" she asked.

"Sienna, I notice everything about you," he said. He was about to say more until they were interrupted.

"Your table is ready, Mr. Garrison."

They laughed together as they walked behind the hostess.

As hard as he tried not to, he couldn't keep his eyes off of Sienna as she walked with purposeful, very feminine strides. She was all woman which was something that had drawn him to her back when they were in college. Back then, when some women would get up in the morning and head to early classes in sweats and sneakers, Sienna would stroll around campus as if she'd stepped right out of the pages of a fashion magazine. She loved being cute and sexy and to his delight, he loved watching what exciting outfit she'd have on next.

"This place is nice. I've heard a lot of good things about it from clients and I've been meaning to check it out," Sienna said as she sat with Carter's help before he took the seat across from her.

"I'm glad I could make that happen for you," he said.

"You're making a lot happen for me and you don't have to. Is it weird? Do you feel awkward with us sort of sliding into a place of comfort as if we didn't go through a divorce and avoided each other all this time?"

"Nothing about being around you would make me uncomfortable or weird. Yes, we're divorced and it was a bad breakup, but we had a lot of good years together and because of that, the level of comfort comes naturally. I've thought about you every day since we split and I knew that you being away from me was what you needed. I was hoping it wouldn't be forever. At one time, you were my best friend. I never thought we'd be best friends again because of what happened, but I would like to be able to say hello, call and check up on you and celebrate you when you have successes. I don't want to be the typical angry divorced couple. I know I messed up, but we had a lot of wonderful times together. Besides, neither of us are hateful people. I respected your anger and gave you the space I felt you needed, but I was hoping it wouldn't be like that forever. I don't want you hating me and if there was ever anything I could do to ease that hate, I was willing to do it to at least get us to the point where we could speak."

Sienna wanted to say she agreed. She'd spent enough time angry and now, she didn't want to be that woman anymore. In order to be able to move on, she had to let go of what happened and leave it in the past. It happened, nobody died, and they were looking to find love for themselves out in the world again. She didn't know which of the two of them would find another mate first, but she couldn't worry about that. It shouldn't matter or bother her, but when she had thoughts about Carter, which seemed to be a lot lately, she saw him still as hers.

"I'm glad we're here and that we can sit across from each other and have dinner while talking cordially. It was a long time ago and it's in the past. I'm not angry and I don't hate you. I never hated you. I feel good that we are at a place in our lives where we're not those angry divorcees who can't stand the sight of each other. I'm enjoying the sight in front of me very much," Sienna said.

As soon as the words left her mouth, Sienna was embarrassed. She didn't mean to say out loud what she had been thinking. The words slipped out. She knew Carter had seen the uncomfortable look on her face and knew that they were words she was thinking and didn't mean to say.

"Take a sip of water Sienna and relax. I know you didn't mean to say it, and though I loved hearing it, I won't hold it against you that you can describe me as a sight you enjoy looking at. You already know the feeling is mutual, so I'll let it go this time. If you happen to let it slip again, I may not dismiss it as easily," he joked and laughed with Sienna when she chuckled louder than she had planned and had to put her hand over her mouth. He caught her looking around to make sure others weren't staring at her.

"Well, it's not like you don't know that you're handsome," she added.

"True and that's not ego. I know what I look like. I'm happy to know that when you look at me you don't see a monster," he said.

"Never, ever that," she said.

Carter was about to come back with some clever retort when their waitress walked up to take their order. The band began to play and they settled in to listen to some great music until their food came. They were out to have a good time and he couldn't think of better company.

As people began to sway, clap and sing along with the band, Sienna joined in, loving that for the first time in a long time, she was out with someone without wondering what was next. She didn't have to wonder about whether they liked each other because she was far beyond like. She didn't have to wonder if the man across from her enjoyed looking at her. The way Carter could barely take his eyes off of her was enough of a message that she felt flattered unlike ever before. They were already having a good time.

"This band is really good," Carter said leaning over toward Sienna's ear.

The moment the words left his mouth and landed on her ear, they had a caressing appeal. It wasn't just any words or any person, this was Carter and his deep, sexy voice. The music had her feeling some type of sexy way and with Carter, that sexiness was heightened.

"They are. How did you find out about them?" she asked.

"Remember Lance? He and Dexter play in a band together sometimes. Dexter gave me a list a few weeks back of all of the bands coming to town and when I checked, I heard this one was really good."

"Great choice," Sienna said and winked. Before she could capture Carter's reaction to her out of the blue wink, she turned back to the band. In the next second, she felt Carter's breath near her neck.

"First you call me handsome and now you're winking at me. A brother could develop a complex from all this flattery you're tossing at him," he said.

Sienna leaned back and laughed with such jovial pleasure, she almost didn't recognize herself.

For the next fifteen minutes, they enjoyed the band without talking, though they both sang when a song was played that they loved.

"The bad was so good," Sienna said as she savored the fresh salmon with parmesan and dill sauce, rice pilaf, and her favorite mixture of kale and collard greens. "This fish is absolutely delicious. I wonder if they'd do catering for big events. I want to have a grand opening for the center and if the owner does outside events, I'd love to think about using him. I heard this is a black-owned restaurant. Is that true?" she asked.

"Yes, and they do catered events. I went to a fundraiser a few months back and the first time I heard about this place was when I asked who the caterer was for it. I'm sure if you checked with him, he'd be open to supplying your event. He seems to be a guy who likes supporting causes to enhance the lives of Chicago residents."

"Maybe I'll ask about the band, too."

"They were good. I'll have to keep them in mind if I ever throw a party and need a live band."

"Like at a party for your parents, perhaps?" she asked.

"Party for my parents? A party for what?" he asked.

"Carter, I can't believe you aren't considering having a party for your parents' anniversary. They will be married for forty years soon and that should be celebrated. I know you're an only child and it would be a lot to take on, but they deserve it. I love your dad and you know how I feel about your mom. They are incredible people and should be celebrated in a big way. You really haven't thought about it?"

Carter shook his head and lowered it in shame.

"I don't know anything about throwing a party. I wouldn't know where to begin," he admitted.

"Well, you just mentioned a band and a caterer, two things you could check into right here. For everything else, you could hire an event planner."

"Event planners are so impersonal and don't know about my parents and their history together. If I were to do something like that, I need someone who knows them and make the night as if my mother had planned it out herself," he said.

"An event planner can do anything you ask them to and put together all of the details from the first to the last."

"I don't know. I can't say it's about money because that's not an issue. I'm not good at those things. When you and I were married, you took care of the social aspect of our lives. I was the business half making sure I covered whatever you wanted to plan. What if I screw a party up and it turns out awful? How would I know who to invite? Where do I start? I would love to do something like that for them. They've done everything for me. I am as successful as I am, not just because I made right decisions, but because of the people around me; those who supported me. I had you by my side during those years of building an empire and my parents were there every step of the way encouraging me with all I ever wanted to do. I'm seeing this party thing in my head and I agree, it would be a great idea. I'll think it through and perhaps reach out to someone this week. I hope it doesn't take long to pull it off. Their anniversary is in two months. That's not a lot of time."

"You only need a couple of weeks to work out the

preliminaries of where you want to have it, a theme, and getting out invitations after pulling together a guest list. Then there is working with a caterer, and keep in mind, an event planner can help with all of that and more. They can do everything you need."

"You did all that when we had catered parties and events? I don't remember seeing a lot of planners helping you," he said.

"Yes, I did all of that myself. I knew what we wanted and no one would know better than me the kind of planning needed for whatever we were having."

"You are a remarkable woman. You always made things happen."

Sienna went back to eating her food and glancing across the table. She could see the struggle within Carter as he tried to quickly think through how to pull a party off.

"Carter, would you like my help?" she asked.

Though she knew he could easily hire someone, she knew his parents and knew that he wanted that personal touch.

"With the party?" he asked.

"Yes. I'm sure I can pull something together in a couple months. I know all of your family and most all of your parents' friends. Between you and me, we can pull a guest list together, that is if you want me to help. It sounds awkward, huh? You have helped me in so many ways that I don't think you understand and I would love to return the favor. Let me help you," Sienna said and waited. Once again, she'd taken a leap and wasn't sure where it would lead, but listening to Carter, she knew he would like nothing more than to have a party for his parents and she didn't want to see him struggle. That was definitely her lane. As she watched several emotions cross his face, she didn't know what he was thinking. Had she gone too far? Did she finally cross a line with him that she should not have? Perhaps, she was taking liberties that she should have kept quiet about. Before she embarrassed herself, she opened her mouth to pull the offer back and apologize to him for assuming he needed her help.

"Yes," he said while never taking his eyes off of hers.

"Yes?" she asked.

"Yes. If you have the time, I would love your help. You have always thrown the best events and I'd be like a fish out of water."

While they ate, they talked more about what he wanted to have.

"I'll write down some ideas this week and see if you like any. The first thing I need to check into is the when and where. Any thoughts right now? Their anniversary is the first Friday in April. What about that weekend?" she asked.

"I'm good with that," Carter said.

"You don't want to check your schedule to be sure you're available?"

He looked over at her questionably. He didn't care if he had something that weekend or not. His parents were a priority and they came first.

"It's for my parents. I'm available even if my schedule says otherwise."

"Okay, what about the where?"

"I have the perfect location for where. My condo has a beautiful banquet hall that would be perfect for the party. It's on the lower level of my building in the level above the garage and below the gym and other businesses located on the second floor."

"Do you want me to check into the availability for you?" she asked.

Sienna was getting excited. As they talked, she took out her cellphone and typed a few ideas and things to do in the notes feature.

"I'm going to let you run with whatever you think is best to make sure it's a night they won't forget. I appreciate you offering to help. I know I should have done more than buy them a vacation of a lifetime, but I didn't know anything about pulling together a party. It would be something more for my sister, if I'd had one. Not that parties are a woman thing, but, still, if I had a sister, I would have given her a blank check and supported her with whatever she thought was best."

"Well, to get this done in the timeframe we're working with, you'll need a blank check," she said.

"I'm going to give you my black card and you can do whatever you need to do. I'll need to contact them to let them know you'll be making large purchases for me. Since you've gone back to your maiden name, and it's no longer Garrison, they may deny some purchases that don't match my name. I'll contact them tomorrow, first thing."

Sienna realized Carter didn't know. She thought back to the last court date before the final divorce papers were signed when she requested to go back to using her maiden name. The judge granted it, but she never made the change. Every piece of identification, credit cards, accounts, etc. were all in her married name. She still carried the name Garrison. She had never signed the final papers for her name change. When she received them, she wasn't prepared to part with the name and then she went on with her life and never thought about it again. She also realized there was no way he would know because when he'd helped her with the car, his business manager handled all of the paperwork, not him.

"My name still matches yours. I still go by Garrison," she admitted.

Again, a look of shock. She was doing that to him a lot all in the same night.

"You're still Sienna Garrison? You didn't go back to your maiden name?" he asked, perplexed.

"I never got around to it and I knew how much of a pain it would be personally and especially professionally. I had plans to do it and never found the time. Yes, I'm still Sienna Garrison. Are you upset about my still having your last name?"

"Are you serious right now? Why would I be upset? If that name works for you, keep it as long as you like. It has been your name for many years and I don't see any need to change it. Tomorrow, I'll have your named added as a signee for the next couple of months while you plan everything, so that you won't need to get my approval while you're planning. Get whatever you need and let me know if I need to do anything."

"Are you sure?" she asked.

Carter reached across the table and took both of her hands in his. He waited to see if she would pull back and when she didn't, he looked her straight in the eyes.

"Sienna, I've never been surer of anything in my life. Check into the condo banquet space and see if you can reach out to the owner of this place and get a band contact for the one that played tonight. They played a lot of oldies and my parents will love that. As for food, you already know what they're favorite things are. Whatever date and time the hall is available around that weekend, let's take it, Friday or Saturday night. I'm leaving all of the decisions up to you and I'll add my two cents in wherever you need. I'll make sure my parents are available, which I'm pretty sure they are. They're leaving for the trip that next week, so I'm sure they don't have plans to be out of town that weekend. Is that good for you?" he questioned.

"Yes, as long as it works for you. I don't want to overstep."

"You could never do that. I appreciate your offer to help me out."

"Your parents have always been wonderful to me and despite the divorce, when they see me, they still call me daughter and I still love hearing it. I would do anything for them."

Carter didn't know what to say. First, he finds out that she still goes by his last name and now that she still loved being called '*daughter*' by his parents.

"They have always loved you and at one time, I thought they were going to disown me and try to adopt you during the divorce proceedings. They'll be happy about the party and even more so when they find out you're helping me with it. It may be easier for your planning if I got you a key to the condo so that you could set up in my place for all the things you'll need to have delivered. That way as we're getting closer to the date, you won't have to pile stuff in your car and get it to the banquet hall."

"Carter, that's not necessary."

"No? What if you have bags and boxes of things you need to work out of? You know I've experienced your event planning and I remember what our house looked like when party supplies began arriving. You're telling me it won't be easier for you to have a space for set up at my place? The banquet hall is right in my building and I have two large spare bedrooms where you can pile stuff up."

Sienna got a tingling feeling thinking about being in Carter's condo, especially if he'd be there when she was. She exhaled and inhaled deeply, but not so that Carter would sense her hesitation. It wasn't that she didn't trust being around him. No. She didn't trust herself being that close to him and his things. She was already having a hard time keeping her legs closed under the table knowing how close they sat to each other. She watched his tongue move as he talked and she knew how titillating it could be delivering pleasure all over her body. She admired how sexy he looked in his all black suit and pink shirt and wondered if he still wore those sexy boxer-briefs she loved seeing him in and out of.

"Sienna?" Carter asked when she didn't respond.

Sienna looked across the table and locked eyes with him and any defense she was trying to put up faded away. This was Carter Garrison, a man she'd loved and been married to and he was right, having a place to set up and have deliveries sent to that she would need would be a good idea. She was thinking too hard about what all of this working together meant.

"I'm sorry. You're right. That would work out okay. Let me know if there are times when I shouldn't come by, like if you have friends or company over or perhaps a date or something. I don't want to be in the way or make it so that you would have to explain my presence," Sienna said and then looked down at her food, moving things around on her plate, but not eating them.

"I'm not worried about that, okay?" he asked.

"Okay," she said and smiled.

"Thanks for having dinner with me tonight."

"I'm glad I'm here," she said and turned her attention back to the band as they took to the stage again after a brief break. She came out for a nice dinner and found herself planning an anniversary party for his parents and soon, in the possession of a key to his personal space. This was the kind of stuff that romance novels were written about. She and Carter in an enclosed place with a bed in it. Her only thought was that the temperature in the restaurant seemed to get a lot warmer suddenly. Looking around, no one else seemed to be having the same effect as her and she knew it wasn't about the temperature. It was her body and her reaction to Carter. She would soon be in his place and spending more time with him to plan to party and one thought crossed her mind; she was in trouble. She was already falling for him all over again. Yeah, she was in trouble.

13

Sienna entered her house after her early morning workout at the gym. She woke up with her nerves on edge knowing all that had to be done in order for the party Carter was planning for his parents to turn out perfectly. Tonight, was the night of their anniversary party, and she was a bag of nerves. For two months, she'd been spending her days in the office and her evenings planning the party. Thankfully, everything had been falling into place and she didn't have anything that had her worried.

She'd secured the banquet hall on the lower level of the building where Carter lived in his top floor, penthouse level condo. The facility provided her with the decorator who was setting the tone with shades of blue---the colors of his parents wedding forty years ago. There going to be beautiful flowers everywhere and the table decorations were going to be out of this world.

She was able to get the supper club to be the caterer for the evening and the meal they were planning could rival a world-renowned professional chef. She locked in the band from the night a couple months back when they'd heard them over dinner. All of the responses to the invitations that went out were now in and she'd been up late the night before working with Carter on seating arrangements. She couldn't even begin to think about how easy it was to fall into a routine of hanging out at his place. They moved around it together as if they were still married, yet the idea that they weren't still lingered in the air. For two months, she'd been able to come and go even at times when he wasn't there. He told her she had free reign to come and go and he meant it. Tonight, she knew he was tired after a long day at work, but after midnight when she was ready to go home, he still insisted on following her home to be sure she got in okay and then driving back to his place which was over forty minutes one way.

Life for the both of them had changed dramatically since they'd had dinner that first week in February. True to his word, he'd given her a key to his place and a code to enter the building through the garage where he consistently left one of his two assigned parking spaces available for her, opting to park either his car or his truck in one of the visitor spaces which were not as close to the building elevator as his spaces were. He even allowed her to clutter up his place with paper, decorations, and planning boards with no complaints. Not once did he complain about the clutter. She thought it would be awkward being in his home, especially when he wasn't there. If he were seeing a woman on a romantic level, she saw no signs of one over the past two months that she'd been using his condo as ground zero for party planning.

Being in the building where the party was going to be held helped. She didn't worry about hiring anyone to help plan the event. She prided herself on her knack for all things event planning. She smiled remembering her conversation with Carter about the four large boxes that blocked his doorway one day when he arrived and she wasn't there. He didn't know what to make of the boxes and had called her to inquire. She told him she was planning on making some of the favors herself, something she'd learned to do in her spare time. He'd never seen her do it and wondered what she was making. The next time they crossed paths at his place, she showed him an example and he loved them. That same night, he'd cooked them dinner, something they argued playfully back and forth over. She didn't want him waiting on her, but he had insisted. That evening, she put work aside and helped him cook pan seared lamb chops, brussel sprouts, and a sautéed vegetable medley, which he cooked in a wok which held and blended the flavor perfectly.

As they ate and sat across from each other at the island in the kitchen, she couldn't help but think back to times when they were married and Carter enjoyed cooking for her.

He was a master in the kitchen compared to her, though she knew he loved whatever she made for them. They talked about old times, fun times, and plans they each had for the future. Nowhere did either mention anything about seeing other people or relationships in general. They stayed clear of a topic that may still be uncomfortable for each of them.

A few times, Carter had to go out of town for a few days and she worked alone at his house. He never gave her a reason to question if he wanted her there when he wasn't. Life went on with her around him all the time without issues. When he was busy with working from home, she'd plan quietly in one of the two spare bedrooms while the fourth room which he'd turned into an office became his cave. What surprised her was the fact that no one mentioned how odd it was that she was the contact for the party or that she was planning everything considering she and Carter were divorced. She expected someone in his family to ask about the odd circumstance, but no one did. It was as if everyone expected it to be her. She brought it up to Carter and he told her it was because his family still loved her and some probably didn't even know they were divorced. It wasn't exactly a conversation topic for the family over the holidays and he mentioned he had not had time for many family events like reunions where he would have to explain why he was in attendance without her. He chose to avoid those conversations all together for now. He didn't want to have to explain the divorce and then get hit with a barrage of questions.

She began questioning why she felt empty whenever she left Carter's place to go home. She enjoyed being around him again and their time together allowed her to see that if she had given her full attention to their therapy sessions and tried to talk through how to repair their marriage or if she'd gotten beyond what he'd done, then the results would have been different. She would have been happy.

With Carter's presence back in her life, she was able to see that she wasn't happy. If fact, one night she thought he'd be home at his condo when she got there to work on the seating arrangements only to walk into an empty home. When she'd sent him a text letting him know she was there, he sent a message back that he would be out for the evening but hoped that she wouldn't find it inconvenient to wait around. He'd follow her home later for her safety. Then she had felt some kind of way that he never invited her to stay in his guest room but made a point of escorting her home every night that she was there late.

Later that night after he followed her home, she could kick herself for being jealous when this was the life she chose. She felt like a stalker when he made the U-turn after she went inside, watching him as he drove way. She wondered if after following her home, that was the time he connected with a woman, late in the midnight hour. Perhaps that was why.

She noticed every little thing about him since they'd been spending time around each other. One thing she noticed was that of all the times he'd followed her home, she'd watched him when he left and he always made the right turn out of her community because it was the quickest way back downtown. Recently, he'd started making a left turn, not going in the direction of his home. Again, jealously settled in as thoughts and images of him with a woman haunted her, keeping her from getting a restful sleep. She had no right. No right at all to make demands on where he went after following her home or who he spent his personal time with. She knew there had to be someone because the Carter she remembered turned heads of women of all ages, all races, all sizes, and shapes. There was no doubt in her mind that he was keeping time with someone or perhaps a few women since he was free and single to do so. She was mad at herself because, bottom line, whoever the woman or women were, she was jealous.

She hadn't expected her feelings for Carter to resurface as though they had never really died. This morning she needed to work off the frustration she was feeling over not being able to turn her feelings off and focus strictly on the planning of the party. Instead, she found herself in various stages of heat whenever she was near him and nights when they spoke late going over additional details, she struggled to get to sleep and found herself taking one cold shower after another just to calm her sexually sensitive body.

Carter's deep voice had a way of coming through the phone and covering her like a soothing sheath. Each time they talked and when she saw him, her body never let her forget how long it had been since she'd made love and her traitorous body turned on her at the mere sound of his voice. She couldn't stop thinking of the husky sounds he made in her ear as he made love to her, the way he would tell her exactly how her body felt enclosed around him. She was in trouble and she knew it. She was lusting over her ex-husband, a man she'd left and divorced.

Once, he'd gotten caught up in how easily the ball players around him made it seem and for a few minutes, he lost his sense of judgment. She didn't want to hear anything from him. Her anger over the embarrassment of what he did impacted her more than what he'd actually done. She figured the events of that weekend would get out, and she'd be the laughing stock of her friends and all the women over the years who'd tried to hit on him and hadn't succeeded. They'd use that time to say they told her so. All men cheat, people said, and so do most women, but was divorcing going far only to prove a point to others than to herself? She never had to answer to anyone, but herself. She didn't have to justify working things out with her husband to anyone else and she could see how remorseful Carter was. He didn't try to hide it, though he probably could have. He chose to stand up for what he'd done and suffer the consequences.

Sienna prepared to take a shower to get dressed and head

over to Carter's condo. She'd packed an overnight bag the night before and the dress she'd bought for the party was already hanging near the door to the garage. The plan was to get dressed at the condo so that she could spend the day getting the banquet hall all set up, and when it was time to get readied for the party, all she had to do was go up to the condo, get a shower and dress. Carter had already told her to use the spare bedroom to shower and dress. He wanted to be sure she had everything she needed, especially easy access to accommodate going back and forth between the hall and the condo.

Just as she reached her bedroom to jump in the shower, her cell rang. Other than her mother and Reese, who often called at the break of dawn, the only other person it could be was Carter. The thought of it excited her. Reese was out of town, so it couldn't be her.

"Calm down, Sienna," she said to herself when she took a running dive for the phone which sat on the other side of the bed. "It's not like you can't call him back," she said and laughed at herself at the image an invisible person would see of her sprawled flat out on her bed.

"Good morning, beautiful."

Sienna shined from ear to ear. Divorced or not, the way he always called her beautiful still had the same sexy impact on her.

"Good morning to you. You're up early."

"Well, I knew you would be. Let me see, you are probably just getting back from or on your way to the gym."

Sienna laughed at how predictable she must be.

"How did you know?"

"How soon we forget that we were once married. I know

your routine when you have something major occurring in your day. With the party on tap later on, I figured you'd be a bag of nerves. I was calling to see if you needed me to hang around all day to help? I know you told me to not take the day off because you have it all under control, but I feel like I should be doing something. You've done everything," he said.

"Not everything. You helped with the seating, the menu, gave me your advice on the decorations, and let's not forget the fact that you paid for everything. You helped even when you thought you didn't."

"You are so amazing doing all of this. I don't know if there are words to express how grateful I am. I can't thank you enough for all you've done. Tell Constance that I want to personally thank her for covering you while you were out of the office this week wrapping things up for the party. Make sure you make yourself comfortable in the guest bedroom and take a nap if you need one before the party. I want you to feel at home at my place," he said.

Carter tried again and again to offer more help with the party, but he wanted her to have full control over it and promised only to step in where needed.

"You didn't have to do that, offering up the room. I could have found a corner someplace to change," Sienna said.

"Now that's just crazy and you know it. I have two spare bedrooms and they both have connected bathrooms if you want to shower and there are clean linens in both. If you need anything, call down to the concierge and he'll get right on it."

"Now, that's what I call living. I should have let you have the house in the divorce and I should have bought a condo."

Sienna stopped talking abruptly when she realized how dry her attempt at humor was. She hated bringing up the divorce and her comment was in poor taste. "I'm sorry. I don't know why I said that," she added.

"Don't worry about it and anytime you want a condo, let me know. I have a guy," Carter joshed.

"You've already done so much for me and I haven't said anything, but I know that price was way below cost on the Mercedes you sold me."

"It was and I would have given it to you for free if I thought you would have accepted it, which you would not have," he said.

"True. You also got Jankowsky to sell to me at below my asking price. I'm still not sure how you were able to do that. I don't even want to think that you paid the difference in the price considering you also gave a large donation to help with the start-up costs and the donation of all of the computers and software for the community center."

"I can tell you that I didn't do that, I promise. Jermony is to thank for that low price and the donation of the construction supplies and manpower. That was all him. You know I'll donate more if you need it. I have friends who want to donate not only money but some of their time. The kids will love getting lessons and advice on basketball and football plays from professionals. I'm working on getting some of the guys I know to volunteer some time at the camp this summer when you have your grand opening. You know I want to help the community as much as you do, so any help I can offer, let me know. You do know that I would do anything for you, right? All you have to do is ask, and if I can wield it and make it happen, I will," Carter said.

"I know you will and I thank you for that. Is this whole situation as weird for you as it is for me? I mean, we've always worked well together, but after not seeing or speaking for so long, it's odd how easily we fell back into talking every day and seeing each other several times a week."

Carter took a moment and chose his words carefully. He didn't want to scare her off by admitting how much he still loved her. God knew he wanted her in his life for more than just this casual friendship they'd fallen into. He liked where they were now and hoped that he could build something with her again. Surmounting the biggest hurdle of getting her to trust him again would be his greatest achievement in life.

"The way you've come onboard and handled this party for me, no one else could have done it. Sure, I could have hired an event planner, but you have always been a daughter to them and no one other than me know them the way you do. You're saving my life here. I've never had a party for them and I wanted to do something special. Thanks for helping me."

Sienna grinned cheekily.

"Well, it looks like we are helping each other. I'd say we make a pretty good team, huh?" Sienna said and once again, smacked herself upside the head. She needed to think before she blurted out what was on her mind. She waited to see what Carter would say about her last comment.

"I'm going to let that one go by. You're trying hard to not say certain things that you're blurting them out anyway and it's okay. I know what you mean and to answer your question, I think we make a *perfect* team."

"I agree. Now, get off the phone so that I can get all of my things together and get over there. Decorators are meeting there at nine this morning and I have lots of deliveries coming in for the day. Thanks for letting me use your condo. I was actually thinking through making time to run back home to my house to change before the party and now I can put on a sweat suit and not worry about that. Now, you're sure you don't mind me being there? I mean, I don't want to explain my presence to anyone."

That time Sienna knew what she was saying and hoped he got the message. She didn't want to pry into his private life, but just in case he was seeing someone and they happen to show up, she didn't want there to be an issue.

"Sienna, there is no one you would have to explain your presence to and I wouldn't do that to you. I've been in the doghouse with you for two years and I'm not trying to ease back in there. You're fine and feel at home. I have a few things to do today, but I'll be there by two in case you need anything. I'll be a phone call away and I'll call you to check in. Good?" he asked.

"Perfect. I'll see you later.

"Yes, you will."

Exhaling, Sienna rolled over on the bed to lay flat on her back and tried to gather her wits.

"Am I ever going to be able to talk or see him without needing to change my panties?" she asked herself out loud and then laughed as she ran for the shower.

14

Sienna sighed as she began the longest walk of her life and though she shouldn't feel depressed about it, that was exactly what she was feeling. Her emotions had nothing to do with how wonderful the party for Carter's parents had gone. That had gone off without a hitch. For the past four hours, she, along with Carter's family and friends, had partied heartily while celebrating his parents' forty years of love.

After making sure everything was set up exactly according to her instructions, she went back up to Carter's condo three hours before the start of the party and found herself exhausted enough to take a quick nap. It wasn't until he came in and woke her up that she realized exactly how tired she was. Her cat nap was refreshing and after waking and getting a shower, she was ready to rock and roll.

For the party, she'd bought a royal blue dress that had a full rhinestone choker that served as the collar and at the end of the long sleeves, the cuffs were also made of rhinestones. The only jewelry she needed were the dangling rhinestones she wore in her ears. She was able to find in her own closet a pair of Christian Louboutin heels with rhinestone straps. After fixing her makeup, which she always applied herself knowing that she only needed a little, and pulling her hair up into a loosely pinned style, she grabbed her bag and walked out of the bedroom to find Carter standing near the door waiting for her. Afraid to move another step and end up accidentally running into his arms, she waited for him to make the next move. Damn did he look like a Greek god in a navy-blue tuxedo with a crisp white shirt, and even from several feet away, she could see how his platinum accessories added to the debonair style that was Carter Garrison.

"My goodness, you sure can wear a suit, Carter!" Sienna exclaimed and she meant every word of it. No feelings of embarrassment or shying away from expressing her opinion. He was freshly shaved with his goatee trimmed to perfection and with the close cut of his hair adding to that his one-thousand-watt smile, she was standing before any and every woman's perfect man. Carter Garrison was flawless and Sienna knew he always had been. He wasn't quite the perfect man, which is the level she'd put him on and when he stumbled off of it, she couldn't handle it. What Carter was? He was and still is perfect enough for her.

"Thank you. You look amazing and that blue is another perfect color for you. If the circumstance between us were different..."

Carter let the rest of his statement fade away as he used his eyes to do a slow perusal up and down her body allowing her to see what he was feeling and not just hearing him say it. There was no need to wear his heart on his sleeve right now. They had a party to get to.

The past few months of seeing Sienna all the time was

confirmation that he needed to talk to her about how he really felt. It would either be that she felt the same way he did or she was never going to forgive him for what he did, and therefore, they would be through as far as being anything other than friends. He wasn't sure he could handle it, but if after he laid it all out on the line and she had no interest in being more than friends, then he'd live with it. He would hate it, but he'd survive. For now, he was happy they were back to communicating.

"Are you ready for the party? Your parents will arrive in thirty minutes and we want to be there before they do," Sienna said. What she didn't do was ask him what his statement meant. She was actually afraid that his innermost feelings would cause her to face hers and though she knew what she wanted, she wasn't ready to express it.

"I am," Carter said and held his arm out for her to link her arm with his.

They rode in the elevator in silence. There was no need for either to say anything about the obvious sexual tension between them. Thankfully, the elevator ride wasn't a long one and once the doors opened, they followed the sounds of music playing and people talking. Once they entered the hall, they spent the next four hours making sure everything went well and that his parents were having a great time. They had family from out of town that they hadn't seen in a long time and more than once, someone mentioned how good it was to see her and Carter still happily married. Carter's words rang true when he said there were still family members who were clueless to the divorce. Rather than dispute the assumption, she smiled her way through and continued as hostess for the night.

The atmosphere was festive and the food was delicious. Music either by the band or the disc jockey that Carter had hired played all night long. Several times she'd danced with Carter and when the time came for speeches, she went back into hostess mode and worked to keep the night flowing.

At the end of the evening as people began to leave, she joined Carter's family thanking everyone for coming. Once the place had cleared out, she and Carter gathered the gifts for the night together and made sure there were no loose ends to tie up. Sienna stood out of place as Carter talked with a few of his relatives who were still there. She walked over to let him know that she was going up to gather her things so that she could get home before it was too late. When he nodded his agreement, she figured he didn't want to get into a conversation at that moment, so she headed toward the elevator.

On the ride up to the condo, she had never felt more alone. The reality settled in that once she left for the night, her life without Carter would begin again, and she didn't like how that felt. The possibility that they would only talk when needed and not because they wanted to was disappointing.

How could being around Carter every day, all day and most evenings have such an impact on her? Going back to life without him was going to be hard. As she walked slowly down the hall toward the door of Carter's condo, she was dreading the fact that she was entering it for the last time. After that, any interaction with him would be over. Would they go back to having no contact at all as if the past weeks hadn't happened? Was she the only one struggling with leaving as if she were reliving the day she'd left the house, moving out after making the decision to file for divorce and not giving her marriage a try?

She felt alone in the cool brick walled hallway. Her mind was playing tricks on her because she was positive she could smell his favorite cologne, so strong and playing tricks on her sense of smell, as if he'd just breezed by her.

Using the spare key he'd given her to use so that she could enter and exit as often as she wanted, Sienna opened the door, stood still, and looked around. When they left for the party, he'd left one lamp on that sent a cascading glow throughout the space. Looking around, she loved that she saw him in every piece of furniture, art, and piece of wall décor her eyes landed on. When they split and he moved out of the house, letting her have it, he hadn't taken any of the furniture. Instead, he opted to start anew and she loved how he'd decorated.

Sienna was suddenly pulled out of her trance by the rapid beeping of the alarm pad which meant she only had seconds before it would begin blaring. Remembering the code, she turned to the wall beside the door and entered it. She smiled knowing that was all she needed was for the alarm company to notify Carter, and he'd come running. Shutting the door behind her, she placed the key on the table next to the door and walked toward the spare bedroom where he'd let her reside when she spent time at his place planning the party.

Walking toward the bedroom her steps slowed and she didn't know why. Was in dread of the reality of the situation? She figured Carter would be a while with the remaining guests and she would be home before he returned. There was no need to drag out the inevitable. There was no longer a reason for her to be around. Her time was officially up. She shouldn't have a feeling about it, but she did, and it wasn't a happy feeling. She should be pleased about getting back to her own life, but she suddenly had a glimpse into how her life would continue from this point on and it didn't make her happy. She was miserable since being back in contact with Carter, but it wasn't because she didn't want to see him or couldn't stand the sight of him after what he'd done. It was because she was still in love with him, despite the divorce. She was reminded daily of the good times they had and it made that one incident that ended their marriage seem so small in comparison.

This was her punishment for not giving them the chance they deserved.

He made a mistake and she made him pay for it by leaving him. What really happened was that she *too* was paying for it. As much as she wanted to, she couldn't move on from him and deep down inside, she didn't want to. The answers didn't rapidly come to her mind, but the pain of walking away again was a powerful punch to her gut.

Gathering up the last remnants of the items she'd left on the bed when she'd changed into her party attire, she found her overnight bag on the floor beside the bed and haphazardly threw everything inside of it. She took one last look around, grabbed the bag and headed back to the front door with the feeling that she wanted to cry welling up inside of her.

She exited the bedroom just as she heard the door to the condo open and close. When she made her way to the main living space, her eyes connected with Carter's as he tossed his keys to the table. She'd left her key there too---a beacon shining out her intent to leave. Sienna watched as Carter sat back on the edge of that table. She walked further into the room on shaky legs, nervous about what they would say to each other. There was a connection going on between them that neither had addressed. She was afraid to and she assumed he didn't want to nor felt what she was feeling.

All evening she'd watched him and, even divorced, she marveled at how sexy he was. Tonight, for a few hours, they were family again and, in a few minutes, they were going back to living completely separate lives. Life and love weren't about the outer image, but the total package of inner and outer beauty and she'd missed that when they split up. He erred, but he was still the most caring and most incredible man she'd ever met. The fact that he went all out for his parents showed how much he loved and cared for them. She knew there was nothing he wouldn't do to make them happy because he loved that hard. He'd loved her that hard and she knew it.

"I think that's everything," she finally said, walking toward him.

Carter stretched his neck moving it from side to side and massaged the back of it with his hand. Sienna stood before him looking like something out of his dreams. Lately, they had all been focused on her. The dreams had been going on since the day she left him and it's why he'd never been able to move on. He didn't know what the correct words were to say to her, but he couldn't let her walk back out of his life. Not having any contact with her since they split had practically killed him and he couldn't go back to that. Sienna was still his everything and he didn't care what he had to do. He needed her to find some space in her heart for him again.

"That's it, huh? Have everything?" he asked.

His mind raced with a way to have her with him a little

longer.

"Yes."

Sienna wanted to say more, but the words wouldn't come. She felt like if they continued talking, she was going to cry.

"Your help was absolutely invaluable to me throughout all of the planning for the party. My parents were smiling all night," he said.

"Yes, they were. I'm glad you trusted me with your vision," she replied.

"It was our vision. You had the idea for the party and I had the idea for the location and the food, decorations and all of the planning was all you. We did this together," he shared.

"It was easy to do when someone gives you a blank check," she smiled.

"Only the best for the best parents in the world. I always wanted to be able to do things like this for them. Thank you for making it happen."

"It was my pleasure."

Sienna started to walk toward the door with her purse over one shoulder and her overnight bag over the other. When she reached for the door handle, she felt Carter grasp her right hand in his right hand. His back was to the door as he still sat on the edge of the entry table as she faced the door.

"Don't go," he whispered without turning to look at her. There it was, he thought. He was putting all his cards out on the table and hoped and prayed he wasn't alone in his feelings.

Sienna kept her eyes on the back of the door for a few seconds before looking over at him. Instead of seeing his face, she saw him looking down toward the floor as if he couldn't look at her and speak at the same time. She couldn't see his full face, but she could still tell that he was in pain; not physical pain, but a deeper pain that emanated from his heart. She recognized it every time she looked at herself in the mirror.

"Carter," she uttered and stood still at the door.

"Please, don't go. At least, not yet. Can we talk?" he asked.

Sienna wanted this, but she still struggled with leaving or staying. They couldn't go back even if something in her wanted to and she didn't know how to go forward without the past creeping up reminding her every day of what they no longer had. She wasn't sure she would be able to survive that.

"I'm not sure that's a good idea," she said softly.

"Why? I've missed you. I've missed you so much I ache in a way I never thought possible. I ache so much some days it's like my heart struggles to beat regularly. I miss you, Sienna. I miss you so much and I don't know how to keep dealing with that. Do we now go back to having no contact at all like after the divorce? I don't know if I can live through that," Carter said somberly and turned his head to the right to look up at her. When their eyes locked, he saw a sadness he wasn't expecting. Was it possible she was struggling as much as he was?

"What do you want me to say?" she asked.

"I don't know. I wasn't expecting to tell you how much I missed you, so I don't know what kind of answer I was looking for. All that I can tell you right now is I don't want you to walk out the door and leave, again. I just want to talk. Please?" he pleaded and then looked away.

Keeping her hand in his, Sienna dropped her overnight bag to the floor and stepped back until she was standing in front of him. She moved back a few steps, still afraid that she would reach for him if she stood too close. They were both hurting and it was clear that she wasn't the only one who had been hiding it all this time.

"What are we doing, Carter?" she asked.

His focus on her grew more intense.

"I know I shouldn't say anything and I'm sorry if this makes you uncomfortable, but I have enjoyed having you around recently. It was hard, so very hard not seeing or talking to you after the separation and divorce. I accept that punishment for what I did to you and to us. Working with you on the party stirred up feelings I never let go of and I never wanted to. I've missed you something terrible. My head aches, my heart aches, and my body aches, all for you. If you want me to apologize for saying that, then I'm sorry for saying it, but not sorry for *feeling* it. After all this time, I *still can't let go*. I can't be without you," he admitted.

Carter waited for some sort of reaction of Sienna being uncomfortable or looking like she was trying to make an escape out the door. As their eyes locked, he waited and waited, watching her as she thought over his words.

"You did let go just as I did. We agreed that the divorce was best. We got out before we ended up hating each other."

"No, you let go and at that time, I gave you what you wanted because I loved you and didn't want to see you hurting every time you looked at me and imagined the worst about that night. I apologized, went to counseling with you, and tried to figure out a way to fight for us, but you wanted out so badly. I could never hate you and it pains me that you hated me."

"Carter, I didn't hate you. I was hurt and disappointed,

I CAN'T LET GO

but there were never any feelings of hatred. Despite what happened, we have a deep, long lasting connection and I could never hate that or you. If I did, I never would have agreed to help you with your parents' party."

"I'm glad you don't hate me. I guess that means you just can't stand the sight of me on an ongoing basis, or you wouldn't have avoided me all this time."

"I didn't want things to be awkward for either of us," she said.

"It will be awkward for me seeing you happy and in love with someone else. You looked happy with your date at the wedding."

There it was. He put it out there, though his original plan was not to bring it up because he would only be torturing himself. Seeing her at the wedding, smiling, laughing and having fun with another man tortured him not only that day, but for days following it. That night, he left, came home, changed, and went to the gym. He loved working out, but that was the first time he worked out in the middle of the night. He felt the need to punch someone or something and decided to work off his anger at the gym. He searched her face for any acknowledgement of that night and the man she was with. He wasn't sure if what Reese told him was true or not about Sienna and the guy being friends. He hoped it was true. All he could do was hope. He hadn't seen her with a man or even remembered one contacting her the many times they were together at his place or any other time. That didn't mean she wasn't seeing that guy or some other guy.

"That wasn't a real date or a date of any kind. Brien is a pharmaceutical representative that I've become friends with. I didn't want to go to the wedding alone and I asked him to go as my guest, not as my date. Brien is happily engaged to a wonderful *man*," she stressed.

Carter's head jerked with awareness.

"Man?"

"Yes, Carter. Brien is gay and has no interest in women at all. He was there as my friend. Is that why you were weird that night?"

"I was weird?" he asked.

"You were and you know it. Reese told me she talked to you and told you Brien and I were friends. You didn't believe her?" Sienna asked.

"Reese says a lot of things and no, I didn't really believe her. You two looked cozy and it ate me up inside."

"Well, you were weird, but you hid your true feelings pretty good."

"I didn't want to appear jealous. People were already watching every move you and I made that night. No one had seen us around each other since we split."

"Brien is in love with his partner, so you have nothing to worry about."

"I do have room to worry though, right? Someday there will be a guy that isn't me and I'll have to find a way to live with that. I'm not sure I can. I meant it when I said I couldn't let go. I still love you as much as I always have and in fact, more because I know what it feels like to lose you and I took that love for granted. I will never forgive myself for that. I would never pry into your personal life, but I know there have probably been others that you've dated and one day, I will have to get over the image of you being with someone else. I did want you to know how I feel."

"What am I supposed to do with this information?" she

asked.

"I don't know. I don't know what I expected. I'm operating in the moment, nothing planned or thought out. You're here, I'm here and I didn't know if we would ever have a chance to talk again."

Sienna looked at Carter and his sincerity was like a beacon of light. It was as clear as a bright sunny day. He never could hide much from her. Since they were talking, she wanted to share a little honesty as well.

"There haven't been any others, Carter," she said.

He looked up at her curiously.

"What?"

"Men. Guys. There haven't been any others. I haven't dated anyone."

"Are you saying you haven't been with anyone at all since we split?" he asked.

Carter tried to hide his delight because he didn't want her to see him take pride in her lack of a dating life.

As the words left his mouth, Carter looked her over from head to toe. The most beautiful woman he had ever met in his life did not just admit to him that for the past eighteen months, she hadn't been with any man at all. He wondered if she knew what he was thinking right now. He needed to know if that meant no physical contact at all; meaning no sex.

Sienna paused and thought about why she was revealing private, delicate information to him. They were divorced and he wasn't entitled to know about her private life. She also didn't want him torturing himself thinking about her being with other men. The time for that would eventually come, but she couldn't stand to see him dealing with the image. She knew how that felt because she'd experienced it time and time again.

"I know what you're getting to and yes, you can let that image go. I haven't been with anyone since you. Not that I want your chest all swollen or anything or to see you beating it like King Kong on top of a mountain, but you are still the only man I have ever been with. I went out on a few dinners and nothing came out of those other than some good conversation."

Carter sat straight up.

"Why?" he asked. He knew for sure that she would have moved on, wanting to put everything about them behind her.

Sienna exhaled, looked away and then gazed back into his eyes.

"I haven't been able to get over you. I've missed you, too," she said.

15

Carter sat stunned. He wondered if he'd heard her correctly state that she missed him.

"Sienna?"

"I know it's crazy right? I've been thinking about it for a while now, but more since walking up here from the party. Watching you tonight entertain and mesmerize all those people, I remembered why I fell in love with you many years ago. I realized that even though we've spent a lot of time together lately planning the party, I've missed you. I've also been struggling with the idea that you've moved on and met someone else, though I haven't seen anyone. I can't imagine there's no one. You're an incredible man, not to mention something you already know which is, how fine you are," she smiled and then looked away. She was going for broke sharing her feelings and didn't know if she was catching Carter off-guard or not.

"I could say the same thing about you and you've already told me you haven't been with anyone which puzzles me. If your reason is anything like mine, we are in the same boat together. We're still emotionally connected."

"I'm sure you've been on many dates and before you say anything on that topic, that's not a subject I can handle; at least not yet."

"Sienna, I haven't been out with anyone," he admitted.

Carter waited as Sienna digested what he'd just revealed. He needed her to know he meant it when he said he hadn't let go of her yet.

"You mean recently?" she asked.

"I mean at all. Since we split, I have not been out with any woman for any reason that wasn't in some sort of a group setting. I meant it when I said I haven't been able to let go of my love for you. I messed up so bad and ruined the best thing about my life where nothing and no one could fill that space, not even temporarily."

Sienna didn't know how to respond to that. Carter, a man that women had no problem being disrespectful in front of her over him had been celibate? No dates? Nothing? That can't be what he meant. He may have cheated on her, but she knew his love, need, and desire for intimacy was voracious. She remembered how intense their lovemaking was and images of their bodies locked and writhing around sent a tremor through her. Like him, she had not been intimate with anyone, and being alone in a room with him looking handsome, virile, sexy, and absolutely delicious in his tuxedo was doing all sorts of things to her psyche. Though he looked tired from the stress of the entire evening, the way he appeared sitting on the edge of the table had her mind and body wanting him. She quickly shook it off, having no right to imagine more; to hope for more.

Carter spread his long legs and clasped his hands in front of him as he leaned back against the wall. He never sat on the edge of the table at his front door before, but he knew it would be the perfect location to be in when Sienna walked past him and out of the door. Before sitting on it, he noticed the spare key he'd given her was on the table. She must have sat it there to make sure he'd see that she'd left it and their time together was over. The finality of her leaving was finally hitting him and he was overwhelmed with a sense of dread, taking him back to the day she'd finally left him and then, months later, filed for divorce. Now, they were engaged in a staring contest and for an instant, he saw a glimmer of hope. His chance was now or never.

"Why are we torturing ourselves? I haven't gotten over you, you haven't gotten over me, and yet, we've been avoiding each other," he shared.

"We're divorced is why," she said.

"I know we're divorced. Trust me, it's been my reality for a while now. Does that mean we shouldn't talk or even see each other?"

Before he knew what he was doing, Carter reached for her hand and pulled her snug between his legs.

"We can't," Sienna whispered, even though she didn't believe it herself.

"Can't what? Be this close to each other? Admit that we have missed each other and then figure out what to do about that? You feel good in my arms and you always have. I know I ruined what we had, but it didn't ruin how much I loved you and I still do. You're trembling," he whispered the moment he reached up and caressed her arms from her wrists to above her elbows.

"We haven't been this close in a long time," Sienna replied. The way her words came out, she was more nervous than she could ever remember being around Carter.

"Is it too close?" he asked. When Sienna tried to look away, Carter reached up and turned her face back to his. He no longer wanted to avoid what he wanted most in the world. He wanted his woman back. "Sienna?" he asked.

"No," she said breathlessly.

Carter's brow creased as he looked at the pain on Sienna's face. It wasn't a pain as if he were hurting her, but the inward pain that he himself had been feeling since the moment they split.

"We don't have to be in this kind of pain, Sienna. We don't. We're grown and can do whatever we want. If it's speak, date, make love without labels, then it doesn't matter because right now, right here is all you and me."

Carter looked at her reaction and watched her shift a little from one leg to the other. One thing he remembered being married to her was how her body reacted to being aroused. She said she hadn't been intimate with anyone since him and when they were married, they'd made love almost every day, so he knew what was happening.

Sienna gazed into Carter's dark eyes, seeing the liquid pools that reflected a deep, passionate love for her. She didn't know how she had ever planned to walk away from him twice.

"Make love?" she said and then realized she's skipped over the other words he'd said.

Carter smiled. Of everything he said, she honed in on that and he was ecstatic about the possibility. He leaned closer to her, a mere breath away from her lips.

"If that's what we want. I know I do. I have missed being inside of you. I can tell by how you're twitching---rubbing your thighs together---that the idea of us in bed, releasing eighteen months of not being together intimately, means you miss us making love just as much as I do. You haven't let a man touch you in all this time. You love making love. I know how much you enjoy it," he said, allowing his voice to caress the intimacy of the moment between them.

Sienna was going crazy inside. Carter was right, her body was on fire and standing this close to him, she was ready for the talking to stop and hoped he would end the ache between her legs by picking her up and taking her to bed. She had missed making love, but only with him. She couldn't imagine another man touching her. She still wasn't ready for that.

"It's been a long time," she uttered quietly, avoiding eye contact. She had never felt more vulnerable, but she felt comfortable in her feelings because this was Carter.

"Let me help you," Carter said and leaned in even closer. Instead of going for her lips like he wanted to, he placed a soft kiss on her cheek. Leaning back, he looked for a reaction that said she didn't want him to touch her and saw none. What he saw was a woman who had a need, one that he was more than willing to take care of.

"Carter," Sienna said softly.

To his ears, her calling his name was like a plea. Hearing her say his name drove him on. He leaned forward again and this time, kissed the other cheek. When he did, he felt Sienna shiver in his arms and from the way she shifted around again, he knew she was getting weak in the knees. The moment she reached up and gripped his shoulders, he knew it was because she felt herself getting weak and needed to hold onto something. He was glad it was because of him.

They had been together for many years. He had been her

first back in college, sharing her virginity with him and knew everything about her movements, reactions, and, especially, when she was in need. He knew what to do to help relieve the pressure gathering and pooling at the apex of her thighs. He already knew it was happening. Her breathing was ragged and she was aroused. What he knew was that she wasn't in that boat alone.

He leaned close to her ear, taking the lobe gently between his teeth and sucking it into his mouth slowly and softly, knowing it would drive her wild. She hadn't been this free in almost two years and that was far too long for any woman, especially her.

"So, in eighteen months, you haven't been with another man?" he asked.

Sienna shook her head.

"No."

"No one has touched you? Made you come apart with an explosive orgasm, like the kind I loved experiencing with you? I know you know how to do that for yourself, but giving yourself release and having someone else focus on giving you the ultimate release aren't the same. The feeling isn't the same, is it? Do you remember how much I enjoyed watching you pleasure yourself for me? Remember how hot it made you to know I was watching and loving every minute of the show? How you would close your eyes and concentrate on touching those places that caused you to quiver and then knowing what I was doing to myself as I watched you? Remember how you would hold your breath as you came as I told you what watching you made me feel?" he said in with a rough, husky voice full of ardent passion.

Sienna opened her mouth to respond, yet no words came

out. She couldn't do anything but focus on Carter's words and the soft, wet feeling of his tongue circling around her ear now moving down to her neck. She didn't even try to resist when she moved her head slightly to one side, giving him more access to her neck. The feeling was amazing and something she'd missed feeling. He was right, none of the toys she'd used to pleasure herself with since they split could compare to the feel of being touched, kissed, caressed and made love to by a man---*this* man. Those times of self-pleasure, it was his face she saw and his body she imagined being near and giving her what she needed.

Carter moved his hands up and down her sides, caressing the curve of her behind, reacquainting himself with the feel of her.

"Uhh," Sienna moaned and gripped his shoulders tighter. She didn't know what else to do with her hands because her body was in total control of her actions, not her mind and all she could think about was feeling.

"I've missed kissing you, feeling you against me, under me, with me inside of you. Do you have any idea how torturous it's been to not have you in my arms like this for all this time? I've been slowly dying inside from not having you," he said as he hummed against her skin, allowing the vibrations to resonate between them.

"Yes. I've been feeling the same torture," she whispered quickly.

"We don't have to do this to ourselves, baby. We don't. I'm here anytime you need me for anything you need. If you need a caress, a kiss or an orgasm, I'm right here. Keep the key I gave you and come by here anytime you want to and especially if you need to. This is our business; me and you and no one else. Can I give you one now?" he asked slowly kissing a path across her neck and lightly blowing on the wet path he left behind.

Sienna's head was foggy. She didn't know what he was offering her; the caress, the kiss or the orgasm. She wanted them all. She was so turned-on, she couldn't find the words to pull together to form an intelligent thought let alone the right question or response.

"Whi...whi...which one?" she stuttered out.

Carter smiled as he kissed from her neck around to her chin, nipping at the area just below her lips. He wanted her more turned-on than she'd ever been in her life. He wanted her need to be so great that she would be more than ready for an orgasm the second he touched her sweet spot, something he was about to do.

No longer torturing either one of them, Carter moved his lips slightly higher and encountered hers. In the next breath, he kissed her sweetly at first, planting soft pecks along her lips, first on top and then on the bottom. Every time Sienna moaned, he was driven on to give her more, licking his tongue across the seam from one corner to the other, getting more turned-on by the second by the hot breath coming from her partially opened mouth.

"Can I give them all to you?" he asked and this time, captured her lips in a kiss that told her everything he wanted to say and do, but he figured showing her would be more convincing.

The kiss was electric. It was fire and pulsed back and forth between them. It was hot and steamy and Carter could feel the effervescence of pure desire which was bringing his body to life. He could feel from the way Sienna was trembling in his arms that she was feeling it, too. The want was mutual and undeniable.

"*Yesss*," she said.

Carter deepened the kiss again when her mouth opened to respond. He made love to her mouth in a way that he knew would have her remembering how his mouth and other parts of his body could please her if that was what she wanted.

As the kiss grew to an extreme level of passion he thought they'd had before, but now knew they hadn't. This need was bigger than breathing. He reached down to caress her outer thighs. At the same time, she took control of the kissing, going at him like a mad woman. He let her take the lead, allowing her to get everything she needed from him. Almost two years was too long for anyone to go without this kind of passion; this kind of connection; this kind of loving. Her need was great and he was glad he was the recipient of her overwhelming desire. She was indeed kissing him like a woman who hadn't been touched in a long time.

"Get what you need, baby," he said between kisses and he thrilled when Sienna heeded his permission.

As they kissed, Carter let his hands slide up under her dress, moving the dress higher until it was over her hips. Holding the perfectly shaped round globes of her behind in his hands, he caressed her, kneading the mounds, pulling her closer to the hardness he knew she could feel between his legs. As much as he wanted her, this wasn't about him---it was *all* about her and her pleasure. She needed him to satisfy the yearning in her and he would do that and only that. He hoped there would be time for more if she was willing, but if not, his focus was on her pleasure.

Moving his hands around, he encountered the thin strap

of her thong and ran his finger along the barely-there piece of string. Moving one hand back to hold her in place by her behind, he used the other to slide his opened right hand around and down between her legs. He knew what she needed and how much she needed it the moment her legs instantly widened for his hand to have a better fit. Her hips had already begun a slow grind under his touch and he wasn't touching his favorite spot yet. He softly caressed her through her thong, which was now drenched with the liquid essence that seeped from her body.

"Mmmm," Sienna uttered against his lips.

She broke the kiss and laid her head on his shoulder.

"You are so wet for me," he said against her ear. "More?" he asked.

"Yes," she groaned into his neck.

Carter gave her more when he let his finger slide beyond the barrier of her panties as he stroked his finger across her wetness, spreading it all around. When he felt Sienna's hips move in a more precision like circular motion, he increased the pressure and used first one and then two fingers to enter her sweetness. He was tight and still, she was all his. Her body was telling him so.

"Look how much you've missed me and you didn't have to. I'm always here for anything you need, including this. Never forget that, baby. Don't deny what you need because I'm around to give it to you, night or day, seven days a week even if I have to take off work."

Sienna barely heard words because her body was on overload. She could feel Carter's fingers moving and caressing all of the right places and at the same time, she could feel his hot breath on her neck. The onslaught of pleasure points being hit all over her body was driving her mad with need. She had no idea how much she really missed having him touch her until he was actually touching her.

"Carter, please," she begged.

"I know, baby. Trust me, I know what you need and you're not leaving here until I give it to you," he groaned softly.

He stopped talking to briefly kiss and then suck on her neck in the place he knew she loved the most, the one that would send her flying. With his fingers going in and out of her body as his thumb stroked her hardened nub, he knew she was close and couldn't wait to see her let go in his arms. He needed to watch her face as she did.

"Mmm," she moaned again as her hips quickened their movement. "I need...I need," she groaned.

"I know, baby, but I want you to know something first. Look at me," he said and moved his head back so that they could look into each other's eyes, even with hers straining to remain open. She was in her zone and he could feel her about to tip over the edge. "I want you not just today, but every day. Having you in my arms like this tonight can't be it for me. I wish you could see the glow on your face and how turned on you are. I can see how close you are to letting your essence flow and I want it all. Most of all, I want you. I love you, Sienna. Baby, I love you," he groaned out, getting as much pleasure from her as she was getting from his touch; his caress.

Sienna couldn't hold on any longer and knowing that Carter, a man who had a sex drive that was off the charts had not been with anyone else drove her to the edge and over. She kept her eyes locked on him and even when her orgasm slammed into her like a two-ton truck, she didn't break the stare. She kept her eyes on him even as she felt her mouth open to scream out her pleasure.

"Let go, baby!" he screamed.

Sienna did and flew higher than she ever had before. Her legs shook and were about to give way as she trembled through the explosion that had rocked her to her very core. His fingers stroking her intimately, his lips kissing her tenderly, and his hand caressing her behind was full body pleasure. The flow of ecstasy went on and on as if it were never-ending. Her body was releasing months and months of pent-up, sexual tension and the feeling was powerful, illuminating, and commanding as his fingers worked their magic.

As her body slowly calmed, she didn't have the strength to stand and so Sienna did the only thing she could do; she collapsed against Carter who caught her body in his arms and held her close.

"Oh my," she said softly, still unable to move.

Carter leaned his forehead against hers while still stroking her intimately, not just for her, but for him too. He needed to be this close to her. Nothing else mattered.

"I love you, Sienna. I always have and always will. Stay with me tonight. If in the morning, you want to leave, I won't stop you again. Please don't leave tonight. If all you will allow me to do is hold you in my arms, I will do that. Just stay with me. Let us both have this night in each other's arms. It's been too long," he pleaded.

Sienna leaned up and searched his face through the haze of cloudy vision after a powerful orgasm, looking for what she needed to be okay with his request. She wanted to spend the night with him, more than anything, but she wasn't sure she'd be able to walk away in the morning. Finding her strength, she reached beyond Carter's shoulder to the alarm pad and keyed in the numbers to activate the system. Taking his hand, she turned on shaky legs and pulled him along with her to the bedroom. Perhaps she could only get one night, and if so, she wanted the whole night. Carter wasn't the only one who didn't want their time together to end.

16

Carter didn't know who to thank for the fact that for the first time in a long time, he and Sienna were on the same page. As they entered his bedroom together, he was still holding on to the image of watching her face as her release took hold of her and he could see her immersed in one of the greatest pleasures he could help her reach. He wasn't going to take for granted the fact that she wanted to spend the night with him. His greatest hope was that, by morning, he could convince her to give them more than just a night of passion. His one and only plan for the night was to allow her to take the lead. There was no doubt he wanted his wife back, but in the end, it wasn't going to be his decision.

Everything was solely in Sienna hands.

Reaching for a switch on the bedroom wall, the lights came on and illuminated not only the room, but the image of the two of them in his bedroom together. He'd thought about and literally dreamed about having her in his room and in his bed.

"Your room is amazing. I had no idea it was this big,"

Sienna nervously said. She didn't want to tell him she was nervous. It wasn't like they'd never been in a bedroom together and the orgasm he'd just given her should have assuaged any uneasiness.

Looking around the room, she took in everything from the extra-large, king-sized bed with a headboard that sat up against the wall between two large bay windows that overlooked the downtown Chicago night, to the beautiful view of the skyline shimmering through the windows. She smiled when Carter pushed another switch on the bedroom wall and a fireplace came to life on the wall across from the foot of the bed. All around the room, she marveled at various African-American art sculptures and wall décor from paintings to canvases to hanging tribal masks. The décor fit in nicely with his hues of brown and beige colors.

"You didn't check it out all the times you were here? You've been in and out of my place for the past two months," he said, pulling her back against him with her body snug against his front. He wrapped his arms around her body and kissed her neck sweetly.

"I was here, but not in this room."

"I wouldn't have minded you taking a look around."

Sienna looked back at him and smiled.

"Can I admit that I wanted to look in your room, but then I didn't want to see where you were possibly spending time with other women. I wasn't ready for that," she said tensely.

Carter let her go as she walked slowly about the room. He leaned against the wall near the door as he watched her walk in a small circle taking everything in.

"I meant it when I said I haven't been seeing anyone. You are the first woman other than my mother who has been in any part of the condo and obviously, no one has ever been in this room. I wasn't ready to take a woman to bed who wasn't you," he said.

Sienna turned to look at him and he smiled. He loved being able to prove to her that though they were no longer married, he was still committed to the love he felt for her.

"What does this mean? Me being here?" she asked.

"It doesn't have to mean anything or it could mean everything. No pressure. You hold the cards. We can relax, listen to music, watch television, or just talk. Whatever this night is, it's up to you. All I ask is that you stay, let me hold you and then eventually fall asleep with you in my arms. I want you to relax with me."

Sienna smiled. "I already feel relaxed," she said. "That is also your doing from what you did in the living room just now," she said with a sneaky grin.

Carter grinned knowing he helped get her to that point.

"I took as much from that as you did," he said.

Carter watched Sienna's eyes travel to the area between his legs before she looked back up at him.

"Looks like I was the only one who achieved satisfaction," she said.

Carter looked down at his straining arousal and didn't shy away from his want for her.

"This is what you do to me."

"I love what you did to and for me," she gleamed.

"There's a lot more where that came from if you want it. You already know I do desire you without question, but we don't have to do anything. I've been controlling my body for a long time now. If you want, there is a television that rises up out of the foot of the bed. We can get up in my bed, fully clothed and watch anything you want. I want to hold you. I've missed that. I've missed you and over the past few months, I haven't been able to think of anything else other than holding you again. What do you want?" he asked and waited as Sienna focused on his face, not looking away. He wasn't sure if she was trying to read his thoughts, but if she had a question, all she had to do was ask.

Moving from the wall, he walked over and sat on the brown leather bench at the foot of his bed. He felt awkward and towering standing near the door looking down at her. He sat and watched as she walked closer and stood right in front of him, all within arm's reach. Still, he fought the temptation to reach for her. He was ready for a repeat of what they had done in his living room and knew that's what would happen if he tried to touch her again.

"Whatever I want?" Sienna asked softly.

"Yes."

Spreading his legs, Carter leaned forward and placed his elbows on his legs and waited.

"Even if all I wanted was one night with you?" she asked.

Carter opened his mouth to agree and then thought about it. Could they really have one night and no others? He was questioning if he could.

"Is that what you want? Only one night?" he asked.

Sienna looked at Carter and then looked way, biting her bottom lip nervously. Could she really ask Carter for one night knowing how intense his lovemaking was? No one would be able to have one night and not crave for more and she was no exception.

"I don't know if I have a right to ask for more," she admitted.

CHERYL BARTON

"You can ask me for anything, and you know that. If you want one night, then I'll give you one night. If you wanted once a week, I'd give you once a week. If you wanted every single night and day, I'd be tired and worn out, but I'd do it and be happy about it," he grinned.

When Sienna laughed, he knew he was getting her to relax and be open with him.

"You are the only person I have known intimately. I know you weren't a virgin when I met you, but I was, and all I know is you. I'm trying to be honest with you, but it's hard telling you the truth because I feel stupid. I mean, I was the one who walked away in the end and I shouldn't have a right to any wants when it comes to you, but I do. I really, really do and I feel ashamed that I'm standing here in your room and you're looking sexier than ever. The only thing I can think about is seeing you completely naked and making love to you so many times that I pass out from exhaustion. Not just tonight either, but more than tonight would be crazy, right? You have to feel some type of way about me after leaving and ending our marriage and yet here we are in your bedroom looking at you like I want to devour you. I already know that's the look on my face because it's what I'm feeling inside."

Sienna looked away avoiding eye contact. For two months, she'd been walking around him on egg shells every time she was at his place, and they were all business-like because of the party planning. From the first day, she wanted him and that desire grew more and more as each day passed. As the day of the party drew nearer, she dreaded more and more that their time together, even if it was to plan the party, was coming to an end. Would they go back to texting sometime or seeing each other at parties or events? Is that what she wanted? She knew she didn't, but what kind of woman divorces a man and then stands before him asking him to give her what she hadn't allowed another man to give her in years?

"Look at me, Sienna," Carter said.

Sienna turned her eyes so that they were gazing into those light brown eyes that had once tamed her with desire she never wanted to be without.

"This is crazy, right?" she asked again.

"Nothing about you and I being here right now is crazy. Yes, you left me and yes, we're divorced, but right now, at this moment, all I know is I want you like a kid in a candy store after a parent has barred them for having candy for years. It's not about the sex---it's about being here with you in any way I can have you. You want one night?" he asked.

"No," Sienna said softly.

"Two nights and weekends?" he asked playfully.

"Tonight, I want all of you and if you still want to do this for more than tonight, I want that. Actually, even if you don't, I still will. No need to start doubting myself now that I'm standing here," she declared.

"You know, we are actually living what has become a nightly dream of mine," he said.

"Is that so? Is the real as good as those dreams of yours?" she asked lightheartedly.

"Oh, you here, before me, and in living color? It's so much better," he replied blithely.

"Well, I've had some pretty steamy dreams about you, too."

"Really? If you'd like to share any of them with me, I'll

promise to get them all in before the sun comes up."

Sienna broke out into a fit of laughter.

"Well, what about after the sun comes up?" she asked.

"Anytime, anywhere. I'll even make you a bat signal to send up for me and I'll come running. As for tonight, let's see what I can do about right now. Does that work for you?" he asked.

"More than you know."

Carter didn't need any more words. He reached in front of him and pulled Sienna forward slowly until she stood between his opened legs. Not taking his eyes from hers, he lifted her arms high above her head and reached for the zipper that ran up the side of her dress. He pulled it down slowly until the dress loosened enough for it to slide over her hips to the floor. Turning her around, he pulled her back and down onto his lap, snug against him, making sure she could feel his long, hard desire for her.

Sienna shivered with longing to feel more than just the impression of that long, steely part of him that she knew would douse the hot, burning flame that was brewing inside of her.

"You are absolutely gorgeous, fully clothed, sort of clothed, or naked," Carter whispered against the back of her neck. He ran his hands up and down her arms until he found himself caressing her outer thighs.

"Open your legs for me," he whispered in her ear.

Sienna moaned knowing that something enticing was coming next, and to her delight, he didn't make her wait long.

The minute her legs were open, she looked down and followed the path of his hands as they first caressed the top of her thighs before moving further in between them her parted, trembling legs. She shuddered when she felt his lips caress the curve of her neck from behind. She felt ready to let go on the spot when his mouth opened and his tongue snaked out to lick a wet path from one side of her shoulder to the other, all while his fingers began doing remarkable things between her legs. She was so wet from before that she could hear the wet sounds her body made when his fingers encountered the drenching moisture he found there.

Sienna didn't know what to focus on more because elicit feelings swirled all through and around her. Unable to control herself, her hips moved on their own accord, gliding back and forth across the hardness between Carter's legs. Unable to even hold her head up, she laid it back against him as his mouth made love to her neck, nipping and sucking while moaning and whispering her name. This caused his mouth to tremble and send vibrations from him to her, driving pulses to the area between her legs that needed and wanted him the most.

"I'm dying, Carter," she whispered softly.

"Not before I get inside of you, and then, feel free to do anything you want. Come on," he said standing and walking around to the side of the bed, moving until the back of her legs rested against the mattress. Leaning down, he captured her lips softly, nipping and going between the top and bottom lip.

Sienna was on fire and was thankful Carter was using one hand to hold her up and with the other, he slipped his hand inside of one of the cups of her bra, finding her pebbled nipple to roll it between his fingers. She moaned, encouraging him on. Her mind and body longed for what she'd been missing and she knew Carter was the only man who could stoke the embers of her desire again and again. Feeling his hand slide down to unhook the front clasp of her bra, she exhaled into his mouth, playing sensually with his tongue for all she was worth. She needed to be a participant in making him feel as good as he was making her feel.

Reaching for the buckle of Carter's belt, she quickly pulled it open. When the sides fell away, she carefully unzipped his pants feeling the hard ridges of his shaft pressing against the soft material of his briefs, which could no longer hold in the massive length and width of him. With her perfectly manicure nails, she stroked the large head, causing Carter to sigh into her mouth. She already knew that meant he was enjoying the feel of her hand on him.

"You know, since we have all night, I would love to say I'm going to take my time loving you, and I will, but not this first time. It's been too long since I've been here with you and inside of you and right now, that's where I need to be. Any objections?" he said moving his head back so that he could look into her eyes. Her alluring eyes had now changed colors to a deeper brown.

Sienna tried to speak, but she was so stimulated, she couldn't find the words to express how much she wanted to put the foreplay to the side and get to the good, good stuff. Instead of speaking, she pushed his pants and underwear together down his legs, and when he briefly stepped back to remove them, she slid her soaking wet panties down her legs and to the floor and she kicked her heels off along with them. She now stood fully naked in front of him and in seconds, Carter had removed his shirt leaving him naked, long, and hard before her. This was better than any night she had suffered being away from him.

"No more foreplay. I'm ready," she uttered, sliding up onto the bed and moving back until she was in the middle. The moment she spread her legs and opened her arms, Carter came to her, covering her body with his as his powerful hardness rubbed her in all the right places, causing her desire for him to increase on a scale that had no measurement. She could feel his body being guided as if by radar into her moist place. She was already wetter than she could ever remember being in her life, first from the earth-shattering orgasm he'd brought her to in the living room and now from his kisses, caresses and being in his arms again.

She was more than ready for the feel of him deep inside.

"Ready for me?" he said in her ear as he used his arms to lift her legs higher around his hips as he rose to his knees.

"Love me," Sienna moaned feeling the head of him at her entrance.

Carter didn't need much more of an invitation than that. He also knew he didn't have to check to see if her body was ready for his. He never forgot how dripping wet she got the minute he touched her and moving the tip of him across her womanly folds, the wetness coated is hardness. Knowing how aroused she was, he was hoping her wetness and the gloved feeling of being inside of her didn't make him fly over the edge of pleasure as soon as he entered her body. His mind wanted to prolong it, but his body was ready to shoot off like a rocket flying into space.

No longer waiting, Carter pushed forward into her body slowly, grinding his hips in a slow winding motion while he was rational enough to still understand that even her wetness wouldn't completely help give way to his large size instantly. After all, he wanted her to enjoy what they were doing without pain. He could feel how snug she was and as much of a turn-on as that was for him, stroking his need for going into her fully, he took his time.

Going in a little, he pulled back out slightly, easing himself inside of her pleasure palace a bit at a time. He moaned, she groaned, and together, they made sweet music to go along with the sounds of him sliding into her moist womanhood.

"You're tight, baby," he said clinching his teeth to keep from surging inside. Sienna felt so good, he wanted her completely covering him.

"Two years, Carter. No one for two years. Love me, please," she begged. To prove that she didn't want slow or soft, Sienna raised her hips and pushed hard causing Carter to slide all the way in. The minute she felt him as far as he could go, she opened her eyes and looked into his, the moment he groaned out loud. With the room well lit, she could see the restraint he was practicing. She already knew he was close, but worked to hold out. She could feel him moving, knowing that he never just had sex by going in and out, but he turned lovemaking into an art, into a dance and his hips moved from side to side, in circles, all in an effort to give her the ultimate pleasure.

Their eyes locked and stayed that way as if both were using their minds to solidify their love. They were no longer in solitude torturing themselves with the want and need they'd always had for each other, but denied themselves. They were letting go and giving into a love that was deeper than anything that could tear them apart as it had done in the past.

The room was alive with the sounds of their love as the

fire in the fireplace blazed hot, casting a glow about the room and turning the sounds of their bodies mating into sweet, sweet music.

As Carter moved his hips faster and surged into her harder with longer strokes, Sienna knew she couldn't hold out much longer. She wanted the feeling to last forever, but more than anything, she wanted to come apart in Carter's arms with him buried deep in her body. Before her mind could register what was about to happen, her body quivered and her womanhood zinged as if every nerve-ending in her body was standing at attention and making a bee-line for the area between her legs. She gave into the feeling and could no longer hold in the scream that had been threatening to deafen them both the moment he entered her body. She would apologize to Carter and his neighbors later, but for now, she let go and screamed as her body gave in to the pure bliss of feeling like she was floating higher and higher above them. Her hips stayed in rhythm with Carter as they increased the pace, riding each other as if this one time would be their one and only time. The sweet sounds of Carter grunting and moaning fueled her passion even more. Her orgasm went on and on like it knew she needed to hold on to it to never forget how good Carter could make her feel. She needed and wanted all he had to give her. She reached down and grabbed his behind, feeling it move around as well as in and out as her hands gripped his hips tighter.

"Sienna!" Carter shouted and let go. He let go of the very essence of himself and gave every drop of it to Sienna. He'd held out for two years, not wanting any other woman to get what had always been meant only for her. Gripping her hips a little tighter, but not too tight to cause pain, he kept her in place as he rocked in and out of her. He let his release take control of his actions. His head exploded as white lights shot across his eyes as his hips pistoned forward with great powerful strokes. He wanted to keep his eyes locked on Sienna's, but he couldn't see anything save for the white lights shooting before his eyes. His was so high on loving her that he never wanted the feeling to go away, never wanted to come down from it. He wanted to stay in the plateau high above them where only his love and lovemaking with Sienna lived.

Carter could feel Sienna using the muscles between her legs to stroke him and unlike ever before, he felt his body rising even higher, though he had yet to come down from the first orgasm. Another one ripped his body apart as he now surged into her wildly, screaming her name over and over again feeling free to do so feeling Sienna's arms holding him tight as her hands caressed his overheated flesh. The bed creaked and groaned from the unfamiliar workout it was getting. Carter was thankful that the windows in his bedroom were thick and solid because he had no doubt the howling that sounded like a wild animal that escaped his lips surely would have shattered a thinner glass. He rode the wave of pleasure until his body began to calm, and he could feel Sienna's lips kissing his chest and up around his neck. He held on to her still with her legs locked tightly around him.

This, he thought, *is what home feels like*. This was the feeling he'd missed for the past two years. This is what he'd missed out on by ruining what they had, trying to be someone he wasn't then and would never be again. If he could, he was going to get his wife back or die trying.

17

Carter woke startled, trying to focus on his surroundings. Before he could panic, he felt a body next to him shift and knew his night with Sienna hadn't been another one of his hotter than fire dreams. He tried not to move around too much remembering their activities that lasted throughout the night and well into the early morning. Daylight had come up just as they had fallen asleep from sheer exhaustion. Sienna had asked for that, and he gave it to her as many times as she could stand. The thoughts of the night before stirred his body to life once again.

He smiled knowing now wasn't the time to deal with his body's hardened reaction to having her naked and in his bed. He should still be asleep like she was considering he knew they had only been asleep a few short hours. The clock on the nightstand told him that the exact amount of sleep he'd had was about two hours. Still, he was wide awake.

They talked throughout the night in between making love the four or five times they did, and though they hadn't resolved all the world's problems, they did agree that they would have no regrets in the morning. They each got what they wanted and needed and there was no looking back. He wasn't able to bring up the subject of moving forward, afraid it would put a damper on their time together. He was planning on having that talk before she left. For now, he needed to get out of bed before he woke her again because his want for her was about to get the best of him.

Kissing her on the one bare shoulder visible under the comforter that he had no idea how it ended up over them when he remembered moving it to the floor when it got in the way the night before, he slid out of bed, walked into the bath suite and pushed the door so that the sound of the running water from the shower wouldn't wake Sienna.

As he waited for the water to warm, he walked over to the mirror and noticed several red spots that appeared on his chest and neck. The thought of how they got there had him reaching to stroke himself. His mind wandered to the night before when Sienna licked, kissed, and sucked her way all around his body and the resulting affect was evident in the passion marks she left behind.

Their love had been intense and the proof that they missed each other and needed the closeness was evident in the number of times they'd reached for each other time and time again, without exhaustion.

As steam rose, he walked into the shower, closing the glass door behind him. Water cascaded over his body as he grabbed shower gel from the holder above the shower head and completed covered his body while he thought about their next step. Could he allow her to walk away from him again after their night together? It wasn't about the sex because if he chose to, he could get that from a lot of places. He only had a desire for Sienna. He would love nothing more than for her to seek him out when she wanted intimacy, but that wasn't how he wanted things to be between them. He didn't want the focus on sex but on the love that still thrived between them, evident in the way they made love to each other all night long. It was hotter than anytime he ever remembered between them. The time away from each other had heightened their desire for each other. Neither seemed to be able to get enough. Either he was reaching for her or she reached for him again and again, until they could barely keep their eyes open. Their bodies had been overworked though their minds wanted to give and get more and more. He finally decided to let her sleep and give her body some rest.

Lathering his body up, Carter shook his head at himself because no matter what he could try and think about, his thoughts wouldn't turn from Sienna being in his bed. Meanwhile, his body, rock hard, solid as steel reminded him that he hadn't had enough of making love to her. Contemplating between going back to joining her in bed or going into another room to take his mind off of her being naked, he turned when he heard a tap on the shower glass door. Wiping the dew from the glass, he smiled when he saw a very naked Sienna on the other side of the glass. He moved back as the door opened, inviting her in.

"Want some company?" she asked before stepping inside.

"You have no idea how badly I do. I was just thinking about you."

Sienna stepped inside, closing the door behind her and looked down his body.

"Is this what happens when you think of me?" she asked,

eyeing his arousal.

"Every single time, baby," he acknowledged.

"The bed seemed cold without you in it," she said taking some of the gel and rubbing it over his body

"I was trying to let you sleep," he said leaning down to kiss her sweetly. Her lips still had that thoroughly kissed look about them from the way he suckled at them all night long.

Following her lead, Carter reached for more gel and while she massaged his body, he rubbed gel over hers, paying special attention to her breasts, a part of her he loved caressing every chance he could.

"I see a part of you that's wide awake and not thinking about sleep," Sienna said looking down his body to his protruding manhood.

Before he could get a word out, he felt Sienna's hands grip his member and stroke him from tip to base, soaping that part of him up making her strokes more delightful. The feel made him fall back against the shower wall as he tried to breathe and not release himself just as she began caressing him more intently and focused. He was already on the brink, focusing on how soft and thorough her hands were.

"You're trying to kill a brother, I see," he strained getting out, gritting his teeth to survive her touch a little longer.

"Not at all, but I love how you feel in my hands."

Carter was barely holding on and knew as much as he loved the feel of his hardness in her soft hands, he had a better idea.

Reaching down, he lifted Sienna up by placing his arms under her knees and raised her up high enough above his straining penis. The throbbing was so powerful that the beat matched his own heartbeat, which was beating faster and faster.

"Do you know what I like better? I like the feel of being inside of you," he uttered.

Before sliding into her body, he took her lips in a powerful kiss, something he never wanted to get enough of. Her kisses blew his mind, the kind of kiss that only two people deeply in love could share. As the kiss deepened and grew wilder, he slid her waiting body slowly over his hardened flesh and exhaled the breath he'd been holding. The feel of her soft, pliant body covering his hot hardness took everything out of him.

"You feel delicious," Sienna said, moving up and down while at the same time winding her hips to increase the pleasure for them.

When she woke to find him not in bed with her, she could hear the shower running and her mind and body were on the same page when she decided to join him. The fact that she'd had little sleep didn't matter when it came to what she knew she would find waiting for her in the shower. As she moved up and down on him and delighted with the feel of him growing thicker, she held on, giving him all she had as he did the same.

They moved in sync with each other as only two lovers could.

Carter turned so that Sienna's back was against the shower wall, and once she was braced there, he surged even faster into her body until the only sounds were of their equal moaning and their bodies smacking against each other.

"I'm, I'm....," Sienna screamed.

"I know, baby. I'm right there with you. Come with me! With me, baby!" Carter screamed and gave into the salaciousness of the moment.

Together, they had a shared experience of exploding at the same time.

Carter continued to hold her body up in his arms, barely able to will his own legs to hold him up. His mind was spent, his body was spent, but his desire for Sienna never wavered and never lessened. She was everything to him.

"You know, I'm not sure I'll be able to walk after a night and morning of making love with you," Sienna finally said when she could find her voice again.

"Well, then spend the day with me, here. I promise to let you get some rest. I'm not ready to let go yet," Carter said, sadly and showed her his pouty face as he carried her with him from the shower toward the bench in front of the mirror where he sat and tried to gather his strength.

Sienna laughed. "What's that face?" she asked reaching for a towel and toweling his body dry.

"I want you to feel sorry for me and spend it here. It's Sunday and your office isn't open today," he said.

"Well, I didn't have anything planned for today."

"Does that mean you'll spend at least the day with me? We can talk about the possibility of the next weekend before this weekend is over."

Wrapping a towel around his waist and handing her one to wrap around her body, Carter stood and placed Sienna on her feet.

"Don't you have to work? I'm sure the dealership isn't closed today," she said.

"Since I'm the owner, I don't have to be there to run it. I wasn't planning on going in until later today anyway because of the party last night, but if you're going to be here, then I'm not going anywhere. I have you here with me and I don't know how long that will last until you decide you've had enough of my company and leave me. We can get dressed in as little as possible, of course, and cook breakfast together. I have all the fixing for those veggie omelets you like. There's fresh fruit and bagels with cream cheese and apple jelly. Yes, I still love apple jelly and if I remember correctly, you do, too. Come on and say yes," he pleaded.

Sienna thought about what it would mean for her to stay any longer. They had talked about a night together, but a night and a day hadn't been on the agenda. She had to admit to herself that the sex was mad crazy and explosive. If all they had was this time, she wouldn't mind getting her fill. She looked up at him as he pulled her into his arms.

"I am hungry," she said.

"That's because you worked up an appetite."

"I don't have any clean clothes to put on."

"If I'm doing my job right, you won't need any, but I do have a t-shirt you can wear. I'll get it for you to put on and while you do that, I'm going to throw on some shorts and start working on breakfast."

Sienna turned to leave, only to be pulled back and the kiss that landed on her lips had her remembering why, like him, she wasn't ready to leave.

**

"This omelet is amazing. What kind of cheese did you use?" Sienna asked.

She spoke in between chews practically inhaling the large omelet he'd made, one for her which was all veggies and one for himself that had three types of breakfast meat along with piles of veggies.

"It's an Italian blend of cheeses, something my mom uses in her baked macaroni and cheese. Sometimes I make just a cheese omelet because of the flavor."

"You still love to cook, huh?" she asked.

"A brother has to eat. You know I've never been one to eat a lot of fast food. That means I either have to have fine dining every night or I have to cook."

"Well, this omelet is everything."

"Another bagel?" he asked.

"I already had one, but I do love bagels. Just a half and this time only jelly, no cream cheese.

Carter moved about the kitchen making sure he was doing all he could to satisfy her pallet.

"So, you're staying all day. What will we do besides make love all day? I don't want to overstay my welcome in your body, but you know, I can't make any promises that I won't try all day to get there," he laughed.

"I desire you just as much as you desire me, so I know something of what you speak. You know what I want to do? Watch television and catch up on my episodes of *Chicago P.D.*"

"I do love that show. I have On-Demand so you can watch as many episodes as you'd like. I may step out in a little while to grab some food for lunch and dinner. I have some stuff, but I want to go all out with lobster tails, shrimp skewers, lamb chops, ingredients for a salad and some ice cream."

Sienna's eyes lit up.

"With whipped cream?" she asked. The minute she did, she could see from the look on his face that his mind went to the same naughty place as hers.

"I would never forget the whipped cream. It has several

uses, in case you forgot," he said with that extra spice to his words.

"Oh, I haven't forgotten. I remember the number of sheets I had to replace because of your need to bring whipped cream to bed."

"It's a good thing I have plenty of sheets then," he joked and placed her bagel in front of her.

"Then I say get two cans instead of one."

Sienna loved how comfortable they were with each other now, in the light of day. Before last night, things were still pretty awkward between them even throughout the party planning, but now, they were as they had been before their marriage fell apart.

"Two it is. Anything else you want me to get?"

"No, but can I use your washer and dryer to wash the clothes I wore here before I changed into my party dress?" she asked.

"You can use anything here, including me," he insinuated in his attempt to ooze as much sexiness as he could muster up.

"I'll remember that," she smiled mischievously.

"Detergent is on the shelf between the machines in that door at the end of the kitchen island. Let's take our breakfast and get comfortable in front of the television. I'm not promising I won't fall asleep on you at some point because I only had two hours of sleep, but feel free to wake me up if you see something you want," Carter said and winked.

"Sounds like a plan."

Sienna hopped down from the chair in front of the island and carried both of their plates to his media room, a place she'd fallen in love with over the past few weeks. The large, tan leather sectional was the most comfortable spot to sit back and relax. She'd never seen an entertainment system like his before and since she was also a technology hound, that was saying something.

Carter joined her on the sofa after grabbing their glasses of orange juice and a few bottles of water from the refrigerator. After placing everything in front of them, he left the room briefly to grab a thin blanket since he figured that they would both be asleep before the first episode wound up. Now that he knew she was staying the whole day with him, he wasn't as anxious to get a lifetime of time together in one night. He now had a day of convincing her that she needed to give them a second chance at more than just steamy nights. He wanted forever.

18

"Spill it, bro. Whatever it is, I need to hear the whole story."

Carter continued walking to his office and kept his face hidden in a way that no one would see the smile of content on his face. Today, he was feeling better than he had in a long time and it wasn't just that he had spent Saturday night and all-day Sunday making love to Sienna and laying around like couch potatoes talking, watching movies, cooking together, and tuning out the outside world. Today, he was practically walking on air.

Going around behind his desk, he picked up the mail that had been left for him by his assistant and sat down, still ignoring Dexter who he forgot was stopping by for a meeting.

"Dex, what are you talking about? I'm the same Carter you see all the time. What's gotten into you?" he asked.

"The question is, what's gotten into you or should I say who you've gotten into? Who was it? I know the look and the walk and I haven't seen either in a long time. She must be someone new because if you were seeing someone, you would have told me. After your drought, I want to hear about this woman that has you walking around here like John Travolta in *Saturday Night Fever*. You know he is the king of the strut. What gives?"

Carter looked up from the mail he was pretending to read and smirked.

"Nothing."

"Stop digging for something that's not there in that pile of mail. You couldn't care less about the damn mail. You're avoiding my questions," Dexter chided jokingly.

He moved away from the door frame, shut the office door behind him and sat in the chair in front of the desk. Raising his feet, he crossed them at the ankles and planted them on the edge of Carter's desk.

"Get your crusty feet off my desk!" Carter quipped.

"I'm staying for the duration until you tell me what's up. I know you and somethings going on. You've been missing since your parent's party on Saturday. I thought you were coming in yesterday and when I called here, I was told you called and said you would be unreachable until today. It must be a woman. Nothing else would keep you from work," Dexter exclaimed.

"We have a meeting about the new inventory in five minutes and you know I don't want these guys off the floor too long. I appreciate you taking the time away from *Chi Brothers* to help out with getting the dealership up and running. The cars are coming in soon and due to the good weather we've had this year, construction is way ahead of schedule. Did you look over the list of what's coming in and when?" Carter asked, trying to change the subject.

Dexter chuckled.

"Stop playing and tell me already. I know something is up

because I called you yesterday about this new inventory and not only did you not pick up, but you didn't return my call. You're usually catching up on work on Sundays. You're always ready to talk business any day, any time. I'm going to sit here until you tell me or feel free to lie and tell me it's nothing and I'll let it go," Dexter lied. "Okay, I lied because I'm not moving until you cough it up.

Carter faked a cough. "We good?" he laughed.

"Funny!"

"We have a meeting we are about to be late for," Carter said, trying to move the conversation on. He was trying anything to end the conversation. He didn't want to jinx what he and Sienna shared hoping there was more to come. Right now, she held all the cards, and he was at her mercy.

He watched as Dexter picked up his phone and pushed the line for the receptionist.

"Tawny, can you get everyone together for the meeting and let them know Carter and I will be there shortly?"

He hung up and went back to relaxing.

"I guess you're not letting this go, huh?" Carter assumed.

"Dude, you walked in here like you won the lottery jackpot. I haven't seen this Carter in a long time and trust me, I'm not complaining. I know that cocky, bowlegged stride and it's a sign that some woman brought you back to life. If I didn't know any better, I would say it was Sienna because I believe no other woman will ever make you happy again, but her. Since that's not possible, who..."

Dexter didn't finish his sentence. There was something about his last statement that brought a slight difference to Carter's demeanor.

Carter coughed again, cleared his throat and pretended to

look for something on his desk.

"Let's get to the meeting. I have a lot of customers coming in today according to the pre-scheduled appointments."

Carter was hoping to throw Dexter off track but was sure it wasn't working when he saw the questionable look on his face.

"Sienna! Sienna? It was Sienna? Say it isn't so. Bruh, it was Sienna? You slept with Sienna? What!" Dexter shouted.

Carter tried to quiet him, but Dexter would let up.

"I didn't say anything like that and you need to shout softer. Remember this is a place of business."

"You didn't have to say her name. As soon as I said hit, everything about you switched up because I figured it out. It was Sienna!" he hollered.

"Keep your voice down," Carter whispered and looked toward the door.

He started to deny it and distract Dexter onto another subject, but he knew that he was like a dog with a bone and was never going to let it go.

Carter briefly closed his eyes and remembered Sienna in all of her glory roaming around his condo all day in one of his shirts. There was no need for him to put up a pretense of even wearing that much because every time she came near him, he would have taken off any clothes anyway. Having her pretty much naked was easy access for them both. If he didn't think he needed to give her body a rest from his amatory thoughts and actions, he never would have let her out of bed. He leaned back and smiled. There was no need to hide anything from Dexter. His next move probably would be a call to Sienna to get answers.

"She stayed the night after my parents' party Saturday

night and it was like it was when we were married. No, let me change that, it was better than any time during our marriage. I woke up this morning and she was gone after the most incredible weekend ever. She left without a note or anything."

"She put it on you like that to the point that you were knocked out dead and didn't feel her moving around or hear her getting dressed? Man, you are so sprung it's ridiculous."

Carter exhaled, hating hearing the truth, but Dexter was right, though he wouldn't admit it.

"I'm not sprung! I'm in love and there is a big different. What I don't know is what her leaving like that meant. I'm feeling pretty good about the weekend we had, but now we're back to life and interacting with the world, and I think she may be having regrets. By the time I got up, it was late. I called her, but she didn't answer. I'm chalking it up to a busy schedule at work. You know I have never stopped loving her and this weekend was like the past year and a half never happened though I know it did."

"True, but she forgave you enough to spend the weekend with you and I believe that's something. Maybe she used you for your body?" Dexter joked.

"I'll take that anytime. Sienna does it for me, man. I hope the weekend wasn't the last time I'll get to spend time with her whether it's in or out of bed. I want her and I'll take her any way I can get her."

"I'm pulling for you. I know you've been waiting for her. It'll be fine. Give her a little space and let her work through whatever she's feeling. The way I know you still feel about each other and yes, I can see that Sienna is feeling you again, too, I'm sure it'll work out," Dexter said.

Dexter stood up.

"Oh, what? We can go to the meeting now?" Carter asked, standing and grabbing what he needed from his desk.

"I got the scoop. We're good."

Carter followed Dexter out and in the back of his mind, he knew Sienna would be on his mind until she returned his call.

**

"Dr. Garrison, did you hear me?"

Sienna snapped out of her stupor and turned to one of the dental assistants.

"I'm sorry. My mind must have drifted off."

"I wanted to let you know that your last client for the day is here. This should be a quick one so that you can get out of here early. You've been yawning all day. Are you alright?"

Sienna nodded in the affirmative and knew that her day had been off. She was still reeling from her weekend with Carter. She couldn't believe she stayed until it was time for her to get to work this morning. She started to wake Carter to let him know she was leaving, but he was sleeping peacefully. She laid in bed and watched him doze for a while before finally getting up and heading out. She had lost count of the number of times they'd made love from Saturday evening until the early morning hours of Monday morning. She tried focusing on work, but images of Carter's handsome face and naked body were distracting her.

"Go ahead and get her settled in one of the rooms and I'll be right in. I'm fine. I didn't get much sleep last night. I'll be happy to get out of here a little earlier than usual and make my way home. Sleep will be my best friend tonight."

"Okay. I forgot to tell you that Ms. Reese is here to see

you. I told her I would check to see if you were busy. Would you like for me to send her back?"

"Yes, thank you."

Sienna wondered what Reese was doing dropping by. She never did that without calling. While she waited, she grabbed her phone and noticed she had two missed calls, two voicemail messages, and three texts. Checking the texts firsts, she smiled seeing that all of them were from Carter. From what she read, he was hoping that her leaving wasn't a sign that she woke up with regrets. He also wanted her to know that that he'd had a memorable weekend with her and hoped to see her again soon. Sienna couldn't contain the huge smile that felt as wide and bright as her heart. Carter wasn't the only one who'd enjoyed their time together. She woke up wondering what their weekend together meant. They hadn't talked about it while she was there, but knew that they needed to really discuss it. She was still grinning when she looked up and saw Reese standing in the doorway.

"So, you are alive?" Reese said.

"What?"

"I said you are alive. I was beginning to question that. If you weren't here today, I was going to call SWAT to track you down. I've been trying to reach you since Sunday morning. I know you were knee-deep in the party planning and then the party, but I thought you would have called me with some gossip afterwards. I want to know what you wore, what did Carter wear? Did he make a pass at you? Did you finally jump him? Where did you disappear to all weekend?" Reese asked, tossing one question after another at her.

Sienna started to respond when she couldn't suppress a huge yawn.

"I'm sorry about that. I'm exhausted," she explained.

"Are you tired for a good reason that I want to know about? Is this a tea or a glass of wine reason? A sister needs to be prepared and I need details. Bring on the details woman!" Reese said with jubilance.

"It's neither. You can't have wine in the office and you don't need any tea. You put more sugar than tea in it and from where I'm sitting, you don't need anything else to excite you more."

"So, where were you?" Reese stopped Sienna as she was about to answer. "And before you answer with some untruth, let me make you aware that you should have worn a turtleneck today."

"I don't wear turtlenecks. I hate that they rub against my hairline. Why would I need a turtleneck? It's cold out, but it's not that cold," she said.

"Oh, that comment had nothing to do with the cold. It did have everything to do with the love marks all over your neck. Did you not look in the mirror this morning? You didn't check yourself out? You know you have to do that after you spend the night with a man sucking all over your body, especially parts visible to the naked eye. I can see those marks from the parking lot," Reese clowned.

Coming all the way into the office, she shut the door and pulled a chair as close to a shocked Sienna as she could get. She laughed when Sienna tried to pull the collar of her jack up higher.

"Why must you exaggerate," Sienna said.

"Exaggeration or not, you didn't deny what I just said and there must have been a man because your first reaction was to try and hide your neck. Girl, you've worked all day with that love all over you. Everybody knows you've been gettin' your *freak* on. I won't even ask who because I already know. You wouldn't let anyone else hit that *but* Carter."

Sienna laughed. "I can't with you today," she said laughing even harder. "You actually said *'hit that.'*"

"Laugh all you want. I'm glad somebody cleared those cobwebs away and it's about damn time. I was tired of you lusting after that man when he has always been yours anyway."

"We're divorced."

"Didn't stop you from giving him some, did it? Whew! Girl, I'm exhausted for you and I hope you got your two-year's worth?"

"I have no words for you right now," Sienna said trying to ignore her.

"Chick, you better come up with some. How did you end up on your back with a man you divorced two years ago?" Reese asked and leaned forward, resting her head in her hand as she did so.

Sienna exhaled and sat back.

"Okay, well, it just sort of happened."

"If you were still married to him and you said that, I wouldn't disagree. You went almost two years without talking or seeing him and then you plan a party and decide to give him some? I'm not hating and you know that, but things like that don't just happen."

"Well, it happened after the party."

"At his condo?"

"Yes. I went back to it to get my things since I got dressed for the party there. We talked, and the next thing I know, it's Monday morning and fifteen or twenty orgasms later---I lost count---and here I am barely able to keep my eyes open and I'm sore in places I forgot I could be sore. I'm so tired today!"

"Does this mean you're together, like a couple? Was this a one-time thing?"

Sienna held up her hand to stop the millions of questions.

"I don't know what it means. The only thing I can tell you is that I had a wonderful weekend and it wasn't just about the sex. That was amazing of course and luckily there is only one other owner on the top floor next to Carter. That neighbor is out of town. I don't know if the walls are thick enough because there was no way to be quiet through what that man did to my body. It was out of this world!" Sienna exclaimed.

"Girl! That's what I'm talking about. That's how it *should* be. He kept you on lockdown all weekend? Since Saturday?"

Sienna nodded her head when words would not explain the intense weekend.

"He knew I was off yesterday and asked me to stay that night and all-day Sunday. That led to Sunday night fun and the next thing I knew, it was this morning and I needed to get home, change and get to work. I was rushing to get here on time and no, I did not think about checking for love marks, though I'm not surprised."

"I don't even want to know where else he left them," Reese joked.

"And, I'm not going to tell you. Is the reason you came by here today to check on me was to be all in my business?" Sienna remarked.

"You forgot we had a shopping date yesterday? I came by the house and called you countless number of times and I got nothing."

"I forgot about that. I'm sorry. I got caught up," Sienna explained.

"From what I hear, no need to apologize. I have no problem being stood up due to you spending time with Carter. It's about time. I've been waiting forever for the two of you to get back together."

Sienna looked at Reese questionably.

"I didn't say all that. We're not back together. I don't know what this was. Hot, passionate, probably illegal in some states, sex that still has my toes curling just thinking about it and great conversation and cuddling, but he didn't say anything about us getting back together and neither did I. We talked some in between all that loving, but nothing in depth about getting back together. What if this was just a roll in the hay for him?" Sienna questioned.

"Is that what it was for you?"

"I don't know what it was. What would people think if it was more than that? He cheats on me, I divorce him, and then I go back to him? People will think I'm out of my mind, and that I'm a doormat."

"Why the hell are you worried about what anyone thinks? If you want that man and he wants you, you're entitled to him. Love rules and conquers all. Don't deny yourself anything based on what someone else thinks about it. I have my own thoughts about it and though all of them are in support of you and Carter working it out, my opinion doesn't matter either. This is about you and Carter and what you want from each other. Wait until everyone hears about this," Reese said.

"You can't tell anyone."

Sienna was dead serious. Whatever happened with Carter,

she didn't want anyone knowing about it until they figured it out.

"I'm not, but if this isn't a one-time thing, people will find out and again, follow my lead when I say, don't worry about what anyone thinks. If you don't know what this means, you need to go talk to Carter. Have you talked to him yet today?" Reese asked.

"No. I've been busy since my day started. He's called and texted a few times, but I haven't reached back. I have another client, which I need to get to and then I'm heading home to get some sleep."

"I bet you need it. Get yours, girl!" Reese shrieked. "You should call him back or better yet, go see him. You need to talk this out and you know I'm a vault when it comes to your business. Mum's the word, but tell Carter I said good move," Reese said and stood to leave.

"I'll pass the word along. Shopping later this week?" Sienna asked.

"I don't know. If you're able to walk after this week, let me know and I'll meet you for some shopping," Reese wisecracked.

"Very funny. I'll call you later."

Sienna went in the opposite direction of Reese, still shaking her head from their conversation. She was right on one point. In order for her to know what the weekend meant, she needed to talk to Carter and she preferred to do it in person.

19

Carter walked around the dealership greeting customers and making sure everyone was being helped. His dealership had been awarded dealership of the year and most of that was contributed to his requirement of his staff to make great customer service the priority. He was about to head towards the service center when his assistant called his name.

"Yes?" he asked.

"Your, uh," she stumbled. "I mean your...."

"Tawny just say it," he said, losing patience.

"Your---Ms. Sienna is in your office. I wasn't sure what I should call her."

"Sienna is here in my office? How long has she been here?" he asked turning in that direction.

"Just a few minutes. After settling her in, I came right out to look for you. I didn't want to call you over the speaker system. I hope that was okay," she said.

"It was perfect and thanks for making her comfortable. Hold all calls and visitors until I come back out."

Walking swiftly, Carter opened the door to his office and

sitting easily on the sofa was the woman he'd been thinking about all day.

Sienna stood when he entered.

"Carter, hi," she said.

"Hello and have a seat. I'm happy to see you. I woke up this morning and you were gone like a thief in the night. Is everything okay? Are you okay?" he asked, joining her on the sofa.

"Sorry about that. I had an early morning client and I needed to get home to change. I thought about waking you, but you were sleeping peacefully."

Carter smiled, happy to know that she hadn't left out of regret.

"I had a busy weekend," he said and reached for her hand, kissing the back of it.

"Yes, you did and it was wonderful."

"Great. Now that I know you didn't leave with regrets, let me do this first."

He didn't want to say another word before he got the kiss he'd been thinking about all day. Capturing her lips and mating with her tongue was first on his agenda and then they could talk."

"Whew!" Sienna said when he released her.

"I needed that. I hope the fact that you didn't leave my place with regrets means this weekend wasn't the only time I'll get to see you and I don't mean sex. I enjoyed spending time with you talking, laughing, and especially cooking."

Sienna looked down not sure of how to bring up the subject of the future and what impact the weekend would have on it. It was two days of great sex with her ex-husband and a sane person wouldn't expect too much since they were divorced because of her. She didn't know where they were going next and if she were going to sleep at night and focus during the day, she needed to know.

"So, this weekend wasn't just about the great sex?" she asked.

"No. Nothing with you could ever be just about sex. I want to be able to see you and spend time with you. If that's too much for you, let me know and I'll back off, but you have to agree this weekend was stress free and relaxing. You work as hard as I do and I know you needed the break. What I really want, you wouldn't be ready for and let's leave it at that. I want to be able to take you out and have fun, no pressure for anything. You have no idea how much I've missed just being able to talk to you. I don't know where you are when it comes to me, but I have been on cloud nine having you around again, and I want more. Is that too much?" he asked.

"No, not at all. I didn't know if the weekend of sex was what you wanted and then that was it. I didn't know what to think other than how incredible the weekend was, and it *was* relaxed. I look forward to spending time with you. I thought it would be awkward, but it's not."

"I'm happy to hear that. Would you like to join me for dinner tonight? I promise not to keep you out late."

As tired as she was, Sienna knew she wasn't too exhausted to see Carter tonight.

"Dinner sounds great. I need to get home, shower, and find a blouse to cover up more of my neck."

"Your neck?" he inquired and tried to look at it.

Sienna showed him what Reese pointed out.

Carter chuckled at the signs of love all over her.

"I would say I sympathize with what people seeing that

will think, but you are not alone sweetheart. The only reason why you can't see what you did to me is because I'm wearing a shirt and tie. I guess we both got carried away, but I liked it!" he exclaimed.

"You are certifiable, Carter," Sienna laughed.

Carter's heart swelled even wider. He knew he would never tire of seeing his love laugh like this in his presence.

"Only about you. You go ahead home and catch a nap if you want. I'll come pick you up around eight? Is that good?" he asked.

"Eight is fine. I look forward to it."

"You already know," Carter exclaimed and grinned. "You already know."

**

"Thanks for a wonderful evening," Sienna said as they drove through the streets of Chicago and headed toward her house. They'd gone to a restaurant outside of Chicago, someplace neither of them had ever been to. Though she wasn't looking at him since she relaxed back with her eyes closed, she could feel his eyes on her and assumed if she looked at his heated gaze, she would wonder if he was dropping her off at home or joining her inside. What had her a little on edge was the fact that he had not been inside of the house they once shared since he moved out. The last thing she wanted was an uncomfortable moment for them, when the night had gone so well.

"I'm glad you didn't decide to stay in for the night. I know you were tired," Carter said.

"So were you."

"True, but the thought of seeing you gave me new life!" Carter lovingly admitted.

Sienna opened her eyes and turned to him.

"Thanks for taking us outside of Chicago. I know why you did, and I appreciate it."

"Nothing to it. I want to be sure you're comfortable and running into any of the gossips we know around Chicago would be odd for you."

"Wouldn't it be odd for you?" she asked.

"Absolutely not. I don't care what anyone thinks about seeing us together."

"I don't either. That's not my issue."

"Would you like to share what the issue is if you have one?" he queried.

Carter knew the moment he told her where they were going originally that the location didn't sit well with her. Changing their plans, he called in a favor and got a reservation at an out of the way, five-star restaurant. They had to drive an hour to get to it, but the food was well worth the ride. He had a feeling Sienna didn't want anyone they knew to see them together.

What he didn't know was why.

"It's not that I care about anyone seeing us together. I need to know for myself if this is something for now or if it's leading to something more. Haven't you been wondering that? I realized we need to clear that up. It came up a few times over the weekend, but we never really talked in-depth about what was next. What should be expect from each other?" she asked.

After leaving the dealership earlier in the day, she'd gone home and thought deeply about what being with Carter again meant and she was finally honest with herself. She wanted him. She wanted back in his life and not just on a friendship or friends-with-benefits level. She wanted love because she was still in love with him. He'd already told her he was still in love with her. They were on the same page; at least she hoped they still were.

"Baby, what I want is you. I can't speak for you and where your head is, but I want you. When I say that, I mean all of you. I want to date, actually be in a relationship again with you. I know it sounds crazy, but I have never been able to let go of what we had. *Never*. I didn't stalk you or hound you, but I always hoped that one day, we'd find our way back to each other. I didn't plan on spending the night with you or anything else that has occurred since the day I saw you at the wedding, but that did confirm the fact that my love for you never changed. I don't know where this is going between us, but I'd like to say I'm in it for the long haul. You have to decide what you want out of this. If this is something more than dinner and talking occasionally, then tell me that and let's not care what anyone thinks. If you want to keep what we are doing a secret from everyone, I'm good with that, but only for a while. We can't hide forever. Still, I believe we should know what we're doing before we share it with anyone. I need to know if we are working on a clean slate and you're interested in seeing if we can have more again. Are you willing to take a chance on us?" he asked.

"I am. I think I knew that the moment I walked back to your condo the night of the party. I was thinking about you while I took the elevator ride up and I struggled with knowing all the time we'd been spending together planning the party was coming to an end. I'd grown accustomed to talking to you every day and seeing you several times a week. It felt good, comfortable. It felt as if it was supposed to be that way. When you came in and I saw you sitting on that table, the only word that came to my mind was *mine*."

"I like knowing you felt that way. That means I wasn't in this alone; this desire to want our love back," Carter said.

"Here we are now. What are we going to do?" Sienna asked. She was glad they were having the conversation.

"We let whatever happens with us go a natural course. For now, I agree that we shouldn't share it with anyone, though Dexter figured it out when he stopped by the dealership earlier today. I tried to keep it from him, but you know how he is. I know for a fact that he'll keep it under his hat."

Sienna snickered. "That's hilarious because Reese did the same thing. I forgot I had a date to go shopping with her yesterday and I accidentally stood her up because I was with you. She was the one who pointed out the marks on my neck and she put it together with the fact that I was at the party on Saturday night. Plus, she knows I hadn't been seeing anyone since we separated. Of course, I wouldn't let some random guy love on me like you did."

When Carter smiled, she smiled with him.

"I'm happy to hear I'm not some random guy," he said chuckling.

"You've never been that---never," she said. "Did I tell you how good that dinner was? I thought the only place to get a perfect crab cake was in Maryland, but that place took me back to the time we drove through Maryland and stopped at that restaurant Oprah Winfrey recommended and declared was her favorite to eat crab cakes."

"Yeah, that place had the best crab cakes and this place was almost that perfect. I hear the Baltimore spot actually ships crab cakes to her. I'll have to inquire about that and get some for one of our romantic dinners." He laughed when Sienna sat straight up in her seat.

"Don't tease me with a good meal. You know I'm a foodie," she declared.

"I can't tell since you stay in perfect shape without an ounce of fat on you."

"I got my workout ethic from you. I still get in some type of exercise every day."

"I do, too."

Their eyes locked when Sienna looked him over as the corners of her mouth turned up into a sexy grin.

"Yeah, I can tell," she said.

Carter started to counter with a sexy remark, but decided against it. It would lead to him pulling over and sliding her onto his lap. So, for now, he kept things rated PG.

"We didn't get dessert at the restaurant. Would you like to stop someplace and get one of those big ice cream sundaes I know you love to devour. You may be a workout junkie like me, but I'm sure you still indulge in those from time to time," Carter remarked.

Sienna gave him a look like she was about to deny his assumption but instead smiled.

"I do indulge from time to time, but tonight, how about ice cream at my house. That is, if you're up for that."

Carter was glad he pulled up to a light that had just turned red because he wanted to be sure he could turn his head to respond without crashing the car.

"I'm always up and ready for anything, especially if it has to do with you," he said slyly. "Ice cream at your house it is, and we're only a few blocks away. I see the neighborhood has some new development," Carter remarked. Since he moved out, he'd only driven through a few times and most recently on those nights recently when he followed her home to be sure she got in safe.

Pulling into her driveway, Carter pulled in front of one of the two garage doors and turned the car off. Hopping out, he walked around and opened her door, extending his hand as he watched Sienna's sexy, long legs slide out. His body crackled to life the moment he watched her feet in five-inch heels hit the ground. In contrast, his feet felt like clay, unable to move as they were mesmerized by her sexy walk. He moved faster behind her when she turned to see that he was falling behind.

"Are you coming?" she asked over her shoulder.

Carter started to say something hot and spicy thinking of the multi-meaning her statement carried, but instead, he walked faster.

Once inside with the door securely locked behind them, Carter kept his eyes on Sienna as she removed the black leather and fur coat and hung it up in the closet. He'd left his coat in the trunk of the car. He could hear Sienna talking jovially, but for the life of him, he couldn't concentrate on her words. He was too busy checking out how deliciously sexy she looked her form-fitting dress.

Throughout dinner, he'd complimented her more than a few times on her attire, but what he failed to say was he kept picturing her without the dress on. He preferred it as a heap around her feet as it dropped to the floor. All thoughts then turned to the visual of her long, sexy legs wrapped around his head as he pleasured her to completion with his mouth. He already knew she had on some type of sexy lingerie in either lace or silk and if he knew her as well as he felt he did, it was skimpy sensual. If only he could get under that dress, he knew it would make his mouth water.

When Sienna looked over at him as he still leaned back against the front where he never moved once they were inside, he assumed she must have asked him a question. It was one he had no idea about so he couldn't answer.

"Are you alright? Did you hear me?" she asked from several feet away from him.

With the exception of the entryway light that she'd turned on when they arrived, they were standing in the dark. The soft glow of the light shown like a spotlight around her, and his heart swooned at the magnitude of her beauty.

"I'm fine. What did you ask?"

"I asked what kind of ice cream you wanted for your sundae. I have vanilla, chocolate, and mint and yes, those are still my favorite flavors."

Carter couldn't think about ice cream. For the first time in almost two years, he was back in the house he'd shared together with the love of his life. Now, all he could think about was making love to her in the same house and enjoying the feeling that he was back home, even if it was just for the night.

"None," he replied, crossing his legs and his arms as he turned and leaned sideways on the back of the front door.

Sienna stopped cold. Did Carter just say he didn't want any ice cream? That was the reason for him coming inside after she'd made the offer in the car. Looking at him, there was an inpatient, mysterious expression on his face that she couldn't read. Though she was in the light, he stood in the dark nearer the door.

"You don't want any ice cream? Does that mean you're

ready to leave already? I see you're still standing at the door."

Sienna didn't know what had happened since they talked about ice cream in the car. Perhaps, he wasn't ready to be back in the house and now he was ready to high-tail it out.

"No, I don't want any ice cream. I thought I did and maybe I will later, but not at this moment."

Sienna moved nervously in place, not sure what to do. Should she offer him something else or should she continue to stand still, while looking at all the manliness he exuded?

"Well, I can make us some coffee and a snack. I have some fruit and cheese if you want to nibble on something," she said and then wished she hadn't. The idea of him nibbling had her body going through all kinds of feelings. In the still of the room, she was already on fire. There was no doubt from the look on Carter's face that he wasn't thinking about food.

"Nibble on something is exactly what I have in mind, but it has nothing to do with food," Carter said, deep and sexy.

"It doesn't?" she said as the words stumbled out of her mouth.

"No. I told you all you have to do is tell me what you want and when and I'm there for it. If you want ice cream, I will definitely eat ice cream with you. I still love it as much as I always have. You tell me," he crooned softly.

The air between them electrified as the meaning of his words cascaded across the floor to her. All night she could only think about whether the night would end in more explosive orgasms or if they were simply having dinner. Truth be told, she didn't want any damn ice cream. Instead, Sienna had a gorgeous, vibrant, and overly sexual man standing in front of her and the only thing she wanted was him.

"I don't want ice cream either," she admitted.

"Are you sure?" he asked.

"I am."

"What do you want?"

"You."

"Are you sure?"

"Yes."

"Come here, baby," Carter murmured with undertones laced with titillating voracity. He didn't want to waste any time giving them both what they needed and desired. True, their coming together was amazing, but it wasn't what drove him. Knowing that she wanted more than casual rendezvous with him was more than enough and any intimacy was a bonus. He wanted it all.

20

Sienna hurried to Carter as he pushed away from the door the minute she was within arms-reach.

"You are extraordinarily beautiful and I want you, but I want to be very clear that I meant it when I said I didn't want just this because this isn't only about sex with you. Don't get me wrong, the sex is amazing and mind-blowing even, but what I said in the car, I still mean. I want more. I *want us* again. Are you all in? I want to sure that there is nothing from the past that is still bothering you or that would make you question getting involved with me again on more than just an intimate basis. I love making love to you and you know that, but like I said, I want it all. You have to be in with me and have no regrets or doubts."

Sienna could feel her body's temperature rising as she watched Carter's eyes darken from their usual light brown color to a darker, more intense brown. There would be no hesitation in her response.

"I'm in. I'm all in. No reservations about the past at all. I think we've both learned a lesson from our history and for me, I learned that nothing in this world is perfect, not even relationships. I never did and never will give you or any man a pass to cheat on me, but what we had should have survived what happened. I found out from someone else's story that it could have been a lot worse, a lot longer than a few minutes, and I could have lost you for good. I want to know if we have a chance. Having you back in my life is like a breath of fresh air. I know that I've grown in the past two years and so yes, I'm all in. I still love you, too. I know you've been saying it, and I love hearing it, but I also want to be sure you hear it. I love you," Sienna said with assurance.

Carter smiled and kissed her passionately, pouring the love they shared equally into it. When he needed to give them room to breathe, he pulled back and lifted her head so that there was no mistake in what he wanted her to see in his eyes and not just with his words.

"I was dead wrong for what I did and it didn't matter if it lasted a few seconds, a few minutes or a few hours, it was wrong. I hope you believe me when I say that given another chance with you, I will never, ever take you or our love for granted again. I may make mistakes, but any other woman will never happen again. I've seen and lived my life without you and I never want to repeat that," he confessed.

Sienna shook her head in agreement.

"I don't want either of us to have to go through being apart like that again," Sienna agreed.

Carter crooned against her cheek. "That's good because tonight, I want to worship you because for a long time, I could only do that in my head and in my dreams."

"You did a pretty good job over the weekend," Sienna murmured when her lips came in slight contact with Carter's.

"And I will again, trust and believe, sweetheart."

Carter allowed his gaze to take her in from head to toe as all of the blood in his body rushed to that area of him that hungered to satisfy her in the most primal way.

Pulling Sienna tightly into his arms, he kissed her passionately, going deep not only into her delectable mouth but also into her very being where he always wanted to be. His head was still spinning when she moved her head back slightly and their eyes locked.

"I get an amazing amount of pleasure being in your arms. I've missed that more than I've been able to even tell myself."

To show her appreciation for all that he was to her, Sienna followed her words up with a caress that turned into a perusal of his body from his head where she let her hands move over it, down the back to his neck, and around to his chest where she opened the buttons at the top that were keeping her from his breadth. When Carter moaned, she knew that he was feeling the same heightened intensity that she was feeling and wanted to always feel. Pulling his shirt completely out of his pants, she unbuttoned it all the way and pulled his shirt down his arms. Sienna didn't care that the two of them were still in the entryway. She had a need to touch and feel all of him that overpowered any sense of worrying about getting upstairs to the bed.

When his shirt was off and her hands were moving across his hot skin, she leaned forward and kissed a line from one side of his chest to the other, leaving a wet trail in her path. When she blew on it and Carter's moans grew louder, Sienna threw caution to the wind and worked to get him naked by unbuckling his belt and making swift work of pulling everything down his legs. She smiled up at him when he willingly kicked his shoes off so that she could finish removing the rest of his clothing.

Standing up and getting her fill, she would never, ever tire of seeing Carter in all of his glory. He was modest, but self-assuredly, all man.

"I appear to be the only one naked and you're not missing even one piece of clothing," he said reaching for her. "That's not fair."

Playfully, Sienna moved out of his reach and walked into the living room, beckoning him to follow the sexy sway of her behind.

"I can remedy that," she said.

"Oh, go ahead and threaten me with a good time, will you!" Carter exclaimed and followed like a moth to a flame.

Seeing where Sienna was going, even in the darkened house with the moonlit sky sneaking through the windows, Carter followed, anxious to find the comfort of the soft couch to make love to her on until neither of them could take anymore. As Sienna turned when she reached a chair, she spun round and stopped his advancement by planting her hand solidly on his chest.

"Not so fast, lover," she joked with the sexy undertones in her voice that could not hide how much she wanted him. Looking down at that part of him that was long and hard, she had no doubt about how much he wanted her.

Any minute, Carter knew his heart would stop beating. He'd never been this aroused before, standing in a room with Sienna fully clothed and him openly baring all of himself to her. It wasn't just about his flesh. He was vulnerable to anything she needed and wanted. He had to move back slightly when Sienna pushed him backwards.

"You stay right there," she said.

Before he could register what was happening, his eyes lowered to where her hands were reaching for the hem of her dress. The moment she pulled the garment up and over her body, instinctively, his hand reached for his manhood which was painfully engorged and wide awake. When Sienna threw her dress to the side, his eyes moved wildly, covering every inch of her from the red strapless bra that was overflowing with her large mounds, down over her flat stomach, landing on the small scrap of a juicy, bright red thong. With his mind, he willed for her to turn so that he could feast his eyes on her apple bottom, remembering how her behind felt in his hands as he caressed the globes at times when he wanted her closer... so much closer to him.

He didn't have to wait long for his wish to come true. Not losing eye contact, he watched her slow turn in her high heels like she was a model on a runway. As she turned, his mouth felt like the Nile River was running through it. Any minute, he knew foam would soon form as his longing for her rose to a new level high in the stratosphere.

"Like what you see?" Sienna asked as she bent over a little to give him an even better view from behind.

"I love what I see and I would enjoy it even more if I could touch," he said making a move to get closer until she wagged her finger at him to not move any closer.

"It's just as much fun to watch, don't you think?" she slurred her words, adding an extra spicy, sauciness, laced with naughty devotion and desire.

Carter started to respond, but then Sienna leaned back up and quickly removed the bra and tossing it behind her at him. Carter, alert with want, reached for it and grabbed it mid-air. Not letting the toss go to waste, he wrapped the silky, lacy material around his manhood and stroked himself with it.

"Watching is fun. Your eyes are watching my every move, especially where your bra is. I see you're staring at me," he said in a rugged, yet aroused voice.

"I'll never wash that bra again," she laughed.

"You won't have to worry about that because now that I have it, I'm not giving it back. Nights when you force me to sleep alone in my bed, I'm going to lay it on the pillow next to me and see how hard I can use ESP to get you to join your bra, in that spot without me asking."

Sienna watched his long, pleasure-filled strokes.

"That is one lucky bra," she said.

"You can be this lucky too if you let me touch you. You're killing me here, baby," he groaned.

Not giving into how steamy he looked using her bra to caress his hardness, Sienna reached for the thin strings at the side of her thong that held it in place. She teased and then slowly slid the garment down her legs.

"Goodness, if I die right here, make sure you cover my body up before the paramedics get to me. You are slaying a brother right now. What are you trying to do to me?" he begged and groaned like a man on the edge.

Now, naked except for the heels she still wore, Sienna spread her legs and leaned forward, resting her hands on the back of the sofa, moving her hips from side to side as if she were a dancer on stage, tantalizing her audience---an audience of one. Not taking her eyes from him, she dipped her hips, twirled them and watched the show of emotions on Carter's face while his hand moved faster and faster. He was definitely holding back on what he really wanted to do. She didn't want to torture either of them any longer.

Raising one hand, she beckoned for him while staying in position. She watched Carter's long, powerful legs as he moved closer, coming to stand directly behind her.

"No pretense," she said.

"I aim to please, baby," he commented while leaning down and placing hot, open-mouthed kisses across her behind, dipping toward her womanhood with a teasing, soft lick before skipping over it, which caused her to purr with anticipation of what she thought he was going to do.

"Mad?" Carter asked, joking.

"Mmm, no, as long as you hurry up. You want me to beg?" she cried out softly.

"Oh, no, baby. Never that. You never have to beg for my loving, though the pouty face is working. You know I got you covered," he said, giving her rump a quick, light smack.

When Sienna wiggled at him, he knew he was on the right page.

Dropping the bra to the floor, Carter reached down and spread Sienna's legs even wider so that she could be fully balanced for what was to come. Reaching in front of him, he caressed her arms from her wrists up to her shoulders, circling his hands and feeling her skin go slick under his touch. At the same time, he moved so that his front was snug against her bottom, sliding his hardness between her legs, caressing her heated skin with it and moving in sync with the sway of her hips

Sienna pleaded not just with her words, but with her eyes as she looked over her shoulder at him.

"Carter?" she questioned what was prolonging what she

needed.

"So, only you get to tease?" Carter asked, moving against her, heightening the sexual force behind the moment.

"Carter?" she pleaded again.

"Okay, baby. I got you."

Positioning himself, Carter surged forward and the power of his stroke caused them both to raise up on their toes.

"Yes!" Sienna screamed and moved with each strong stroke given to her. She loved how he knew what she liked and how she liked it.

"You holding on tight to the chair? You're going to need to!" he hollered.

Gripping her hips with the strength in both hands, Carter loved her over and over, harder and harder, while giving her what she was screaming for. The moment was so delicately hot, spicy and damn near explosive from their cat and mouse game that he knew he wouldn't be able to last long.

Pushing deeper with steady pumps and controlled surges, together they raced toward the moment of pure ecstasy. The sounds of their lovemaking combined with the trembling that rose in Sienna's legs had reached back to him, letting him know she was close. Carter gripped her hips tighter, pulling her back into him and intensifying the image of Sienna bent in front of him, as she grabbed the sofa with all of her might. He knew the second her release slammed into her as her hands slipped from the back of the sofa to the cushions and she masked her howl of pleasure by letting it out into the pillows. He could feel the excess essence of her release as it soaked him and ran down his legs.

The moment came for him right after as an orgasm caused his entire body to shudder. He had no control as his hips moved about wildly. Carter closed his eyes and let it take him higher and higher as he stroked deeper, longer and harder until the weight of the explosion caused them to collapse together in a heap onto the sofa with him on top of her. He tried to take in deep gulps of air to catch his breath, but he struggled with focus. The air around them was electrified with their hunger for each other and not just from the great sex, but because of something even greater: *Love*!

When he could move and breathe again, Carter stood, reached down and picked up Sienna's limp body. Only because he knew they needed to move off of the sofa did he find the strength in his own limbs to move.

"I would love to stay right here, but the floor is hard and I don't want mess up your sofa. Why don't we find a bed?" he said in Sienna's ear as he wrapped her legs tight around his waist.

Sienna laid her head on Carter's shoulder and was thankful that he'd picked her up. She had no energy to move and barely had enough to walk.

"A bed sounds good about right now. I needed that. I needed you something crazy. I always have," she said soft and lovingly.

"I know, baby. Me, too and I already know that I have a lot to prove to you, but you can trust and believe, I'm never letting go of you again. Believe me when I say I am yours, you are mine and never will there be anything that I will allow to come between what we have."

Carter turned and walked up the winding staircase with Sienna in his arms, applying kisses to her face and neck and whispering over and over again how much he loved her.

"I trust everything about us," she said, letting him know

she had faith in knowing they understood how precious real love was.

"Are we ready to tell anyone about us? I know you wanted to wait to see what we were going to be, but if we're both all-in, it's time to be open about it and not have to feel like we're sneaking around. We were once married and we're two, grown ass people," he said as he entered the bedroom.

Without thinking about a light, he walked to the bed and followed Sienna down to the soft mattress, not even bothering to pull the blanket back to get under it. They turned so that they were facing each other.

"I'm ready. I don't know why I wanted to wait or keep this from those who love and care about us, especially our parents. We know that Reese and Dexter already know and when our other friends find out, I think we'll get mixed emotions."

"Do we care?" he asked.

"Should I care that people will wonder how I could forgive you or that it should take longer for me to forgive you than the time that has passed?" Sienna asked as she moved closer into his embrace.

"No one else can live our lives for us, but us. I only care what you think and no one else. I've suffered wrath from people around us for what I did back then and you know what? I didn't care what they thought then and I don't care now. I only care about what you think and how you feel. Do you really care what other's think?" Carter asked.

"I don't, but I don't want anyone trying to throw you under the bus from something two years ago that's dead, buried and stinking now. We've let it go and for those who know what happened, I want them to let it go and leave it in the past, too. We're in a better place and know how fragile love can be."

"Well, we will have the opportunity in a few weeks if you want it."

Sienna thought and knew what he was referencing.

"The party for the house warming," she said.

Sienna remembered that now that Keith and Kim were married, they had also purchased a new home and were having a blessing done in a few weeks. She'd forgotten all about that.

"Yes, the party. Everyone will be there. Did you get an invitation that said that you can bring a plus one?" he asked.

"I did. I take it you did, too?"

"I did. What are we going to do about that?" Carter asked.

When he received the invitation earlier in the week and saw the plus one, Carter knew he wouldn't be bringing a plus one if it wasn't going to be Sienna.

"Well, it's weird that they are allowing a plus one for a house blessing, but okay. They've been married a few months and have had more parties than anyone else I know," Sienna joked.

"So, what are we going to do? I'm not bringing someone else. I want to be your plus one."

Carter knew he would go bat crazy if Sienna showed up with someone else after they've already been reconnecting. That wasn't the way to put on a façade that they weren't seeing each other. He wanted to shout it out to the world that their love was worth the fight.

"I want to be your plus one, too," she said.

"Then that's what we will do. Our friends will either sink or swim with us. I can tell you that it won't be a dry party after we arrive. So, we're doing this?" he asked.

"Yes, we are. I think for now, we should both reply that we're bringing a plus one because we have to reply by tomorrow. We don't need to say who. That way between now and the party, we can talk to our parents and tell them first. How do you think your parents will react?" Sienna asked.

She should be asking herself that same question. She remembered her mother's story that she would never share with another living person and she knew that her father had once been raving mad at Carter for what he'd done, but had since warmed and even gone back to speaking to Carter since their breakup. She was still not convinced they would be okay with them being back together as a couple. Telling them would be challenging. It wasn't that they wouldn't support her decision. It was more about their concern that emotionally, she wouldn't survive something else breaking them up a second time. She was already determined to not let it and knew that neither of them would test their love again.

"My parents will be ecstatic. For months after the split, every time they saw me, they reminded me what an immature fool I was for ruining our marriage and they hoped that I had learned a hard lesson. Trust me, that's a lesson I never want to be on the other side of ever again. What about your parents? Do you think they'll accept me back into your life as more than just a friend? I can go with you to talk to them if you want. I have no problem begging and groveling with them as I did with you, so that they'll allow me back in. I'm not one to worry about seeming weak; I know my manhood is intact," he said and kissed her on the lips to solidify his assertion.

"Yes, it is," Sienna said and to hone in on how sure she was, she reached down and stroked that part of him that instantly came to life under her touch.

"Mmm, don't start *nothin'* and there won't be *nothin'*!" Carter groaned out.

"I have no problem starting something. You are lying here naked in my bed. I'm hoping to start stuff all night long."

Carter kissed her again, this time deeper.

"I like the sound of that. Before we get this party started again, parents soon?" he asked.

"Yes, soon. I want you all to myself a little longer. Is that selfish of me?" Sienna asked.

"Not at all. Just know that I am ready whenever you are," he replied.

21

Pulling up in front of her parents' house, Sienna said a silent prayer hoping they would understand when she shared with them the news that she and Carter had been seeing each other since his parents' anniversary party. It had actually started during the party planning with all of the time they were spending together acting like a couple, but neither of them addressed it. To her, that time felt like the re-getting to know you phase before they jumped into all the hot and heaviness that they still hadn't gotten out of their system. She would have some explaining to do to her parents.

They had been by her side every step of the way when she had gone through her divorce and they knew what it took out of her. Only her mother knew of an additional secret that she never wanted her father to know about, one that she knew one day that she would have to tell Carter about if they were ever to move forward. She wasn't ready to deal with that yet. That pain, she still dealt with every day and would wait for the right time to talk about it with him.

What she wanted most was her parents' support or at least

their understanding. When she shared with them that she had agreed to help Carter with his parents' anniversary party, neither of them commented. Her mother simply told her that she was glad that after the divorce, his parents never treated her any differently than they did during the marriage. They still loved her as much as they always had.

Her parents had been invited to the party even though they were no longer in-laws, but they had a previous out of town engagement, so they couldn't attend, but sent a very nice gift. She knew that both sets of parents still stayed in contact and enjoyed dinner together occasionally.

She looked over at the house a few times trying to plan out what she was going to say by way of explanation. What she and Carter had been working on since the party was absolutely wonderful. Since their steamy weekend of reacquainting themselves with each other's bodies, they were dating again, going to the movies, out to cozy dinners and even mini-road trips. They had taken two short weekend trips away in order to tune out the world and focus on rebuilding what they'd lost over the past two years. Their relationship was strong, and to her, could only get stronger. Having their parents as support would help greatly and she was hoping to get that today from hers.

She was about to exit her car when she heard her cell phone ringing somewhere in her purse. If she hadn't already turned the car off, she could have used the console to answer. Searching for it before the ringing stopped, she smiled when Carter's handsome grin graced the phone screen.

"Hey, you!" she said.

"Hi, beautiful. I was checking one last time to see if you wanted me to come with you to talk to your parents. I want them to know how serious I am about us and how I will never hurt you or us again. I think I owe them a face to face if we plan to have any success of them supporting our decision to try dating again."

"Don't worry about it. I got this. I need to talk to them alone. If you want a face to face, do that, especially with my dad. I think he would appreciate that after my talk with them tonight. My mom, I'm pretty sure I can read and know how she's going to react. My dad will be hesitant, but he'll want whatever involves my happiness. It would be a good idea for you to sit down and talk to him."

"I'll do that later this week. I would do anything to make sure there are no reservations on his part. Come see me after you leave there. You know I will be nervously pacing until I hear from you," he said.

"I'll come by your place when I leave here. Will you be there by then? I didn't know if we would see each other tonight. I know you have that incentive thing going on and business has been booming all week especially with the new dealership preparing to open."

"Nothing will keep me from seeing you tonight. I promise no all-night love session, but I can't promise it won't happen at some point after seeing you. You will probably be done before I'm finished here, but you still have your key from when you used my condo during the party planning. Park in one of my two spots. Call me when you get there and I will have one of the guys at the security desk come and escort you. We don't have any problems, but I want to be sure they are keeping an eye out for the most precious person in the world to me."

"Charmer," she said adding feistiness to her voice.

"It's all fact, baby. See you later tonight?"

Sienna knew she could never deny him and all day, she hoped they would see each other.

"Yes, I'll be there and if you're not too late, I may plan a special treat for you."

"Tease," he responded. "I may be sort of late. After we close, I need to go over the latest inventory list for the new shop and read over and sign the paperwork for new cars I have coming in here. Make yourself comfortable."

"You enjoy me being a tease."

"More than you will ever know. You got my mind reeling, and now I have to wait a few minutes before I leave my office, or I'd embarrass myself with this hard-on you just gave me with an image of you as my treat. Good luck with your parents. What happens if they are against it?" he asked.

Carter knew that was a possibility, but he'd tried to push it out of his mind all day. After all, he couldn't stand losing her again.

"I meant it when I said it won't change anything between us and it won't. Don't worry. I know my parents were upset when everything went down, but like your parents are with me, they never stopped loving you. It's not the same as them being disappointed in you. You told me your talk with your parents last night went easy. I expect the same."

"My parents have always loved you and never wanted anyone for me, but you from the moment I brought you home to meet them when we were in college. You sure you don't need me to come there? I can leave right now and be there in twenty minutes."

Sienna sighed out loud.

"First, no I got this, and second, your dealership is forty

minutes away and I don't want to know that you can get here in twenty minutes. Stop driving that fast! I have to keep telling you to slow down. As much as I want to see you and I know you want to see me, I'll always be waiting even if you have to drive like you're driving Ms. Daisy!" Sienna exclaimed.

Carter laughed knowing he wouldn't get there in twenty minutes, but he wanted her to know he was in her corner and a phone call away.

"Okay, okay. I hear you and I promise to slow my driving down. I'll see you soon."

"Yes, you will," she said.

**

"Is she still sitting in her car?" Connie asked, knowing her daughter and that once Sienna pulled up, she wouldn't get right out.

"Yup. She's either rehearsing what she wants to talk to us about or she's speaking with Carter, who is most likely reassuring her that the talk will turn out okay," Lars replied.

"Will it?" Connie asked, putting down the paper she was reading and stretching her neck to see if she could see Sienna sitting in her car in front of their house.

"Connie, don't worry so much. The talk will be fine."

"Lars, you know what she wants to talk to us about, right? I know she thinks she can hide stuff from us and sometimes she can, but this time, not so much. You know Carter's mother called me the day after their anniversary party and told me that she could sense something was happening between our kids again. I told her I thought once they started working together on the party, the sparks would fly all over. She said they couldn't keep their eyes off of each other and only looked away when they thought someone would see."

Lars peeped out of the front window of their house again, waiting to see if Sienna was close to getting out of her car.

"I know you can't see her, but I can tell she's nervous. She's probably wondering if I'll be open to accepting Carter again after what he did. I was angry with him as any father would be, but you and I know I'm not the one to judge in this kind of situation."

Connie looked at Lars lovingly.

"If we got through what our marriage went through many years ago, and we're still together, she and Carter will have a better marriage this time than before," he continued.

"Marriage? You think she's here to talk about marriage?" Connie asked, hopeful.

"No, but I think that subject will come up again and probably soon," Lars said.

"Did you see her when she came for dinner last Sunday? She was walking around here talking a mile a minute, all bubbly singing and humming. When was the last time we saw that in our princess? If what Carter's mother says is true and she saw something between them, then I believe it's been going on since back during their anniversary party. Isn't that something?" Connie asked, suddenly smiling, happy that Sienna was once again happy herself.

"That's been months ago," Lars replied.

Connie thought about the length of time and hand an inkling that something had been going on from the many conversations that she'd had with Sienna. What also triggered her thoughts that they were together again is that, though Sienna still dropped by often, she never stayed to long and there were times when she would get a text message and the look she saw on her daughter's face let her know that the text had come from a man. It wasn't just any man either. She had no doubt it was from Carter.

"True, but I think they've been taking the time to figure out what they were going to do now that they've reconnected," Connie said. "You remember what we went through and the time it took for forgiveness," she added.

"Yeah. The difference is you didn't divorce me and we dealt with it each day here, under this roof. They had too much time apart."

Connie thought about that and didn't necessarily agree. Some things took more time to heal than others.

"Well, now that they found their way back to each other, I think they saw the value in keeping it to themselves until they were sure there was still love," Connie stressed.

Lars hadn't thought about that sad time in their own marriage since Sienna told them she was leaving Carter for an indiscretion. He stayed out of the decisions she had to make and allowed her to decide for herself. He never told her about his own indiscretion and now wondered if telling her back then would have made a difference. It was possible she wouldn't have had to go through the heartbreak to get back to the love.

"There always was love between them," he said.

"That first day when she called us from campus to tell us about this guy she met, I'd never heard her talk that way about any guy. When the separation and divorced happened, I wanted to tell her to stick with it and work it out, but that would have been wrong if it had turned out worse for her to stay than to leave," Connie said.

"You stayed with me after what I did."

Connie turned to him and smile. Staying was the choice she made and the best choice for her. She knew Sienna needed to walk her own path.

"Right, but no one told me to do that. I had to make that decision on my own and Sienna had to do the same thing. I wanted their marriage to work, and I still want happiness for them, but it has to be on a level where she has internal peace and acceptance. It can't be forced on her," Connie explained.

"You're right. I was wondering when she would make that call saying she wanted to talk to us. I was surprised she didn't just show up and spring it on us before now. It's not like we would be surprised. I may be a little hard of hearing, but my vision with these glasses is pretty near perfect," Lars laughed.

"It was obvious to me when she shared party ideas with me and told me how close they were working together on it. I was expecting a visit about him and I'm honestly surprised it took this long. When she wouldn't tell us over the phone, I knew it was about Carter. Anything else, she would have shown up unannounced and told us. This is special to her and she wanted us to know how much by planning this talk. What do you think?" Connie asked.

"I think that boy never stopped loving our daughter just as she never stopped loving him and tonight, she's going to ask for our support of her decision to go back to him. Not that she'll need it. She'll want it though. I remember when you and I first fell in love and how deeply I felt about you back then. I can honestly say the only time I've seen a deeper love was between Carter and Sienna. I know he screwed up and I could have choked him, but I've been there. My affair lasted a lot longer than a minute or two like his did. Mine was months and yet here we are still madly in love, forgiving and understanding each other. I love you for loving me and staying with me during my stupid phase. If Sienna is asking for our support, she will have mine one hundred percent without reservation. I wouldn't want her to miss out on the kind of love I know they share. I wouldn't want her to miss out on having thirty-five years of love and passion like we've had. I know you have always wanted them back together, though you supported her decision to file for divorce. The boy messed up and he's paid for it. People make mistakes. I know some people find it hard to accept and stay together after an indiscretion. You hear women and men talk about it every day how saying they would leave immediately and file for divorce. Wrong is wrong, but forgiveness will extend your life, removing hatred and doubt."

"I want her to be happy," Connie exhaled while saying a silent prayer.

"She is, you know. Our baby is happy again and in love," Lars said. "I've prayed for the day when I could look in her face and see happiness like never before. I think they've both finally found what it means to really be in love and work at a marriage through the good, the bad, and the very ugly. Marriage isn't perfect and it takes more than most people are willing to give these days. I think they've found it," he added.

"She will get our support and love and we'll make sure Carter knows he has it to. I suspect you'll be hearing from him in the coming days."

Lars shook his head. He had a feeling when Sienna pulled up alone, that he and Carter would have a separate conversation. He looked forward to it. He may even share with him what he and Connie had gone through and how they survived. Carter needed to know that love conquered everything else, even imperfections. He would make it clear that he would drag Carter through hell if he ever hurt Sienna again, but he'd do it in a supportive, positive way. He loved Carter, but Sienna was his baby and nothing surpassed the love he had for her.

"I look forward to talking to him. Women are different, and he knows that you're the sweetest, most loving woman alive. If anyone was going to be open to them being back together, it would be you. As a father, he may think that it will take more of a man to man talk to convince me of his sincerity. I'll let him have his say and then I'll remind him how precious my only child is and if he tries anything else in the future, he won't have to worry about divorce a second time. I've been looking for a reason to pull the new gun out and give it a test run," Lars said and smiled when Connie rolled her eyes at him and chuckled out loud.

"Stop threatening to shoot somebody. I know what those words mean and you wouldn't hurt a fly."

Lars huffed and stuck his chest out.

"Yeah, okay. He better not mess over my baby girl, I know that much. He's a great guy," Lars admitted.

"Yes, he is. He's learned his lesson and he loves Sienna. That's enough for me," Connie said.

Looking out of the window again, Lars moved away from it, sat in his favorite chair and acted like he was reading the paper that he'd read earlier.

"Looks like she's made up her mind about what she's going to say. She just got out of her car and is walking toward the house. Try to look like we haven't been scoping her out," he said.

"Hmph. I will not. This has been a long time coming and I want her to know I already knew this day would come. I'm sure she saw you occasionally looking out of the window at her. You wouldn't last a day as a spy. Who looks out of a window and moves the curtain each time?" she laughed.

"Well, I was worried when she didn't get out. I was praying she wouldn't lose her nerve and drive away."

Connie smiled brightly.

"Oh, no, this is about love---the greatest love of her life. I'm just as ready for her to get back to it as she is."

Connie sat in her favorite chair with her eyes on the door. Within seconds, it opened and though she didn't want to reveal her obvious state of knowing, she couldn't hide it. When Sienna smiled bright, she could already feel tears welling up in her own eyes. Her little girl was back. The light of life was back in her eyes.

22

"You're awake?" Sienna asked exiting the bedroom and finding Carter sitting in front of the television without it being on. He was instead on his laptop working away. She smiled when he looked up at her.

"You shouldn't be. You have a busy day tomorrow. We didn't spend all evening going over the specifications for your office park, getting you in bed early only to have you up in the middle of the night," he said.

"I was sleeping until I realized I was sleeping alone. I'm a little antsy about signing the final papers tomorrow. Constance and I are meeting early for breakfast before the meeting. Right now, I'm dealing with butterflies in my stomach. This is really happening, isn't it? Something I have dreamed about since I was a young girl is about to come true. Months of waiting and we're finally here," Sienna said joining him on the sofa.

"Yes, and they should be coming true. You've worked hard for this and now that it's finally here, you're nervous? Don't be. It's all falling into place. Look at all of the donations from around the country that have come in from those who love and support Chicago and the work you're trying to do. While I was sitting here working, I got an email from Jermony, who's going to donate all of the sports equipment for the community center and he's sending a big check. I've also recruited him to help teach the kids some ball playing techniques during the summer hiatus from playing."

Sienna bounced for joy like a little kid.

"Really? What's that, twenty professional athletes that have already agreed to donate their time to the center? That's amazing! Maybe I'm not nervous, but just excited."

"You'll have a lot of time for excitement with all the work that'll be involved. I understand with the upgrades that need to be done to the entire complex inside and out, it's going to take quite a few months to complete," Carter assumed.

"Oscar Jankowsky has already reached out to Constance and me, letting us know he has a large team ready to begin once the final papers are signed tomorrow. I saw the invoice for the computers you and Dexter are donating. Thank you for that and for bringing in college students who are available to tutor seven days a week. This is more than I could have ever dreamed," she said.

"I want you to always dream big. Don't hold anything back. Together, we'll work on it."

"That goes for you, too. Three more weeks and your new dealership is opening, the largest dealership in Chicago and the only one offering the high-end vehicles that you're offering. You have bigger names attending that than those who attend major awards ceremonies every year."

"Of the two hundred cars in the initial shipment, over half have already been secured by a deposit, which is crazy. The shop hasn't even opened yet."

"What are you up so late working on?" Sienna asked, trying to get a look.

"Final selections on new employees. I allowed my current staff to have first pick of positions at the new dealership and now, I'm working to fill the extra slots and also back-filling for those who'll be changing locations. I came out here so that I wouldn't wake you."

"We haven't had a chance to talk these past few days, not even the night after I went to talk to my parents. We've been like ships passing in the night."

Sienna began to notice earlier in the week that, though they had been spending a lot of time together previously, this week they'd struggled with finding time for each other because of other commitments.

"I know and it's been bothering me that we've both been too busy for any real quality time. I do love that we get to sleep in each other's arms at night either at your place or mine. That time is important, but not enough. We need to disconnect from the Matrix and find some time away where we're not thinking about work."

"I agree," Sienna replied.

Carter closed his laptop and turned to her.

"I think we should go away for like a week to an exotic island where there is nothing to do but focus on each other and having fun. I need to see that body in a sexy, tiny bathing suit, swimming and lounging around. I want to drink those fruity things you love and eat without any worries about working out or watching our weight. We work and work out like maniacs and we need a break. What do you say?" he asked.

Carter had been thinking about going away for an extended trip for a few weeks. The perfect time would be after the new dealership opened, letting his team handle everything, trusting in their ability to do the jobs they were hired to do without him hovering.

He remembered having a boss years ago who was the king of micromanagers and a narcissist to boot. He never understood that not everyone needed to constantly have their ego stroked or a pat on the back to make them feel better about themselves. They never got along and it didn't matter how many times his egotistical boss tried to make him conform, since Carter had his own way of working and getting through life. He refused to be led on a string. He vowed he would never be that kind of boss, knowing one day he would run his own show. He was making a major move and now it was time to enjoy more of the life his moves had created for him.

"That sounds heavenly. We've already added on additional dentists and other staff to have in place when the office park opens and to accommodate everyone. Constance and I are vowing to work less hours to not only get the new location up and running, but to also exhale and relax more. Where are you thinking about going?" she asked.

"I'm going to work out all of the plans and the only thing you'll need to do is pack a suitcase full of everything sexy you own and be ready to go. Now, since we haven't had a chance to talk a lot this week, tell me what happened with your parents. I'm hoping to have a sit down with your dad this weekend. I'm going to invite him out to dinner."

"That's a good idea. He's been waiting to hear from you."

"Oh? Is that a good or bad thing?" Carter asked.

He hadn't asked sooner about what happened with her parents, instead giving Sienna time to share what she wanted about the meeting when she was ready.

"Well, I saw my father watching me through the window. When I got in the house, he was acting like he was reading the newspaper and I already know he reads it first thing in the morning. I didn't waste any time telling them that you and I reconnected and were seeing each other. I told them no one could predict the future but that we are enjoying being comfortable around each other again."

Carter leaned over and kissed an area on her neck that was exposed. He was happy she was fighting as hard for them as he was.

"Did you tell them you have been tiring a brother out several times a week since the night of the party?" he joked.

Sienna pushed him slightly on the shoulder.

"Not a conversation I would ever have with them, but if I'm doing that, you're letting me."

"Anytime, every day! So, they're good and not out for my blood?" he asked quizzically.

"I told them about how we saw each other at the wedding and the party planning and how we connected again. I was talking a mile a minute and they sat across from me at the kitchen table and just listened. When I tired myself out from talking, my dad asked one question. He asked me if I was happy. Without any doubt, I said yes. They agreed that the only thing that mattered was if we were making each other happy. They asked if I had any reservations at all because of what happened in the past and I told them that you and I have both matured and grown up to realize how precious love and life are. When you love as hard and deeply as you and I do, it's meant to be for always."

"You did that, huh?" Carter asked, holding his hand up for a high-five.

"I did, thank you very much and my dad won't hurt you, so go ahead with your meeting. Just as your parents still loved me, my parents still love you. No more talk of the past, only the future. Right now, I need something to help me sleep," Sienna said softly, making sure he understood she meant him.

"I got you, but remember this when you're tired in the morning," Carter said, standing and lifting Sienna over his shoulder as he carried her into the bedroom while she giggled away.

**

"You're wiggling," Carter said as he looked over Sienna's shoulder to the window where daylight was just coming up over the Chicago sky.

"That's because you're close behind me and I can feel you," she moaned as her body immediately reacted to him pressed up snuggly against her.

"You felt me in the middle of the night and you're supposed to still be asleep. You have a big day today."

"I know, but I feel you and I can't think of a better way to start my day. Can you?" Sienna slurred and moaned, already stimulated as her body stirred to life. She went willingly as Carter reached for her, pulling her even closer to his body.

Though Sienna had been sleeping for the past few hours after making love, he was still wide awake, and, in the solitude of the early morning hour, he'd laid quiet with her in his arms, while marveling at how lucky he was to be given a second chance with the only woman he'd ever loved. In all the years that they'd dated and then been married, he thought he had appreciated Sienna, but it wasn't until they got back together that he realized he now knew what real appreciation of a good woman meant. He stayed awake listening to her breathing softly, and when she would turn or move away in her sleep, he would pull her back close to him. When he did that, she'd reach out for his arm, pulling it tighter around her body. All he wanted to do for the rest of his life was make her happy.

Leaning forward, he kissed her shoulder and placed a line of opened mouth kisses down her arms.

"I know how to start and end the day when you're in bed with me and naked as a jay bird as you are now. I'm always ready and you know it," he said softly.

Before Sienna could come back with a response, she sighed the moment she felt Carter lift her leg slightly and without moving her, he entered her from behind as they spooned.

"The feel of you and looking out over the beautiful sky makes this is a perfect morning," she moaned as her body rose to the occasion and as the power of love flowing through her consumed her. Moving her hips slowly, she joined in on their sensual act of early morning lovemaking. She reached for Carter's hand where it gripped the side of her hip, and she held on as he increased the pace. With the feeling of him inside of her and his full lips and tongue doing sexy things to her neck and shoulder, she thought she might possibly last long this time, but it wasn't possible the moment she felt his teeth nip her softly causing a shiver to creep up her spine, causing a sizzling feeling throughout her body.

She clung to the feeling that this was what her perfect life looked like. When his hand moved up and cupped her breast, she let her hand travel with his as he caressed her nipple. The moment he gave the hardened peak a little pinch, her body let go. She reached her arm behind her head and held on to the side of his face as her body exploded in pure ecstasy.

"I love you, Sienna," Carter crooned in her ear. "I love you, baby!"

He thought he was prepared for the onslaught of the orgasm that had been building and building, but the moment it hit, an exquisite moan escaped his lips as he buried his head in the area between her head and shoulder while his hips didn't move wildly, but slow, and penetratingly deep. Her inner muscles flexed and stroked him to completion. He loved how she milked him as the sensation of his climax had him soaring to heights he'd never been to.

"I love you, too!" She exclaimed.

Once their bodies calmed, Carter said a quiet thank you that he was once again right where he belonged. In the arms of the woman who was taking a chance on loving him again.

"It's time to get up and get all that paperwork signed. It's time to see your dream come to fruition," he said.

"Now, my day is officially starting," Sienna whispered.

23

Carter zipped through traffic to get to the party knowing they were already an hour behind. He'd spent more time preparing for his grand opening which was occurring the next day and was late picking Sienna up from home after she'd gotten off work for the day.

The past few weeks had been busy ones and all of the work he'd put in that kept him away from her a lot of days and nights was finally paying off. Not only was he more than prepared for the grand opening, he and Sienna were going to be flying off to spend a glorious week together. He had yet to tell her where they were going and she didn't seem to care as long as they were together. Two days after the celebration, they were flying off and leaving everything about work behind. For now, they had to get through an evening where they were finally showcasing to their friends that they were a couple again. It's been months since his parents' anniversary party and the months had also been the happiest of his life.

"Did I tell you that Reese has been bugging me about you being my plus one for the party ever since I replied to the invitation? I didn't realize she would be helping Kim with the invitations. She said word had gotten out that you and I replied and that we were both bringing guests. They're wondering if there was going to be some kind of tension with us showing up with separate dates."

Carter looked over at Sienna and smiled. Dexter had been feeding him the same information.

"They're trying to find out who we're bringing. Reese didn't tell anyone the truth, did she? Dexter was being asked the same questions. He told me he kept answering that he didn't know but assumed everyone would find out the night of the party when I showed up with my date," he replied.

Carter looked over at Sienna and smiled because he was finally free to love on her without worrying about who was watching. They loved their friends, but like most friends, they could be judgmental.

Tonight, he didn't care.

"What do you think is going to happen when we show up together?" Sienna asked. She'd been thinking about it ever since she left the office early. She typically did that on Fridays and today was no exception. She wanted to look extra special knowing what was in store.

"Some will be in shock and others will claim they knew it all along. I don't care what they say as long as they don't bring any drama."

Carter was serious. He would check anyone who made Sienna feel uncomfortable.

"Yeah and you know Angel will be there. You didn't tell me she made a pass at you after we split up."

Carter turned again in surprise.

"Wait, what? She made a pass at me? No, she didn't, at least not that I remember. When did it happen? Are you talking recently? I swear I can't recall that," he said, thinking back on every interaction with Angel.

"A year ago."

"A year ago?" he questioned.

"Yes, a year ago."

Carter tried to think back to a time when he was in Angel's presence. It didn't take long before that time registered.

"Oh, that? That was Angel being Angel, buying a car she couldn't afford and I peeped her motive from the start. Her flirting was unmistakable and I never thought anything about it, including her very low-cut and very short dress. Her heels were so high, she could barely walk in them. She even showed up once with something like a wiper broke or something crazy like that. Rather than go to the service department, she asked to see me using the story that she was a close friend of mine. I sent her right to the service department anyway. Before she left, she came back again, flirting and acting all crazy. I let her know to not even try it right before I told her I was still and always would be in love with you. She said something like you had moved on and something about some guy you were involved with and how I needed to move on too. I laughed at her, which seemed to really piss her off. That was a year ago. I never thought about it after that day even when I've run into her at other times. She brought that up to you?"

Sienna knew how much of a snake Angel could be. She was getting a good lesson on who her true friends were that she could really trust. Angel wasn't one of them. She'd heard stories of Angel going after men who were married, involved, or had been involved with someone close to her. She should have known she would have set her eyes on Carter.

"She was at the spa when Reese and I went last night. I went to get a massage, my nails and hair done and she was a little more talkative than usual. You know Angel is all about drama. She tried to slide the fact into the conversation that you were coming with a date to the party tonight. She wanted to see if she could get a rise out of me. She started talking about how she never would have allowed a man as fine as you to get away for anything, trying to feel out the conversation to see what the sensitive points were. She claimed you flirted back with her as hard as she had flirted with you, which I don't believe, but I still let it get to me. I couldn't stand the sight of her being phony and when I got up to leave, she said something about how if you were her man, she wouldn't leave you alone. I flipped off on her, telling her what I really thought about her trifling ass and then I bunked out!" she declared.

Carter laughed so hard, the car swerved.

"You almost made me crash with that one. Did you just say bunked out? Who are you woman and how come I didn't know about this side of you? I like it. I'm pretty much turned-on by it," he exclaimed happily.

Sienna chuckled and laughed harder.

"Yeah, that was my *Ice Cube* quote of the day," she joked. "Angel is just one big nightmare of a person. I've tried to be friendly to her for a long time and I don't even know why. She doesn't deserve it. She tried me."

Carter could only imagine Sienna letting her claws come out. He knew what it was like to be on the other end of her being pissed off and it wasn't pretty.

"I'm sure you set her straight. Don't let her get to you. Never let a woman who isn't married or even in a relationship set you off about anything when it comes to love. She's lonely, pathetic, and always has been. She has always tried to do things to upset you."

"I know. Reese once told me that Angel said that I didn't deserve a man as handsome, rich, and successful as you, while she struggled to make ends meet with men who never measured up to anything and could barely hold jobs," Sienna shared.

"Baby, you know Angel isn't worth the brain space," Carter replied.

"I said that exact thing to her. We're too old for childish games like that. She was being petty and I was playing into it."

"You know I have no interest in Angel and I never have. There isn't a woman around that I want who isn't you. Do we have issues with trust? I have eyes for you and you only," he said.

"I know and I don't have any doubts about you or about us. I was upset because she's always faked being my friend, and I knew it. She showed her true colors and she'll be the one with the biggest shock on her face. At the spa, it wasn't me that she had to worry about. When I left, Reese was ripping her a second hole and we know Reese."

Carter snickered. If there was a person on earth who always looked out for Sienna, it was Reese and if Angel deserved it, he knew that Reese brought it.

"Great minds think alike, baby, because I would have done the same thing. Don't waste any time on anything Angel says or does. My love for you is intact."

Carter made the last turn onto the street where the party was in full swing. There were cars parked all the way down the block.

"Do you want me to let you out here while I park the car? I see a spot a few cars down."

"No, I'll walk back up with you. I have on high heels, but they're comfortable."

Carter quickly found a space and went around to help Sienna as she exited the car.

"This is it, huh?" he asked.

"This is it. You ready?"

"Baby, I've been ready since the first day. Let's do this!" he said taking her hand in his and walking to the house. As soon as he reached the door, which was opened, Carter stood back and let Sienna walk in first, ahead of him. When he came in behind her and looked up, all eyes were on them and with the exception of the music playing in the background, no one made a sound or made a move. He looked around and saw people stopped midway before letting their glasses filled with drinks touch their lips as if they were attempting the mannequin challenge. Others who had been talking just stopped and stared. Sienna turned and looked at him with questionable eyes and he hunched his shoulders, not caring that they were now the center of everyone's attention. The silence was broken the moment Reese knew they were there.

"Hey, you two! I should have known it was you. Everyone is standing and staring like this is the second coming of Christ or something. Either stop staring at them or take out your phones and snap a picture!" Reese screamed at the group before turning back to them. "I love these guys, but they get on my nerves!" she stressed and then smiled at the happy couple.

"Sorry, we're late. Carter had final touches for the grand

opening that couldn't wait."

"Girl, don't apologize. I'm glad I arrived before you did so that I could peep the look on everyone's face. They've been waiting for the two of you to show up with your dates. They're shocked to see that you're each other's plus one, but I knew because I'm the best friend!" Reese boasted.

Now that Reese had softened the blow, others began welcoming them and congratulating them on being together. That is, everyone except Angel, who scowled at them from a corner. The look on her face was priceless and Sienna smiled and tried not to gloat.

"You're so crazy!" Sienna said.

"Girl, I'm serious that every time someone came in the door, everyone looked to see who it was and if it was you or Carter, there seemed to be a collective sigh of frustration that they were still waiting. I'm glad I don't have to keep that secret anymore. So, are things still hot and heavy with you two?" she asked Carter.

He didn't answer, but shook his head. Only Reese could ask him a question like that.

"No words for you, Reese. No words," he joked. "Sienna, do you want a glass of wine?" he asked.

"Yes, thank you," she said.

"Can you get me one, too?" Reese asked. "While you're gone, I'm going to question her about everything that she's been unwilling to share because of your secret relationship."

"Stop teasing him, girl!" Sienna said and blew a kiss at Carter as he walked away. When she looked around, again, all eyes were on her and a few stood with their mouths wide open after she blew Carter a kiss.

"Go back to what you were doing!" Reese yelled into the

crowd. "These people are maniacs," she whispered to Sienna.

"You act as if you're not! You have your days, too, girl. How's the party so far?" Sienna asked.

"Better now that you're here. Things are still good with you two?" she asked.

"Things are better than good, they're great. We have found our way back to each other and the love we always should have had. I couldn't be happier."

"Are you still going away in a few days?"

"We are and I still don't know where. He only told me to make sure I brought my passport. I haven't told him that I'm already packed. We've taken a few weekend getaways, but we'll be gone for eight long, glorious days and I can hardly wait. I have a doctor's appointment in the morning to finally get a birth control shot so that I can get away from taking this pill every morning. I was taking it to control my cycle and not to prevent pregnancy since I wasn't sleeping with anyone, but now I'm realizing I need something more effective."

Sienna had been worried about getting pregnant with the number of times she and Carter had made love without condoms. Her current dosage of birth control wasn't necessarily for pregnancy prevention.

"Aw, he's putting in overtime on you, huh? Get yours, girl. I'm happy for you. When you get back, I'll tell you about someone I've been seeing. He's someone you'll remember from back in college who I was madly in love with, but didn't really know that I was. You know how I was back then. I wasn't exactly the kind of girl who was committed to a particular man," Reese said.

"I remember those dark days of seeing you go through one

man after another. I can't believe you let that life your mother led impact you to the point that you thought that was considered some kind of relationship. You could have had one, but you messed that up. Who is it that you may have had a serious thing for other than Torrence Allen?" Sienna asked and waited.

"Who else could it be?" Reese asked.

It couldn't be, Sienna thought to herself. There was a twinkle in Reese's eyes that made her think that she may be on to something.

"Who? Is it Torrence? You're seeing Torrence Allen from college? Since when?" Sienna shrieked and quieted when Reese moved them to a quieter spot in the room.

"You are so loud. If I wanted everyone to know, I would have put up a sign. Since a few weeks ago. It's been sort of off and on and nothing too serious. He recently moved here and is the owner of the new casino that's being built right here in Chicago."

"Wait. I heard about that. Carter mentioned something about hearing Torrence was connected to that somehow, but we've been so busy that we never talked about it again," Sienna said.

"Right. The company I work for just won the contract for the marketing and promotion of the casino and when I went for the first meeting, he was sitting across the table. It's been a wild ride, but we can talk about it when you get back from your trip. He's been spending more time out of town than here in Chicago, but when he's here, we've been kicking it a little. I have too much to tell you and this isn't the place. Tonight, we're here at the party to have fun sipping on wine and pretending it's tea with all of the shade that'll be thrown at you and Carter for coming together. I think just about everyone in our circle is in support of the two of you and your rekindled loved, but not everyone. Angel is still hating, but let her. Maybe she'll find a man soon and she won't have to go after everyone else's. Speaking of men, here comes yours."

They turned toward Carter as he walked toward them.

"Ladies," Carter said handing them each a glass of wine. Sienna was about to take a sip when she felt as if the room was spinning. Gathering herself before anyone noticed she was a little off-kilter. She handed her glass back to Carter.

"Hold this for a minute. I need to find the bathroom. Reese, don't pry as I know you'll try to do the minute I walk away."

"Don't make me promise what I can't deliver to you," Reese teased.

"I'm already pleading the fifth to whatever you're going to ask me," Carter said turning to Reese.

"Only because my girl loves you will I leave you alone and not give you the third degree, but you already know, don't mess up again."

"I hear you and Sienna is blessed to have a good friend like you."

"When you return from your trip, we should go out on a double date and really have some fun."

"Double date? I thought you were swearing off men to showcase in public. This must be someone special," Carter said.

"You remember Torrence from school?" she asked.

"Torrence Allen? Casino owner Torrence Allen that you dated or whatever that was when we were in school? Yeah, I remember him. He's big time now," Carter said.

"Yes, he is. I've been seeing him the past few weeks and it's been going well. Nothing serious, but the past doesn't have him hating me," she said.

"Right, he's in town building his new casino. What's that number two or three?" he asked.

"Number two and it'll be the biggest one yet."

"I saw something about it, but haven't done much more than read about it. They haven't even broken ground yet, but I hear it's going to be spectacular," Carter said.

"From what I know so far, it will be the biggest opening Chicago has ever seen," Reese said.

"What else has Torrence been doing besides running a successful casino in Las Vegas? He's blowing up!" Carter cheered.

"We're still connecting and getting to know each other again. He's been in and out of Chicago over the past few weeks, but will soon spend more time here after the actual construction begins."

"I hope that works out well. I remember the two of you were hot and heavy back in school and then it ended sort of abruptly."

"Yeah, there was some drama, but that's behind us now."

They turned when Sienna returned.

"Are you okay?" Carter asked. "You look a little out of it."

"I'm okay. I think I'm just exhausted," she said.

"Well, you'll soon get plenty of rest on our trip."

"I'm looking forward to that."

"Call me before you leave. I'm going to go make the rounds before all the blessing of the house starts and then things can really get wild!" Reese exclaimed.

"I will and don't hurt anybody tonight," Sienna said as Reese walked away.

"Are you sure you're okay?" Carter asked again.

"I am. I'm starving and I don't want any more wine. I could use a bottle of water."

"Okay, baby. Let's go find you some food. Come to think of it, I'm pretty hungry myself," Carter said leading them toward the room with all the food.

Sienna looked tired and he knew it was because of the extra hours she'd been putting in with signing contracts and making decisions on the new office park. He couldn't wait to whisk her away to a place where all he was going to allow her to do was lay around, sip her favorite drink and allow him to cater to her and love on her for eight days.

For now, his plan was to feed her in hopes that the food will give her the energy she needs. He was concerned when she returned from the bathroom looking like she was going to be sick. Food will do the trick, he thought and escorted her through the throngs of people who still looked shocked at seeing them together. He already knew that it was time they all got use to it because he and Sienna together again was not temporary. This was long-haul kind of love.

24

"Pregnant? What? I can't be pregnant! That test can't be right. Check again, Dr. Jan. I'm serious, your test is wrong," Sienna said stunned and feeling a little faint. She couldn't have heard her doctor correctly.

"I'm sure it's right and I wouldn't kid you like that."

Sienna felt like the world was spinning all around her, and any moment, she was going to pass out from shock. She had to be dreaming when her doctor informed her that she was pregnant.

She'd made the appointment to see Dr. Jan, her gynecologist in order to get a more dependable option for birth control since she and Carter couldn't seem to keep their hands off of each other and she was hoping to have it in place before their trip. All Carter had to do was look at her and her body would tingle with want that wouldn't go away until he doused the flame of her desire. The last thing she expected to hear was that she was already pregnant.

"I'm serious, you have the tests mixed up or something. I cannot be pregnant. I'm about to go on vacation," she said out loud again, trying to convince herself more than her doctor.

"Sienna, you can be pregnant and you are and you can still go on vacation. You're not having the baby tomorrow," Dr. Jan quipped.

Sienna felt like the room was caving in on her. Her vision was starting to get blurry.

"Pregnant? Me?" Sienna asked as if saying it again was going to change the outcome.

"You don't look well. Sit back down and let's talk."

Sienna could hear her doctor talking, but she failed to comprehend anything coming out of her mouth. She simply couldn't get beyond the word *pregnant*. The idea of pregnancy would not sink in. It had to be something else. She sat down and looked back up at her doctor with pleading eyes.

"It's some kind of stomach flu or something," she said, trying to convince herself it was anything but a baby.

After enduring a gamut of tests before she got the birth control shot and also informing her doctor that she'd been feeling dizzy for no reason recently, she waited in the examination room for what seemed an eternity. She was expecting to be home and preparing for her flight with Carter the next day where the destination was still unknown to her.

The day before, on Sunday, she'd spent a busy day at the pre-grand opening for his new car dealership where they had to shuttle people in from a nearby parking lot. The crowd of people was massive and had included family, friends, and coworkers. There had also been celebrities and professional athletes from all over the country. Carter had made a lot of connections over the years and many had come out to support and to see the new line of cars that were available for purchase. By the end of the event, she was beyond exhausted. She decided to leave a little early and went home to wait on Carter. He would officially be on vacation for the next two weeks, something he had not done in years, according to him. By the time she got home, she had yawned a million times in her car. The only way she knew that Carter had actually spent the night with her was because in the morning, he'd left her a note saying how much he loved her and that he was happy that she was finally getting some sleep. She hadn't been feeling well after the party and then they had an exhausting time at the dealership. If the pre-grand opening was that huge, she could only image what the grand opening for the public would be after they returned from their trip. She couldn't wait to get some rest and ended up sleeping the evening away and into the next morning. She was disappointed that he didn't wake her up when he came over and she was angry at herself that she was so tired, she didn't hear him come in or join her in bed.

Now, here she was listening to her doctor proclaim a pregnancy.

"It's not the flu or a virus. You, my dear, are pregnant. Once you get over the initial shock, let's talk about what's next. The last time you were here about six months ago, I asked you about sexual activity and birth control and you said you weren't actively engaging, but that you wanted to continue the prescription for the pill because they were doing a great job of regulating your cycle. It wasn't a strong enough dosage that I would have given you if I thought you were active."

Sienna couldn't think. The only thing repeatedly flowing

through her mind was she was going to have a baby.

"I'm not. I mean I wasn't until a few months ago; actually, about five months ago, right after I was last here for an appointment. I was coming in for more dependable birth control, which is why I made this appointment. I had no idea I was pregnant already. I've been so busy with work that being pregnant never would have occurred to me. Now that I think about it, I haven't had a cycle in two months. I've been so busy that I didn't notice."

"I'd say you've been busy---busy getting pregnant," Dr. Jan laughed. "I'm trying to cheer you up so that you don't pass out on me. I can tell you're still shocked. So, you've gotten back out into the dating realm with a zest after your split from Carter. I still miss him being with you at appointments. Sorry if that's still a sore subject. You know how I felt about him. Of course, I understand why you split. Still, I've never seen a man love a woman as much as he loved you, not even my own husband," she kidded.

Another realization just smacked her in the face. Not only was she pregnant, but she was pregnant with Carter's baby. *They were going to have a baby*, she thought silently to herself. It was real---as real as the baby growing inside of her. She placed both of her hands over her stomach and no longer in shock, an immense amount of love surfaced for the baby they'd made together.

"I'm going to have a baby," she said, with awe welling up in her words.

"Yes, you are. I want to do an ultrasound and a few other tests to see how far along you are. I would go by your last period, but you said you've been getting them except for the past two months. I take it you've been active back before that?" Dr. Jan asked.

"Yes, before that but after my last appointment with you. To be more exact, since April. The pills have helped to regulate my cycle, but it didn't do so well with me having lots and lots of great sex. I mean, the best sex of my life!" she happily proclaimed as an image of Carter, naked and powerfully aroused crossed her mind.

"Whoa, don't have sex right now! You look like you're thinking about that man right at this moment," Dr. Jan laughed. "Well, it looks like you've been successful in getting pregnant with this new man in your life. Are you excited?"

Sienna knew that there was no need to think hard about that.

"Yes! You're sure, right? This couldn't be some mistake and during the exam or ultrasound, you're going to find out it's actually something else?" she asked with caution.

Sienna smiled when her doctor, who had been her gynecologist since she was a teenager, laughed again.

"I'm quite sure. I'm glad you're happy about the baby. I know how much you wanted to have one before."

Sienna knew her doctor was thinking about Carter as much as she was and the fact that when they had split up, she found out a week later that she was pregnant and just as fast, she had miscarried within another week. Sienna had never told him about that loss. Now, she was pregnant again, yet they were no longer husband and wife, but still together.

"I did and that was a rough time for me."

As soon as she thought about the baby she had lost long ago, fear settled over her.

"What if it happens again? I can't go through that, not another time. What if something happens?" she asked, now frightened and already overprotective of the baby.

"I see great fear on your face and I can hear it in your voice. Don't do that to yourself. Positive thoughts only. I'm going to have you settled back into a room for the exam, but first, since you seem so happy, who is this new guy? Have you been seeing him long and how will he react knowing you're pregnant?" Dr. Jan asked.

How ironic was the name she was about to reveal to her doctor?

"Well, see the story is this," she started and smiled so bright at the thought of being pregnant with Carter's baby, she couldn't get the words out. Before she could, her doctor interrupted her.

"Oh, my. Look at how you're glowing. He must be some guy."

"He is and the past four or five months have been nothing but amazing and now a baby. He's going to be over the moon. He's always wanted children and though this news of a baby is unexpected, I have no doubt he will be as happy as I am," Sienna expressed. She was feeling nothing but pure joy. She was going to have a baby. She and Carter were going to have a baby.

"Ah, sounds like someone is in love, again. I'm happy for you and sad because I had hoped that you and Carter would one day find your way back to each other. So, mystery aside now, who is this new man in your life who makes you happier than I've seen you in a long time?" Dr. Jan asked.

Sienna bit her lip nervously.

"Carter," was all she could say and waited for a reaction

"You are seeing another man named Carter? How ironic is that? That name is so rare," she added.

Sienna looked at her facetiously.

"Really, Dr. Jan? That's your first go-to response? Think about what I just said. It's *that* Carter," she repeated.

"Wait, you're serious? I thought you were joking because you know how much I like him. We're really talking about Carter Garrison? Your ex-husband?"

"Not a joke at all. I'm pregnant by my ex-husband. We've been seeing each other again for the past few months and like I mentioned, it's been wonderful. We've been keeping it under wraps and just last week shared our new status with family and friends."

Sienna wasn't prepared for her doctor to leap out of her seat, come around the desk and hug her tightly, but that's exactly what happened.

"Best news ever! So, things have changed for you lately, huh? No wonder you are over the moon with happiness."

"They have and I forgave him a long time ago and chastised myself for not doing so before the divorce. By then, I felt like I had to go through with it, even though I didn't want to. Recently, we ran into each other at a wedding and I also helped with a party for his parents and that's what brought us back around each other again," she clarified.

"I would say so with that bun in the oven. I'm happy for you both. Let's get the exam done and then come back to talk. When you were pregnant before and miscarried, you were going through a very stressful time in your life. There was nothing medically wrong with you that caused it, so this time, I'm going to demand that you take it easy and focus on everything good, less work and more time being loved and catered to by that wonderful man of yours. You said you were going away and that's good. My prescription is relaxation and I mean it. I don't want to hear anything about work or other stresses. We want a healthy pregnancy."

"Believe me, I'm not going to do anything other than eat and lay on the beach. I actually get to eat and not have to worry about gaining any weight!" Sienna laughed.

"True, but still, eat healthy. I'll get you some pre-natal vitamins and set you up for another appointment in about six weeks. Come see me earlier if you're not feeling well or if you just want to talk. Let's finish up your appointment and then we can come back and I can answer any other questions you have. First, let's get a look at this little one and see how far along you are so that when you tell Carter, he'll know when to expect his status to change to daddy!" Dr. Jan said.

"Oh, he's going to be happy – at least I hope so. It's unexpected and we just got back together," Sienna said, now worried again for a whole different reason.

"You said things were going well. Sounds like you shouldn't have a worry in the world. I mean it, no stress, Sienna."

"I hear you doc," she replied and stood and followed the doctor out. She couldn't wait for their secret destination trip where she would tell him about the baby. They hadn't talked about anything long-term like marriage or babies, but knowing they were in love was enough for her. Well, knowing she was carrying his baby personified her love and solidified her decision to focus on the here and now.

**

The jewelry store was the last stop on Carter's to-do list. It was the day after the pre-grand opening of his new car dealership and that day couldn't have gone any better. It was closed to the public with the opening for everyone taking place in a few weeks. Thanks to the best marketing team, recommended by Reese who worked for one of the top PR firms in the country, his event was promoted to reach as many interested parties as possible and it was a major hit.

Bigger than that, an even bigger event was about to take place in his life. He was planning on asking Sienna to marry him again. If she said yes, it would be the best day of his life.

He had been thinking about proposing for a few weeks, but it wasn't until he met with her father that he knew the time was right.

After Sienna told him that the talk she had with her parents about them being involved again had gone well, he called her father and asked him out to dinner. He had secured a private room in one of the finest steak restaurants in the city. One thing he had learned from years of being involved with and married to Sienna was that her father loved a good steak. It was over that dinner that he explained all that had happened that caused him to hurt Sienna in a way that he would always regret. To his surprise, her father wasn't as angry as he thought, even back when it occurred. His reason was an even greater shocker.

Sienna's father shared a life-long secret with him, one that he wasn't sure Sienna knew about, but it was important for him to tell Carter in order to explain why he didn't hate him for what he'd done. Carter listened quietly as Lars told him a story of his own infidelity and how he'd gotten caught up in a long affair with a woman he never had any intentions of leaving his wife for. However, he had still carried on hoping his wife wouldn't find out. He kept the affair from getting out and the only reason he stopped was because his wife had found out when his mistress came to their home, angering him. His affair didn't mean he didn't love his wife but that he got caught up in intimacy that didn't involve the heart. Lars had been young then and thought he was a big shot and could do anything he wanted, but he never thought of the consequences of his actions, which could have been losing his wife and daughter had Connie chosen to divorce him. He was grateful that after counseling and a lot of apologizing, eventually, they had worked things out. He'd never stepped out on her again.

What Carter appreciated about the conversation with Sienna's father was that neither judged the other, but both understood what it felt like to hurt the women who had always been by their sides and how much they would have lost if they hadn't come to their senses. For Carter, he did lose Sienna and he would never forget that. He never wanted to feel that bad again. He wanted to make sure every day of Sienna's life was filled with love and happiness and whatever he could do to make that happen he would.

After they talked and ate porterhouse steaks and extra-large, over-stuffed baked potatoes, they enjoyed after dinner drinks in which Carter went into a speech about how Sienna was his world. He added that, though they had been together for months, he didn't want to waste time being in a relationship if they could have more. He wanted to ask Sienna to marry him again and this time, it would be a forever kind of love. He asked Lars for permission to marry Sienna. Carter could even admit to himself that, deep down, he was more nervous than he had been the first time he asked many years ago. Lars had every right to be concerned about the depth of his commitment to marrying Sienna again. Lars surprised him and didn't show it. Carter barely had the words out of his mouth when Lars told him it was about time. He had always thought of Carter as a son and welcomed him back into their lives as a son-in-law. From that point on, for the rest of the evening, they talked sports, family and how blessed they were to have such incredible women.

As he drove home that night, Carter called Sienna from the car to let her know that his talk with her father went well. She didn't ask for details and he didn't want to break the confidence they shared about Lars's mistake long ago. Besides, Sienna was just happy things had gone well.

His focus now was on their trip the next day where he intended to love on her for eight days while away and then more when they returned home before they both went back to work. He was planning a major staycation for them and it involved not answering the phone and never leaving the house. He hadn't taken any kind of vacation since they were married the first time. He'd dived full speed ahead into work, lonely without Sienna. His passion for work became his wife. His plan was to actually get her back, body, heart, and soul.

A week ago, he'd made an appointment with his favorite jeweler, who was working on an exclusive design of an engagement ring just for Sienna. Joshua, the jeweler, was a god-send, able to design the ring and have it ready before his trip in the morning. Carter hoped Sienna was just as ready as he was to get back to their real life together, not merely being involved and seeing each other, but actually back to planning out their lives as husband and wife again.

Making his way to pick up Sienna's ring, he wondered how her appointment at the doctor's office had gone, knowing she had not been herself for a few days. He hoped she wasn't coming down with some kind of bug that would keep her from really enjoying their time away. He was taking her to a sexy, exotic resort which is a place they had talked about going to many, many years ago. They were leaving very early in the morning and since he wouldn't be seeing her until he picked her up in the morning, he dialed her as he drove.

"Hey, beautiful!" he said the moment she answered.

"Hi! I was just thinking about you. I was going to call you to confirm the time you'll be here to pick me up in the morning. I'm planning to get in bed early tonight so I can be up and refreshed for our trip. I'm really excited in case you can't hear it in my voice," Sienna said.

Carter could almost see her excitement through the phone.

"I take it the appointment went okay and you're not coming down with a summer flu or cold or anything? If you were, I am all ready to play doctor," he teased.

"I love your version of playing doctor, but no, I'm fine. No flu or cold or anything. I'm good. In fact, I'm better than good. I'm ready for this time away with you and leaving everything about work here in Chicago. You know this business park is really jumping off with construction about to begin in a few weeks. I'm glad it's happening, but I need to separate myself from it for a while," she said.

"It shouldn't be too stressful with all of the help you're getting. Thanks to Reese and to the marketing firm she works for, the word has gotten out. You know her firm did an extraordinary job for the dealership. You mentioned even more money and tangible donations have poured in. You know I'm here to help with anything you need. I don't want this to feel like a burden to you," Carter said.

"I don't know how I can thank Reese for all of her help, getting us this partnership with her firm to do the marketing and promotion from now until a year after we're up and running. It's exciting. They did do a great job with your opening yesterday. I hope it was everything you hoped it would be."

"It was that and then some. You know I'm already thinking about the other new locations, one in Florida and one on the west coast. We've been ready to move beyond Chicago for some time now. I'm going to spend some time after we come back on what that expansion will look like and I also want to be sure I'm giving you just as much of my attention. I don't want our lives to be all about work. Thankfully, Dex and I are talking to perspective partners and that will help take the weight off of us in trying to run businesses in other states. This dealership is my baby, but more than that, you're my baby and my priority."

"We are each other's priority and that means we each get to follow our dreams. We won't lose focus on what's important and that is us. We're getting this time away and we can take more trips whenever we feel we need our time," she said.

"I'm down with that. I love you so much, Sienna. Have I said that today?"

"Yes, baby you have and I'm so proud of you, Carter. Baby, you are all about goal chasing and I love it. I adore that energy you have that poured into me many years ago. You have always been driven and because of that, I'm there with you dreaming the next dream. I love you," Sienna said.

"I love you, too. I love you more than anything in this world. Have I thanked you lately for loving me again?" Carter asked.

"No amount of thank you is ever needed. We are a power couple and we love like a power couple."

"Yes, we do, and though I love goal and dream chasing with you, I want to be sure that it doesn't take us away from making our love the first priority. I would be happy being broke and living in a shack with you as long as I know I have you by my side. The only goal I want to get lost in would be in loving you like never before."

Carter could feel himself making a case for them to get married and so he pulled his thoughts in because the next words felt like they should be his proposal instead. For that moment, he wanted to be in Belize.

"I think we know how important our love is and so I'm not worried," Sienna said.

"I agree. I have a feeling this trip is going to be one of the most memorable of our lives," Carter exclaimed, thinking about the moment he'll slide the ring on her finger. He was planning to do it their first night.

"You and I are on the same page. I was thinking the exact same thing," Sienna said rubbing her hand across her stomach. She couldn't wait to share their news and hoped he would be as happy as she was at the idea of being parents.

"I'll see you in the morning and get some sleep."

"I will. I have a feeling I'm going to sleep like a baby," she said.

25

"This place is amazing. I've never seen so much beauty and elegance. This is definitely what I call living," Sienna said as she gazed around her home away from home for the next eight days. She walked around their luxurious suite excitedly checking out everything.

After getting to the airport and finally finding out they were going to the Turtle Inn Resort in Belize, she couldn't be happier. This was someplace she always wanted to travel to, but they had both been too busy years ago while married and building careers to actually go once they could afford to.

This place was their Shangri-La, their peace of heaven on earth. She captured every image as they traveled from the airport to the resort and each image was more breathtaking than the last. She may have grown up in Chicago, but she loved the water; Sienna was a water baby. Her first view of the blue ocean water was spectacular. She was in a place for lovers with the love of her life. No moment could be more perfect for everything she had planned.

"I'm glad you like it. I told them I needed the best for the love of my life," Carter replied.

CHERYL BARTON

He sat down and watched as Sienna went from one room to the next rushing back and forth around him. He loved making her happy and hoped that over the past few months, she could see that he loved her unconditionally and wanted a life with her, uninterrupted by anything that would seek to upset their happy life. This trip was his do or die moment, no more waiting. He wanted to marry her again.

"You outdid yourself. This view of the ocean is incredible," Sienna boasted excitedly.

Barely able to contain her jubilance, she walked over and planted herself right in Carter's lap, wrapped her arms around his neck and kissed him with the appetite of a she-devil.

"If you don't stop kissing me like this, we're going to see very little of this island today and I want to sightsee, but tonight, you are all mine," he swooned against her shoulder.

"Okay, only because I can't wait to check out the island. What shall we do first?" Sienna asked, more excited than she expected she would be.

"Let's first get unpacked and I will get our day started. I have a full day of fun planned," Carter said.

He was happy he could keep the destination a secret. Behind the scenes, he had his travel agent make all of the arrangements including their activities. More than anything, he wanted quiet nights sitting out enjoying the peaceful silence of the ocean and the sheer beauty of the starry, moonlit sky. They were in paradise.

"You thought of everything, huh? You don't need me to do anything?" Sienna asked.

Carter pulled her into his arms to once again remind her that he didn't want her lifting a finger to do anything other

310

than enjoy the time away.

"All I want you to do is have a great time in this nirvana we have here and let me spoil you."

"Thank you for this trip. I really needed this," she replied, snuggling close.

"I could tell you needed a break. I know when you need something, especially a respite. You seemed a little distracted and in need of some rest and relaxation. I take it work has been crazy with the new project. The other night, you fell asleep before the movie started and in the few minutes it took for me to go in the kitchen to make us a late-night snack, you were down for the count as if you were worn out."

Sienna pouted and then smiled. She wanted their quiet time that night, but she could barely keep her eyes open and she tried really hard to do so.

"I'm still sorry about that. I love that leather sectional you have. I sink into it and all I can think about is sleep."

"It's okay. I loved having you with me even when you're sleeping and snoring!"

"I do not snore," she punched him lightly on the arm.

Sienna held back on revealing that their son or daughter growing inside of her was also responsible for her being tired lately, even though she had no idea that was the cause. Her plan was to tell him about the baby later in the evening, but she was losing the battle over keeping it from him any longer. She didn't like secrets and this one was going to change their lives. Before she could share her good news, she had something from her past that she needed to tell him and she didn't want to wait to do that because she wanted to brighten up what she knew could be a tough conversation about the baby.

Sienna moved from Carter's lap and sat on the edge of the table in front of him. The table was low enough, even with the seat he sat on, where they would be looking at each other face to face.

"I need to tell you something," she said, nervously. Other than her parents, she had never told another soul what happened to her, not even Reese. That was a time in her life when her world was spinning out of control and that one vestige of beauty of finding out that she was pregnant had dissipated as quickly as I had arrived when she lost the baby.

"Okay. This sounds serious. Your voice sounds so grave," Carter said, concerned.

Sienna reached out and took his hands in hers, looking down at where their fingers were now laced together. She then looked up into his eyes and though part of her news wasn't the greatest conversation piece, it was needed if they were going to keep moving on together.

"Let me start by saying, I love you and I always have, even though our bad time, though I wouldn't admit it then. I figured if Beyonce could forgive Jay-Z, who am I to not forgive, right?"

Sienna chuckled, hoping to lighten the moment a little. She was about to share something and hoped that it didn't put a damper on the love that had begun to blossom between them once again, a love that had never really gone away.

"Hey, they are the king and queen!" Carter clowned.

His attempt to join her in a little humor was to help her ease into whatever she was struggling to sharing with him.

"I know we've talked about all of that and it really is water under the bridge for me and after today, I never want that time to come up and interfere with our lives again."

"I'm with you, baby," Carter said.

Sienna moved nervously.

"There is thing about back then that I still need to share if we're being open and honest about everything. No secrets between us, right?" she asked.

Carter hesitated before he agreed, something he was fearful about acknowledging as he feared her words meant another man or something else that would shatter him. He would have to get over it because he prayed hard over the past two years to get his wife back and he would accept her with everything---the good and the bad.

"Yes, baby. No secrets and nothing that would ever hurt one of us ever again. When you're ready to share, I'm ready to listen with no judgement," Carter said, bracing himself for the worst.

Sienna fell in love even more. She always knew Carter was the perfect man for her and she was glad she was able to accept him for his imperfections as well.

"When we split, I know I made it look like it was easy for me to walk away, but it wasn't. It was the first hardest thing I've ever had to go through in my life."

"There was something after that?" he inquired.

Sienna nodded her head yes as she fought with the memory of what she went through.

"After I left and the separation began, I didn't sleep well and I stayed with my parents until you told me to take the house and you moved out. Before that, I was depressed because the weight of everything was so much to deal with. A week after we split, I found out I was pregnant, but two weeks later, before I had a chance to digest the pregnancy, what it meant and the fact that we weren't together anymore,

I miscarried. I lost our baby," she said and waited.

The minute the words left her mouth, tears fell from her eyes. She hadn't spoken the words in a long time and hearing herself say it again brought the weight of that moment back on her. The loss was still heavy. As the tears fell, she felt Carter's hands stiffen in her own. The same feelings she had experienced back then were hitting him for the first time. She held his hands tight while he processed what she said. She didn't have him to lean on back when she went through it because she had left him. She would now be here for him while he experienced the various emotions she remembered going through as well.

"What? You were pregnant?" he asked tensely.

Carter had taken a few minutes to prepare himself for whatever Sienna had to say, but he wasn't ready for this. *Nothing* could have ever prepared him to hear that not only did the love of his life lose their child without his knowledge but that the loss was his fault. It had been spurred on by the hurt and depression his betrayal had inflicted on her.

"Yes. I didn't know I was pregnant when I left. You know how crazy my cycle has always been. I was so self-absorbed in what I was going through that it caught me by surprise. Before I had a chance to figure out how I would bring up the subject with you, the baby was gone just as fast."

Carter pulled her closer to him and cuddled tight.

"Baby, I'm so sorry. I'm sorry you went through that and I'm even sorrier that what I took us through sent you into depression and eventually, the loss of our child. Why didn't you tell me? Were you going to tell me?" he asked solemnly.

"I was so overwhelmed when I found out and so much was going on, I hadn't thought about it and when I figured I would, I woke up one morning with bad cramps like I've never had before. My mom drove me to the hospital and that's when they told me I had miscarried. Between that and us just having split up, I spent months trying to get myself together to deal with anything again. I thought about telling you and then I thought that it would come out as if I were blaming you because of what we had gone through. I didn't want to throw the loss in your face and place that blame on you. I was angry at you, yes, but I still loved you and so I went through the loss without you. My doctor said it wasn't anyone's fault. Things happen," she said.

Sienna leaned forward and laid her head on his chest. They sat that way with his arms around her, both letting the weight of that loss sink in.

"I know things happen. That was major and you should have told me. I know you were livid with me, but it was my baby, too and you should not have gone through that loss without me. You needed someone else to shoulder that burden. I just...you didn't have to be alone," Carter whispered against her skin. He knew that he needed her close to him at this moment and felt that she needed the same thing.

"I lost our baby," she murmured and when she felt arms pull her tighter, she released cries that were more like wails. She let go of every feeling she felt when she heard that the baby was gone and Carter wasn't there to hold her like he was now.

"You told me the doctor said it was no one's fault. If there is fault, it lies with me for taking us through that when I knew better. I was thoughtless, careless, and sorrier than I have ever been in my life. That baby wasn't meant to join us at that time," he said. Carter loosened up, trying not to live in a moment of sadness. If she would have him, they would have a life time of having and loving their children together.

"Are you sure you're okay? I'm sorry for not telling you back then."

Carter didn't need either of them feeling sad or sorry for something neither of them could control.

"Baby, I understand why you didn't. Thank you for telling me now. I will never, ever take my love...take *our* love for granted again. I hope you know I mean that. You will never have to worry about me doing anything that could cause me to lose you. Don't move, okay?"

Carter jumped up and rummaged through the backpack he'd carried on the plane. He would never trust a precious gift in his luggage. Finding what he was searching for, he walked back over and this time, instead of sitting on the chair across from Sienna, he instead knelt down in front of her. Before Sienna could ask what he was doing, Carter held out the black velvet box that he'd brought along with them. He didn't immediately hand it to her, but searched her face for any signs that now wasn't a good time.

He didn't see any, at least not that he could tell.

"Carter? What is this?"

Sienna sat so still, she wasn't even sure she was still breathing. Carter was on his knees in front of her holding a box. She would have reached for it, but her hands wouldn't move. Her heart wouldn't slow down and she couldn't find any other words as she looked from his eyes to the box in the palm of his hand and then back to his eyes again.

"I prayed so hard for an answer to how to win your love back. I mean, I prayed, and prayed, and promised myself I would never give up on trying. I didn't know when the right time would be to connect with you again, but I didn't have to find the right moment. It showed up in the form of Keith and Kim's wedding. When I saw you that day, my heart felt like it was going to burst out of my chest. My heart was so filled with love for you. I was hesitant to approach you, but I knew that I had to try. Once I did, I already knew that was the first day of the rest of our lives. I just had to work on proving that to you and I hope I've done that. I brought us here to this beautiful island to surround us with love in a paradise away from everyone else. I wanted to be alone with you with no work on the horizon for me or for you. I wanted it to be you and me. I wanted that because I didn't want anything but beauty around when I told you how much I love you and how much I would love for you to be my wife once again. I know we can't go back and I don't want to. No. I want to go *forward*, and I want us to do that together. These past months have been some of the best of my life and it wasn't anything big that made it significant. The significance was me and you together having fun, getting acquainted again and being in love. It was a big deal every moment reconnecting because I was connecting with the love of my life. I love you so much it hurts that I can't call you my wife like I once could. I want that again. I don't want to overshadow what we just went through with me now knowing you had lost our baby and went through that without me. I understand why and never again will you ever have a reason to go through another moment in your life, good or bad, without me. I want to always be here for you, starting from today; starting from this very moment," he said.

"Carter," Sienna sighed through tears that were now falling for a happier reason and not the sad moment they'd just experienced.

"When I had dinner with your father, I told him I wanted to marry you and asked for his blessing to prove I was the man who would love you the way you should be loved and cherished. Now, I'm here with you and asking. Sienna, will you marry me?"

Carter watched her closely, not knowing what she would say. Unlike the first time he proposed, he knew she was ready and there had been many hints that she was expecting a ring. This time, they'd gone through a rough patch, found each other again and found that love was still alive between them. If she loved him as much as he loved her, then he had no reservations about asking right now.

Sienna leaned forward and kissed Carter, reigning in her tears so that she could clearly answer him. Leaning back, she looked again at the box and then into the face of the man who was her prince and always had been.

"Yes. I will marry you. I love you and will marry you a million times," she said.

Carter, ecstatic, wanted to get the ring on her finger as fast as he could, even as he fumbled with opening the ring box.

"I love you too, and I can't wait to have lots and lots of babies with you. We'll always remember the one we lost and cherish every new baby that comes into our lives," he said.

Sienna smiled even though she knew he couldn't see her face clearly. She took his hand, since he was having a hard time trying to remove the ring's ribbon. Then she placed the flat of his palm on her stomach.

"Well, we are well on our way, daddy."

She waited and waited, but never let go of her smile. Before she could react or drop a further hint, Carter darted up so fast that he dropped the ring box and stared at her.

"Breathe, Carter. You look like you're about to pass out."

"Uh, did you just call me daddy? I mean I love when you're saying that at the right time, if you know what I mean, but we weren't in the middle of you know what. So, what did you really mean?"

As he talked, Carter paced back and forth across the carpeted floor, forgetting he'd left the ring box on the floor by Sienna's feet.

"First of all, you're breathing like a madman, so inhale and exhale easy. Second, I'm going to need you to find my ring," she laughed.

Remembering what he was doing, he went back to the floor and picked up the box. Finally undoing the ribbon and opening the box fully, he slid the ring on her finger, kissed her, and then placed his hand on her stomach as he smiled. It was either that or keep fighting the urge to hyperventilate with the news.

"You're pregnant!" he shouted and shook as if he couldn't control his body's movements.

"Okay, you look like you've won the lottery and are about to pass out all at the same time. Maybe you should sit down."

"I...I can't sit down. I'm going to have a baby...I mean you're going to have a baby...wait, we're going to have a baby. Are you sure?" he asked and kissed her again. This time, he went back to his knees, lifted her shirt and kissed her bare stomach.

"Yes, we're going to have a baby in about seven months. I found out right before the trip. I was planning on telling you when we got to our destination and I even bought you a 'Daddy' gift. Then, you proposed and I thought it was the perfect time to tell you. I take it you're as excited as I was the moment I found out?" she asked.

"Are you kidding me? Have you met me? This is amazing news and I can't wait. I'm going to be a daddy!" he shouted. "After hearing that we lost a baby and now finding out we're having one? I couldn't be happier that we're getting this second chance, not just at love, but at having a baby."

"The timing is perfect," Sienna said. She smiled as Carter kept kissing her over and over again.

"I love you so much. Thank you for making me a daddy and a husband again. We need to get married soon. I don't want our baby born when we're not married. I know that sounds kind of crazy since we were married before, but I'm sort of old-fashioned guy on some things and this is one of them."

"I will marry you anytime you want," Sienna exclaimed, basking in the excitement of marriage and motherhood.

Carter jumped up and started looking for clothes.

"Let's do it now!" he exclaimed, not waiting for an answer.

Sienna laughed and followed behind him.

"Carter, I need you to slow down. I would marry you anywhere, anytime, but if we're going to do this, we can't do it without our families. Our parents would strangle us if we didn't have a ceremony, even if it's a small one with just us and them."

Carter exhaled and moved around haphazardly like a wild man. He didn't know what to do next. He was on a high and didn't know what to do with all the energy he found he now has.

"Okay, you're right. I'm going to be a father, Sienna! I'm going to be a father!" he shouted and danced around, pulling Sienna into his arms as they danced together.

"I'm glad you're excited. Now that we both know and it's real, I want to find a way to help you sleep," she said with a sexy spiciness to her voice.

"Sleep? Now? I'm too hyped up!" Carter said, clearly over the top with excitement still dancing around.

Sienna stopped dancing, stepped back, and started removing her clothes.

That was all the incentive Carter needed. Sienna was right, they needed to slow down and focus on the moment. They could tell their families about the engagement and the baby. Then, they could plan a quick wedding. He wouldn't wait until after the baby was born. He wanted his child to be born to parents who were in love and married. Again, he was just that type of guy.

"I love you, baby," he said, picking her up and carrying her into the bedroom.

"I love you, too," she said.

Epilogue
Over a Year Later

Dexter tried to keep up with Carter's long strides as they rushed through the airport to get to baggage claim, but nothing was stopping his friend from his determined steps to get out of the airport and home to his family.

"Seriously, if we didn't ride in the same car, I would tell you to leave me and go ahead. I'm out of breath trying to keep up with you, bro!" Dexter hollered from behind him.

Carter turned quickly and looked behind him at Dexter clearly huffing and puffing. He laughed, but didn't slow down.

"Man, I've been away from my wife and daughter for three days, the first since Symone was born and at six-months-old, she's growing and doing more each day. I don't want to miss anything," Carter said, talking without slowing his strides.

At the thought of his baby girl and wife, Carter smiled like a crazy man. Talking to them on the phone wasn't enough to satisfy him. Seeing Symone grin via his phone or iPad wasn't enough. He needed to have her in his arms as she playfully slapped his cheeks. He needed to get back home to them and hold both of his girls in his arms.

"I understand, but how would it look if you have to attend

my funeral from a heart attack. My goddaughter will not be happy if I'm not around to see her grow up and also to threaten her first boyfriend. Slow down and we can get you home in one piece. Rushing won't help the luggage come down faster and you know how that is," Dexter countered.

Carter wasn't thinking about that. The moment his plane landed at O'Hare International, the only thing on his mind was getting home to Sienna and Symone. Thinking about Symone had him smiling from ear to ear. He'd never known a love like the kind he gave and received from his baby girl. Life for them had been a rollercoaster after Sienna revealed her pregnancy in Belize.

Three months after returning, they had a small church wedding and three months after that, almost a month before her due date, their little bundle of joy came bouncing into the world like a ball of fire yet, deceptively looking like a tiny, peaceful and beautiful clone of her mother. He had never experienced a more perfect moment than being by Sienna's side for the delivery and as their daughter was born, she cried with lungs that rang out notifying the entire ward that Symone Garrison had arrived.

As the hospital staff cleaned her up and weighed her, she continued to scream until he walked over and told her that her daddy was here and would always be with her. Carter had reached for her little hand and for a few seconds, her eyes opened, looked at him and she'd quieted. Then Symone had gripped his finger so tightly, he'd been afraid to move away. She needed her daddy right by her side and that was where he stood until they wrapped her up and placed her on Sienna's chest. Since the moment he found out Sienna was pregnant, he had spent night after night talking to their child through her stomach. He wanted the baby to know and to remember his voice. Clearly it had worked. The hospital staff in the room admired the already intense connection between father and daughter.

He never left Sienna's side throughout her stay in the hospital. Each time she breastfed, he would climb up in the bed with them and talk directly to Symone, joining in on the intimate moment. He was happy that the new wing of the pediatric ward at the hospital allowed for fathers to stay with the mother and baby the entire time. Sienna was in a private suite which included a large bathroom where he could shower and change each day. Because he had to rush Sienna to the hospital for the birth, he had left his own overnight bag at home. His mother had taken care of that and brought him what he needed. Nothing was more important than being with them. He discovered a brand-new level of love every time he looked into Symone's beautiful face.

Once they were able to take her home from the hospital, nothing could keep him away from being there every day to help care for her and to bond with her. He and Sienna had made the decision that, though she was opening the office park and community center, she was stepping back from being a dentist until Symone was much older. She looked forward to spending time at the community center where she would be able to take Symone with her each day.

In the midst of preparing for the grand opening of the office park and community center on the south side, he and Dexter had worked out a business arrangement to expand their dealerships and auto customization business outside of Chicago. To allow him time with his family, Dexter agreed to do a lot of the traveling to handle business out of town, accompanied by their new businesses' office managers and attorneys. Success was following him in life and Carter felt his biggest success was his priority to his family.

Now that he was back, he wanted to see his loves and then head over to the office park to see how things were coming along. They were one week away from one of the biggest events the south side of Chicago had ever seen. They were expecting big named politicians and celebrities along with as many children who were interested in enjoying a day of fun. Following the opening day events, the community center would be open seven days a week and would be fully staffed, including off-duty police officers who would make sure the kids had a safe place to come. Most important to Sienna was the ability to open medical offices and a clinic in the office park for the citizens on the south side who found it hard to afford health care costs. One additional inclusion in the event was his surprise for her.

He smiled remembering the day Sienna mentioned being able to provide dental services on the go with a bus that would travel throughout the southside providing free dental checkups for residents, young and old, who couldn't get to the community center or another place to have regular checkups. Through some of his connections, the bus would be arriving about an hour after the opening, surprising Sienna and her staff.

"Luggage!" Dexter shouted the minute he saw their bags coming down the belt.

"It's about time. I was ready to leave it here and come back for it later. I miss my girls!" Carter shouted.

"I'm sure you called her every hour of the day that we weren't in meetings. They probably needed a break from you hovering," Dexter quipped.

"Remember those words one day when you have a wife and children of your own and you see that cute little face look up at you, smiling because you love them and they love you and the harshness of the world hasn't taken control of their minds yet."

"I see how Symone reacts to you when you're around. You're already her hero and no matter what the world is like when she grows up, she'll remember the love you've always had for her," he said.

"I plan to keep being her hero, too; hers and Sienna's. I told you I wanted my wife back. I got that and more and I don't think there's a man anywhere who is as happy as I am. There can't be!" Carter yelled and drew the attention of others in the airport. He apologized as Dexter laughed uncontrollably.

"You are a nut, bro. You did and you got her. I'm happy for you. You were always meant to be together."

"I meant it when I said I was never letting go."

Carter's phone chimed with a facetime request. He already knew who it was as he grabbed his suitcase and headed toward the parking garage.

"Hey baby! How are my girls doing?" he asked the minute Sienna's face appeared on the screen.

"You need to come and get your daughter who is being a little feisty today. I'm trying to get her dressed to drop her off with your parents for a visit and she's not cooperating. You're back, right?" she asked.

"Yes, we just landed. A visit? Did you remember I was coming back today? The two of you won't be there?" he asked, disappointed.

"I know, but I won't be long and your parents called and asked if they could come over today. I said yes until Reese had some kind of drama with Torrence. He was supposed to come to town to be her date for the office park opening, but something happened. You know they've been seeing each other and she has trust issues. I think they had some kind of argument and aren't kicking it anymore. It's been kind of sketchy for months anyway, especially since he's been around more with the construction starting."

"So, they are still doing the on-again, off-again thing? I thought they had actually stopped seeing each other all together a few months back. Is it serious with them?" Carter asked.

"I don't think so. I think it was fun in the beginning, but then he was gone out of town a lot. For the past two months or so, he's been in Chicago a lot more and they've been seeing each other more steadily, but she's pissed at him about something. I don't know. You know she's always been there for me, so I need to do the same for her. I asked your mom if she could keep an eye on Symone until your flight got in and she was happy to do it. When I talked to you earlier, you said your flight was being delayed. I didn't know you were coming in on time."

"It was last minute. The original flight was cancelled and I would have gotten in about five hours later, but we were able to get on another flight that was leaving and we just made it to the gate on time."

"Do you want me to wait on you?" Sienna asked.

Carter could hear Symone crying in the background.

"At six-months old, she sure does have a big set of lungs. Let me talk to her. Let her see me on the screen," he said, carefully crossing traffic to get to the garage. He smiled the moment Symone's face flooded his screen and he took in her light brown eyes, the perfect match for his.

"Here she is," Sienna said. "Look at this pretty face all torn up from crying," she added.

"Hey, baby girl. What's wrong with daddy's baby, huh? Why are you giving mommy a hard time? You miss your daddy?" he asked.

The minute Symone figured out his voice and face on the screen, she stopped crying and started cooing at him and playfully hitting the screen. They had that special kind of relationship. She was no longer being fussy, but she wanted to play and giggle at him.

"Ugh, you and your daughter are a perfect pair," Sienna said smiling.

"I have the perfect touch. Stop giving your mommy a hard time and Daddy will be home shortly," he said. "Go ahead and take her to my parents. I'll take a moment and stop by the dealerships to see how things are going. That will give her some time with them. I'll pick her up in a few hours. Don't be long, baby. I've missed you and Reese will always have some kind of man drama," he expressed and smiled, not meaning any harm in his assessment of Reese and her personal life.

"I won't. You know how dramatic Reese can be, but this is different. She's really upset. I pumped plenty of milk for Symone, some in the fridge and some in the freezer. I don't plan to be too late. I've missed you."

"I've missed you, too."

"Planning to show me how much you've missed me?" Sienna asked, lowering her voice in order to sound more erotic. She had plans for her husband.

"The minute you get home, I'll be ready. Now, our little blocker there may take that moment to decide she would prefer to be wide awake rather than sleep, but when she's out and you're home, it's on baby. Go take care of Reese and tell her I'm sorry about whatever is happening with her. Smooth-talking Torrence finally messed up, huh?" Carter asked.

"I don't know, but deep down, I sure hope things calm down and they figure it out. She sounds pretty through to me, but she did about six or seven other times since they reconnected. You know Reese," Sienna said.

"Baby, we're talking about Reese. She's the queen of drama. If I know her, she'll be crying a river all night and tomorrow, she'll be someplace with him and her feet will be pressed up against a front window," he laughed.

"True, true. One day, she'll have the kind of real love that you and I have, but until then, when drama calls, I try to be the friend she needs."

"I need you too and as soon as you get home, you'll see how much. Hey, you know when we talked about having children back to back. You still up for that?" he asked.

"We just had Symone and you want another baby? What are you doing to me, Carter?"

"Nothing like what I want to do to you and I'm not talking about literally right this second, but I want our children to be close in age. I want everything when it comes to us. I want the children, the white picket fence and as perfect as a life as we can have together. I could have lost our love forever," he admitted.

"I know, baby, but you have me and Symone now and forever. I want a lot of babies with you and with as much as we both love Symone, I can imagine all of our children would benefit by sharing in that same love. I'm ready for more babies as soon as you are. Let's talk about it and we can definitely practice it if you can talk your daughter into letting us have a night of uninterrupted love."

Carter laughed out loud.

"My daughter and I will converse the moment I get to her. She loves her daddy and will do anything for me."

"Yeah, good luck with that. She's our little shady baby who plots for us to never get another moment alone. I think she's trying to make sure she's an only child, keeping all the love for herself," Sienna chuckled.

"Don't worry your beautiful head about it. I'll see you when you get home. I'll be ready and waiting for you," he whispered, dropping his tone an octave to a deep bass, knowing she loved the sound of his deep voice.

"Mmm, you're making me second guess going to help Reese," she moaned in the phone screen.

"See? Baby number two is on the way!" Carter happily shouted.

"See you in a bit, lover boy!" Sienna said before ending the call.

Carter hung up as they got to the car.

"What happened with Reese?" Dexter asked. "I heard you say something about Torrence messing up?"

"It sounds like Torrence messed up again. There seems to be issues ever since they hooked back up again. I think Reese is actually falling for him this time and then finding the least little thing to complain about. First it was that he was never in Chicago and now that he's here more because construction on the casino has begun, she's pissed about something new,"

Carter explained.

"Wait. Tough as nails Reese is not going to give her heart to a man. Remember back in college what she did to Torrence? I mean I love her like a sister, but she's got issues with enjoying a man who really likes her," Dexter said.

Carter shook his head in agreement as they walk up to the car.

"I don't know what's going on this time, but you know, I heard a thing or two about Torrence. He's no angel. He's been living the playboy life in Vegas since he moved there. He's the male version of Reese. I wonder if she knows he's a player," Carter said.

"I love Reese, but serves her right. Torrence walked in on her screwing some guy in her dorm and she shrugged it off like it was nothing that he saw her. I can't imagine being in his shoes back then," Dexter said.

Carter huffed.

"I can't imagine being in his shoes now. Reese is not the commitment type and if that's what they've been trying to do, it may not work until she really decides to let go of her thought that men are not meant to be committed to."

"I heard a thing or two about Torrence too. I remember a story about him and a beautiful daughter of a very rich guy from Dubai or someplace like that. Reese may not know about that unless she did a google search of his life. Another friend of mine said he knew Torrence to never have a cold bed in Las Vegas. Reese may not be about committing, but she won't tolerate a guy messing around on her either," Dexter said as they got in the car that Carter had left when they flew out for business a few days ago.

"Well, whatever it is, Sienna will get her through it and

then prepare for the next time she'll get another call from Reese. I still can't believe they have been back kicking it after what they went through in college. If Torrence is playing her, he had better put on a full armor and shield because Reese doesn't play fair when she's hurt. She's going for the jugular," Carter joked.

Dexter grabbed his own crotch and imagined Reese launching a swift kick on Torrence.

"I feel for that brother. Reese is a hard sell on forever, but if she's decided she finally wants it with him, he better come correct."

"I know that's right. I'll drop you off on my way to the dealership. I'm going to do a drive by and then get home and wait for my wife to get home. I have three nights to make up for," Carter said as they pulled out into traffic.

"Ugh, another crazy in love couple. I prefer staying single and not depriving women of all of this," Dexter said and doubled over in laughter.

"Dude, you just haven't found your Sienna yet. I pity you when you do. You won't know what hit you," Carter said.

"Never gonna happen," Dexter said.

"I bet Torrence is saying the same thing."

Get the second installment of the *"The Brothers of Chi Town"* book series, "Swagger and Baggage"

It's not a coincidence that casino owner, Torrence Allen, ran into his college sweetheart, Reese Michaels again; it's fate. As his memories unfold, he had tried everything to keep her in his life and his bed back then and failed at both. She wasn't ready for him then, but he hopes she is ready for him now.

Reese Michaels never thought she'd see Torrence again. Their split in college was dramatic and hurtful and still, no man had been able to win her heart. She considered herself the permanent third wheel to friends who had found love and marriage.

Their whirlwind affair, quickly turned into love just as it suddenly crashed and burned when a woman shows up to claim Torrence as hers. When it's also revealed that this woman isn't the only 'other woman', Reese finds herself left with a broken heart, shattered love and dreams of forever beyond her reach. How did she not know about the other part of Torrence's active and amorous life?

Torrence isn't ready to give up on having Reese in his life after his deceit. He finds himself in the fight of his life to finally have the love and commitment he wanted only with her. His swagger had always won women over, but it's his baggage that's causing his life to spiral out of control and he could once again find himself without the woman he has always loved.

Find out in *'Swagger and Baggage'*, book 2 in "The Brothers of Chi Town" romance book series coming in 2019.

Get other romance novels from Cheryl Barton on her website at www.cherylbarton.net

Upcoming Release - "True Lies or True Love"

FBI Agent, Quintin Bell was sent to work undercover at Tee King Investment Securities to get proof that Carlos King, owner and hedge-fund boss, was embezzling money from his own employees' retirement accounts. In a chance encounter, he noticed Carlos' daughter, Meadow and before he could keep his heart from getting lost in her beauty, he found himself at a crossroads between doing his job and following his heart.

Meadow King wasn't looking for love that day in the café, but there was no way she could resist the handsome, rugged looks of a stranger when the intoxicating vibe between them became undeniable and irresistible. Unbeknownst to Meadow, the man she's fallen in love with has a secret that could not only ruin the love that grew between them, but it could topple her entire world.

Quintin knows that love can be real and it can be true, but his lies are what create a façade of their love affair and could cause it to crash and burn just as it has begun to heat up with passion that neither of them had ever experienced before nor could they see themselves without ever again.

Quintin is running out of time in trying to find a way to do his job and hold on to the woman he loves. His biggest hurdle will be if he does his job, can he convince Meadow that his lies may have been true, but his love is truer!

Enjoy this excerpt from "Heartbeat", book 2 in "A Lovers' Heart" series.

Navy SEAL, Calvin Lymon's body purred to life with a desirous hunger unlike anything he had ever experienced before. The word, stunning, streaked like lightning across his mind the moment the statuesque beauty came into his line of sight in the overcrowded pub in the heart of Colombia, South America. The essence of her tantalizing aura radiated so far out from her actual body that everything about her engulfed his very being like a tight embrace that covered him completely.

Calvin couldn't take his eyes away even if he wanted to. Even though the room was packed with patrons from one dusty beige wall to the next, from across the room and through every person that covered the path between them, the woman of his admiring gaze stood out. He watched every scrupulously slow move as she danced and swayed to the Latin music playing loudly through speakers that were place in all four corners of the large, spacious room.

A lump formed in his throat causing him to gulp in disbelief at the immediate impact her loveliness had on him. He had seen and indulged in his share of beautiful women before, but none compared to the woman his eyes were locked on.

Slowly changing the direction of his stare, he looked downward toward the gray and black marbled tiled floor where she stood and his eyes covered her from her brightly painted red toe nails that peaked out at him through strappy white high-heeled stilettos and up her long-toned chestnut brown legs which were visible because of the short white body hugging dress she had on.

From there, he let his eyes continue on their path to hips that flared out, just below her slim waste showcasing her hourglass figure. The way she moved had his mind traveling to a place in time where he imagined himself holding on to all of her curves tightly as her legs wrapped snugly around his hips allowing his body to sink into hers in the most intimate and provocative way. He shifted in his seat as his manhood jumped when his eyes continued an upward path landing on her full, large breasts, the part of a woman that he admired first when it came to the physicality of a sexy woman. His mouth felt as dry as the Mohave desert with a tongue that was as heavy as lead as lascivious thoughts around all he could do with a body like hers flooded through him.

Anxiety overtook him when those in the crowd walking by blocked his view of her as if the very life was being sucked from his body. A sheer moment of disconnect had his heart racing while he stretched his neck as if keeping his eyes on her was what kept his heart beating, giving him life.

Finding an opening, again, the beauty once again came into focus and this time, as she danced, she turned around and he finally got the chance to see her face. To say she was beautiful didn't quite capture the full, powerful punch of her exquisiteness. He had never seen a more perfect woman in his entire life and he had a feeling, he probably never would again. He couldn't focus on anything else other than his life depending on him getting his fill of looking at her.

Her long dark hair flowed down around her shoulders moving in sync with her body's movements. When she raised her hands above her head and slowly swayed down toward the floor, Calvin almost fell off of the chair he'd been sitting on, snapping him briefly out of the trance the beauty had him in.

Remembering to breathe, he looked around and checked to see if anyone else saw what he did and by the look on every guy's face in the pub, he wasn't the only one who noticed her; he wasn't surprised.

A feeling of possession overcame him as he turned his face up in a sneer at every man who looked at her the way he was looking at her. He wanted her, yes, and he assumed every man in the place did as well and he didn't like it one bit. Little did they know that he was Calvin Lymon, Navy SEAL and he had enough confidence to overshadow everyone in the room. This woman was his and there was no way he would lose out on an opportunity to meet her nor would he watch another man spend the night getting to know her the way he was planning to do. No one knew, but she was meant for him.

"You okay, Cal?"

Somewhere in what seemed like a distant place, Calvin heard someone addressing him as Cal, what family and close friends called him, but he couldn't focus on the words because he didn't want to take his attention away from the woman of his dreams. The voice had to be that of Mason, his best friend and fellow Navy SEAL. No one else from their team had accompanied them on their one day off from surveillance in the foreign country. He tried his best to tamper down the intrusion of Mason's voice because it was distracting.

Turning back to the woman who had already stolen his heart, he watched as she moved left and then right until she was again standing tall. The moment she threw her head back and laughed at something, what he didn't know, his libido went off the charts like never before. His body hardened like impenetrable steel.

"Cal, can you hear me?"

He heard the voice again, but didn't want to focus on it just in case the woman in front of him wasn't real, but possibly a mirage. Can any woman really be that beautiful? She was perfection and she would be what a man would call a total package. Everything about her was flawless and the way she carried herself, her magnetism wasn't just externally, but he sensed a strong, confident woman internally, something that meant more to him than what he could see with his eyes.

"Cal? Give me a sign that you hear me?"

Now annoyed that he was being interrupted, he huffed out a response.

"Yes, I can hear you," he said in his head because his mouth wouldn't move. What was wrong with his mouth? He tried again to form words to actually speak, but nothing came out. He could only hear his answer in his head, perhaps due to the loud music wafting out from the speakers.

In an instant, for some reason, the crowd milled back into focus right in front of him, thereby blocking his view of her. He slid down from the stool and tried to find her again as his heart beat sped up and uneasiness put his nerves on edge at the thought that he may have lost his chance because he allowed himself to be distracted by a voice. He didn't want to lose sight of her because he needed to meet her. He needed to tell her that though he'd only set eyes on her for a few minutes, he never wanted to live another day without seeing her beautiful face over and over again.

Calvin wasn't sure he'd actually been living until the moment he'd spotted her. Now, the word, complete, came to mind because that would be the state of his love life if he were able to convince her that they were meant for each other.

"What are you thinking about, Cal?" he heard as he started making his way through the throngs of people who gathered and were now in his way.

Calvin knew he was thinking one thing and one thing only and that was to get to this woman and start a connection he hoped would lead to him showing her that he could be the man of her dreams.

As he pushed his way forward, the crowd seemed to thicken even more as he forced his way through to her. He could hear voices calling out to him and though he wasn't focusing on them, they were familiar. Dismissing them, he didn't want to talk to anyone other than the woman who was the focus of his full attention.

Coming to the point where he thought she had been standing, he couldn't spot her anywhere. Anxiously, he looked around as his heart began to pound in his chest with the thought that she had indeed left and he would never get the chance to talk to her, to get to know her or to let her know that she had such an immediate impact on him that his life would be nothing if he didn't have her in it.

Not seeing her anywhere, he held his head in disappointment as he turned and made his way back toward his seat at the bar. Coming through the crowd, he walked up to the stool, turned and when he looked up, there she was right in front of him and smiling. When she wiggled her finger at him to come closer, he pointed to himself to be sure she was talking to him. When she nodded yes, he was ecstatic with delight thinking that she must have been watching him as he was watching her and maybe even feeling the connection he'd felt.

As if from a scene in a movie, the crowd parted, clearing a path straight to her. As he began to move in her direction, the smile on her face turned into a frightening frown, one laced with fear and overwrought with terror. He watched as her hand reached up to the side of her neck covering it as her eyes beamed with dread. Looking from her face to where her hand landed, he could see bright red blood begin to seep through her fingers, covering her hand and sliding down to stain the white dress she was wearing. He looked on in horror as she then reached to her stomach where another big red patch of blood began to form and coat the fingers of her other hand. What was happening, he thought as he felt helpless at coming to her aid?

Without thinking, Calvin began running to her, reaching her at the moment when she collapsed to the floor. Holding her in his arms, he could hear her plead with him to help her. He looked around and was stunned to see people were still dancing as if the most beautiful girl in the world was not bleeding to death on the floor right in front of them. He looked for Mason and called out to him for help, but the music was so loud, he knew Mason wouldn't be able to hear him.

Calvin tried to lift her up to get her to a hospital, but her body felt like lead. As her eyes began to close and her hands dropped away, Calvin was puzzled as to what happened. Had she been stabbed? Was it a shooter? He looked around for anything and saw nothing, but crowds of people dancing to the music, laughing and drinking. He tried putting pressure on her neck and then on her side and screamed for anyone to help him. He reached for the person closest to him, but he couldn't get a good grip on his pant leg. His hand, covered in blood seem to go right through the man next to him without even leaving a smear of the blood that now soaked his hand.

Turning back to the woman in his arms, he watched as her body went lifeless while he screamed again for someone, for anyone to help him.

"Cal? Can you hear me? Come on, Cal, calm down. I'm here. Can you hear me?" a voice said.

Calvin struggled to focus on the voice calling out to him. Perhaps that was the help he needed, but the voice he thought he was hearing wouldn't be in Colombia, South America with him. He was on a mission and far away from the glitz and glamour life his brother Cade lived, but he was quite positive that the voice now calling out to him was his Hollywood, superstar brother, Cade Weston. What would Cade be doing in Colombia, he thought? He looked around and didn't see him. Where was he? He tried to speak, but something painful was preventing him from making a sound. His throat felt like it was on fire. It felt blocked with something that was keeping him from speaking.

"Hold on, Cal, the doctor is coming," he heard.

The voice that time was Cameron's, his baby brother who shouldn't be in South America, but in Florida finishing up his last year of his undergraduate program before he started graduate school to continue with his advanced degree in Journalism. What was going on? Why are his brothers in South America and why weren't they coming to help him with the dying woman in his arms? He struggled to move and to talk, but could do neither. He felt helpless and weightless as if he was fighting against forces that wanted him to remain still, unable to do anything on his own.

"Mister Lymon, can you hear me? This is doctor Bell. Give me a minute and we'll get the tube out, but I need you to stop struggling with me."

Calvin could feel hands holding him down keeping him from moving.

"Everything's alright, Cal. You're alright, bro."

Cade? That was Cade's voice again, this time a lot closer than before. He wasn't hearing things. How could this be? Cade was in California or Texas or Florida or someplace else with his wife, Callie, but he definitely was not in South America.

"Cal, it's Cam – can you hear me? I'm here, I'm right here. We're all here and you're going to be okay."

Again, he heard Cameron's voice and he knew he must be in the twilight zone. All of a sudden, he felt his body jerk as he struggled to move and breathe. He felt like he was about to regurgitate, but it wasn't quite happening. He couldn't breathe even though he tried with all of his might to do so. Like a man trying to get his last breath, he inhaled and coughed as hard as he could as his eyes suddenly opened. His eyes did a quick, frightening scan and didn't recognize where he was. What frightened him most was he no longer had the beautiful woman in his arms. Where did she go?

"Breathe easy, Cal. Just breathe easy, bro. That's it."

Being able to see clearly now, he looked around and saw both of his brothers, a guy in a white coat and several other women surrounding him. Where was he?

"Calvin, it's doctor Bell. We took out your breathing tube

and it's going to be a few minutes before you'll be able to speak and even then, it will be a strain. Can you look my way? Can you hear me? Do you understand me?"

Calvin couldn't take his eyes from his big brother, Cade. Wherever he was, he felt calmer knowing Cade was there, but he still needed to know why?

"Cade, talk to him. He seems to only want to focus on you," Dr. Bell said.

Cade walked closer to him and Calvin's eyes widened sensing something wasn't quite right.

"Hey, bro. You're woke. I know it's hard to talk and I can see you struggling to do so. The doctor said it's going to be hard, so just nod if you can understand me. Nod, Cal," Cade said sternly.

Shifting his eyes to the left he saw that standing next to Cade was Cameron who was also encouraging him to remain calm. Something was wrong if both of his brothers were standing over him and a doctor was talking to him. Was he in a bed?

Doing what Cade asked, he nodded. He looked to Cameron who cheered with excitement, no longer with a worried facial expression.

Calvin couldn't get his thoughts to line up to explain what was going on. One moment he was back in the bar with Sofia and then all of a sudden, she began bleeding from wounds and he couldn't help her. Sofia? Where was she? He already knew her name? Why was she bleeding like that on the day that they'd met which had been over a year ago? Was that right? He was so confused.

As his thoughts began to clear and the voices around him began to converse with each other, he thought back to a moment ago when he'd held Sofia's lifeless body in his arms. He couldn't make sense of the scene that had played out. Sofia hadn't died in his arms in the pub and not on the day that they'd met. Now that his memory was clearing up, he remembered that she may not have died in his arms in the pub, but she had died and remembered seeing her body and being overwhelmed with grief.

He now knew that for a year and a half, he and Sofia had been in love and then it all ended the day she died. She was gone and the thought startled him. Something else was wrong as a sudden pain pierced his heart. They have a son! He and Sofia have a son and his name is Camico. Where was Camico? Sofia was dead, but where was their son? He'd promised her he'd look after Camico, but, where was he? If he was in a hospital or some facility where his brothers were and doctors and nurses were tending to him, where was his son? A feeling of trepidation overtook him as he tried with all of his might to form the words. With everything in him, he screamed at the top of his lungs.

"Camico!"

Everyone in the room turned toward him. Before he could decipher what was happening, where he was and when, the room went completely dark. Calvin had passed out.

Coming up next from "A Lovers' Heart" book series, "***HEARTBREAKER***", Cameron Lymon's story.

In book 3, *Heartbreaker* of *A Lovers' Heart* steamy romance series, Cameron Lymon, the sexy, youngest brother of Hollywood heartthrob, Cade Weston and Navy SEAL, Calvin Lymon, with his Master's degree in Journalism and a minor in Communications and Sports Management in hand, landed his dream job in Denver, Colorado as the co-host for a new morning talk show. Women love to call him the "Heartbreaker" because of the bevy of beautiful ladies he's left in his wake, not interested in giving up being a bachelor for falling in love. He enjoys taking after his big brother's old lifestyle of being a playboy.

Dakota Kane sacrificed a personal life and fought hard in her career to be the lead personality on Denver's top television morning show, but she was about to risk it all for passionate, steamy encounters with her new, much younger co-host, who is ten years younger and fifty shades hotter than any man she'd ever encountered. All he had to do was smile at her and she was a goner.

Cameron didn't know what he was in for when what he thought would be casual, behind closed door romps with the ever-so-sexy Dakota began to turn into much more when his heart became as invested in her as much as his body had. As things turned serious, his heartbreaker status came back to haunt him and his relationship with Dakota was threatened by his past.

Cameron and Dakota have to decide if what they are beginning to feel for each other is worth the risk of their careers when their secret love affair becomes the topic of public opinion and ridicule.

Book One - Bachelor Not for Sale – Now available

Even self-proclaimed "bachelors for life" meet that one woman that makes them want to slow down and second guess bachelorhood. After suffering through the heartache of what he thought was true love, Duron Knight meets and becomes enchanted with bombshell Taija Charles.

Taija has heard a lot about Duron and all of her body senses are on overdrive when she meets the handsome bachelor face to face. As the sparks fly, Taija plans to show Duron how she can help him mend his broken heart with real love and the right amount of lust.

Book Two – A Designed Affair – Now available

In the follow-up to "Bachelor Not for Sale", Loren Knight has been engaging in a secret love affair with her brother Duron's best friend and business partner, Michael Bailey. He is everything she could want and more in a man, but she believes the risk is too great for any type of relationship with him beyond the bedroom door.

Michael Bailey has been fighting his attraction to Loren for years. He has stayed away from her out of respect for his best friend and business partner. Now that he and Loren have finally given into passion that they both have been craving, can Michael convince Loren that what they share is worth the risk?

Book Three – A Perfect Combination – Now available

In the third installment following "Bachelor Not for Sale" and "A Designed Affair", Tyrone Davis is the king of one-night stands; nicknamed, Mr. Love Them and Leave Them. He learned to perfect it from his two best friends, Duron Knight and Michael Bailey. He never imagined a one-night stand would have such a lasting impact, but that's exactly what happened.

Victoria Alston couldn't forget the incredible night she spent with Tyrone Davis, someone connected to one of her best friends. The next day, she disappeared, returning to reality and the fiancé she'd left in Boston while on business travel. They both soon discovered that it wasn't just a one-night stand, but a perfect combination for love.

Book Four – Love at Last – Now available

They had the perfect love...That's what Brian Knight thought of his relationship with Sherry Braxton until he looked up one day and she was gone and never wanted to see him again.

Two years later, he discovered that there is the possibility that Sherry may have been pregnant with his child. Hurt and angry at her deceit, he takes a flight to Baltimore to fight for his rights as a father and realizes that the love and passion they once shared had never died.

Is it possible he could still have the kind of love he thought would last a lifetime? Can he still have his love at last?

Un-Break My Heart – Now Available

Dr. Mackenzie Ellis suffered a loss so great, she never thought she'd fall in love again, especially with someone close to her.

Travis Blackwell, III never dreamed of crossing the line with Mackenzie until his heart would no longer allow him to deny the love he has for her and the passion he wants to share with her knowing that he is the key to mending her broken heart.

Bossy – Now Available

Cassidy 'Bossy' Bostic came from nothing, but knew she would be something. Pregnant and alone, she was forced to run from her past in order to have a future. Her rise to the top as the owner of a fashion dynasty is what dreams are made of, but her hard, icy persona could have her living a lonely existence.

Drake Montgomery, a rising attorney heading toward the political arena, has fallen in love with the 'Bossy' mogul only to discover it's 'Cassidy' he loves, but 'Bossy', not so much.

Can their hot, steamy romance melt even her cold, icy heart? Only time and love will tell.

Heartthrob – Now Available

Cade Weston, Hollywood's most eligible bachelor and named the world's sexiest man of the year, lives life at the top with a bevy of beauties at his beck and call, people providing his every desire and more money than any one person should have.

Callie Hurston struggles to make it as a stylist to the stars in a world where women are intimidated by her beauty and men are interested in her body and not her talent.

Cade thought he had it all until he has a chance meeting with Callie and decides to take a chance on her talent and ends up taking an even bigger chance with his heart.

Can the playboy turn in his player's card and give in to love?

A Better Man – Now Available

Phoenix Graham is living her best life with the best man, her fiancé, Carson Stone, heir to the Stone Tower Hotel Empire. Her perfect life is shaken up when a handsome, rugged and extremely sexy mysterious man moves in across the hall and she begins to see that the rose-colored glasses she had been seeing life through were blinders. She soon discovers that Carson was the best man for her until she takes notice of a better man and his name is Gavin Black.

What's a girl to do when the best doesn't get better and better is what she craves?

Home for Thanksgiving – Now Available

Firefighter Nicholas Sullivan is going home for the holiday after he was sidelined due to an injury on the job. Guilt over a life lost has kept him away from his family's ranch in Montana and now he's forced to face his past demons and deal with a self-imposed life of regret.

Veterinarian Parker Wingate's first encounter with the handsome firefighter was less than pleasurable. She sympathized with his hurt, understood his pain and before long, felt his love.

Knowing the holiday season is ending soon, can Nick go from living in love for the moment to allowing himself to finally live in love forever?

His Halloween Promise – Now Available

Dylan Kennedy and Savannah Eaton-Kennedy may be divorced, but that doesn't stop them from indulging in some pretty hot and sexy encounters.

A divorce decree may mean that their life together is over, but Dylan has a promise to keep that could bring his wife back where she belongs; in his life permanently.

ABOUT THE AUTHOR

Cheryl Barton lives in Maryland and in her spare time she loves to read espionage novels, cook, watch Sci-fi movies, spend time with family and friends and enjoy Maryland steamed crabs.

Indulge in more romance and inspirational novels by visiting her website at www.cherylbarton.net.

Cheryl is a member of the Romance Writers of America – National Chapter and the Maryland Romance Writers.

Connect on Social Media:
Facebook
https://www.facebook.com/authorcherylbarton/

Twitter
https://twitter.com/AuthorCBarton

Instagram
https://www.instagram.com/authorcherylbarton/

www.ingramcontent.com/pod-product-compliance
Lightning Source LLC
Chambersburg PA
CBHW031149020726
47499CB00002B/300